"Ingenious and entertaining . . . chilling and inventive . . . [an] addictive book." —*New York Times Book Review*

"A gripping narrative. Trussoni has created her own distinctive, smart, and sly style evident in her rewarding new novel." —*National Review*

"Inventive and entertaining." —*People*

"Danielle Trussoni's vivid and uncanny tale *The Ancestor* makes the most of her signature blend of science, myth, and mystery. As the pages turn, family secrets come to light against a gothic backdrop that will keep readers following the startling twists and turns all the way to the end." —Deborah Harkness

"Danielle Trussoni's *The Ancestor* is a lushly written, dreamlike modern gothic with as many dark turns and twists as the Montebianco family tree has branches. Welcome to the family." —Paul Tremblay, author of *A Head Full of Ghosts* and *The Cabin at the End of the World*

"A surprise inheritance, a remote castle in the Alps, and a cursed family bloodline? Yes, please! *The Ancestor* is a gloriously modern Gothic novel, blending mythic monsters with modern science in ways that gave me a thrill. Danielle Trussoni has written one hell of a tale." —Victor LaValle, author of *The Changeling*

"*The Ancestor* is a wonderful shape-shifter of a novel. One minute you'll suppose you're in a haunted house: think Shirley Jackson. The next, you're transported into the sort of world Mary Shelley might have created for *Frankenstein*. Danielle Trussoni is an immensely gifted literary descendant of both storytellers—they are among her ancestors—which is one of the many reasons why I savor her work so very much."

—Chris Bohjalian, bestselling author of
The Flight Attendant and *The Red Lotus*

"This smart, suspenseful thriller is at once an age-old tale and a fresh, scarily relevant trapdoor into our current genealogical obsession. Danielle Trussoni has written a biological and narrative labyrinth that you will happily get lost in, even as you question everything you think you know about yourself."   —Benjamin Percy, author of *Suicide Woods,*
Thrill Me, The Dark Net, and *Red Moon*

"Deliciously creepy. . . . Trussoni plausibly and expertly combines an intense, darkly gothic narrative with elements of mystery, the paranormal, and legendary tales. This odyssey of monsters and family will enrapture readers."

—*Publishers Weekly*

"An opulently romantic horror tale, with a plucky . . . heroine who discovers she is part of a family whose dark secrets have been sheltered from the world at large. . . . A gothic extravaganza."   —*Kirkus Reviews*

THE
ANCESTOR

ALSO BY DANIELLE TRUSSONI

Fiction

Angelology
Angelopolis

Nonfiction

Falling Through the Earth
The Fortress

Danielle Trussoni

THE
ANCESTOR

A NOVEL

CUSTOM
HOUSE

P.S.™ is a trademark of HarperCollins Publishers.

HarperCollins books may be purchased for educational, business,
or sales promotional use. For information please email the Special
Markets Department at SPsales@harpercollins.com.

A hardcover edition of this book was published in 2020 by
William Morrow, an imprint of HarperCollins Publishers.

FIRST CUSTOM HOUSE PAPERBACK EDITION PUBLISHED 2021.

Designed by Fritz Metsch

Photo retouching: Dimi Lazarou

Library of Congress Cataloging-in-Publication Data
has been applied for.

ISBN 978-0-06-291277-0

21 22 23 24 25 LSC 10 9 8 7 6 5 4 3 2 1

To my ancestors, whose lives made mine possible.
And to Hadrien, for the future.

THE
MONTEBIANCO
FAMILY TREE

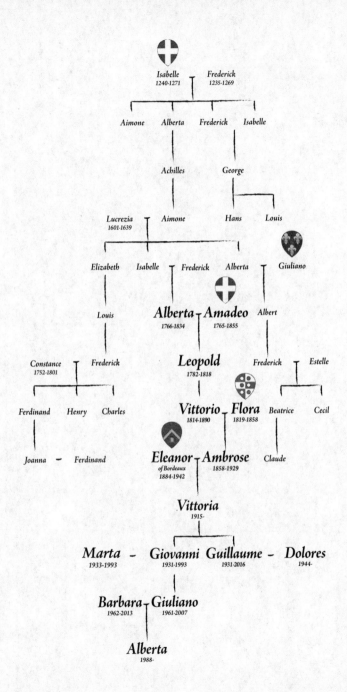

THE
ANCESTOR

ONE

❧

To DISCOVER YOU are the heir to a noble title in the twenty-first century is like winning a fortune in the lottery, the Mega Millions or a Powerball jackpot, only to find your prize will be paid out in francs or liras: suddenly you are rich, but rich in a currency that has no value in the modern world.

Or so it seemed to me upon learning that I was the last living descendant of the ancient house of Montebianco, a family whose power, from the Middle Ages to the unification of Italy in the nineteenth century, was immense; whose sons— because only sons mattered in those unenlightened times— had fought religious wars and married minor princesses and sired noble children, but whose fortunes (and fertility) had diminished as the modern world rose, leaving me, Bert Monte, a twenty-eight-year-old American woman with few social graces and zero knowledge of European history, the sole blood heir to an ancestral domain in the mountains of northern Italy.

It all began early one Saturday morning just before Christmas. I was living alone, although Luca's things were still at the house. He'd been taking clothes to his new apartment slowly, week by week, a pair of jeans here, a T-shirt there, in an effort to keep our lives intertwined. His plan was working: we saw each other often, and had even gone out for dinner and a movie the month before. While we'd been separated for six months, and it had been my idea for him to move out, I found it comforting to have my husband around. We'd been together for nearly ten years, and despite the problems—which were mostly my problems, as we both would agree—it was hard to imagine life without him. My parents were both gone, and I had no brothers or sisters, aunts or uncles or cousins. Luca was the only family I had.

Until, that is, the letter arrived from Italy. A knock came at the door, and I left off decorating the Christmas tree—a three-foot fir festooned with tinsel and blinking lights—to answer. It was a cold, sunny December morning, the sky so bright that the envelope glinted like a mirror in my hand. I signed my name on an electronic pad, wished the delivery man "happy holidays," and was back inside before I saw that the envelope was addressed not to me, Bert Monte, but to someone named Alberta Isabelle Eleanor Vittoria Montebianco.

I sat down at the kitchen table, pushing aside tinsel and glass bulbs, so that I could get a better look. The return address was from Torino, Italia. A parade of bright Italian stamps floated at the top right corner of the glossy envelope. The words "Alberta Isabelle Eleanor Vittoria Montebianco" scrolled across the center. Although everyone called me Bert, my given name was Alberta, so that part made sense.

I was hesitant to open something that might not belong to me, but Alberta was my name, after all, and the address was my address, and so without further debate, I ripped the envelope open. A sheaf of thick, A4-sized pages fell into my hand. The top page was covered in calligraphy, and in the bottom right corner, gleaming like a first-place medal, shone a golden seal of a castle floating above two mountains. The paper alone was something to behold—heavy bond linen stock, creamy and thick, with an ink signature pressed into the fiber by the nib of a fountain pen. The text was dense and entirely foreign. Turning the pages, I tried to find something I could understand, but aside from the name Montebianco, which appeared about every other line, it was entirely incomprehensible. Holding up the envelope, I said the name out loud, "Alberta Isabelle Eleanor Vittoria Montebianco," fumbling over the syllables as if I were a child learning to read.

My first thought was to call Luca. He always knew what to do. Logical, reliable, sane—these were the qualities I loved about him, and the qualities that bound us still, even after all the rough times we'd been through. I'd known Luca most of my life—we had attended the same schools; we had practically grown up together—and he knew me better than anyone. He had grieved with me after the last miscarriage, and he was the one who suggested we go to therapy, volunteering to join me, even when it was clear that I needed it more than he did. Luca had always believed that with a little work and preparation, we could survive anything. But one thing was certain: neither of us could have prepared for a letter like the one from the Estate of the Montebianco family.

I remember sitting there, in my kitchen, turning the envelope over in my hands. A strange feeling came over me then, clear as a voice in my ear. It was a warning, a premonition of danger. I wonder now, after all that I've learned about the Montebianco family, and all that has happened since that snowy December day, what my life would be like had I tossed the envelope into the recycling bin with the junk mail and old newspapers. But I did not throw out the letter, and I did not pay attention to the creeping sense of danger slithering up my spine. I simply slipped the papers back into the envelope, grabbed my jacket, and went out into the cold, bright morning to find Luca.

MY HUSBAND OWNED a bar called the Miltonian, a local hangout on Main Street in the hamlet of Milton, New York, a river town of about two thousand people two hours north of Manhattan. I'd made the drive to Luca's bar a thousand times at least, marking the way by the rolling hills and apple orchards, the pumpkin patches and cornfields, the nail salons and roadside fruit stands. Milton had not been hit with the great Brooklyn migration that had revitalized Hudson or Kingston or Beacon in recent years. It was small, the population static, which was fine with those of us who grew up there, but difficult for business owners like Luca, who needed city traffic.

I parked on Main Street, in front of the Miltonian. My husband's bar was a short, squat brick saloon with a neon beer sign in the window. Inside stretched a long, polished nineteenth-century bar, an antique pool table with gryphon claws gripping the hardwood, a jukebox full of old jazz standards, and a series of low-hanging Depression glass light fixtures that cast a soupy glow everywhere.

I went inside and sat on my favorite barstool. Bob, my soon-to-be ex-father-in-law, had just finished eating lunch. He slipped into his coat and gave me a quick smile. "He's in the back."

"Thanks, Bob," I said, giving him a kiss on the cheek on his way out. Luca's mother had died when Luca was in fifth grade, leaving him and his father to fend for themselves. Bob felt Luca's disappointment about the state of our marriage as much as Luca did, and I loved him for it.

"Hey," Luca said, returning from the backroom with an armful of bottles—Hudson Baby Bourbon, Catskill Curious Gin, and others I couldn't name.

He was surprised to see me there; I hadn't been to the bar since our separation.

"Want some lunch?" He hadn't shaved in a while, and a thin blond scruff covered his chin and cheeks, giving him a disheveled look I'd always found sexy.

"A drink," I said, sliding the envelope onto the bar. "Gin and tonic, extra lime."

In the past, I wouldn't have had to tell him. Luca knew what I liked to drink and usually had it ready before I could order. But lately, this man I had known most of my life looked at me as though I had become a different person and all the things I used to like—black coffee, and long walks by the river, and suspense novels, and a strong gin and tonic with extra lime—might change as easily as my mood.

As he mixed my drink, I spread the pages out on the bar, smoothing down the edges, trying (and failing) to understand a word or two of Italian. They looked like official documents to me—at least the top one did, with its large golden seal and colorful calligraphy.

"Are you back in school?" Luca asked, placing the gin and tonic and a bowl of peanuts on the bar.

I had been working toward a degree in early childhood education, and had even completed two semesters of a program at Marist, but everything had unraveled when I lost another baby, this one five months along, older than the others, developed enough that we knew he'd been a little boy. I couldn't bear to read about the physical milestones during the first year of a child's life or the development of language in toddlers when it was becoming more and more clear that I would never have a child of my own. So far, no one, not even Luca, knew how to help me get over that.

"It's not for school," I said, meeting his eyes. He poured a pint of IPA for himself, which was unusual: Luca didn't drink at work. He had realized I needed company and broke with habit to join me. I tipped my glass at him—*cheers*—and drank the gin down. It felt good, the slow, sure rush of alcohol, the inevitable flood of blood to my brain.

"What is it, then?" Luca asked, looking down at the documents spread over the bar.

"I'm not exactly sure," I said, taking another long sip of my drink. "It came to the house today."

"Looks like Italian." He picked up the envelope and read the flowery Italian names aloud, each one like blossoms on a branch: "*Alberta Isabelle Eleanor Vittoria Montebianco.* Who the hell is that?"

I shrugged. "I know as much as you do."

He looked at the return address. "Torino?"

Something surfaced in my mind, a memory rising from an obscure depth. "Didn't our grandparents come from Turin?"

"They were farther north," Luca said. "Up in the Alps."

Our grandparents had been born in the same small village in northern Italy. They had immigrated to New York City after the Second World War, lived in a tight community in Little Italy, and then moved to Milton in the fifties, drawn by backyards and good public schools. Luca and I had grown up in the shadows of this migration—the elaborate Sunday lunches that went on all afternoon, the Catholic school education, the way we looked as though we were part of the same clan. Our heritage was northern Italian, our skin washed pale as a snowdrift, our hair white-blond, and our eyes watered down to the lightest shade of blue. Our ancestry held fast in our genes like the clasp of a fob to a chain, even as our grandparents, then our parents, became Americans.

Despite my shared heritage with Luca, our families had not been close. In fact, I always felt that they had disliked each other, especially the older generation, although I had nothing concrete to back this feeling up. Luca's paternal grandmother, Nonna Sophia, had never been particularly warm to me, not even at our wedding. When Luca and I took her to church on Sundays, as we used to do before the separation, she never sat near me on the pew, but between her son and grandson, as if I might rub off on her.

"How is Nonna doing, anyway?" I asked, fingering the documents on the bar. Nonna had been born in Italy, and it struck me that she might help me understand the letter.

"Eighty-six and healthy as a horse," he said, taking a handful of peanuts.

"That woman will outlive all of us," I said, feeling both admiration and dread.

"She hasn't been doing very well since the move, actually," he said. "My dad says her mood is worse than ever."

Bob and Luca had moved Nonna to a condo at the Monastery, a retirement community on the river, earlier in the year. It had been a big production. Nonna hadn't wanted to leave her house, but Bob had insisted.

"She doesn't like it there?"

"Not really. It's hard to get used to a new environment." Something in his voice told me he was talking more about himself than his grandmother. "She misses her old life, but she'll be okay. She's resilient."

He met my eyes, and I knew that he was waiting for me to discuss his move back home. He wanted to let everything bad that had happened between us slide away. He wanted to start over.

"I'm working on things," I said, an edge creeping into my voice that I hadn't meant to be there. "You know that."

"I know, I know," he said, giving me a sweet smile. "But it might be easier with a little help, don't you think?"

I pushed the papers toward Luca to shift his attention to the problem at hand. "Do you think Nonna would take a look at these for me? Maybe she can tell me what this is all about?"

"She might," Luca said, glancing again at the papers. He seemed as intrigued as I was about them. "Why don't you stop by the Monastery and see what she says?"

I bit my lip, wondering if I would regret bringing Nonna into the situation. Things were hard enough between Luca and me without getting his whole family involved. Maybe it was time I solved my own problems, especially now that we were living apart.

"Do you think she'll be able to understand this?" I asked, but I knew perfectly well that she would understand all of it. The older generation had spoken Italian all the time. My grandparents had been dead for years, but I still remembered the melody of their voices when they spoke their native language.

"I'll give her a call," he said. "Let her know you're coming."

TWO

꙳

THE MONASTERY RETIREMENT community sat high on a riverbank, an immense brick structure with copper drainpipes, dark windows, and a moss-covered slate roof. Built in the mid-nineteenth century, it had housed Catholic priests until the eighties, when a developer cut it into twenty-two independent living condos, some with river views, others giving onto the woods.

I parked near the entrance and then sat in my car, a wave of anxiety running through me. Nonna was a formidable woman, and I was a little afraid of her, especially because I hadn't seen her since I'd asked Luca to move out. She hadn't been crazy about me before—she had always seemed to look down on my family—but now she would have a real reason to hate me.

Bracing myself, I tucked the envelope under my arm and walked up to the reception desk, where a bearded nursing assistant took my name and then led me to Nonna's apartment.

"There's someone to see you, Sophia," he said. He showed me into the room before slipping back into the hallway, leaving me alone with Luca's tiny, fierce grandmother.

When the battle to relocate Nonna had begun, Bob argued that Nonna would be more comfortable at the Monastery, that it wasn't as antiseptic or medicalized as the other retirement homes, and it was true: Nonna's apartment was warm and comfortable, with art on the walls and books piled everywhere. There was a small kitchen, a private bathroom, and a stunning view of the river, its snowy banks blanketed by a thick gray mist. A Christmas tree blinked in the corner, a few presents tucked underneath, and I remembered, suddenly, that it was nearly Christmas. I should have brought a gift. It would have cast this whole thing in a better light.

"Nonna," I said. She didn't seem to hear or see me, so I took another step closer. "Is this a good time?"

Nonna, small and frail, a jet-black wig perched on her head like a nest, sat on a sectional sofa near the window, a magnifying glass in one hand, a paperback in the other.

She turned the glass in my direction, and a single blue eye expanded under the thick lens, as hard and bright as a blown-glass marble. "Come, sit down," she said. Her English was heavily accented, her voice clear and direct, forceful, not at all the voice one would expect from an eighty-six-year-old woman.

I sat across from Nonna on a wobbly recliner. Up close, her skin was mottled with moles and freckles. A few hairs grew from her chin and ears, and her hands were dappled with liver spots. She looked me over, skeptical, and I wondered if she'd forgotten me.

"It's Bert," I said, feeling my cheeks go warm. "Luca's wife."

"I know who you are, child," she said, glancing back to the door, looking for her grandson. "Is Luca here, too?"

"He's working," I said. "He told me to tell you he'll be here Sunday, with Bob, to take you to church."

"Oh," she said. She focused on me with a strange intensity, as if trying to understand why I had come without Luca. "So remind me: Who do you belong to?"

The older generation always asked who your parents and

grandparents were, as if you were nothing more than a weak reflection of an ancestral original.

"My parents were Giuliano and Barb. I'm the grandchild of Giovanni and Marta Monte."

"Giovanni's granddaughter," she said darkly, her brows settling into a furrow. "Of course, I see the resemblance. You look just like your grandfather when he was young. Around the eyes. Attractive, your grandfather. *Nessus dubbio a riguardo.*"

I barely remembered my grandfather. He had died when I was five years old, and only fragments of him remained with me: the smell of his cigarettes, the glimmer in his blue eyes as he laughed, the shiny leather shoes he wore, the tassels flopping. I was about to ask what other similarities she found between us when Nonna pulled herself up off the couch and walked to the kitchen.

"Coffee?" she asked. "Milk or sugar?"

"Black," I said, eyeing the paperback she had been reading: *Amore proibito.* A bare-chested hulk of a man held a redheaded pixie in his bulging arms on the cover.

Nonna returned with the coffee. She had trouble managing, so I took the cups, set them on the coffee table, and helped her sit. When she had settled in, I pulled out the envelope from Turin.

"I was hoping you could help me with something, Nonna," I said, slipping the papers from the envelope and giving them to her. "This came in the mail, but I don't know what it says."

Nonna spread out the pages over the table and picked up her magnifying glass. The lens tracked over the lines, the words popping into view. She paused at the golden seal and a blaze of foil exploded at the center of the glass.

"My goodness, I never thought I would see this again," she said.

I leaned across the coffee table to get a closer look. She angled the magnifying glass over the seal and I saw it again: the castle above two mountain peaks.

"This was everywhere in Nevenero," she said. "All over town. In the post office, on street signs, on the door of the café. Everywhere."

"What is it?" I asked.

"The Montebianco coat of arms." She put down the magnifying glass. Her face had gone ashen. She lifted her eyes to meet mine. "Where did you get this letter?"

"It came this morning," I said, sipping my coffee. "Registered mail."

"I shouldn't be surprised, I suppose." She sighed a deep and resigned sigh. "It was only a matter of time before they found you."

I considered this a moment. *Before they found you.* The way she said it, her voice accusatory, her eyes filled with a sudden wariness, made it seem as though this was my fault and that I had been hoping to be found.

"Who is *they*?"

"The House of Montebianco."

The name on the letter flashed in my mind. *Alberta Isabelle Eleanor Vittoria Montebianco.*

"According to this letter, the Count of Montebianco died six months ago." She tapped her magnifying glass against the edge of the coffee table, as if the rhythm helped her think. "The lawyers representing the family estate looked for his heir." *Tap, tap.* "They have come to the conclusion that there is not one Montebianco left in the world." *Tap, tap, tap.* "Except you."

I must have appeared utterly baffled, because Nonna said it again, only more slowly.

"This letter is from the legal team representing the House of Montebianco. They claim that you, Alberta, are the last of the Montebianco family line. They want you to come to Turin for an interview regarding your inheritance, which is explained"—Nonna shifted through the papers and pulled out the fancy-looking one with the golden seal—"here, in the Count of Montebianco's last will and testament."

"What else does it say?" I asked, a mixture of wariness and wonder bubbling up in me, the same restrained hope I felt when a pregnancy test came back positive: a new possibility was forming in my life.

Nonna bent over the pages with her magnifying glass. "I can hardly read this, there is so much legal language here, but this page outlines what you could inherit if you are proven to be the heir. There is the title and a property." She bit her lip, her expression going somber. "Montebianco Castle," she said, her voice little more than a whisper. "A death trap, to be sure."

"But there is obviously some kind of mistake," I said. "My name is Alberta Monte, not Montebianco."

She leveled her gaze at me. "You are Giovanni's granddaughter, yes?"

"Yes," I said. "I am."

"Then you belong to the House of Montebianco as sure as that seal does."

Although I had heard everything she said, I could not process what was happening. Pieces of information were coming to me, but they didn't make sense. There was the Montebianco name, an inheritance, my grandfather, a golden seal. The facts collected in my mind, but I couldn't read them.

"You knew about this before?" A shade of an accusation slipped into my voice.

"Of course we knew," she said, dismissing my question with a shrug. "Your grandfather Giovanni was born a Montebianco. He shortened his name when he naturalized as a citizen. Many of us did that, you know, to fit in. Jews. Eastern Europeans. Italians. But he had a more specific reason, of course. Oh, he was a proud man, your grandfather, not one to speak badly about his family, but we knew he'd run away from them. Who were we to blame him for trying to bury the past? We were all doing the same thing."

As she spoke, I felt more and more confused. Who had he run away from? And why would he speak badly about his family? "But what was there to bury?"

A shadow passed over her features. "It has been almost seventy years since I left," she said at last, her voice trembling. "And nearly that long since I have spoken of it."

"Of what, Nonna?"

"*Nevenero,*" she said, emphasizing each syllable. "The village we left behind. Do you know what it means?"

I shook my head. I had no idea.

"Black snow." She gave me a dark look, as if the words pained her. "*Neve,* snow; *nero,* black. Such a cruel place, Nevenero. An ice village, so cold, so brutal you froze to death if you wandered too far from home. We ate what we killed—ibex and rabbit. We wore goatskin trousers and marmot furs. Our houses were made of simple materials—wood and slabs of granite—with high, wedge-shaped roofs that kept off the snow. Simple but strong. And always, no matter the position of the sun, the village was trapped in the shadow of the mountains. Day and night, it was dark. But the castle, built higher than the village, built right into the rock of the mountain, was even darker still."

Nonna leaned forward, her eyes filled with emotion. "The

village was so dominated by the mountains that roads were nearly impassable, so narrow that trucks jammed the sheer, glacial passages. It is a miracle we were able to leave at all. But we did leave: brothers and sisters, aunts and uncles, friends and rivals—we all fled. We all came here to start over. And that is why we all forgave Giovanni. Despite his name, we forgave him. Forgiveness, however, is not the same as trust."

I sat back in the recliner, trying to understand why so many people had fled Nevenero and what my grandfather had done to require forgiveness.

"Does Luca know about this?" I asked at last. "Or Bob?"

"We came here to start over," she said. "We didn't want the children to know."

Nonna pushed her glasses up her nose and adjusted her wig. "I have photos somewhere around here," she said. She pointed to a cabinet near her bed. "Look in there."

I went to the cabinet, found an album in a drawer, and brought it to Nonna. She flipped through the pages, and I saw a series of black-and-white images of stone houses, miserable-looking children, goats knee-deep in snow. There was a family portrait of people whose features were a half rhyme to Luca's—Nonna's brothers and sisters, I guessed. Her parents. Her grandparents. Nonna pulled out a photo of a narrow valley carved between two snowcapped mountains. At the center of the valley, lifting like a sinister wedding cake, was a castle. It stood dark and solitary, surrounded by sharp peaks. All else was ice and shadow.

"That is Montebianco Castle," she said, her expression filled with fear. "I never saw it up close. We were not allowed to go anywhere near it."

I took the album and looked at the picture. "My grandfather lived *there*?" I asked, astonished.

"They didn't mix with the villagers," she said. "I didn't meet your grandfather until we made the crossing."

She turned the pages until she came to a yellowed newspaper clipping. "Here it is," she said, pulling a photo from a page and giving it to me. A young man stood before a steamer, the words "S.S. *Saturnia*" painted on the side. The quality of the photo was degraded, so grainy that Giovanni seemed little more than a stain of sepia bleeding through the page, but I could see that he was packed for a voyage. There was a suitcase in his hand and a steamer trunk sat at his side. An expression of wonder colored his features, a reckless readiness, the kind of expression that accompanies an act of faith. I could see that Sophia had been right about our resemblance: my grandfather was tall and broad-shouldered, with a wide forehead, large hands, and a deep cleft in the chin. Like me.

"That was the ship that took us from Genoa to New York," she said, running a yellow fingernail over the picture. "I didn't have the same class berth as your grandfather—I was down below—but we played cards up on the deck. Look here." She glided the magnifying glass over the photo, so that it hovered about the steamer trunk. There, in tiny gold letters stamped into the leather, was the name: MONTEBIANCO. "It was July 1949," she said, her voice sad suddenly. "We didn't want to go, but we had no choice. After they took my younger brother, Gregor, all of us left."

"Wait," I said, thinking I had misheard her. "Who took your brother?"

Nonna closed the album. "The beast. It watched from the mountains and took the most vulnerable." There was a tremor in her voice. "The smallest children. The ones left alone to play in the village. Gregor was playing in the trees near the mountains when it happened. That's where they hid, where the trees grew thick. They killed our goats, ate them right there and left nothing but bones. We never found the bones of our children, though. The children just disappeared."

"What was it?" I asked, trying to imagine what kind of wild animal would attack goats and children. "A wolf?"

"I encountered it only once, but it was enough to understand that it was not like anything I had ever seen before," Nonna said. "I was fourteen years old when I saw it." She rubbed her eyes, as if massaging away a headache. "The beast took Gregor a few years later. After that, we left. Our homes, our belongings, the graves of our ancestors, everything. We didn't look back, ever. Even your grandfather Giovanni, who had so much more to lose, gave up everything. He knew what was happening in those mountains. He knew!"

Nonna's eyes had become large and wild. I picked up the letter and shoved it back into the envelope.

"There's no need to get upset, Nonna," I said. "It happened a long time ago."

"Yes, a long time ago," she said, leaning back into the sofa, exhausted. "A very long time ago. But tell me, child, do we ever escape the evils of the past?"

A chill fell over me, and although I had no clear idea of the evils to which Nonna referred, I felt the same premonition I had felt earlier that day, a premonition of the past bleeding into the future, dark and deadly, a warning to leave it be and go on as if I had never heard the name Montebianco.

"Do not go to them," she said, meeting my eyes. "Your family has had such trouble. Such tragedy and pain. Let the past die. Look ahead, to the future here with Luca."

I stared at her, wondering what on earth she was talking about. Could she possibly know about the troubles Luca and I had had over the years? We hadn't told anyone about our struggles to have a child. The pregnancies, the miscarriages, my infertility treatments, the specialists—we had tried to spare them disappointment.

"Everything is fine, Nonna," I said. "Don't worry. It will all be okay."

"This is our fault," she said, her voice anguished, her eyes enormous behind her glasses. "We didn't tell our children what happened in Nevenero. We didn't tell our grandchildren. We wanted to forget. We wanted you to be innocent. We thought we had escaped."

Nonna trembled as she spoke. She didn't look well. I felt for my phone. I would call Luca and ask him to come over and help.

"This is nothing to get worked up about, Nonna," I said. "Please. Don't worry. It's just a letter."

"Just a letter?" she said, her eyes growing large. "Don't you understand? They want you back. The Montebianco family has come for you. They *need* you back. I am sure this is not the first time they've tried. Giovanni must have known they would come. He couldn't bear the thought of it. That is why he killed himself."

"My grandfather killed himself?" I asked, astonished. I leaned back into the recliner for support. "He committed suicide? Are you sure?"

"Don't be fooled," she said, narrowing her eyes. "Whatever that family gives you is nothing compared to what you will lose."

It couldn't be true that my grandfather had killed himself. I would have known. My parents would have told me. But suddenly, it struck me how little I knew about my grandparents. My parents had no photos of them, no family heirlooms, nothing at all of our Italian heritage. My parents had never spoken of the past. Could they have been hiding something?

Nonna tried to stand, but fell back into the sofa, wheezing and gasping. I was afraid she would collapse right there and die, on the floor of her living room.

"Nonna," I said, going to her side. "Please, Nonna, calm down. I'm getting Luca. Don't worry."

Nonna grabbed my sleeve and pulled me close. Reaching for my hand, she took it between her cold fingers and brought it to her heart. She looked me in the eye and, her voice shaking with emotion, said, "Listen to me, child. I saw it. The beast came for me on the mountain pass. Its teeth were sharp as razors, its eyes devilish. But worst of all, it was so like us. Monstrous and yet so human. The legends were true."

THREE

❧

*D*EVIL. MONSTER. BEAST. *Suicide.*
These words circled my mind as I walked through the parking lot. *Devil. Monster. Beast. Suicide.* Nonna Sophia had left Italy nearly seventy years ago, and yet her fear remained hard and tactile, so solid I could feel it there beside me as I kicked through the snow to my car. What on earth had she seen that had scared her like that? An animal? A person? What did she mean by "the legends were true"?

Try as I might, I couldn't put her words out of my mind. The way she held my hand to her heart and the beseeching look in her eyes—she had been terrified. *Don't be fooled. Whatever that family gives you is nothing compared to what you will lose.*

At my car, I looked out over the vast grounds of the Monastery. It was three thirty in the afternoon, snowing heavily, the sky a fog of indigo against the river. The days were at their shortest, and dusk had fallen, darkness rising from the river to the heavens like watercolors seeping into paper. I brushed a layer of snow from the windshield, wishing that Luca had come with me. Surely, he would have known what to say to calm Nonna. He was always better at these things than I was.

Yet, even Luca would have found Nonna's reaction to the letter extreme. I leaned against my car, feeling unbalanced, dizzy. Had my grandfather really committed suicide? Why would my parents have kept that from me? Had they, like

Nonna Sophia and the older generation, tried to protect me from the truth?

As I got into my Honda, I heard something behind me. I turned, expecting to find a visitor, maybe even Luca. There was nothing but the empty parking lot, the wash of darkening light, the snow swirling in the wind. And yet, I felt a presence, an eerie human presence, close as breath on the back of my neck. Something wasn't right.

I locked the car door, turned on the heater, and called Luca, telling him everything. After he promised to come to the Monastery to check on Nonna, I threw the car into reverse, did a U-turn, and headed back toward Milton. It was three forty-five. The town hall closed at five.

MRS. THOMAS, HEAD of the Vital Records office, was my friend Tina's mother. In high school, there had been weeks when I had slept at the Thomases' house more often than my own, partially because Tina and I played softball together, but also because, being an only child, I loved Tina's brothers and sisters, the big chaotic family dinners, and the sense that there was always something exciting happening at the Thomases' place. I'd compared her house with mine and, finding life quiet and dull with my parents, chosen to be with Tina.

The Vital Records counter was abandoned, but I could smell coffee from somewhere beyond the rows of metal filing cabinets, so I knew someone must be back there. I rang the bell and waited. Office hours were 8:30 a.m. to 5:00 p.m. Monday through Friday, but even if Mrs. Thomas had left early, someone would help me.

"Well, hello there, Bert Monte!" Mrs. Thomas said, stepping out from behind a cabinet. She was a tall black woman in her fifties with an abundance of gold rings stacked on her fingers. "You looking for Tina?"

I was glad to see Mrs. Thomas. She had a way of putting me at ease. Maybe Tina had told her about my troubles at school, or my crippling shyness, because Mrs. Thomas always made me feel welcome. "Isn't Tina in the city?" I asked.

"Brooklyn," she said, shaking her head. "That girl left the day she graduated and is never coming back."

"I heard you're a grandma," I said, aware, suddenly, how much time had passed since high school. I could hardly believe Tina and I had graduated ten years ago.

"Blessed many times over," Mrs. Thomas said. "Three grandbabies. Two boys and a girl."

Mrs. Thomas reached for a framed photograph on her desk, but I was too preoccupied to see her grandchildren. "I know you're closing soon, but I was hoping to take a look at the Monte family records before you leave for the night," I said. "Birth and death certificates. I'm doing some research."

"Not you too," she said, flipping up a square of countertop and letting me pass into her domain.

"You've had other requests for Monte family records?" I asked.

"No, silly," she said, swatting my arm. "We are totally overrun with genealogy requests. I have been photocopying and mailing records all over the place. Just last week I priority-mailed twenty-three birth records to a lady in Florida. She took a genetic test and realized her dad—the man she grew up with and whose name she carries—wasn't actually her biological father. Her mother told her the name of her real father is Joe Johnson, from Marlborough, New York, so I went through every one of these cabinets hunting down that name. There were twenty-three Joseph Johnsons born between 1899 and 1935." Mrs. Thomas gave me a look of exhaustion. "I know I shouldn't complain. Vital Records revenue is up by about a million percent."

She walked back into the maze of filing cabinets. "Are you making a family tree? Everyone I know has one going on ancestry.com. Or they're doing genetic tests from that other site. What's it called? Two-three something. I just did a spit test and found out I'm not even African!"

"What are you, then?" I asked, surprised by this. Her skin was a dark caramel brown.

"If you ask me, I'll tell you I'm African American. But according to my test, I'm thirty-nine percent Hispanic, forty-one percent Middle Eastern, twelve percent Irish, and eight percent African! I'm more *Irish* than African? I couldn't believe it, so I took it again. I paid another hundred dollars to get the same result!"

"That is crazy," I said. Maybe I wasn't the only one with family secrets. "What a surprise."

"It changes everything and nothing," she said, shaking her head, as if she were ready for whatever life might throw at her. "I mean, I am still *me,* but jeez, it's hard to get your mind around something like that." She went to her desk and pulled out a piece of paper. "Here it is, all official."

The words "Genetic Profile" were written across the top. Below this, there was a sequence of ancestral groups—Northwestern European, Middle Eastern, North African, Southern European, East Asian, Sub-Saharan African, Native American, and so on, with percentages next to them. There were "Maternal and Paternal Haplogroups," a section titled "DNA Family," and another column called "Neanderthal Variants." A chart outlined the ancestral group results Mrs. Thomas had described.

I knew exactly what kind of test this was. Some months before, I had bought a genetic testing kit from the online company Mrs. Thomas had mentioned. The site promised to give a complete profile of my ancestry, including the countries of origin and the ethnicity of my ancestors, all for ninety-nine dollars. I had spit into a plastic tube, mailed it to a lab, and awaited my results.

That had been many months before, in the wake of the last miscarriage, when I'd been desperate to find something, anything, that might explain why I couldn't have a child. I had seen specialists, none of whom had answers for me. The idea struck me, as I watched Mrs. Thomas search through the *M* filing cabinet, that it wasn't a coincidence that I had taken a genetic test when I did. I had been in mourning. My marriage, the baby, my parents, my studies—I had lost so much in the previous years. Sadness and disappointment had subsumed me, ripping out the seams of every part of my life, even the parts I thought were tightly bound. Without Luca, I was alone in a way I had never been before. There were moments—late at night, after drinking too much—when I felt that the universe, with all its billions of life-forms, its bacteria and protozoa, its plants and animals, was broken somehow. How could the world be teeming with life when I felt so utterly alone? I wasn't going to get into it with Mrs. Thomas, but I had needed that test. I needed to believe that a scientific breakdown of my genetic composition—a clean, color-coded pie graph that demonstrated my family heritage scientifically— would tell me something profound about who I was and why I was floating untethered, no family to steady me.

As it turned out, my test results never came back. I guessed they had been lost in the mail, and sent an email to the site's customer service address, asking for information. But then things came to a head with Luca, and I forgot all about the genetic test.

"Here we are," Mrs. Thomas said, pulling out some certificates and bringing them to her desk. "I didn't know you had an uncle," she added, fanning the papers out so I could see them.

"He died before I was born," I said.

There weren't many Monte birth certificates. Just three: my father, Giuliano, who had been born January 17, 1961; his brother, Frank, born March 22, 1966; and me, Alberta, born March 20, 1988. My grandfather Giovanni had been born in Italy, so there would be no birth certificate for him on file. My mother was born in Dutchess County, and her certificate would be there, filed under her maiden name.

Before I could ask her to photocopy them, Mrs. Thomas was off on the other side of the room, hunting through the filing cabinet holding death certificates. While I waited, I pulled my birth certificate from the pile. My Social Security card had the initial "I" as my middle name, as did my driver's license. I read the birth certificate. Family name: Monte. First name: Alberta. Between those names were three others: Isabelle Eleanor Vittoria.

"Hmm," Mrs. Thomas said, her head bent over the cabinet. From the sound of her voice, something wasn't right.

"There should be five death certificates," I said. "My grandparents, my parents, and my dad's brother."

"Come here a sec, hon," she said, lifting the file from the cabinet and carrying it to the back of the office. "Take a look at this."

Mrs. Thomas spread the death certificates out under the light of a lamp. I could see there were more than five. Significantly more. She arranged them into two piles on her desk.

The left pile had the five certificates I had expected to find. On the right, there were ten others.

"What are those?" I said, taking the pile on the right. I sorted through them, one by one. The first eight certificates were dated between 1942 and 1969. The parents were listed as Marta Monte and Giovanni Monte, my grandparents. On the line where the names should have been typed, there was an abbreviation: N/A. Not applicable. The last two certificates were from the eighties, and the parents were listed as my mother and father. Each of those two certificates had a name: Rebecca Monte and John Monte. At the top of each document were the words "Certificate of Death."

I sat down in the chair at Mrs. Thomas's desk, stunned, and looked at them all again.

"Names weren't mandatory with these older ones," she said, pointing to the eight nameless certificates. She picked up the newer certificates. "But these two came after new regulations were put in place. Names were required on all certificates in this county after 1978."

I stared at the death certificates, the typed words and official signatures, my heart heavy. "What does that mean?"

She looked at me, suddenly cautious. "You see here," she said, pointing to the dates. "The day of birth and death is the same. These are all stillbirths."

A heavy, suffocating weight pressed on me. *Stillbirths.* That was what the last miscarriage had been, technically. The first three had happened early, before the eighth week, nothing but blood and some cramping. But the last pregnancy had been twenty weeks along, a boy, fully formed and small as a kitten. I'd held him for a moment, looking at him, knowing it would be the last time. I wrapped him in a cotton swaddle blanket and kissed his forehead. When they took him away, it was as if they took a part of me, too. Luca had taken care of everything at the hospital, and I never saw any of the paperwork. Our baby—our son—must have a certificate there, under Luca's family name. I wondered what name Luca had given him.

"You all right there?" Mrs. Thomas asked.

"I just don't understand how there can be so many . . ." I couldn't say it, the word "stillbirth"; it stuck in my throat like chewing gum. "So many of *these* in my family."

"You didn't know about any of this?"

I shook my head. "I knew that I was an only child, and that my father had a brother who died young. But I didn't know about . . ." I glanced at the papers. "Them."

Your family has had such trouble. Such tragedy.

"Well, sometimes when you start digging into family history, this shit just comes out of the woodwork," Mrs. Thomas said. She patted my hand and gave it a squeeze. "Let me make you some copies."

"Thanks," I said. As she walked back to the copy machine, I remembered why I had come there in the first place. "Hold on a sec," I said, pulling my grandfather's Certificate of Death from the pile and taking it back to her desk. Giovanni Monte, born 1931 in Nevenero, Italy. Died July 1993 in Milton, New York. Running my finger down the page I found what I was looking for. Cause of death: suicide.

FOUR

✣

I KNEW I WAS being followed the moment I pulled out of
the parking lot. There was the same prickling sensation at
the back of my neck that I'd felt at the Monastery, the same
eerie presence lingering behind, only now I could identify it:
a black Porsche with New Jersey license plates.

The car arrived like a sheet of fog sliding over the moon:
there was a sudden darkening of the atmosphere, a tremor in
the air. It pulled out after my Honda, slowed, and drove
carefully, too carefully, behind me. I checked the rearview
mirror, saw the car trailing me, noted its tenacious proximity, and continued onward, trying to ignore it. But a new
Porsche in the hamlet of Milton was an anomaly nearly as
great as a letter from noble relatives in Italy. I fixed my eyes
on the road and drove, determined to get home without having an accident.

A parade of emotions had marched through me that day,
but for the first time I was really, truly angry. What in the
hell was going on? Why had my parents kept Rebecca and
John a secret? Or the other eight stillborn Monte babies?
Hadn't they thought that maybe one day I would discover the
death certificates and figure out that there was some kind of
medical issue in our family? What hurt the most was that my
mom and I had spent so much time together when she was

sick, so many afternoons watching television, so many mornings walking by the river, talking about everything under the sun, and she had said *nothing*. Not one word about Rebecca or John. Not one peep about the name Montebianco. Not a whisper that Grandpa Giovanni's family had a fancy title and a castle and probably a shitload of money.

By the time I pulled up at home, I was fuming. I jumped out of the car, ready to confront whoever was driving the black Porsche, but I found—as I looked behind me, my headlights cutting voluminous sculptural shadows in the snow— no one. I was alone. My house was dark, the driveway empty. I started to tell myself that all of this was nothing to get worked up about, but of course, it *was* something to get worked up about. With the arrival of the House of Montebianco's letter, the cogs and wheels of an unstoppable machine had been set in motion. I wanted to pretend that it was just another day, and that I could go on as I had before. But I couldn't have ignored the letter, or anything else I had learned that day, even if I wanted to.

My head was throbbing. The sooner the day was over, I thought, the better. It wasn't even six o'clock, but I wanted dinner, a hot shower, and bed. Tomorrow, I would look at the world with fresh eyes and a clear mind. Tomorrow, everything would make sense.

I made my way up the icy drive, keeping my balance the best I could, when, out of the corner of my eye, I saw the black Porsche parked down the street. I stopped, a lightning bolt of fear bursting through me, and ran to the front door. My heart racing, I slipped the key into the lock and pushed the door open. I was nearly inside when a shadow fell across the entrance. I caught my breath, and terror, sharp as a spike of ice, slid up my spine. They had, as Nonna Sophia had warned, found me.

FROM NONNA SOPHIA'S description of Nevenero, I had imagined the home of my ancestors as a place in a fairy tale, a cursed village hidden in the mountains. In my mind, I envisioned ice-glazed gingerbread houses, a haunted castle, a ring of spiked granite peaks looming at the periphery. I imagined the Montebiancos as a cruel Italian Mafia family whose vicious crimes had pushed the villagers to flee. The one thing that never crossed my mind was that the House of Montebianco would send someone after me and that this someone would be so disturbingly, so disarmingly charming.

"Really sorry," a man said, stepping from the shadows. "I didn't mean to frighten you."

I'd jumped away from the door and dropped my keys. I may have screamed, as well, and although I can't remember hearing my voice, the expression on the man's face told me that my reaction had startled him.

He held up his hands to show they were empty. "I'm harmless, I promise," he added, giving me a big smile. "Unless you have a legal problem. In that case, I can be quite devastating."

Devastating to say the least. He was thirty-something and handsome, with dark, unruly hair, very shiny oxfords, and a well-cut suit. Not winter attire in rural New York, to be sure. He spoke with a strange accent, one that I later understood to be British English softened by the fluidity of his native Italian.

"Who the hell are you?" I said, recovering my composure enough to retrieve my keys from a snow-filled planter.

"Enzo Roberts," he said, offering me his hand. "I realize this is an unconventional way to approach you. But . . ." He shivered and looked past me, into the house. "Could I possibly . . . ?"

"Come in?" I said, ignoring his extended hand. "No way."

He looked wounded. "I'm here to help you, if you would let me explain."

"Help me?" I said. "Help me with what?"

"With the details." He tapped snow from his oxfords on the edge of the concrete step. "I'm a lawyer with the Montebianco Estate. You should have received some rather complicated legal documents. I want to clarify some points that may be . . . confusing."

"Not necessary," I said, stepping into the foyer of my house and gripping the door. "Thank you very much."

"Just let me explain . . ."

But he didn't need to explain. The letter had caused too much pain and confusion already. I didn't want to speak to Enzo Roberts. I didn't want to shake his hand or hear his explanation. I wanted Enzo Roberts to turn around and walk away, so that I could hold off thinking about the Montebianco family, and the bundle of death certificates in my purse, for one more night.

I pushed the door closed and latched the lock.

"Truly," he called from the other side of the door, "I'm sorry to approach you this way. It is an odd situation, to be sure, and you must want to think it all over in peace. But please allow me to come inside for just a few minutes and explain. There is more to this than you might suspect. Give me five minutes. Then I will leave you alone. I promise."

"Wait there," I said, pulling out my phone and dialing Luca. "My husband will be here in a few minutes."

TEN MINUTES LATER, Luca's Jeep pulled into the driveway. By then, I had googled Enzo Roberts and found, according to his profile on LinkedIn, that he was a thirty-seven-year-old lawyer who lived in Turin. Outside, Luca asked a few questions before he rapped on the door. As he brushed by me, he squeezed my arm to reassure me that everything would be okay. Although I had explained the situation on the phone—namely, that there was a strange man on the front steps and that we might want to call the police—it was clear that Luca was going to handle this the way he handled everything else: with a cool head and a generous pour.

"I think we all need a drink, what do you say?" he said, leading Enzo Roberts into the living room.

A drink was exactly what we needed. Sometimes, I wondered if I wasn't divorcing a saint.

"I'll make them," I said, heading to the kitchen, where I dug out a bottle of my favorite gin from the cupboard, sliced a lime, and grabbed a bottle of tonic water from the fridge. The sound of the ice cracking and the smell of juniper and lime calmed my nerves. No need to panic, I told myself. Nothing bad was happening. We would have a drink with Enzo Roberts, hear him out, then send him on his way.

Enzo and Luca were laughing by the time I joined them in the living room. Luca had begun his usual charm offensive, telling Enzo about one of the regulars at the bar, a guy named Butch who got drunk and used the bar phone to prank call his ex-wives. With his silk tie and buffed oxfords, Enzo looked nothing like the locals at the Miltonian, but Luca was a barman through and through, and could talk to anyone about any subject. No matter where you came from or what you looked like, Luca could make you feel at home in five minutes.

I put the tray of drinks on the coffee table. I hadn't finished decorating the tree, and tinsel and ornaments were strewn here and there, making the room cheerier than it had seemed in a long time. I sat down next to Luca and looked at Enzo more carefully. He had black hair and large, dark eyes. His cheeks were still pink from the cold, and his elegant hands were folded over his wool trousers. There was a briefcase at his feet, its calfskin polished to a shine. It struck me that I needed this guy. He might be the only person who could help me understand the story of my family.

Enzo gave me a big, charming smile, took a sip of his gin and tonic, and said, "As I mentioned, I'm here to help you with the documents you should have received."

"I did receive them," I said, taking a sip of my drink.

"And is there anything I can help you understand?"

"You can start by telling me what in the hell is going on." I could hear my voice rising, and felt Luca tense up at my side, but I didn't care. In the past few hours, everything I had believed about myself had been turned inside out. I wanted answers.

"Well," Enzo said, straightening, his voice turning lawyerly, as hard and cold as a winter morning. "You've inherited a legacy that is worth a great deal, and you will need to travel to Italy to meet with the estate lawyers to claim it."

Luca said, "What does that mean—*worth a great deal?*"

"It means," Enzo said, looking over the living room, his gaze settling on the small, sad-looking Christmas tree, "life-changing."

I kept my expression neutral, hoping to mask how curious I was about what he could tell me. But in truth, I was dying to know everything about the Montebianco family. I wanted to understand my parents' silence, my grandfather's suicide, Nonna's strange warnings. I wanted to know if my family history might explain the void that had formed at the center of my life.

"That said," Enzo continued. "There are a few circumstances

you should be aware of." His voice became soft, as if he were telling us a secret. "This isn't just about money. The Montebianco family is more than just another wealthy family. They are a rather special family. *Were* special, I should say."

"Special?" I said, suspicious. "Special how?"

Enzo took a sip of his drink, swirled the ice, and took another. "What I'm trying to say is that your inheritance is not simply a matter of cash. It is comprised of quite a few other . . . elements."

"The letter mentioned a list of assets," I said. "A property in Nevenero."

"Yes, there is that, of course. But I'm not referring to Montebianco Castle," he said, finishing off his drink and putting it on the coffee table. "The Montebianco family is an old one. There are very few families like it in the world. Your first noble ancestor was born in the thirteenth century. You are the twenty-ninth generation to inherit the family title."

"Wow," I said, trying to imagine it. "I guess everyone has to come from somewhere."

Enzo laughed. "Yes," he said. "They do. That is certain. And you come from a very particular somewhere. The estate would like to speak with you to discuss your position. To offer guidance. The sooner the better."

"It can't hurt to get more information," Luca said, and, if I hadn't known him better, I'd have said he was warming to the idea of the Montebianco fortune.

"Okay," I said. Maybe he was right. Nothing wrong with more information. "I'd like to speak with them."

"Perfect," Enzo said, looking relieved.

"What's the time difference in Italy?" I asked. "Is it too late to call now? Or we could do it tomorrow?"

"It *is* too late, as a matter of fact. And besides," he added, giving me a serious look, "the estate will need to speak with you in person. Everything has been arranged. The estate is waiting for us in Turin. Transportation has been scheduled. We can go whenever you're ready."

"What? *Now?*" I said, startled. "As in right this minute? There's no way I can go now."

"Why not?" Enzo asked. "Luca, you are more than welcome to join us, of course. Clearly, this inheritance affects you both. The two of you can spend Christmas in Turin. There is a lovely hotel in the old part of the city. The estate will arrange everything."

"I don't even have a passport," I said. Luca and I had been meaning to travel abroad for years, but the time had never seemed right. "Neither of us do."

"Not a problem," Enzo said. "We anticipated that and found a solution."

I glanced at my husband. For the first time in our marriage, Luca was at a loss. Once, a surprise trip to Italy for Christmas might have thrilled him. Now, as we were navigating our separation, it was a minefield.

"I'd love to," Luca said at last. "But New Year's Eve is our busiest night of the year. That doesn't mean you shouldn't go, Bert. Actually, it might be good for you to get away from here for a week or two. It will help get your mind off things."

"You don't think this is totally crazy?" I asked. It was all happening so fast. I relied upon Luca to be reasonable, but he didn't seem to think it was such a bad idea.

"Sure, it's a little out there," Luca said, giving me a smile. "But it hasn't been the easiest year for you. Maybe this is what you need to get back on track."

I turned to Enzo Roberts, perched at the edge of the couch, watching us with a cool, sharp gaze. I wanted to trust him, but couldn't quite yet.

"Lawyers are used to dealing with false claims," I said, eyeing the briefcase. "I can't imagine you came all this way without some kind of evidence."

Enzo bit his lip, considering my request. Then he pulled out his briefcase, slid it onto the coffee table, and flipped it open. "As a matter of fact," he said, "I do have something." He pulled out a piece of paper and handed it across the table. "Do you know what this is?"

It took me a full minute before I understood the charts and numbers on the paper in my hands. But once I got it, things began to fall into place. There was a genetic profile of my ancestry, the kind of basic breakdown Mrs. Thomas had shown me. On a separate page, I found columns of numbers and symbols, a bunch of terms I didn't understand. The words *"DNA Test Report"* were written across the top of the page. The Montebianco family estate had used my DNA to find me.

Just then, as my eyes jumped down the ladder of data, a memory opened in my mind. I was a child, not even five years old. It was winter, and I was walking with my grandfather on the snow-covered land behind his house. I tried to keep up with him, but he moved at a pace that seemed impossible to me. At last, he stopped at a pond, frozen over and dusted with snow. He took off his boots, first one, then the other, until his large, wide feet were bare. He nodded to my boots and told me to take them off. *It's too cold,* I said. *Where I come from, this is not cold,* he replied. I didn't want to take off my boots, but I did anyway, one at a time, then my socks, until my bare feet stung in the snow. We walked on the pond, slipping over the ice until my feet burned with a white-hot fire, then went numb.

In my living room over two decades later, reading the document that changed my life, I felt the same white-hot fire in my body. I was frozen but burning up.

"How in the world did you get this report?"

"Apparently, it was quite easy," Enzo said. "When you sent in your saliva sample, you checked a box allowing your information to be released to the company's DNA specialists, so that they might include you in their so-called DNA Family Tree. This allowed your DNA to be analyzed and recorded in a database. A private genetic research company pays to access this database. To be fair, the research team we hired acquires genetic information from multiple online sources. There are a few major databases, but online ancestry companies are the most efficient. And streamlined."

"Is that even legal?" I asked, trying to remember the release I had signed. It was just some form online, endless legalese with a box to check at the bottom. I hadn't even read it, just clicked through. At the time, it had seemed innocuous enough.

"Very much so," Enzo said.

"And so according to these results, my DNA matches . . ."

"The Montebianco family." Enzo pulled out a second report. "This shows your relationship to your now-deceased great-uncle Guillaume Montebianco. The match is indisputable."

I stared at the papers. I couldn't argue with a DNA report, but I didn't quite trust it either. It was like watching a magic act. You know it's all sleight of hand, but the trick is so smooth you accept it as real. I finished my drink, all of it, in one gulp.

"You okay, Bert?" Luca asked, touching my hand.

"It's just a lot to take in," I said, wanting, suddenly, to go back in time to that morning in the kitchen, when the pre-monition of danger had been so vivid, and dump the envelope in the recycling bin.

"I'm sure this is all quite disorienting," Enzo said, taking the DNA reports and sliding them back into his briefcase. "But it doesn't have to be. The estate will go over everything with you in Turin. I assure you, there is nothing to worry about. It will all be clear soon enough."

He snapped his briefcase shut and stood to go.

"I can't believe my family kept so many secrets," I said quietly, speaking more to myself than to Luca or Enzo.

"Every family has its secrets," Enzo said. "But nothing reveals the truth like DNA."

FIVE

✦

WE FLEW TO Italy that night.

Enzo Roberts went to get dinner in town, giving me time to talk Luca into coming with me. I explained about my grandfather's suicide and what I had learned at the Vital Records office. He must have sensed how much I needed him, but he also must have realized that if ever there would be a moment of reconciliation between us, this was it. When he presented the trip in this light to his father, Bob was more than happy to cover at the bar, as it meant giving us time to work things out. We packed a few essentials—pajamas, a few changes of clothes, toothbrushes—turned down the heat, locked the front door, and left everything behind.

At Teterboro Airport, a chartered plane waited on the tarmac. It was impossible to mask my astonishment at the whole thing—the car that ferried us out onto the airfield, the sleek, shining jet, the simplicity and ease of it all. It took all of ten minutes to board. We didn't have to go through security. We didn't wait in lines. There was no taking off of shoes and jackets. No uncomfortable pat-downs. We just showed up, walked up some steps into the plane, and that was that. This, I realized, was the world in which certain people lived, a place where those with money were exempt from the rules.

Once in my seat, a uniformed air hostess poured us each a glass of champagne—the Cristal 2008 label peeking out from behind her fingers—gave us each a bowl of cashews, and assured us that dinner would be served as soon as we were in the air. "But of course, if you'd like anything before then, please let me know."

I leaned back into my huge leather reclining chair, wishing my mother were there. She would have loved the fancy champagne. My father had died in a car accident when I was nineteen, and while his death had been a painful shock, losing my mother had been harder. She had been diagnosed with throat and lung cancer when I was twenty-one, and had lived four more years, each year filled with a Ferris wheel of progress and reversals—she would climb to a state of remission only to fall back into the illness, as if taken down by a sinister gravity. The end was terrible, for her as well as for me. I raised my glass and, pushing aside my feelings about Rebecca and John, and everything else that had been left unsaid, made a silent toast to her.

I was on my second glass of champagne when a TSA agent stepped on board.

"What does he want?" I whispered to Luca, feeling my stomach sink. Surely, they were going to tell me that Enzo was a criminal, had entered the country illegally, and this would all be over.

"Passport control," Enzo replied as he stood and headed to the front of the plane. "Let me take care of it."

I watched Enzo, my face growing hot, sure we would be escorted off the plane any minute. But when the TSA agent asked for our passports, Enzo handed him three maroon booklets. The agent opened them up, glanced at me, then at the passport. I watched this interaction with my stomach in my throat, sick with the tension. But he didn't seem to be finding anything wrong with the situation. He even asked Enzo what the weather was like in Turin.

"Have a nice trip," the TSA agent said at last, giving the passports back to Enzo. Then he turned around and left.

"What just happened?" I asked, as Enzo sat across from me and picked up his glass of champagne. He handed me one of the passports. I opened it. My photograph stared back at me, and the name Alberta Isabelle Eleanor Vittoria Montebianco was typed out clearly on the page.

"Is this a fake?" I whispered.

"No, it is not a fake," Enzo said, smiling slightly.

"But this is me," I said, turning the passport to get a closer look at my picture. It definitely was me.

Nome: Alberta Isabelle Eleanor Vittoria Montebianco
Sesso: Donna
Luogo di nascita: Poughkeepsie, New York (USA)
Data di nascita: 20 Marzo 1988
Cittadinanza: Italiana

"Because of your ancestry, the Italian government recognizes you as an Italian citizen. We began the paperwork after we learned of your identity. The estate has some connections that proved useful to speed things up." He gave Luca a passport. "We got a spousal citizenship for you."

"Wow," I said. And because I could hold the passport in my hand, see my photo, and read my name on the laminated page, for the first time since learning of my inheritance, I believed that all this life-changing business, this Alberta the countess stuff, was really happening.

WE LANDED IN Turin the next day. I knew nothing about Torino, and so Enzo explained that it was a northern industrial city in the Piedmont region, famous for the Fiat 500 and the ancient House of Savoy, of which I was (as it turned out) a distant relation.

A car picked us up at the airport and delivered us to a boutique hotel at the historic center of the city, where we were ushered up a wide marble staircase to a spacious, elegant suite. There was a king-sized bed, a plush carpet, a bathroom with more marble than a monument, and a balcony overlooking a narrow street filled with shops and cafés. I fell into a deep sleep the minute I climbed into bed, a bottomless, disoriented sleep without geography, and woke to fresh flowers on my night table, a bouquet of white roses that filled the air with a rarified fragrance, one that I would thereafter associate with privilege. Tucked into the flowers was a card from the manager: *Welcome, Countess Montebianco. Please call my personal number if you should need anything at all.*

I doubted we would. The place was incredible, so large I almost forgot that Luca was there, sleeping on the couch across the room. I told myself that I shouldn't get too excited. We would meet the legal team, hear them out, and be on our way back home in a day or two. Even then, after having seen the DNA report, I was sure that there was a catch, something that would prove the whole thing to be a mistake.

I was still in my pajamas later that afternoon when a knock came at the door. Enzo Roberts, handsome and composed as ever, stood in the hallway. I stepped aside as he breezed into our room, all efficiency. He carried his briefcase, as usual, but in his other hand he had a fistful of shopping bags.

"I hope you don't mind, but I stopped by a boutique down the way," he said, gesturing to the bags. "Neither of you had time to pack properly. Try them on and let me know if they are acceptable."

I peered into the bags and saw stacks of new clothes. It was true that we hadn't packed much, only carry-on suitcases. There was a black silk dress, a pair of black suede boots, some brown wool trousers, a white silk blouse, and a charcoal suit jacket. I glanced at the price tags and almost choked. The dress alone cost more than my mortgage payment. And the charcoal suit jacket? It could have paid a good portion of my college tuition. Later, after I saw Italians walking in the streets near the hotel, I understood that the clothes were a necessary gift. What we had brought—a few sweaters, jeans, and tennis shoes—would be wildly out of place. If we were to go out wearing such attire, we would be visibly foreign. Enzo had bought the clothes in an effort to help us feel comfortable.

"This is beautiful," I said, pulling the black silk dress from the first bag. I held the dress out at arm's length. It was silk crepe with a low V in the front. The tag read size 46, the Italian equivalent to size 10. "Looks like it will fit."

He looked me over with an appreciative gaze. "I have an eye for beautiful things."

I gave him a sidelong glance. Could it be that Enzo Roberts was flirting with me? I glanced at Luca, who was too busy looking at a new leather jacket and some dress shirts to notice.

"Thank you," I said, folding the dress carefully and setting it on the edge of the bed. I picked up the trousers. "I'll wear these at the meeting. The estate won't know what hit them."

Enzo walked to the center of the room, stopping under the chandelier.

"Did you sleep well?" he asked. He met my eye a moment too long, and I wondered if he knew that Luca had slept on the couch. I had no idea how aware he was about our marital problems. "Are you happy with the room?"

I looked around at the ridiculous opulence of my suite. It was hard to believe he was serious. He'd seen my lackluster living room and my sad Christmas tree. This hotel was nicer than any I'd ever seen; the sheets were thick buttery cotton, almost liquid against my skin. "Everything is perfect. Beyond perfect."

He looked relieved. "Wonderful," he said, as he set his briefcase on a table and opened it. "Because you will be here for the next few days. The estate would like to set the meeting for tomorrow afternoon." He pulled a leather pouch from his briefcase and handed it to me. "Which gives you a little time to rest and see the city. If you are up for it, of course."

I unzipped the pouch and found a phone, a room key, and a wad of euro bills. I kept the phone—my phone had died and I didn't have an adapter for the charger—and handed the pouch to Luca. He looked inside, his eyes wide with surprise at the sight of all that cash.

"I've programmed my number, as well as the number of the hotel, into the phone. There is no passcode—you can create one if you want, of course. I've also added a list of places you might want to visit—the Egyptian Museum is amusing—as well as some of my favorite restaurants. It might snow, which will be a treat, as we rarely get snow at Christmas. I've downloaded the Google Translate app, in case you get stuck ordering dinner. I've called already, and they are aware that you might drop in. Just mention my name and they will take care of you."

THAT EVENING, THE manager sent up a complimentary bottle of wine—a dry prosecco that smelled of apricots and ice. We drank it on the balcony, watching the people below: an elegant woman in high heels and a tight, tailored overcoat; an old man reading the *Corriere della Sera* under the light of the bus stop; a child walking with her grandmother. Everyone was as elegant as Enzo Roberts. It was my first time away from home, and perhaps I was easily impressed, but I could have spent the whole night like that, watching the passersby on the street.

It had been dark for an hour when it began to snow, flakes drifting down over us and melting on the wrought-iron balcony. Luca slipped his arms around me, and it seemed, suddenly, that I had been summoned home.

I glanced at my watch. Twelve o'clock. For a moment, I was confused—was it dark at noon? Or could it be midnight already?

"We lost six hours," Luca said, noting my confusion. "It's lunchtime for us, dinner here."

"You hungry?" I asked.

"Let's go out and do something fun," Luca said. "Something totally new."

"It feels like forever since we did that," I replied.

"Well, it's been forever since we've been happy," he said, which was an understatement.

"I'm happy now," I said, pulling him closer, taking in his scent.

He leaned over and kissed me, and it was as if we were who we used to be, unguarded, me and Luca with the whole of our future ahead of us.

"I'm sorry about asking you to move out," I said, resting my head on his shoulder, feeling the scruff of his beard against my cheek. "I just didn't expect everything to be so . . . difficult."

"It isn't your fault." A bus stopped on the corner below, its brakes squeaking. "But maybe we should think about adoption."

"Of course, yes, we should," I said, closing my eyes and feeling the snow on my cheeks. We kissed again, and I felt, suddenly, that I could be happy with the life I had then and there and could forget about the futures that might have been.

Back inside, we fell into bed together and made up for the months of separation. As I lay in Luca's arms, I thought back to the moment I had opened the letter and the sharp feeling of foreboding that had fallen over me. If the letter had not arrived, we would never have had this time together. The premonition of danger had been wrong: the letter had brought me and Luca back together.

We showered and changed into the clothes Enzo had left. Luca put on a new shirt and the leather jacket, while I zipped into the silk dress. Everything fit except the black suede boots. This was no surprise. I had inherited my grandfather Giovanni's feet, wide and flat, and it was never easy to find shoes that fit. I sat on the bed and looked at them, wiggling my long second toe. My ugly feet had caused me no small amount of embarrassment growing up. I never allowed anyone to touch them, and aside from Luca and my parents, no one had ever seen them. As a child, I had avoided swimming. In the summer, when I wore sandals, I always kept my socks on, something Tina, who knew how much I hated my feet, had teased me about. Luca always said I was too sensitive, that nobody would even notice, but I had never been able to feel good about them. I slipped on my boots from home, glad the dress was long enough to cover them.

"That dress is perfect," Luca said. "You look beautiful."

As we left, I paused before a full-length mirror. Luca was right: the clothes had the effect of transforming me. From the liquid reflection of the mirror, I saw someone else, the kind of person I'd always imagined I could be one day, after graduating and getting a job—tailored, elegant. Powerful. Alberta Montebianco. It wasn't vanity, but recognition: I knew this woman. She had been waiting for me there, in that hotel room in Italy.

SIX

TORINO WAS NOT a primary destination for most tourists. It didn't have the grand monuments of Rome or the cafés of Paris or the charming bars of Barcelona. But that night, as Luca and I walked hand in hand through the dark streets near the hotel, I had the impression that Turin, with its palazzos and small shops, was the most romantic city in the universe.

We wandered through the city without paying attention to street names, skirting the river Po before turning back in the direction of the hotel. We waded through a crowd standing before a theater and walked alongside a park, where wreaths of Christmas lights hung from lampposts, casting red and green and white halos over the sidewalk.

It was an hour or so before hunger drove us to look up one of the restaurants Enzo had programmed into the phone. We typed the address into Google Maps and five minutes later we walked into a rustic, dimly lit osteria on the Via Guiseppe Verdi. From the outside, the place appeared quiet, but when we went inside, the restaurant was nearly full. Wine racks lined the walls, bottles rising between framed photos of Alpine landscapes—deer and bear and snow-laden mountain huts. As we followed the host to a table in a back corner of the room, I saw plates of pasta, pots of fondue, and baskets of black bread on the tables. Hunger twisted through me. I hadn't eaten for hours. I sank into my chair, in full anticipation of dinner.

When the waiter arrived, we ordered the nightly special from a handwritten card. As each dish appeared, the waiter explained the courses: antipasto, primo, secondo, and dolce. The fondue that I had spotted earlier was called *bagna cauda,* a bubbling bath of olive oil, anchovy paste, and garlic eaten with raw vegetables. Then came a creamy, fresh pasta called *tajarin,* served with a glass of white wine, a smooth, nutty Nascetta. This was followed by steak and Barolo. Then a dessert of hazelnut cake and a shot of espresso.

Whether it was because I had never tasted such food or because it was my first and last meal with Luca in Italy, I have never, not before or since, tasted anything quite like that dinner. I think of it as akin to the last meal of the condemned, one eaten in the final moments of a life to give comfort and strength before an unknown journey. Because a treacherous journey awaited me, and while I had no idea of the difficulties I would face, and the ways in which my life would be forever changed, I did embark well fed. The pasta paired so perfectly with the white wine that I wanted to order a second plate. The grilled steak dissolved into the rich earthy flavor of the Barolo. The sweet hazelnut cake hovered over the meal, a delicate top note. I looked at my husband, happier than I had seen him in years, and I felt a rush of gratitude that we were together. No matter what happened—bad news, good news, tragedy or good fortune—I could get through it as long as we could talk about it over dinner.

As the waiter cleared the plates away, I couldn't help but wonder how Nonna and her family could have left such incredible food behind. But of course, they had never eaten like that. Such luxuries didn't exist in the village of Nevenero. In that remote, barren place, there was little more than dry goat meat and polenta and vegetables pulled from rocky soil. It was the Montebianco family, living in the castle above the village, that feasted on steak and drank fine wine. I know, because I have been in the cellar below the castle, walked through the enormous caverns carved into the granite of the mountain, and pulled a bottle of hundred-year-old Bordeaux from the shadows. I have opened bottles that collectors would pay a fortune to acquire and drunk them alone at the fireplace, watching the moonlight on the snowcapped Alps. My palate has become refined, my expectations engorged, but I have never forgotten the experience of drinking that simple Barolo with Luca on my first night in Italy, its earthiness grounding me, even as the rest of my life dissolved into thin air.

By the time we finished, the tables were empty. Waiters moved from place to place, carrying dishes to the kitchen, removing tablecloths, clearing glasses to the bar. The waiter cleared our table, and when he'd left, Luca slid his hand over mine.

"You're worried," he said. "I can tell."

"I'm not worried," I said, pulling my hand away to fidget with the tablecloth. I was lying, of course, and he knew it. "I'm sure that the meeting with the lawyers will be just fine."

"There's no need to be anxious."

"I'm just tired. Jet-lagged, probably. That's all."

"It's been quite a day," Luca said, signaling the waiter for the check, his eyes gleaming with happiness. It had been a monumental day, the day our futures had realigned.

"I keep thinking about what they'll say tomorrow," I said.

"That's understandable, considering."

"I can't help it," I said, feeling suddenly emotional. "I

feel like I've been deceived. Like my parents weren't honest with me."

Luca took my hand again and squeezed it. "Maybe they didn't know."

"Yeah, maybe," I said. "Maybe my grandfather didn't tell them anything about his family. But if your grandmother knew that there was something odd in my grandfather's past, then surely other people did, too, don't you think?"

Luca stared at me as if he wanted to say something, but the waiter arrived with the check. I pulled out the pouch and paid with euro notes.

"Let's get back," Luca said, standing and helping me with my coat. "We both need sleep."

As we walked toward the hotel, I felt my spirits revive. The cool night air cleared away the anxiety and left me with thoughts of the good my inheritance could bring. "How much do you think the Montebianco family is worth?" I asked Luca.

"Way more than I originally thought," Luca said, smiling in a way that made me laugh.

"A million?"

"The private jet? The hotel and the cash? More."

"Wouldn't it be amazing to pay off the house and my student loans?"

"And the mortgage for the bar?"

"It would feel incredible to have some security." I shoved my hands in my pockets, shielding them from the wind. "There's something I keep trying to figure out, though. Why didn't you tell me what Nonna thought about my family?"

Luca stopped, zipped his new leather jacket against the cold. "Come on, Bert, you must have noticed."

"Noticed what?" I could feel the blood rush to my cheeks, the throb of my pulse in my chest.

"How your family was always . . ."

"Always what?"

"Nothing," he said, and I could see that he hadn't meant to take the conversation in that direction, that he was a little drunk and had said something he already regretted.

I stopped and turned to face Luca. "My family was always *what*, Luca?"

"Shunned." Luca took a deep breath, the kind of breath one takes before diving into a cold pond. "Your family was always shunned."

The word stung like a slap. "That is not true."

"Did you ever wonder why you weren't included in the church youth group?"

"No. Well, I wondered, but I didn't care . . ."

"Or why your parents weren't part of any of the community events?"

"Like what?" I asked, my voice catching in my throat. "The Lent potlucks?"

"Or the Christmas bazaar or the Saint Joe's fund-raiser?"

I hadn't thought of any of these things for a long time, but a sense of shame fell over me as Luca listed them. Yes, my family had kept to themselves, and yes, there was definitely a sense that we weren't welcome, but I had never thought of us as being shunned. No one had ever articulated our status in Milton quite so clearly, and it hurt.

"The older generation wouldn't even talk to your grandparents," he said.

"How do you know that?"

"Nonna warned me before I married you," he said. "She said your family was *tainted*."

I stared at him, shocked and hurt. *"Tainted?"* I asked. "Did you really just say the word 'tainted'?"

"Bert, I'm sorry." Luca looked sad and unsure of himself, but I could see that he had been carrying these feelings around with him for years. "I didn't listen. I loved you anyway, Bert. With everything that's happened, I've always loved you anyway."

"I need a little air," I said, turning away and leaving him standing alone. "I'll see you back at the hotel."

I WANDERED THROUGH the snow-covered streets, tears in my eyes and a headache throbbing at my temples. I was angry but also relieved. In thirty seconds, I understood why there had been such resistance to me in Milton, why I'd never felt a part of the same community as Luca and his family. Clearly, whatever had happened in Nevenero so many years before had not been left there. When our families had immigrated to America, they had carried this bad blood with them.

I walked for a good hour and was about to turn back toward the hotel when, at the corner of a narrow, cobblestone street, I saw a bookstore. It was a small shop with wood-framed windows stacked high with books. The thought crossed my mind that maybe there would be something in the store about Nevenero, a travel guide, or a book of Italian history that could help me understand the place my grandparents had left.

A bell rang as I pushed through the door and walked into a warm space that smelled of tobacco and old paper. A man with gray hair and a matching mustache smoked at a counter, a book open before him.

"*Buona sera,*" he said without looking up.

"*Buona sera,*" I replied. I looked around, at the high wooden shelves crammed full of books, and wondered how anyone found anything in such chaos.

"Excuse me," I said. "Do you speak English?"

He looked up from the book and put out his cigarette. "A little."

"Do you have a book about a place called Nevenero?" When he looked at me blankly, I added, "It's a village in the Aosta Valley."

"Valle d'Aosta." It sounded beautiful when he said it. "I think . . . no. But follow me."

He walked through a narrow passage between bookshelves, stepping over stacks of magazines on the floor, until we came to a shelf filled with travel books. He ran his finger over the spines—Francia, Grecia, Roma, Sicilia—stopping at an oversized hardcover, *Fortezze della Valle d'Aosta*. Fortresses of the Aosta Valley. He slid it out and gave it to me, then turned, leaving me to page through black-and-white photographs.

Mountains dominated every picture. There were fortresses and castles framed by mountains, herds of goats on limestone crags, stone village houses nestled into valleys. Ibex, with their long, sharp horns, stood on granite precipices. I couldn't read much of the text, but the images gave the impression that the region was stark and breathtaking, all steep inclines and vertiginous descents. It made me wonder at my grandfather, how his character must have been formed by such high and low points, his personality shaped by extremes. I remembered his propensity for long hikes in the Catskills, the cold of his farmhouse in the winter, and skating on the pond in our bare feet, and I understood that these traits had to have been carried with him from the Alps.

I flipped through the pages until I came to a map of the region, a splotch of land with Mont Blanc at the northern extremity and the Gran Paradiso National Park to the south. I searched the map, looking for the village of my ancestors, but Nevenero wasn't anywhere to be found. It must have been too small and insignificant. I tried to remember what I'd found online on the drive to the airport the day before: that Nevenero existed somewhere in the northwest corner of the Aosta Valley, hidden in a fold of alpine granite south of Mont Blanc and north of the commune of La Thuile, one of the least populous communes in the least populous region of Italy.

I closed the book and was on my way out the door when the bookseller stopped me. "I found another book about the Valle d'Aoste. You want to see it?"

I didn't have time to answer before he walked ahead, to the opposite side of the store, to a shelf labeled *Occulto*.

"This can't be right," I said, studying the books with pictures of pentagrams and reverse crosses, the tree of life and the ouroboros. "Nevenero is a *town*."

"Here," he said, pulling down a book, checking it against his notecard, then handing it to me. The title read: *Mostri delle Alpi*. Monsters of the Alps.

I thanked him and fell into a chair in the corner. It may have been the fight with Luca, or perhaps the events of the past few days were starting to get to me, but my throat was dry and my hands trembled as I turned the pages. The book was filled with pictures of the greatest hits of Alpine monsters—a half goat, half devil called Krampus that supposedly terrorized mountain villages each Christmas and dwarfs called cretins. I later learned that, in the nineteenth century, explorers to the region found entire communities of cretins tucked away in the mountains. These small beings were not monsters at all, but people afflicted with an iodine deficiency. When iodized salt was introduced, the disease disappeared.

I had never heard of Krampus or cretins, had never seen the twisting, serpentine dragons drawn by the Swiss naturalist Johann Jakob Scheuchzer in the seventeenth century. I had never imagined a gryphon, with its lion body and eagle head, or any of the devilish hybrids I found in the book that evening. But even if I had, none of the bizarre life-forms that allegedly existed in the icy crevices of the Alps could have prepared me for an image near the end of the book. It was a black-and-white photograph of a man—at least, I thought it was a man—his skin unnaturally pale, white hair long and tangled over his shoulders, a coat of fine fur covering his chest. He stared out from the photograph, his enormous eyes boring into me, as if daring me to turn my gaze away.

I puzzled over him, finding him both monstrous and fascinating. It was as though I knew him already, those haunting, predatory blue eyes living in a corner of my mind, submerged and half visible as a creature of a nightmare. But it wasn't until I read the words typed below the photo that I went cold with recognition: *La Bestia di Nevenero.* The Beast of Nevenero, the very creature Nonna Sophia had warned me about.

I WAS A block from the bookstore before I realized that I was running. I had reacted in a rush of blind movement, propelled by fear, the mechanism of thought catching. When it clicked into motion, I remembered my reaction to the picture and the startled call of the bookseller—*Va tutto bene?*—as I threw a twenty-euro bill on the counter and ran out of the store, book in hand. I was so unnerved I could barely see two feet in front of me. It wasn't until sometime later, when the cold night air left me shivering, that I came back to my senses.

I pulled my coat tight against the wind and walked into the night, oblivious to where I was headed. I moved through the streets quickly, without stopping, hoping to exhaust the anxiety thrumming through my veins. I heard Nonna Sophia's words ringing through the air. *The legends were true.*

I walked alongside a park and, after a series of turns, found myself standing before a large neoclassical palace. At last, I stopped to catch my breath. Brushing snow from a bench, I sat and opened my purse. Inside, I found the leather pouch Enzo had given me. It was no small relief to have it. I had walked blindly, perhaps in circles, and had no idea where I was. I could use the phone and the money to get back to the hotel, make up with Luca, and go to sleep.

And yet, even as I opened the phone and searched Google Maps, I couldn't stop hearing Nonna Sophia's voice: *Let the past die. Look ahead, to the future here with Luca.*

I picked up the book again, trying to puzzle out the meaning of the description written in Italian. I scrolled through the apps on the iPhone, opened the Google Translate app Enzo had downloaded, typed the Italian passage into a box, and, with the push of a button, I had the following:

THE BEAST OF NEVENERO

First documented in the nineteenth century in the village of Nevenero, this pale-skinned Alpine monster is believed to reside in the caverns below Mont Blanc. The Beast of Nevenero, as it has been called, was thrust into the spotlight in the early twentieth century, when British naturalist James Pringle published a series of articles about the creature. Pringle argued that the beast was a distinct cross between man and ape, and thus proof of Darwinian evolution. Pringle was en route to photograph the beast when he was killed in an avalanche below Mont Blanc. The Belgian-French cryptozoologist Bernard Heuvelmans, who came to the village of Nevenero in 1962, built upon this theory, claiming that the Beast of Nevenero was the creature popularly known as the Abominable Snowman.

His claim was ridiculed by zoologists and paleoanthropologists alike, whose published refutations effectively ruined Heuvelmans's credibility. No evidence of the creature's existence has emerged since.

I looked again at the black-and-white photo, taking in the beast's white hair and wide, jutting jaw, its large blue eyes and heavy brow. It was exactly as Nonna Sophia had described. Luca wasn't going to believe it. I closed the book and was about to go back to the hotel to show Luca my discovery when I heard the sharp rhythm of shoes coming up behind me. I turned to find Enzo Roberts, a perplexed expression on his face.

SEVEN

✦

"W HAT ON EARTH are you doing here?" I said, jumping
up and dropping the phone on the sidewalk.

Enzo smiled, elegant and apologetic, much the way he
had smiled when he'd surprised me at my house the day before. He was gracious, well-mannered, even chivalrous. Yet,
there was something inscrutable and persistent about him. I
wasn't sure what he was thinking or, more important, what he
wanted from me.

"Luca checked out of the hotel," he said, bending down to
retrieve my phone.

I felt my heart sink. Luca must have been really angry, and
really hurt, to pack up and leave.

"Where is he now?" I asked, as Enzo placed the phone back
in my hand.

"That I don't know," he said. "But I thought you might
need some company." His voice was casual, as if there were
nothing more natural in the world than running into me in
this out-of-the-way spot.

"But how did you know I was here?"

He gave me a sheepish look and then lifted his phone to
show me the screen: there was a map with a flashing dot. Of
course. My phone had tracking turned on.

"The estate would kill me if you got lost or hurt," he said.
"I hope you understand."

I shouldn't have been surprised. Enzo needed to keep me from leaving Italy before the meeting, and what better way to do so? It would have been careless to give me too much freedom, and Enzo did not appear to be careless.

"I need to call Luca," I said. "This works for international numbers, right?"

"Plus-zero-zero-one then the number," he said.

I tried Luca's number, but my call went straight to voice mail. "He's not picking up."

Enzo looked at me with concern. "You must be cold."

He was right. After walking through the snow, then sitting on a wet bench, I was freezing.

"I know a bar around the corner," he said, taking me by the arm. "Let's warm you up."

Two minutes later, we squeezed into a narrow wine bar filled with the sound of laughter and music. Enzo flagged the waiter and ordered two glasses of cognac. There was some back and forth between them—I imagined it to be about the cognac, but it could have been about politics or the weather for all I knew. I was more interested in Enzo's congenial expression than what he was actually saying. He was so charming as to be unreadable.

The waiter delivered two snifters filled with golden liquid. I lifted my glass and smelled burned caramel swirled with alcohol.

Enzo looked me over. "An argument with your husband?"

"I needed to be alone," I said. "I ended up walking all over the place."

"I've had my share of spousal disagreements," he said, smiling kindly, and I felt a sudden warmth toward him, as if I could confide in him. "Most revolving around family situations."

"I doubt your situation has ever been as complicated as this," I said.

"No doubt you are entirely correct."

"Who are the Montebiancos anyway?" I asked, feeling the cognac warming me. "What do you know about them?"

"Probably less than you do."

"The estate must have information about them. They work for the Montebianco family, after all."

"To be honest," Enzo said, "the estate hasn't been entirely forthcoming with me about the details of your situation."

"But how can that be?" I asked. "They sent you to bring me here. They gave you my medical records."

"The messenger doesn't need to understand the message to deliver it," he said, sipping his cognac. "You can ask the lawyers anything you want tomorrow. They work for you."

This caught me off guard. "They do?"

"Of course," he said, smiling slightly. "You have just inherited them."

"Oh," I said, "I guess you're right." The reality of my position hit me. I wasn't some powerless person being hauled into a legal meeting. The lawyers of the Montebianco Estate worked for me.

"The estate is composed of three lawyers. The head lawyer is a man named Francisco Zimmer. Swiss. Speaks very good English. He's been the Montebianco family's primary attorney for forty years. He knows the family very well, and can surely give you whatever information you want. The other lawyer, Murray Smith, has been part of the team for less time than Zimmer. He handles the daily problems and responsibilities. Bills and taxes and so on. I was hired last year, to oversee the more personal elements of the estate."

"Personal elements," I said. "Like me."

"When I first began working for Zimmer, I was curious about Nevenero," Enzo said, putting his snifter on the table and giving me a look of complicity. "I tried to look it up. There is very little information out there. You'll find a Wikipedia page with the name Nevenero, and you'll learn that it is a town in the Aosta Valley, but that's about it. If you look hard, you'll find a reference to the castle, which once belonged to the House of Savoy. You'll find a line or two about how the village was abandoned around the time of the Second World War. Maybe two hundred people on the planet have ever been there, and I am not one of them. I can't tell you more than that."

As Enzo spoke, I couldn't stop seeing the Beast of Nevenero, its pale skin and ferocious eyes. I couldn't ignore the fact that everything Nonna Sophia had said was proving true. Maybe I should have taken her advice and stayed home. A tight ball of fear and suspicion formed in my stomach. I reached into my purse and pulled out the book of Alpine monsters, turned to the photo of *la Bestia di Nevenero,* and set the book between us. "I found this earlier this evening."

He took the book in hand and read the photo's corresponding passage. After a minute or so, he closed the book and gave it back to me. "Stories like this aren't unusual in northern Italy. The Alps are one of the least-accessible geographical areas on the planet. All those frozen, unexplored mountains have an effect on the imagination. There are reports of abominable snowmen in practically every ski village between here and Chamonix."

"That's what I thought," I said, tucking the book into my

purse. Although his confidence reassured me, and I knew that the *mostri delle Alpi* were nothing more than old superstitions, I couldn't help but feel the shadows of Nevenero creeping over me, the icy Alpine winds coming ever closer, leaving a foreboding in my heart as dark as black snow.

EIGHT

✤

THE NEXT AFTERNOON, I met with the lawyers of the Montebianco Estate.

Three men stood in unison as I walked into the room, Enzo Roberts and two men I had never seen before. They sat in a windowless conference room, some folders piled between them. An enormous bouquet of lilies dominated a side table, filling the air with a heavy, funereal scent. Aside from the morbid odor of the flowers, the atmosphere was antiseptic—impersonal, businesslike. Lawyerly.

The first lawyer, an elegant gentleman with silver hair who appeared to be somewhere in his early seventies, held out his hand. "Countess, my name is Francisco Zimmer. It is a delight to finally meet you." He gestured to a short man wearing a bright yellow tie. "That is Mr. Murray Smith. You know Mr. Roberts already. We're so very pleased you have come to Turin to meet with us."

I shook each man's hand and then took a seat. They sat across from me, hands folded on the table, an air of anticipation in their manner.

"I believe you received the estate's letter," Zimmer said. "And the list of assets."

"Yes, I did receive it," I said. "But as it was in Italian, I couldn't read it."

"You speak *no Italian?*" Smith asked, incredulous.

"'Ciao,'" I said. "And 'spaghetti.'"

Zimmer opened a folder and took out a sheaf of paper. "Let's start with this," he said. "It is an English translation of the Italian documents sent to your home. There is a long version and then a more simplified one." He found the page he was looking for and handed it to me. It had a stamp at the bottom, certifying that the translation was authentic. "This is the simple version."

I took the paper and read the following:

The Montebianco Estate is comprised of the following assets:

1. Ancestral title dating from 1260 as granted by Amedeo VI of the House of Savoy to Frederick Montebianco through marriage to Isabelle of the House of Savoy.
2. Exclusive use of family coat of arms, described as two black mountains and a castle.
3. Exclusive use of the Montebianco family seal.
4. Exclusive ownership of family jewels, furniture, silver, artworks, tapestries, and all other movable goods, etc.
5. Exclusive ownership of the Montebianco ancestral home, namely a 25,000-square-foot castle in the valley of Nevenero and all of its annexes, including wine cellar, dairy, grain mill, abattoir, and so forth.
6. Exclusive ownership of the *maison particulière* in the third arrondissement of Paris.
7. Dividends from the family portfolio of investments, including real estate, forestry business, stocks, bonds, currencies, and precious metals (estimated value to be disclosed in yearly financial report, attached).

I read the list several times, my eyes climbing up and down the list of treasures. I had known about the title, which was probably little more than a nominal hereditary name, without value in the modern world. And I was aware of Montebianco Castle. But I had not expected family jewels and artwork and dividends. I had not expected a town house in Paris. There was no concrete amount attached to any of these items, but I could see that the Montebianco Estate was worth a fortune. *Life-changing money,* I remembered Enzo saying.

"Do you have the financial report?" I asked.

Smith opened another folder, searched through it, and gave me a fat document. I flipped through the pages until I found the family income for 2015. Scrolling down the endless columns of numbers, I found the total revenue for the previous year. It was negative fifty-three thousand euros.

"They are in debt?" I asked, stunned. I thought of the private jet, the fancy hotel suite. How on earth was the family paying for these things when they had negative income? "That is surprising, considering . . ."

"Yes, surprising," Smith said. "But not so unusual. Like many old families, the Montebiancos amassed wealth for generations. Now there is nobody to take care of their assets. The forestry business, for example, could yield great profits, if it were managed correctly. As it is now, the family is without liquidity. I would suggest you start selling some of the assets in order to raise cash. Aside from the Paris apartment, there are parcels of land. We could begin there."

I read the financial report again, unable to fully take it all in. "I don't know what I expected," I said. "But this is really . . . it is all really incredible."

"It must be quite a surprise," Smith said, nodding sympathetically.

"Quite overwhelming," Zimmer added.

"You are in an extraordinary situation," Smith said.

"What is extraordinary is that you found me at all," I said. "My name is Monte, not Montebianco. It must have taken more than a Google search to locate me."

Zimmer and Smith exchanged a look. They had been waiting for that question.

"It was not as difficult as one might imagine. Our research team found your location based on your online profile," Zimmer said. "They looked at photos of you via your social media, pulled up your home address and phone number via the White Pages database online, and determined that you were the person we had been seeking. All told, it took a matter of hours to make a definitive match between you and the Montebianco family."

The silence was thick, stultifying, almost as funereal as the odor of the lilies. I could feel the lawyers' eyes on me, awaiting my response. I didn't like that they knew so much about me, and I hated that they had hunted me down online. But then, if they hadn't, I would not be sitting there trying to work out the value of my inheritance.

"Are you feeling well, Countess?" Zimmer asked. "It is rather hot in here. I could order you something to drink?"

Countess. I looked at them, all three of them, staring at me from across the table. The countess was me.

"All of this has happened really fast," I said. "It's a lot to take in."

"Your feelings are perfectly understandable," Zimmer said. "As Smith said, such news can be quite overwhelming. A shock to the system. But I daresay, this will all feel less unusual with time. Once you visit Nevenero, and take control of the estate, you will become more comfortable with your situation."

"I'm not sure about that," I said.

"You would be surprised," Smith said, adjusting his yellow tie, "how well one *adapts* when a fortune is at stake. Now, if you don't mind, we will move forward with the legal formalities."

Something about his tone—so smug, so confident—irritated me. Who did he think I was, a treasure hunter? "I really need some time to think about this," I said, digging my nails into the palms of my hands and wishing Luca was there. Having an ally on my side of the table would have made it all easier to take in. But he hadn't returned my messages. I could only assume he was back in Milton.

"It is only natural that you are a bit turned around," Smith said. "Perfectly normal."

"Smith is right. Such things don't happen every day," Zimmer said.

"They don't *ever* happen," I said, leaning back in my chair.

Smith and Zimmer exchanged a look. "Countess," Zimmer said. "You are young, and—forgive me for saying so—rather too naïve to navigate such a complicated situation alone. Of course you need time to think. Of course we will give you as much time as you require. But I think it will relieve you to know that you will have some guidance from a member of the Montebianco family."

"I don't understand," I said. "The Montebianco family has died out. I'm the last one. Isn't that why I'm here?"

"The letter you received regarding your inheritance stated that you are the sole living heir. That is true. You are the last surviving *legal* heir to the Montebianco title. But there is, in fact, one other member of the Montebianco family still living. She is quite ill and will not be around for much longer, I'm afraid, which is why we sought you so urgently. She is the wife of your grandfather Giovanni's late twin brother, Guillaume Montebianco, your great-uncle. Not a blood relative, but a relation by marriage. Her name is Dolores. She is not strong, but healthy enough to meet you."

I stared at him, sorting out the relationships. My grandfather Giovanni had a twin brother. And this twin brother, Guillaume, was the great-uncle who had remained in Nevenero.

Zimmer, seeing me struggle, said, "When Giovanni left for America, Guillaume stayed behind. He took over the responsibilities of the family. He died last summer, leaving no heirs, at the age of eighty-four."

"It was his DNA you matched with mine," I said, remembering what Enzo had told me the other day.

"Exactly," Zimmer said. "Your great-aunt by marriage gave us that sample. She has managed things at the castle for the past six months. She and Guillaume had no living children, but she knew that Giovanni may have had descendants. It was Dolores who hired professionals to find you."

"And my great-aunt by marriage," I said. "Dolores. She is in Nevenero now?"

"She is there," Zimmer said. "Waiting for your arrival."

NINE

❧

I T WAS LATE afternoon, the light draining from the sky, when we arrived at the land of my ancestors.

As the helicopter swept over the Alps, lifting and falling in currents of air, I pressed close to the window, straining to see the panorama of mountains in the distance. There were glaciers and gorges, snow-filled valleys, waves of ice lapping against granite, mountain peaks as high as skyscrapers. At the edge of my vision, a range of frosted cones cut into the sky, forming a barrier between this wild, frozen world and the orderly one we'd left behind. How desolate it all seemed from above, with the endless angularity of crags, the expanses of white so vast and uninhabitable. And yet, I knew there were villages deep in the ice, villages where human beings had been born, had lived and died without ever stepping beyond the shadow of the mountains.

We hit a gust of wind and the helicopter fell. I gasped and grabbed hold of Zimmer, who barked at the pilot to be careful. The pilot steadied the helicopter, and the largest mountain of all filled the windscreen: Mont Blanc. It loomed before us, monstrous in its size, the peak so high it seemed to prop up the sky. Its wide, massive body was brown and clumpy, a mound of sculptor's clay scored by a knife, so many cuts and grooves jeweled with ice.

We began to descend. Down we slid, through sheets of fog,

each filmy plateau revealing the landscape in layers: rock, ice, spruce and cedar trees, snow, and, at last, the outline of a stone structure rising up from the scoop of a valley—Montebianco Castle.

"All this," Zimmer said, as we hovered over an outcropping of black granite studded with ice, "belongs to you."

As I gazed down at the vastness and desolation of the valley, a chill went through me. I shivered not from the cold—it was warm enough in the helicopter—but from something else, a swelling fear of what waited below. Some part of me knew, even then, that my inheritance was not the stroke of luck one might imagine it to be.

"There is the family estate," Zimmer said, pointing to the castle nestled in the palm of the valley, the mountains clutching it like fingers. "And over there is the village of Nevenero."

If he hadn't pointed it out, I would have missed Nevenero entirely. There were no lights and no roads that I could see. Not a single car or truck. Just dark houses clustered together like mushrooms on birch bark.

"But there's nothing but snow," I said.

"The road to Nevenero is blocked until spring," he said. "Which is precisely why we are up here."

The whirling of blades shifted as the pilot angled toward the castle.

"The castle depends entirely upon air transport at this time of year. Food, medical supplies, everything they need is dropped in. I will return for you next week, with the helicopter that brings supplies. The castle has seen better days, but Greta, the housekeeper, has been instructed to make you comfortable."

As the pilot descended, I got my first real look at Montebianco Castle. It was a perfect square held by four massive towers, one at each corner. Zimmer explained that the original thirteenth-century structure had been a squat, one-story fortress built to defend the family from belligerent rivals, but was razed in the late sixteenth century and rebuilt in the fashions of the period—an elegant castle with a large, Renaissance-style courtyard filled with potted trees, a jewel-box Baroque chapel at one corner, and a series of outbuildings at the other. The towers were topped with conical slate roofs, the windows fitted with blown glass panes, and an ornate ironwork gate blocked the entrance. Nothing remained of the original fortress except the foundation: the perfect square, each corner held in place by a strong, fortified tower. At the top of each tower flew the brilliant flags of the House of Montebianco, bright streaks of yellow and blue flapping in the wind.

THE HELICOPTER TOUCHED down on the flagstones, and I jumped out. Zimmer handed me my suitcase and gave a terse wave—crisp, impersonal, as if he were sending me on a covert mission. Then the helicopter lifted into a swirl of fog, leaving me alone in a vast, ice-covered courtyard.

Everything was still and silent. Night had come, and banks of fog had fallen to earth, leaving the air heavy, granular, obscuring the mountains in a smudge of smoke. The courtyard was immense and perfectly enclosed. I looked around, searching for the housekeeper. A few lights flickered in the castle's windows, but no one had come to greet me.

I zipped my coat closed, bracing against the sharp wind. The cold was so domineering that it had overtaken the stone: an entire wall of the castle was encased in ice, as if a wave had washed up on it and, in a snap of subzero wind, frozen in place. I had landed in an unwelcoming, desolate place, one that matched the mountains that surrounded it.

I looked up to the star-spattered sky. It was a black bowl filled with diamonds—glittering and inaccessible. The helicopter was gone. I was on my own.

Grabbing my suitcase, I started across the flagstones, the needling wind pricking my skin. I had just passed the main entrance of the castle when I saw it: a flicker of candlelight in a small window at the top of the tower. For a fraction of a second, a face appeared, terrible and twisted by shadow. It was a woman, her brow heavy, her hair wild. I dropped my suitcase, surprised by her sudden appearance. That must be Dolores, I thought. Her illness explained the ravaged visage, her unnatural pallor, the strange features, the monstrous expression. Then, in a flash, the candle went out. The window turned black, and I was left breathless, my heart beating hard, my hands trembling.

A shuffling of feet alerted me that someone was coming. I turned to find a short, fat woman in a heavy wool coat. Greta wore a wool stocking cap pulled down over her ears, and I could just make out a series of scars on the left side of her face.

"Hello," I said. "You must be Greta."

She stared at me, silent. I glanced up at the tower.

"There was someone standing there just now," I said. "Did you see her?"

"That is the northeast tower," Greta said, without answering my question. Her mouth went lopsided when she spoke, as if her jaw had been broken.

"Was that Dolores Montebianco?"

She shrugged and said nothing.

I considered this cryptic response as she continued to stare at me, blankly, without affect. I offered my hand. "I'm Alberta," I said, raising my voice, in case her hearing was bad. "Here to see Dolores Montebianco."

She didn't take my hand. Instead, she grabbed my suitcase and shuffled across the courtyard. I followed her past a row of outbuildings, abandoned stone structures with heavy wooden doors—a granary, dairy, apiary, and abattoir. Zimmer had told me that, once, these buildings had sustained the castle, giving the Montebianco family flour, milk, honey, and meat. Now, like so much of the castle, they had been left to rot.

Greta walked ahead, her thick-soled boots crunching over the ice. The night was bitter cold, the wind slicing through the courtyard, all sharp edges. I was eager to get inside and warm up. It had been a long, frustrating day. That morning, I spent hours trying to get in touch with Luca. When he hadn't picked up his phone or answered my messages, I resigned myself to try again from Nevenero. But from the looks of it, I would be lucky to get even one bar of reception. Zimmer had mentioned the remoteness of the village, but I hadn't had the strength of imagination to picture anything so isolated as this. I tried not to be too alarmed. I would go inside, get some sleep, and figure it out in the morning.

We turned a corner, and—*bam*—I was on the ground. A heavy, hairy beast tore at my coat with its teeth, growling and straining to split me open. I struggled, kicking and pushing with all my strength, but it twisted and feinted, claws and teeth raking at me from every direction. The thing snapped at my face, my ears, my arms. I kicked, landing a few solid thrusts before realizing that I was fighting some kind of dog. I screamed and doubled down, kicking harder.

There was a scurry of feet on the flagstones, and suddenly the dog was jerked away, leaving me gasping, my cheek searing with pain.

"Jesus Christ, what the fuck was that?" I said, pushing myself up from the flagstones. I was shaky on my feet, hardly able to stand. I touched my cheek. My fingers were wet with blood.

A man slipped a rope around the dog's neck. He was talking to it in a language I didn't understand, Franco-Provençal, I would learn, the local patois. The dog was as strange as the language, huge, with long black dreadlocks that gave it the look of an evil Muppet.

The man gave the dog a command, and it sat.

"You frightened her," he said, his tone accusatory. His English was heavily accented, his voice little more than a growl.

"*I* frightened *her*?" I said, incredulous. "Are you serious?"

"This is Sal, madame," Greta said. "He minds the grounds."

Sal turned to Greta and said something that I did not understand, but that I gathered to mean: *Who the hell is this?*

Greta's reply must have informed him that I was the Montebianco heir, for Sal's features softened and he met my eyes for the first time. "Welcome, madame," he said, his voice turning suddenly deferential. "I wasn't expecting anyone and didn't shut the dog in the mews. I am sorry she frightened you. I hope she didn't scratch you too badly?"

Scratch me? She had nearly ripped my face off. I wiped blood onto the sleeve of my coat and looked at the man, taking in his rough leather boots, his battered hands. He wore the same brown burlap trousers and heavy-soled boots as Greta, but whereas Greta was short and heavy, he was tall and muscular.

"Alberta," I said, ignoring his question. "Alberta Montebianco."

"Salvatore," he said, giving a quick nod.

"What is that thing?"

"A Bergamasco shepherd. Name's Fredericka."

"What a terror," I said, touching my cheek and feeling a hot, swollen lump.

"She should be," Sal said. "That's how we trained her."

I glanced back at Fredericka, wondering why they needed such a vicious guard dog when there was no one around for hundreds of miles.

"You've come from America, madame?" Sal asked.

"Yes, that's right," I said, taking a tissue from my pocket and holding it over my cheek. I wanted to get inside and take a look at what the dog had done to me. I had a feeling I might need stitches.

Greta picked up my suitcase, said something more to Sal, and started toward the castle. I followed, not quite finding my balance. The courtyard, the castle walls glimmering with windows, the enormous black sky—everything seemed to tip and waver around me. As I walked away, Sal called to me from behind.

"Welcome to Montebianco Castle, madame."

GRETA LED ME up a set of stone steps, pushed back a wooden door, and escorted me inside the castle. The wind died in an instant, and a pervasive silence filled the air. Over time, I would come to understand this silence, the thickness of it, its almost tangible viscosity, as the defining nature of the mountains—a quiet, choking presence that suffocated one slowly, breath by breath.

But I didn't know that at the time. Then I saw only evidence of bygone greatness. The rooms were filled with ancestral treasures: oriental vases, plush carpets, and Dutch still-life paintings of flowers, fruit, hummingbirds. These were the objets d'art the family had collected over the centuries, the bounty of their years of abundance and power. The family coat of arms had been molded into the masonry at every turn. Plaster medallions of my ancestors' profiles filled an entire wall, perfect white orbs of noble faces. The Montebiancos may have been obscured by time, and their future had dwindled to a single heir, but here was proof that they had once been an important family. A great family.

I shivered as I followed Greta along the hallway of the ground floor. She introduced each room as we passed, and I had the eerie experience of realizing that everything I saw— every room, every carpet, every fireplace, every precious object—belonged to me. We passed a sitting room she called the salon, where embers glowed in a fireplace; the grand hall, where the meals were served; a nook with a couch and an elephantine Bakelite telephone, gray and heavy on a table. We stopped in a wide corridor where a cuckoo clock was mounted on the wall, its face all dials and mother-of-pearl disks, its trapdoors closed, waiting. It was a quarter after six o'clock. It felt like days since I'd left Turin.

We climbed a set of stairs to the second floor, where rooms opened at every turn, many more than Greta could show me, hidden spaces that I would explore over time. It seemed to me, as we walked through the narrow halls, the arched doorways and vast corridors, every space communicating with the next, that we were not only navigating an old musty castle, but that the map of my vast family tree was unfolding before me.

Finally, we stopped on the third floor, on the southeast corner. As Greta unlocked the door to my rooms, I waited at a large window overlooking the mountains. Shelves of ice and granite lifted before me, a dizzying panorama of snow and rock. The brutality of the wind, the torture of subzero temperatures, the distant moon that rose in the sky—this was the world of my forebears. I felt it then, the presence of something kindred in the landscape, an intimate connection between me and the mountains, and I understood that this savage place was in my blood. This vast, stark place, this thin air and soaring sky, this desolation—all of this had produced me.

A bolt turned as Greta unlocked the door to my rooms and disappeared inside. I followed her, finding myself in a series of large and well-furnished spaces that, taken together, were bigger than my entire house in Milton. The first—with windows that framed a series of mountain peaks—was a sitting room with a large stone fireplace, a couch upholstered in striped silk, a writing desk, and shelves filled with old leather-bound books.

Greta went to work building a fire. As she piled up birch logs, I went through an arched doorway, into a bedroom with an enormous four-poster bed, canopied and enclosed on all sides by curtains, a wood-burning stove, and a series of tapestries of hounds and antelopes. At the far end of the room, separated from the sleeping chamber by a green silk screen, was the bathroom. Passing by me, Greta stepped behind the screen and washed soot from her hands in a porcelain sink.

"This here is the marble of Porta Praetoria," she said, gesturing to a pedestal bathtub, its rich gray surface shot through with veins of mica and quartz. "The toilet won't clog if you don't throw paper in it," she added, tugging on a silk cord attached to an overhead tank to draw my attention.

"What's this?" I asked, bending over a low marble sink with gold faucets.

She smirked. "Guess you don't have bidets in America."

Without further explanation, she walked back to the sitting room. The fire was roaring, filling the space with light and the scent of burning birch. Greta unpacked my clothes as I watched, hanging them in a large wooden armoire. She lined up my shoes and stacked the shampoo and soap I had taken from the hotel in Turin on the desk, placing them next to a note, written on Dolores Montebianco's personal stationery, that read: *Bienvenue, Comtesse.*

"Madame Dolores wants to see you tomorrow," Greta said as she shut the door, leaving me alone.

I opened my suitcase and pulled out the phone Enzo had given me in Turin. There was no reception, not even a spark of service. I turned it off and restarted it, hoping it would connect to some local network, but it didn't. The mountains had surrounded me in a curtain of silence. I was cut off from the rest of the world.

I sat at the antique writing desk, opened a drawer, and removed a pot of ink, a sheaf of paper, some old fountain pens, an ink-stained cloth, and a penknife. There were so many drawers, filled with so many old and neglected objects, that I could have unearthed treasures all night, but I was too tired, and too overwhelmed, to do more than stare out the window. Fractals of frost had formed around the edges of the pane, floral, crystalline, but I could see, through the clear glass at the center, Nevenero below, the houses layering down the side of the mountain. Superimposed over this panorama was a reflection of me, Bert Monte, the same person I had been just days before, yet now unrecognizable.

I touched the wound on my face. Fredericka had scratched my cheek badly. It would scar, leaving a long, thin line across my cheek, a permanent reminder of my first night in Nevenero, but I wasn't thinking of that then. Tears filled my eyes. Not out of pain—the scratch didn't hurt that much—or out of vanity offended by the damage done to my face. No, it was something else. A sense of loss filled me as I looked at that person reflected in the window. Perhaps I understood that this was the last of Bert Monte, and that from that point forward, I would be Alberta Montebianco, heir to a sinister legacy tucked into a fold in the mountains. Perhaps I sensed that my fate had been waiting for me, and now that I had arrived, I would never be free again.

TEN

❧

THE NEXT MORNING, a knock at the door woke me. It
was Greta, carrying a tray with a porcelain coffee service.
She left it on the desk and brought me a pot of ointment,
homemade by the look of it, for the scratch on my face. I had
washed the blood from the wound the night before, but it had
grown sore during the night. The right side of my face was
swollen and painful to the touch.

"I might need a doctor for this," I said, dabbing the salve
on my cheek.

"No doctors up here, madame," Greta said.

"No doctors at all?" I said. "What do you do if you get
sick?"

"See Bernadette," she said, gesturing to the salve. "She made
that for you."

"Bernadette is a doctor?" I asked. The ointment smelled of
eucalyptus and tingled on my skin.

Greta shrugged. I took this gesture to mean that Bernadette was a medical person of some sort. As she walked to the
door, she said, "Madame Dolores would like to see you in her
salon now." Without further elaboration, she closed the door.

I climbed out of bed and examined the pot of hot coffee,
bowl of sugar, and pitcher of cream on the tray on my desk.
There was a linen napkin with the Montebianco coat of arms
embroidered in a corner. I drank the coffee as I dressed in

leggings, a sweater, and running shoes. Then I ventured out into the hallway to find Dolores.

With two or three turns, I was lost. The night before, I had followed Greta through dim corridors, up a set of winding stairs, around a corner, and past a large window. I hadn't paid attention to whether we'd gone right or left, up or down. Now the house seemed a maze of mirrors and chandeliers, paintings and tapestries, like some twisted baroque nightmare. The more I walked, the more unfamiliar it all became. I wandered for some time before I heard a voice from the shadows.

"Alberta Isabelle Eleanor Vittoria Montebianco."

A wheelchair sat in a doorway. Like everything about the castle, it came from another century. The frame was formed of bronze, and the wheels were large and wobbly, like the tires of an old bicycle. In this contraption sat a thin old woman, her legs covered with a wool blanket, a pair of leather slippers sticking out at the bottom. Her white hair frizzed in a halo around her head. Two knotty hands—the fingers glistening with gemstones—gripped the armrests. This was Dolores Montebianco, my great-aunt.

"*Mon Dieu,*" she said. "I was sure I would be long dead before you arrived. Come, help me to the tea table. There is much to discuss."

I took the wheelchair by the handles and pushed Dolores into the large salon on the first floor. The room was filled with Victorian furniture—red velvet sofas, mahogany side tables festooned with porcelain figurines, and a richly patterned silk wallpaper that wrapped the room in tangles of cherubs and harps. It was enough to make me dizzy. I didn't plan to stay in Nevenero for more than a week, but the thought had crossed my mind that, should I stay longer, there would be some significant redecoration to be done.

"Near the window," Dolores said, and I steered her to a table covered with a white linen cloth. As I pushed her closer, I saw that the seat of her wheelchair was fashioned of wood, which Dolores had made more comfortable with a stack of pillows. "Open the curtains. I want to get a good look at you."

I pulled back a pair of green damask drapes, revealing a bank of medieval windows. Lozenges of thick colored glass captured the early-morning light. Nonna Sophia had said there was never sunlight in Nevenero, but she had been wrong: there was plenty of light, enough to see that Dolores's eyes were pale green, her hair ashen, and her face so pale and wan, so thin and lifeless, as to give her the look of a skeleton.

A cut crystal bell had been placed to one side of the table, a china teapot on the other, its pattern a Bavarian farm scene with roosters and cows painted in gray-blue. I positioned Dolores's chair near the bell and then sat across from her.

Dolores shook the bell, and Greta arrived to pour steaming black tea into our china cups. Dolores nodded, and Greta stepped back to a corner of the room.

"Those beasts," Dolores said, gesturing at the wound on my cheek.

"There are more than one?"

"Oh, yes," Dolores said. "One can't go outside without fear of losing an eye." Before I could ask why Dolores allowed such vicious creatures at the castle, she asked, "Are you happy with your rooms? They are exceptionally well placed, facing Mont Blanc and the village as they do. The furniture is a bit worn, true. The last resident of those rooms was Maria, *une cousine germaine* of my late husband's father. A Spanish princess. Destitute, of course. But beautiful . . ."

"The rooms are fine," I replied. I sipped my tea. It was bitter, overbrewed. I added sugar and milk.

Dolores held up a long, bony finger, a garnet ring sitting just below the knuckle. "That expression on your face just now," she said, narrowing her watery green eyes. "It is the very likeness of my late husband. He was more masculine, of course, a bit thinner. And your hair is a different shade of yellow, but I see an exceptionally strong family resemblance. There is no denying it."

"Really?" I said. "I know so little about my extended family. Do you have pictures of him? Or of Giovanni?"

"There must be photographs somewhere," she said. "I will ask Basil, my secretary, to look in the library." Dolores took a sip of her tea, then added in a spoonful of sugar. Her hand shook, spilling drops of tea on the linen cloth. "It is rather uncommon that we should meet this way, don't you think? Through lawyers and such."

"Yes, strange," I agreed, suppressing an urge to go back to the subject of the photos of my ancestors. To ask all the questions that were floating through my mind. Questions about my great-uncle and my grandfather's relationship: Had they been close or had they had a falling-out? Was that why Giovanni left Nevenero? I wanted to know why everything in the Montebianco family had gone so wrong. Why I was the last one left. "Not the usual family reunion, for sure."

"Indeed," she said. "You, raised in some *obscure* corner of the world, without hope or resources, childless, divorced—"

I felt myself recoil. After Turin, I had come to see my relationship with Luca in a different light. "My husband and I are back together, actually."

"Suddenly arriving *here* . . ." Dolores lifted her arms and opened them, embracing the whole of the Montebianco Castle. "To us."

I felt my cheeks burn. She made it sound as if I had crawled out of some ditch. "It is all pretty astonishing," I said at last. "I'm still trying to get my mind around it."

"Yes, well, to tell you the truth, even after Francisco Zimmer told me of your existence, I couldn't be sure that you were . . . *one of us*. But Francisco says that the test you took—what is it called?"

"A DNA test?"

"Yes, that's it. Francisco claims that this variety of test is *always* correct. Ninety-nine point nine nine percent accuracy, he claims." She looked down her regal, beaklike nose. "When it comes to family, one must be sure."

"Of course," I muttered, feeling even more uncomfortable than before. I didn't like the sound of my voice—part hopeful, part ingratiating. For reasons I couldn't fathom, I wanted Dolores to approve of me.

"I must ask," Dolores said, leaning close, her voice falling to a whisper. "Did they really trace your relationship to this family through *saliva*?"

"Through a genetic analysis," I said.

"Heredity used to be verified through church records," she said. "Marriages and christenings."

"Now it's done in a lab," I said.

A look of wonder filled her expression. Picking up her teacup, she said, "How strange the world has become."

Dolores lifted a silver spoon and tapped the side of her china cup, summoning Greta. She hurried to the table, filling first Dolores's cup, then mine.

I straightened in my chair, determined to get somewhere with Dolores. However unworthy she thought me, I was the heir of the Montebianco family. I deserved to know about their history. "I was hoping you would tell me more about the Montebianco family. And my role here."

"If there is anyone who can do *that,* it would be me," she said, a hint of bitterness seeping into her voice.

"My grandfather was extremely secretive about his past. I don't believe that my parents knew anything about his family. Did you ever meet Giovanni?"

Dolores waved a ring-encrusted hand. "Heavens no," she said. "I married Guillaume when I was twenty-seven years old and he was forty. Giovanni left Nevenero long before then. But surely you knew your grandfather?"

"He died when I was five years old," I said. "He killed himself."

Dolores froze mid-sip, thought this through, then put her teacup down. "Suicide!" she said. "Well, that figures. He never did have the strength of character to face life's challenges like a man. He ran off and left Guillaume to shoulder the family burden alone. My husband thought Giovanni would return one day to offer his assistance, but of course he never did. It was an enormous betrayal. No one remained to carry the family forward, you see." She looked at me for a long, tense moment. "But now, there is you. *Alberta Isabelle Eleanor Vittoria Montebianco.* Do you know why you were given that name?"

I had yet to learn to spell the name, let alone parse its origin.

"They are ancestral names, passed down from generation to generation. If your parents were unaware of the Montebianco family, as you believe they were, it must have been Giovanni who christened you thus." She narrowed her large green eyes and examined me, as if looking for something to prove me worthy. "Despite everything, he must have felt compelled to continue family traditions. Did your father have an Italian name, too?"

"Giuliano," I said.

"Ah, well, there you have it. There are a number of Giulianos in the family tree, just as there are many Albertas. The first Alberta Montebianco was born in the thirteenth century. You are her namesake. Isabelle, the second of your four Christian names, was the founding mother of the noble Montebianco line, a member of the House of Savoy who married Frederick, a native of this valley. A great beauty, if her portrait is to be trusted. And Eleanor, your great-great-grandmother, was simply extraordinary. French. Came to Nevenero from Bordeaux. Which must have been something of a shock. The weather is so terrible up here."

Dolores had explained all of my names except one. "And Vittoria?"

Dolores closed her eyes. Her cheeks flushed, and I wondered if she felt ill. Finally, she opened her eyes and said, "The family has changed over the generations. The Montebiancos have risen to great heights and fallen to unthinkable lows. But there are some elements of the family that have endured, characteristics that make you *different* from other families. You might say Vittoria is one of those elements."

"Vittoria was one of my ancestors?"

"Yes, indeed," Dolores said. "The mother of Guillaume and Giovanni, as a matter of fact, which makes her your great-grandmother. And although her given name is Vittoria, she has always been known as Vita."

"Vita," I said, rolling the word on my tongue. *Vita.* The sound itself seemed to pulse with energy. Life. Vitality. *Vita.* "It's pretty."

"If only the name matched the woman," she said bitterly.

"Did Vita have something to do with why my grandfather left?"

Dolores gave me a withering look. "You might say that, yes."

I waited for Dolores to continue, but I could see that the topic annoyed her. Finally, she said, "You were raised far from here, far from your birthright, far from the traditions and expectations of the Montebianco family. But now you are here, Alberta, and I will tell you this: You have a duty to fulfill. You have responsibilities to perform. You must come to understand your inheritance and take charge of it. Or you will find that your inheritance will take charge of you."

Dolores lifted the crystal bell from the tea table and gave it a quick shake, its clear, high vibrato ending the conversation. Greta jumped to the wheelchair, gripped the handles, and pushed Dolores away. From the hallway, Dolores called, "Meet me at two o'clock in the portrait gallery, and I will show you what I mean."

ELEVEN

✦

I LEFT DOLORES'S SALON intending to go back to my rooms, but before I knew it, I was walking through a part of the castle Greta had not shown me. With its twisting hallways and staircases, its communicating corridors and bricked-up doors and circular rooms with multiple exits, the castle soon became a frustrating maze. After thirty minutes of wandering, I was thoroughly lost.

As I had discovered earlier in the salon, the castle wasn't as overcast as Nonna had believed. There were flashes of sunlight from time to time, and even whole hours of illumination in the morning. But for the most part, the castle was gloomy. Pools of gray shadow collected in every corner. And by afternoon, the place was dark as night.

This wouldn't have been a problem had the lights worked. But the electricity was a conundrum. Only a fraction of the structure had been fitted with lights and modern plumbing. The main source of heat came from *kachelofen*—German wood-burning stoves made of brightly glazed clay tiles. Stacks of logs could be found in every corner; the scent of burning birch and cedar and spruce lingered in the hallways. Chopping the wood, carrying and stacking it, and cleaning away the ash must have occupied Sal for hours each week.

The west side of the castle, where Dolores resided, my sleeping chamber on the south side, and the various shared spaces on the first floor—the grand hall, the salon, the wide central corridor—these rooms all had *kachelofen*. The rest of the castle sustained itself as it had since the thirteenth century, with fireplaces throwing heat and chamber pots poisoning the air. Parts of the castle were so cold that hoarfrost grew like moss on the stone walls and my breath crystalized to smoke. Kerosene lanterns illuminated the unwired areas of the castle, and I found them scattered in hallways and left on the landings of stairwells, positioned in the darkest corners by Greta.

Much of the castle had been uninhabited for decades, maybe longer, leaving the rooms in shambles, shut up and abandoned. The bolted shutters, the furniture covered in dust sheets, the cobwebs filling fireplaces, the bed frames without mattresses—these neglected spaces were in ruins. The scent of mildew filled the air, and I found whole swaths of ceiling had been eaten by water damage, then infiltrated by mold. When I opened the shutters of a sitting room on the second floor, hoping to let in a little fresh air, a pack of rats ran past my feet, fleeing the sunlight as if it were boiling oil. In another room—a huge ballroom filled with mirrors and cobwebs—I sat on a silk chair, only to disturb a clutter of spiders. They crawled from the crevices in droves, hundreds of legs climbing over my clothes, tangling in my hair.

Dust sheets covered furniture in some of the rooms, while other pieces had been left to the elements. So far as I could tell, there was no rhyme or reason to it. No system for preservation. Objects that seemed valuable—a pianoforte inlaid with mother-of-pearl, a Turkish rug the size of a truck—were left exposed, while an iron candelabra and an ugly bit of taxidermy had been wrapped with care. In any case, all of it would have to be assessed, cataloged by an antiques dealer, and restored. Or sold. It would be an enormous job, I realized, one that Luca, with his systematic approach to life and head for business, might enjoy.

Luca was never far from my mind those first days in the castle. Perhaps it was the fact that he had left Turin angry, or perhaps because we had been so close to repairing our relationship, but I wished he were at my side to see it all. He would have found my sleeping chamber romantic, the bidet fun, Dolores's salon trippy. We could have stood at my window together and looked down over Nevenero, guessing which of the village houses had belonged to Nonna's family or to my grandmother Marta. I wished I could talk to him, so that he knew how important our time together in Turin had been to me. He needed to know that the separation had been a stupid mistake and that whatever had been said and done in the past was forgiven.

I took out the phone and held it near an ice-covered window, testing for a signal, but there was nothing. I had wandered into the east wing, which was even more neglected than the other parts of the castle. It hadn't, from the look of it, been inhabited for a very long time, perhaps because it faced the mountains, leaving it colder and darker than the other wings. A section of the roof had collapsed, showing a slice of black granite and gray sky. Cracked windowpanes seeped cold air, while the shutters, many broken and hanging from hinges, did nothing to block it. I walked for ten minutes, shivering without my coat, only to find myself back where I'd begun, leaving me disorientated and dizzy.

I had just arrived at the farthest corner of the east wing when I heard a strange sound at the end of the hallway. At first, I thought it was the wind, but when I listened more carefully, I could detect the fluctuations of a voice, then a second voice, behind a door. For a solid minute, I stood there, frozen in place, listening. There was a rise of strings and the swell of a piano's crescendo. Someone was listening to classical music.

Creeping to the door, I pushed it open. The music grew louder, filling a small, narrow space without furniture or lights. I was about to turn and get out of there when I saw, in the center of the space, a mound of something fleshy and liquid and very dead. Stepping closer, I found the bloody carcass of a goat, an ibex to be precise, its long gray horns curled against the stone. I crouched down to get a closer look. Its body lay open. White bone jutted from wet flesh where the fur had been ripped away. It hadn't been dead long—the blood was fresh on the stone floor, and there was no smell of decay. Its large, liquid eye stared up at me, wide and lifeless. I touched its side. It was still warm.

I was so disgusted by the goat that I had forgotten the music behind the door. But when I heard it again—the intertwining of violin and piano, an eerie duet—I knew I wasn't alone. I stepped backward, toward the hallway, straining to see in the dim light. There was someone there, close by. Just then, I saw another door at the far side of the room. I had not entered a closet, as I had thought, but an antechamber, one that communicated with a larger room. I didn't have time to consider the uses of such a space, or to question why a goat might have been slaughtered there, because at that very moment the hinges squeaked and the door began to creak open. Abandoning the goat, and whoever waited beyond the door, I turned and ran.

I WAS OUT of breath by the time I made it to the first floor, so unnerved, so turned around that I nearly ran into Greta in the corridor. She sidestepped me, lifted a silver tray above her head, and gave me a look of reproach. "Lunch is served in the grand hall," she said, walking ahead.

I followed her into a long room with wood-paneled walls. I had passed by the grand hall the night before, when it was dark and the outline of the long table was barely visible at the center of the room. In daylight, I found a frayed carpet over the stone floor, and a long, capacious cabinet stacked with silver plates. An enormous fireplace, fashioned of stone and decorated with the Montebianco coat of arms, filled the room with heat.

Greta put the silver tray on the table, turned on her heel, and walked out of the room.

"Hello, there," a man said from the far end of the table. "Fancy some lunch?"

The table might have seated fifty—it was long and narrow, stretching clear from one end of the hall to the other—but there were just two place settings. I walked the length of the room toward the man. When I reached him, I grasped the edge of the table, trying to catch my breath.

"Are you quite all right?" he asked, looking me over.

"I don't know," I said, taking the cloth napkin from the second place setting and wiping my brow. "I just saw something really *strange*."

He was a thin, pale man in his mid-fifties, with precisely clipped hair and a trimmed mustache, wearing a baggy sweater under a tweed jacket. He leveled his eyes at me. "Was it a dead goat?"

"Oh my God, yes, that is exactly what it was!" I said, relieved that I wasn't crazy. "Did you see it, too?"

"No, but I did witness Sal with a live goat in the castle this morning, so . . ." He stood, pulled out my chair, and nodded to indicate that I should sit.

"That isn't unusual here?" I asked. "A dead goat in the castle?"

He gave a quick shake of the head—*no, not so terribly unusual*—and sat down across from me. "You must be Alberta," he said. His face had gone pink. "I'm Basil Harwell, secretary to the Montebianco family. How was your journey?"

"Bumpy," I said, trying to calm down.

"Ah, helicopter transport. There's certainly no other option at this time of year, is there?" Basil shook his head again. "The snow is impenetrable from November to May. We are Old Man Winter's prisoners until springtime. One gets used to it."

He directed his gaze at me, and detecting my disheveled appearance, and the sweat glistening on my forehead, he asked, "Did you get lost?"

"Is it that obvious?" I asked, feeling dangerously close to breaking into tears.

"Don't fret! It happens to everyone," he said, taking a drink of wine. "One guest, a delightful descendant of the king of Sardinia, was missing overnight. Sal and Greta and I searched the place and found her in the second-floor ballroom, on the north side of the castle, asleep on a divan."

I smiled despite myself. "I was in that ballroom."

"What a mess," he said, shaking his head. "But who could possibly take care of so many rooms? There are eighty-five in all. That is not counting the bathrooms, storage areas, or the kitchen."

"You've been here a long time," I noted. It wasn't a question. It was obvious that Basil was as much a part of the castle as Sal and Greta.

"Ages," he said. "Or so it seems. I am in the library every day, if you should ever need me. I keep the archival records organized. Order and invoice for supplies. And I pay Greta and Sal and Bernadette each month."

"Greta mentioned Bernadette," I said. "Isn't she some kind of a doctor?"

Basil rolled his eyes. "Oh, heavens, no," he said. "She's the cook, and because she has a talent with herbal remedies, Greta and Sal go to her for every sniffle. I don't rely on Bernadette for anything but dinner."

I thought of the woman I had seen in the tower. It had not been Dolores, as I had believed. It must have been Bernadette.

"I think I may have seen Bernadette," I said. "When I first arrived."

"You would absolutely know if you saw Bernadette," Basil replied. "Her appearance is, shall we say, *peculiar.*"

Bernadette must have been the odd-looking person I had glimpsed in the tower. There was one mystery solved.

Basil scooped some steaming polenta, mushrooms, and slices of meat onto his plate. Gesturing that I do the same, he said, "Don't let it get cold."

I followed his lead and filled my plate, leaving the mushrooms, which seemed unappetizing, like stewed prunes.

"Anyway," Basil said. "I also coordinate telephone calls between Madame Dolores and her many employees outside the castle. It is like running a hotline, calling Turin and London and Paris as much as I do. That is how I was aware that you would be arriving. Francisco Zimmer rang here nearly every day with updates. Now that the count is gone, I am in charge of nearly everything. Not what I imagined my life to be when I was in my twenties, that is certain! My training was as an educator. Originally, I came to Nevenero as a tutor."

"There were children here?" I asked, but of course I knew the answer to this already. Guillaume and Dolores were childless. There had been no children to teach in Nevenero for a very long time.

"Not exactly," Basil replied, evading my question and instead holding up a bottle of wine. I presented my glass, happy to have a drink. "This is an Arnad-Montjovet, a strong local wine. You wouldn't believe it, but Alpine wine can be quite good."

"I was told the family has an impressive wine cellar."

"Quite right," he said. "The *cave* is a treasure and still contains bottles brought from Bordeaux with Eleanor, your great-great-grandmother, upon her marriage to Ambrose. Five hundred bottles were bestowed to the family as part of her dowry. I have a cellar list somewhere in the library, if you'd like to see it."

I told him I would, and took a sip of the wine. Then I turned to my plate. The food was unfamiliar, without the charm of the meal I had shared with Luca in Turin. Flat. Simple. Without taste. I remembered, suddenly, eating something similar at Luca's family reunion a few years back, something Nonna had made. I pushed a pile of mush with my fork.

"Polenta," Basil explained. "Ground cornmeal. Very typical of this region. You will get used to it."

I cut a bite of meat and tried it. It was dry and chewy. "And this?"

"Goat," Basil said.

I almost choked. The image of the dead goat flashed in my mind. The metallic smell of blood. The rush of fear.

"Not to your liking?" Basil asked. "Yes, well, goat is also an acquired taste, I suppose." I chewed the goat slowly, focusing on a mole above his right eyebrow, a brown circle, big as a dime. "Sal slaughtered this one earlier in the week. You'll meet Sal soon enough. He's a glum, unsociable man. Illiterate as a cow. But good with dogs and guns."

"Sal and Fredericka introduced themselves last night," I said, pointing to the wound on my cheek. "Pretty, isn't it?"

"Detestable dog," Basil said, shaking his head.

I pushed the sliced goat meat around my plate, unable to eat.

"When I first arrived," Basil said, "I was very critical of the local fare, too. I had been living in Rome and had grown accustomed to dining well. But I have found that one comes to accept, even to *appreciate*, what one experiences with regularity."

"You don't mind it, then?" I asked. "Being so far away from everything?"

"Mind it?" he said, finishing off his glass of wine. "I choose to live this way. It makes the truth more bearable."

"Which is?" I asked, curious to know what he meant by such a grandiose statement.

"That we are not separate from all of this," he said, waving a hand toward the window, at the expanse of mountains beyond. "Language and education, good and bad manners, careers and friendships—such social constructs are not important up here. Here, we are a part of nature."

Greta stepped to the table with a pot of tea, poured out two cups, and left the room, her heavy boots clomping.

"Is she always like that?" I whispered when Greta was out of earshot.

"Greta?" Basil said, lifting an eyebrow. "She's been that way ever since Joseph disappeared." He glanced over his shoulder to make sure she was gone. "She took this position some four years ago, after a nasty divorce, and arrived with a child, a boy named Joseph. I think she may have accepted the position without informing the boy's father, or the courts, if you know what I mean."

I glanced out the window at the vast emptiness of the valley. This would be the perfect place to disappear with a kidnapped child.

"I do think such extreme measures may have been justified," Basil added quietly. "Considering those scars on her face. But even here Greta wasn't safe from tragedy. Two years ago, Joseph vanished. One minute, he was in the courtyard playing; the next, he was gone. We all searched high and low for the boy. He was only six years old, all blond curls and rosy cheeks. He brought such sunshine to this place. We never found him."

"My God," I said, feeling sorry for my critical assessment of Greta. "Did he get outside the gate and get lost?"

"My personal theory: the father. He discovered Joseph's location and took him back to Germany."

I felt a wave of empathy for Greta. I had never lost a six-year-old son, but I knew what it felt like to long for a child. Absence had formed a hollow space in my life, one that I still hadn't learned to fill. When Greta returned to clear the plates, I was unable to face her. When the cuckoo clock chimed in the distance, the birds chirruping and the bell ringing twice, I put my napkin on the table and stood to go.

"Finished already?" Basil asked, pushing his chair away from the table.

"I'm supposed to meet Dolores in the portrait gallery," I said, turning to leave.

"Ah, you will enjoy it," Basil said. "It is an excellent collection. Quite representative of the various styles of portraiture through the centuries. Come, let me show you the way."

Basil escorted me down the corridor, stopping at a cloakroom near the main entrance. He dug through layers of coats until he found a long, heavy mink. "Take this," he said. "It is utterly freezing in the north wing."

I hesitated, stroking the fur. It was feathery, soft, the color of chestnuts, the most sumptuous thing to have ever passed through my hands. "No one will miss it?"

"Frankly, there's no one here to miss it," he said, stepping close and helping me into the mink. "If I were you, I would wear this coat and enjoy it. I would take every bit of pleasure you can from this place. The house is full of treasures. Take the paintings to your rooms. Have Greta bring you wine from the cellar, the old bottles. Drink them! No one else will. Find pleasure in what you have inherited. It helps the time pass and renders one philosophical."

"I'll definitely do that," I said, warming to Basil's eccentric behavior. "But Zimmer is coming back at the end of the week. I'll be gone soon."

"That is what he told you, is it?" Basil said, pursing his lips.

"Yes," I said, meeting his eye, searching his expression. "Did you hear something different?"

As Basil put his hand on my back and steered me in the direction of the portrait gallery, he said, "Of course, there is always the chance that Zimmer will retrieve you soon, but I wouldn't count on it. The Montebianco family needs you far too much. They have kept me in their service for over two decades, and I can tell you: once they get their hands on you, they don't let go."

TWELVE

❧

B ASIL'S WARNING ACCOMPANIED me on my hike to the
portrait gallery, his words making me doubt Zimmer for
the first time. Until then, I had trusted what the estate had told
me, not only about Zimmer's return, but about everything
from the DNA test to the state of the Montebianco finances to
Dolores's illness. The thought crossed my mind that I should
have been a bit more wary before climbing into a helicopter
and flying to God knows where without an escape route. And
yet, I told myself, nothing had happened to make me doubt
Zimmer's honesty. Basil was most likely exaggerating, and
Zimmer would be back in six days.

All thought of Zimmer disappeared as I passed through
the enormous double doors of the Montebianco portrait gallery. Basil had been right: it was an incredible collection. From
the ceiling lush with trompe l'oeil clouds to the panels of oil
paintings on the walls, it seemed to glisten and refract with
light. I walked through the long, narrow room, the gleaming
parquet floor reflecting the gilded frames of oil paintings, dozens upon dozens of family portraits, all hanging side by side.

I found Dolores asleep in her wheelchair at the center of the
hall, her wool blanket slipping down to her ankles. I pulled it
up around her waist and tucked it in, taking a good look at
my great-aunt. Time and illness had ravaged Dolores, leaving
her thin and frail. Her weakness was even more exaggerated

when compared to the vibrant portraits. These men—because only men stared down from the frames—were exemplars of fortitude, perfect specimens of strength. The wealth and breeding of each Montebianco count—the hunting trophies, the battle scars, the beautiful wives, the palaces—had given him the bold confidence of an emperor. In fact, one of my ancestors—Heinrich XII, Count of Montebianco—had been painted standing on a chariot before a Roman aqueduct, as if he had conquered the world.

And yet, despite their grandeur, something had gone terribly wrong. All their wealth and power had been unable to sustain their dynasty. Whatever had caused their diminishment—whether it was bad luck or, as Nonna had said, some taint in their blood—time had brought them the same fate as the rest of humanity: obsolescence, death, and obscurity. I wondered what they would have thought, to see the world now, centuries after their deaths. How they would have balked at the idea that a young woman from another part of the world, without the culture or noble bearing of the Montebianco family, was all that remained. Their power and fecundity had dwindled, and now there was nothing left but me.

Dolores awoke suddenly, blinking as she tried to recognize me. "Push," she said at last, pointing a bony finger forward, her voice hoarse, little more than a croak.

I wheeled Dolores past the glossy, dark-hued oil portraits, the sleeves of the mink coat draping over the metal handles. The silence of the gallery was pristine, so clear that the squeaking rubber of the wheels on the floor carried through the space, resounding like a chime in a church. Small brass plates were affixed to each frame, presenting the name of each Montebianco. I strained to read them as we passed, feeling an eerie sense of recognition. Large blue eyes, flat noses, heavy brows that made them look grumpy even when they smiled—there was such continuity in their traits that they seemed like one man, dressed in different uniforms perhaps, sitting before different scenes, but all variations of an ancient original. I had never known any of them, and probably wouldn't have liked them much if I had. And yet I carried them inside me. I found, in the shape of a chin or the mold of a cheek, a reflection of myself. Their genetic predispositions were my genetic predispositions. This, I realized, was the definition of family in the twenty-first century.

"There," Dolores said, as we rolled by a portrait. "Your grandfather Giovanni next to his brother, my Guillaume."

The picture showed Giovanni as a young man. He was pale and stocky, with blue eyes and white-blond hair. A defiant smile gave me a shock of recognition. I remembered his face as an old man, how he had smiled in the same manner, as if daring the world to show him something new and unexpected. I remembered how my parents had always noted the cleft in my chin had come from him. I touched it then, feeling the proof of my unoriginality.

In the portrait, Giovanni wore a military jacket and stood near a horse, a gun in hand. Although the portrait must have been painted just before he left Nevenero, I had a hard time imagining this man, who appeared so similar to the other Montebiancos, leaving the castle and traveling to New York City with the villagers of Nevenero. How had he related to people who were so very different? He must have had trouble finding his place among them. The military uniform, the horse, and the look of steely confidence in his expression—he had changed so much by the time I knew him.

"He looks just like the rest of them," I said at last.

"Well, he should. Giovanni was raised to carry the family

forward. Lessons in comportment, elocution, French and German, etiquette, horses—his formation was extensive, his father made certain of that. The same went for Guillaume." Dolores twisted the rings on her fingers. "After Giovanni left, the family title went to Guillaume. Being a younger son was a problem, of course. But not as big a problem as having no heir at all."

I shifted my gaze to a nearly identical portrait of my grandfather's brother, Guillaume. "Did something happen between Giovanni and Guillaume?"

"If you consider abandoning one's family *something,* then yes, something happened between them. Something irreparable."

"He must have had a good reason to leave," I ventured.

"Good reason?" Dolores gripped the arms of her wheelchair. "He was weak. Weak and afraid. That was his reason."

My grandfather stared from his portrait, his eyes trained on Dolores, and for a moment I imagined him stepping down and joining our conversation to defend himself. He would tell me the real story, rather than Dolores's bitter version.

Dolores tapped my arm and pointed ahead. I pushed her forward.

"You may have noticed that there are no portraits of women in this gallery," Dolores said. "You would think there were no Montebianco daughters, no wives, no matriarchs. Of course, this was not the case. The portraits of the women of the family are all hung in the salons, bedrooms, and sitting rooms—the domestic areas of the castle. There is just one exception. There, along the corridor."

I pushed Dolores past innumerable sets of glistening eyes, to the far end of the room, where a curtain separated a chamber from the rest of the gallery. Pausing, I looked back over my shoulder, as if the great chorus of my ancestors might bolster me, then swept the curtain aside, revealing a small, enclosed space filled with candles, like a chapel. Two chairs sat at the center, positioned before an enormous oil painting framed in gold.

"You asked why Giovanni left," she said. "This is your answer. *She* is why he left."

I glanced at the copper tag: *Vittoria Isabelle Alberta Eleanor Montebianco, 1931.*

"Go on," Dolores said. "Take a good look."

I sat down and gazed up at a canvas almost entirely devoid of color. Vita wore a black silk dress, its fabric arranged around her in layer after folded layer, opening like a black rose around her hips. A hundred tiny onyx buttons climbed from waist to bosom, glossy as the backs of beetles, terminating at a high collar at her neck. Her hair and ears were covered by a black veil. Her skin was pale, almost deathly white, and the background was little more than a wash of gray.

I stared at the portrait, transfixed. Tall and wide-shouldered, she was as strong and commanding as any of the men in the gallery. This strange mixture of elegance and dominance found expression in a cool, supercilious gaze. There was something about the figure that held me captive. I couldn't look away, even for a second. It was not the light glinting from the jewels in her white hair or the piercing, unearthly blue of her eyes that made my heart beat. It was the expression frozen upon her face, an expression of absolute power.

"She was beautiful," I said.

"As a matter of fact, she was *not* beautiful," Dolores said. "This painting looks nothing, *nothing,* like her. Nothing at all! Vita has always had a pale, frightening complexion and an overbearing appearance. She was just as awful when she was young as she was as an old lady. Despite various attempts to help her—experimental therapies and so on—she never did become presentable. This portrait is a work of fiction. The family hired an artist to create a flattering version. The eyes, the enormous Montebianco blues, *those* are Vita's. The rest is propaganda."

"But why?" I asked.

"The truth has never been an easy burden for the Montebiancos," Dolores said. "With power comes pride. Better to hide a problematic child away than to let the world know how very damaged she—and thus the family—was."

Suddenly, I remembered the woman in the tower. The flicker of the candlelight over her pale face. The way she had watched me. It had not been Bernadette in the tower.

"Ambrose, Vita's father, had wanted to kill Vita, but her mother stopped him. I suspect she thought Vita would not survive long, and would take her tainted blood with her to the grave. But instead, Vita remained strong and vital. And, of course, her parents grew old and died, leaving Vita to the family like a cursed heirloom, one passed from generation to generation."

"Vita is alive," I said.

"She will be one hundred and two years old in March."

"And she is the person in the northeast tower."

"She has resided there all her life."

"But I don't understand," I said, trying to work out the consequences of this information. "Why didn't Vita inherit the title of countess?"

"*Mon Dieu*," Dolores said. "Vita would never have been capable of running this place. She was deemed incapable of managing her own affairs and disinherited. The family records are in the library. I would suggest you acquaint yourself with them."

I glanced up at the portrait of my ancestor, the oils gleaming in the flickering candlelight. "Can I meet her?" I asked.

She twisted a large ruby on her finger. "In time, yes. But not now. I'm in no condition for Vita today. She is not easy to stomach, even at her age."

"What is wrong with her?" I asked, feeling a knot of anxiety tighten in my chest as I realized that Vita's medical problems might explain my own troubles.

Dolores gave me a long, steely look.

"The Montebianco family is one that survives by traditions, Alberta. Traditions that have been passed down for many hundreds of years. These traditions might seem outdated to someone like you, coming from a place like America, where people do just as they please. But for us, they are essential. The suits my husband wore were sewn by the same haberdashery in London as his great-great-grandfather used. His shoes? We have a cobbler in Milan who knows the family feet intimately—the width, the length, the *peculiarities* of shape. I don't imagine you have these kinds of traditions over there in America, but for us, certain practices are not questioned."

She coughed again and, pulling a handkerchief from her pocket, wiped her lips.

"For the past hundred years, the most important tradition of your family has been to keep Vita. Keep her from harming herself, of course, but mostly to keep her from outsiders. That has not been an easy task. She is often her own worst enemy. And over the years, there have been instances of trouble. Stories. Rumors. When fear and superstition get hold of simple people, they turn violent. Have you heard the accounts of what happened to noble families during the revolution in France? Such violence has happened often throughout history. Frightened peasants surround a family, burn them out of their home, parade them through the streets, and execute them. They pillage and destroy everything of value. It is savagery. They would have killed us all if they'd got ahold of Vittoria."

Dolores turned her wheelchair to face me, her green eyes suddenly ablaze.

"But now you are here, and there is a higher responsibility to uphold than protecting Vita." Dolores gestured to my ancestors gazing down from their gilded frames. "The Montebianco family relies upon you, Alberta. It is their legacy, *our* legacy, that must be kept. And I will help you do it."

THIRTEEN

✦

THE AIR FELT heavy as I pushed Dolores back to her rooms on the west side of the castle, as if weighed down by all that she had left unsaid. I wanted to ask her to explain what she had meant about protecting our legacy, but the poor woman was exhausted. Even before I handed the wheelchair off to Greta, she had fallen asleep. The morning had been overwhelming for me as well, and I felt the beginnings of a headache. I asked Greta the way to the courtyard and, armed with the mink coat, headed outside to get some fresh air.

Leaving from the main door, I retraced my path from the night before. I walked over the icy flagstones, past the outbuildings and toward the main gate, glancing around, looking for Fredericka. She was nowhere to be found, thank God, but the doors of the mews stood open, wide and menacing. I was surprised to find that the outbuildings, which had seemed enormous and solitary the night before, were little more than one small corner of the vast courtyard.

Daylight revealed it to be as big as a football field, the interior walls lined with windows and doors that opened directly into the castle. A set of stone stairs led up to a second-floor landing, where I could see—through a pane of intricately connected hexagons of glass—a chandelier in the ballroom I had discovered that morning. Above, the entire perimeter of the third floor was lined with shuttered windows. Below, stone

pots stood throughout the courtyard, topped with snow and
ice. I imagined that, come spring, they would be blooming
with geraniums the color of blood.

The chapel, that jewel box that had seemed so small from
above, was in fact quite large up close, with vertical stained-
glass windows and a stone steeple. I peeked inside and found
rows of pews, an altar, a table of burned-out candles, and a
marble baptismal font positioned before the altar. The last
time it had been used, I realized, would have been for the baptism of my grandfather Giovanni and his brother, Guillaume.

Being outside felt good after my strange and disorienting
morning in the castle. The chill was reassuring, its effect simple and predictable. A thick white mist hung over the mountains, leaving the air cold and heavy in my lungs. Smoke rose
from chimneys on all sides of the castle, diffusing the scent of
charred cedar. I took a few deep breaths, filling my lungs with
the smoke-tinged air, the aftertaste of carbon lingering in my
throat as I came upon the castle gates.

Gigantic, iron, and topped with spikes, the main gates of
Montebianco Castle were imposing and impassable, two qualities that had surely served the castle well over the centuries.
The doors were huge iron panels decorated with metalwork,
the family coat of arms blazing at the center, and while I
hadn't noticed them the previous night—it had been dark and
the helicopter had touched down at the very center of the
courtyard—I saw now that these gates were the only way out.
And they were closed tight.

I gave the doors a shake, trying to determine whether I
could push them apart. They were locked, but even if they
weren't, they weighed a ton. I remembered the boy Joseph,
Greta's six-year-old son, who had gone missing. With gates
like that, he couldn't have wandered away on his own. Basil's

theory about the father taking the child seemed like the stronger explanation.

I worked my foot into a groove below the latch, testing out the possibility of hoisting myself up, but there was nothing to grab on to, and the top of the gate was ten feet above me, at least. Even if I were able to scale the door, the top was lined with iron spikes, short, sharp spears standing at attention, as if waiting to display a row of decapitated heads. Dolores, Greta, Sal, Basil, and the mysterious Bernadette. Enzo and Zimmer. Me. Human totems against the fierce elements outside.

The clanking of metal behind me rescued me from this gruesome thought. "Good afternoon, madame." I turned to find Sal walking toward me, a shotgun in his hand. "Need some help?" he asked. His expression was taciturn, accusatory, just as it had been the night before, only now I noticed the intelligence in his sharp brown eyes.

"I was thinking I would take a walk. But the door"—I shook the gate again—"is locked."

"It is always locked," Sal said, his whole manner questioning, suspicious. "What do you want out there?"

"I'd like to get a sense of the property." I gave him the most authoritative look I could muster. "Maybe check out the village."

"You won't find anything down there, madame."

"Nevenero isn't very far, is it?" I asked.

"Farther than it looks. If you want to see the village, let me drive you." He gestured to a Range Rover parked in the far corner of the courtyard, shiny and gray, a snowplow rigged to the front. It was the single modern object I had encountered since my arrival.

"Thanks," I said. "But I'd rather walk."

Sal shrugged, selected a key from a ring on his belt—large

and old-fashioned, bigger than the rest—unlocked the gate, then pushed the doors back. They creaked, the hinges rusty and unwilling, revealing thigh-high drifts of snow on the other side. He pointed to a cleared stone path snaking around the exterior of the castle, wide as a moat. "If you follow that," he said, "you can see the village from the east lawn."

I thanked Sal again and hurried past the gate, happy to get away from him.

Stepping outside the protection of the castle walls gave me the first real sense of the ferocity of the Alpine wind. I was met with a glacial gale, a strong slap of force from the north. Walking into it, I followed the exterior ramparts alongside the castle. In the somber light of late afternoon, the castle, with its gray towers and shuttered windows, felt sinister, identical to Nonna's grainy black-and-white photograph. The landscape was equally foreboding, the mountains casting a desolate shadow across my path. Now I understood what Nonna had meant when she said the castle was always dark. In such gloom, blue skies and sunlight seemed impossible.

Rounding a corner, I made my way uphill to the highest point of the grounds, the east lawn, where I was met by a wall of box hedges. Ducking through a small gate cut into the greenery, I entered a snow-covered expanse with a pond at the center, the surface a perfect circle of ice. In the spring, the pond would be so clear I would see a miniature civilization at the bottom—rocks and fish and frogs and moss. On warm afternoons, I would watch the shadow of the mountains float on the surface of the water, giving it the look of polished silver, convex, like an overturned spoon. But then, on that winter day, the pond was merely an extension of the frozen world, the colorless foreground to a vibrant greenhouse beyond.

After the castle, the greenhouse seemed a miniature

paradise. It was a Victorian structure made of iron and glass, its paint chipped and rusting, the panes fogged, rimes of frost collecting at the edges. I opened the door and a rush of balmy air fell over me, heavy with moisture and fragrance. Flowers and fruit trees grew in clay pots from one end of the space to the other, their waxy green leaves pressing like hands against the windows. Masses of tomato plants climbed wire cones, the fat fruit nudging potted lemon trees. I shrugged off the fur coat and leaned into a lemon tree, inhaling the bright, sweet scent of citrus.

Seeing a wicker chair, I sat and stretched my legs. The sun was beginning to set, the light turning pink and orange on the granite rock face, a liquid light that seemed to drip from the peaks. The scene was beautiful, startling, like something you would see in a picture. And yet there I was, in real life, watching it unfold before me.

If only the truth about my family would unfold with such grace. So far, I couldn't get anyone at the castle to give me a straight answer about anything. That my great-grandmother was alive was a surprise, yes, but it didn't have to remain such a mystery. If Dolores would just explain what was wrong with Vita and why she was such a big responsibility, I would make arrangements with Zimmer to assist her. I would bring the matter up as soon as he returned with the helicopter.

The sunset was in its final moments of brilliance when, across the east lawn, Sal emerged through the gate in the hedge. He trudged past the pond, then turned toward the greenhouse. I didn't have any reason to fear him, and yet I felt that there was something dangerous about Sal. It wasn't only his gruff manner or his behavior at the gate that bothered me, but something else, something I couldn't put my finger on. Perhaps I associated him with Fredericka's attack and the painful scratch on my cheek, which wasn't entirely fair. He was probably a perfectly nice guy who was trying to do his job.

And yet, as he walked toward the greenhouse, I grabbed the mink coat and ducked behind a potted lemon tree, crouching down as he stepped into the greenhouse. He lifted a basket and walked from one end to the other, picking vegetables and fruit. I heard the squeak of a faucet turning, then water splashing. Some minutes went by as he moved past the beds of herbs and flowers, sprinkling them with water, his boots sliding over the colorful mosaic floor. I breathed slowly, quietly, thankful that Fredericka wasn't there.

Soon, Sal hung up the hose and went to a table, above which gardening tools hung on the wall. He took down a clipboard, glanced over it, pulled out a pair of shears, and went to work snipping herbs. He examined each plant with care, taking the leaves in his fingers before harvesting them. When he'd finished, he went back to the table, hung up the shears, and emptied the herbs into a large glass jar. Then, tucking the jar into his basket of tomatoes and lemons, he walked past me and out the door.

When I was sure he'd gone, I stepped out from behind the lemon tree. The greenhouse was tranquil, everything just as it had been before he'd come in, only my peace of mind had been altered, replaced by a nagging sense of unease.

I went to the table and grabbed the clipboard, finding a chart filled with Latin words, perhaps twenty or so. I didn't understand Latin, but I guessed that the chart must be a list of herbs. Sal had checked off those he had harvested—*Cicuta maculata, Atropa belladonna,* and *Ageratina altissima.* He must be collecting plants for Bernadette and her herbal remedies, I thought, maybe even herbs to make the ointment for my cheek. It was incredible, I thought, how self-sufficient they were.

I threw on the mink, went out the greenhouse door, and made my way to the gate in the box hedges. But as I walked past the pond, something caught my eye: at the very highest point of the east lawn, perched on a hill overlooking the pond, sat a squat structure built entirely of white marble. I glanced at the sky, where a deep purple night had fallen to the east. If I wanted to be back inside before dark, I would have to hurry.

I hiked past the pond, following a cleared path lined with white mulberry trees—their gnarled black limbs pruned back to stumps—to the building. It was the family mausoleum, the façade composed of pillars molded with acanthus leaves and sculptures of angels. MONTEBIANCO had been chiseled into the lintel above a wrought-iron door, an elaborate portal that opened into the belly of the family tomb.

I pushed open the door, stepped inside, and found myself surrounded by dozens of names carved into marble cartouches. I examined the graves of the oldest members of the clan first, Frederick Montebianco (1235–1269) and Isabelle Montebianco (1240–1271), then skipped from plaque to plaque, jumping through time: Amadeo Montebianco (1765–1855) and Alberta Montebianco (1766–1834); Leopold Montebianco (1782–1818); Flora Montebianco (1819–1858) and Vittorio Montebianco (1814–1890); Eleanor Montebianco (1884–1942) and Ambrose Montebianco (1858–1929); and Guillaume Montebianco (1931–2016).

As I considered these names, I was drawn to a cartouche that read "Vittoria Montebianco." I knew immediately that something didn't match up. The Vittoria Montebianco lying in the tomb had been born in 1915—the correct birth year for a woman turning 102 in March—but, mysteriously, the date of her death read 1920. Vita was the mother of my grandfather and was, if Dolores was to be trusted, still alive. Yet, according to the plaque, she had died when she was five years old.

I shivered, pulled the mink coat tighter, and turned to go, wondering what it could mean, when I saw at the far end of the mausoleum a tablet, a marble cherub poised above, which read: *Bénissez les âmes des innocents, qui sont partis avant le sacrement du baptême.* Below, in tiny print, ran columns of names. Dozens of them. I leaned in to read them, but the light had faded and only the faintest purple haze lit the stone. As I slid my finger down the cold marble slab, pressing each name, a well of emotion swelled in my chest: these were the names of babies who had died before their baptism. I stepped back, finding it difficult to breathe, suddenly aware of the low ceiling and the narrow walls, the way the cherub leered, his smile mocking me. I knew then that whatever disorder had afflicted my family began long ago, here in the Alps, among my ancestors. It had been cast in my blood like a curse.

FOURTEEN

✦

DOLORES HAD SUGGESTED I acquaint myself with the Montebianco family history by reading the family records, so after a restless night of wondering about Vita—and the plaque I had found in the mausoleum that suggested she'd died long ago—I decided to go to the library the first thing the next morning.

Luckily, I found it more quickly than I had expected—it was on the third floor, in the northwest tower of the castle, a long, chilly hike from the first floor. Built into the turret, the library was a large circular room with bookshelves that followed the curve of the wall, the ceiling high and conical. My eye was drawn to an elaborate family tree painted overhead, the branches and leaves curling upward, filling the ceiling with the names of my ancestors and the dates of their births and deaths.

Basil was at a desk near a window, writing in a thick ledger. It had begun to snow, and a cyclone of white swirled against the window, obscuring the mountains. There was a pot of ink at Basil's side and a black fountain pen in his hand. He appeared to be cataloging books—there were stacks and stacks of them on the table, fifty at least. A history of the Alps, collections of political essays, a biography of Mary Shelley, and a novel by Ann Radcliffe.

As I approached, he put down his pen, gave me a quick

wave, and gestured for me to join him. I dropped into a hard, wooden chair. The room was cool, drafts of air slipping through the windows. I shivered and wished I had worn the mink coat, which I had left hanging in my rooms.

"You must have a lot of time to read," I said, glancing at the biography of Mary Shelley.

"Less than you would imagine," Basil replied. "These books are like living creatures to me. Caring for them takes a great deal of time. I repair damaged spines, watch for mold and worms, and generally keep the collection safe from the all-too-inevitable ravages of time. No one ever thinks that books need tenderness, but they do, quite a lot, in fact."

He stood and walked beyond a row of shelves into a shadowy alcove, returning with a box.

"But the most time-consuming aspect of my work, the one that has been the focus for the better part of a decade, has been archiving the Montebianco family's records. You would think that this would be the work of months, perhaps a year at most. No such luck. While the marriages and births and deaths of the family are well documented, there are ancillary documents that must be dealt with, many hundreds of boxes of personal papers—correspondence, memoirs, diaries, and so on. It is my task to put them in order."

"How many boxes are there?" I asked, gazing back into the shadowy alcove.

"Oh, hundreds. It isn't difficult work, and I could get through it quite quickly, but the entire archive must be translated into English." I gave him a questioning look—were they doing that on my account?—and he added, "Dolores, as you know, is English. She has insisted upon reading every last document in her native tongue."

"Your Italian must be very good to translate all this."

"French, actually. The language of the region was French until the late nineteenth century. Italian was not formally adopted until the unification of Italy, and even then, French—or, more correctly, a dialect of French called Franco-Provençal—was used in Nevenero. I am an expert in the dialect, although I don't use it much. The Montebianco family spoke very correct aristocratic French."

"Is Franco-Provençal still spoken?" I asked.

"Not really," Basil said. "Although who can say? There could be crevices in these mountains that hide a whole community of Franco-Provençal speakers and we wouldn't know. The Alps have the ability to do that—swallow something up and keep it hidden forever." Basil sat down again and took up the fountain pen, as if to continue cataloging the books. "In my work here these past years, I have unearthed information that has been buried for generations. I've found diaries stashed in trunks in the west tower, lists of guests visiting the castle during the seventeenth century, Alberta and Prince Amadeo's last wills and testaments, renovation plans after the fire of fifteen ninety-three. And, of course, the genealogical records. I am the only person who knows the entire Montebianco family tree." He gestured to the murals, the incredible branching and flowering of my family. "All twenty-nine generations, if one includes you."

He stood, grabbed a cane with an ivory handle and pointed it at the ceiling. "We will need to get a muralist up here in the spring," he said. He tapped a white space on the ceiling. "Your name will go right here."

I looked up at the Montebianco family tree, at the names of my relatives painted in a florid cursive and adorned with various coats of arms of noble houses that had, over the years, merged with the Montebianco clan. The branching off of names and dates and family connections started from two names at the top—Frederick and Isabelle—and ended at the bottom, with my grandfather Giovanni and his brother, Guillaume. With the other branches of the family included, the mural funneled up over the entire ceiling.

"We'll need to add my parents, too," I said. "Giuliano and Barb."

"Giuliano must have been named after this Giuliano," Basil said, pointing to a name. "Giuliano, Prince de Condé, a cadet branch of the House of Bourbon, a dashing rake who embarrassed the family with his voracious sexual appetite. He happened to have been married to another Alberta. There were many Albertas, all named, like you were, after the first Alberta Montebianco, born to Isabelle and Frederick in the thirteenth century."

I glanced at the union of Alberta and Giuliano, another meeting of the Montebianco coat of arms with that of an illustrious family.

"We can have your parents painted here, and you right below," Basil said. "Did she have a family coat of arms, your mother?"

I shook my head. "Regular people don't have coats of arms," I said. "Or such elaborate family trees."

"It isn't only about class," Basil said. "It is about inheritance and tribal identity. The family tree as a recording device is thought to derive from biblical sources. It acted as a form of cultural identification, of course, but also was a badge of inclusion. If you recall, Jesus could trace his ancestry to the House of David, and this gave him a legitimacy that he would not have had otherwise. The practice of keeping track of genealogy was more vital to noble families. They were careful to delineate bloodlines, and to avoid mixing with undesirable families. The importance of genealogical records at that time cannot be overestimated. Now, as you very well know, everyone can create a family tree on the internet. What used to be an art is now a pastime."

He pointed up at the top of the family tree, near Frederick and Isabelle.

"The Montebianco family begins with the creation of the House of Montebianco in the thirteenth century with the marriage of Isabelle of Savoy to Frederick. We don't know Frederick's original surname, as it must have been one of the common names up in these mountains. The family was christened Montebianco after the great Mont Blanc rising above the valley. There are many elements of the Montebianco origin story the family chooses to suppress. Most families of their stature were created through an association with royalty or through knighthoods. But Frederick Montebianco, the first of your family line with a noble title, was a goat herder."

"A goat herder?" I said, astonished.

"I thought that might surprise you," Basil said, leaning back in his chair. "It used to be that Nevenero was nothing more than an outpost for goat herders—a few shacks where they could sleep before ascending into the mountains. Before Isabelle of Savoy arrived, there were no stone houses, no shops, and very few people in the village of Nevenero, nothing at all to distinguish this piece of terrain from any of the other ramshackle outposts scattered throughout the mountains. Those poor souls had no aspiration but to survive the winter months. They made cheese from goat milk, ground corn into polenta, and crushed bitter, heavy wine from what grapes they could manage to grow. It was primitive to be sure, but safe.

"Then, one summer afternoon, a herd of ibex were grazing in a valley near the village when along came a small army of men, fifty or so soldiers on horseback, led by a nobleman with a red coat of arms on his jacket. Your ancestor, Frederick the goat herder, knew to stay away from noblemen, especially those wearing fancy labels, and so he led his ibex—those are the big mountain goats, the ones with the curved antlers, not the smaller chamois—away from the trail and into a valley, hoping to escape notice.

"As it turned out, the group came from the House of Savoy in the Piedmont, and the nobleman was Amadeo, a relation of the king of Sardinia. He was on his way to Switzerland to fight some other nobleman—I have never quite been able to discover which offending family he was after—over some perceived insult, got turned around, and ended up in Nevenero, which they described as being akin to ending up in one of Dante's rings of hell. The elements in the Aosta Valley are harsh, to say the least. If the sun doesn't fry you in the afternoon, the wind will flay you when night falls. The air is thin at this altitude, and it was common for travelers unaccustomed to the lack of oxygen to turn blue and die before they dismounted their horse. That is what happened to the prince: as he arrived at the top of the mountain, he became lightheaded and fell from his steed.

"Frederick came out of hiding, revived Amadeo and brought the whole group to the village, where they were given wine, roasted goat, and lodging. When Amadeo recovered, he promised Frederick a reward for saving his life. Frederick, who most likely didn't believe a word of it, said he'd gladly accept whatever the nobleman offered, and pointed them in the direction of Switzerland.

"One year later, Amadeo returned. He had won his duel in Switzerland and believed that Frederick the goat herder had given him the strength and luck he'd needed. As promised, he brought a reward: a wife with a noble title and a fortune. This prize took the form of Amadeo's sister, Isabelle, a beautiful girl of sixteen whose pale blue eyes seemed siphoned from the mountain sky. Isabelle was the youngest daughter of Peter I of Savoy. She was intelligent, educated, and undeniably wicked. She had been sentenced to death for some heinous crime—I believe it was murder . . . Let me check."

Basil stood and dug through one of the boxes until he pulled out a large, thick book, one that appeared—from the loose spine—to have been read many times. On its cover, stamped in gold, were the words *The House of Montebianco.*

"There was no account of the founding union recorded at the time—we have very few documents from that early period in the family archive—but we do have an account set down by a later Montebianco, Eleanor, Countess of Montebianco, a French noblewoman who married Ambrose, a direct descendant of Isabelle and Frederick. Eleanor wrote this history of the Montebianco family. In my opinion, it is the most interesting account by far."

He flipped through the pages, looking for a certain passage. "This is the translated version, of course." He stopped suddenly. "Ah, here it is," he said, and began to read:

Child of the nobleman Peter I of Savoy, Isabelle, the founding mother of the House of Montebianco, was, by all accounts, wild. The fair Isabelle was beautiful beyond measure, and while beloved by her father, the girl was tainted at the core. She was known to torture cats as a girl and, as a young woman, killed a suitor who had overstepped his bounds, stabbing him with a dagger and letting him bleed to death at her feet. For this, she was banished from the House of

Savoy, sent to the treacherous lands of Mont Blanc, her hand given in marriage to Frederick Montebianco, thus beginning the noble line of the Montebianco family.

"So," Basil continued, again flipping through the book. "Isabelle of Savoy was a murderess. But, because of her family's power and influence, her sentence was light—exile rather than death."

"She was sent to Nevenero," I said, glancing out the window at the blizzard. "That doesn't seem to be such a light sentence to me."

"On the one hand, Isabelle was exiled from her home at the Savoy palace, where there was certainly more excitement than could be found in Nevenero. But on the other hand, she found herself free of the restrictions of the highly codified etiquette of her medieval family. And Frederick was not such a bad deal either. There is a painting of him hanging in the portrait gallery. He was quite a handsome man. Very tall for the time. I suggest you go take a look. By all accounts, Isabelle and Frederick were very much in love." Basil closed the book. "In any case, their union founded a dynasty. This castle was a wedding gift from the House of Savoy to Isabelle and Frederick, as was the coat of arms. Multiple family lines grew from Isabelle and Frederick's union. As they had four children, the different lines of the Montebianco family can be traced from each of these descendants. Your branch of the family tree, as you can plainly see, begins with the eldest daughter of Isabelle and Frederick: Alberta.

"As the line moves down through the centuries, and more families join the tree, one's lineage becomes more complex. Family trees, however, diminish complexity. They simplify our origins, smoothing them out so that we can trace our heritage through one bloodline to a single—usually desirable—ancestor. In the process, we discard the less desirable ancestors—the criminals, the bastards, the deformed. The maternal lines are usually forgotten as well, as the mother's name disappears in marriage. Only the most noble maternal lines—those with royal blood, usually—were celebrated."

I looked at my family tree, following the lineage of Frederick and Isabelle's children. Alberta Montebianco had a robust line of descendants. The others were truncated, not even half the size of mine.

"There are no living descendants from the other three offspring of Isabelle and Frederick," Basil said, following my gaze. "Those bloodlines died out by the eighteenth century. The heartiest branch, aside from your ancestral line, grew from Frederick and Isabelle's eldest son, Aimone Montebianco. His lineage produced heirs until eighteen sixty-seven, when all were killed in an epidemic of some sort. Leaving only the descendants of Frederick and Isabelle's second child, Alberta."

Looking over the family tree, I saw that the links between my ancestors were embellished with leaves and fruit—pears and apples and cherries—to display the fecundity of these connections. Most of the couplings were distinguished with a coat of arms, the Montebianco coat of arms being most prevalent, but there were many others, too.

"Those," Basil said, noticing my interest in the family coats of arms, "are from most of the noble families of Europe, many of which are now long gone. The Montebiancos married into these families as often as possible to solidify their position and influence." He pointed the cane at a coat of arms. "Once very powerful families have now gone the way of the dinosaurs. Just as the Montebiancos would have, if they hadn't found you."

"What happened here?" I asked, looking at a branch that had abruptly ended.

Basil looked at the union, squinting to read the names: Charlotte of Normandy and Lars of Denmark. "I imagine they had no children," he said. "Or, wait, what was the date of their union? Eighteen fifty-six? There was a tragedy about that time, I believe. We have a news clipping of it somewhere. I cataloged it myself. Yes, yes, it was this couple. They died on their honeymoon, as a matter of fact. A fire in a hotel in Monte Carlo. But they weren't the only ones to meet a tragic end. The Montebianco family is full of stories of insanity, murder, even infanticide."

"Infanticide?" I said.

"Children born with severe physical or mental defects were often abandoned. Now we would recognize these defects by their medical names—Down's or Prader-Willi or Marfan syndromes. We understand these disorders and can treat them. But then they were believed to be a curse. Sometimes these infants died on their own. Sometimes their families helped them along."

"I saw the tablet in the mausoleum," I said. "The one listing the babies who died before baptism."

"The number of stillbirths, miscarriages, and so on was very high due to interbreeding—first cousins marrying and the like," Basil said.

"You would think they would just stop marrying close relatives," I said.

"That is easy to say now," Basil said. "In the twenty-first century, marrying your cousin is a misguided practice to be sure. But remember, they knew nothing about the hazards of inbreeding back then. Families made choices in order to consolidate power, but also based on pure superstition and fear—

they were afraid what might turn up if they married outside the family. This was especially true in royal families—look at Charles II of Spain, a product of Hapsburg inbreeding. His tongue was so large he couldn't speak and his jaw so deformed he had difficulty eating. Queen Victoria's husband, Albert, was her first cousin, and their children were encouraged to marry within the family as well. There was real anxiety about maintaining superior blood, when, in reality, all that intermarrying made for some monstrous human beings. It's no wonder, I say, that the Montebianco family has had so many problems."

"And what were they, exactly?" I asked. "All these problems?"

Basil froze up, his expression turning hesitant. "I am not at liberty to discuss them at length," he said quietly. "But I can tell you that the Montebianco story is quite *complicated*. I have found that there is much obfuscation, if not downright erasure, around a certain member of the family: Leopold Montebianco, your fourth great-grandfather. He was a naturalist who explored these mountains and supposedly kept very meticulous records—records I have been hired to find. Unfortunately, I have been unable to do so."

Basil turned back to Eleanor's history of the family and paged through it.

"While it has always been more or less speculation, many in the family believed that it was *Isabelle* who brought the trouble into the family."

"Was there something wrong with Isabelle?" I asked, feeling a tight ball of anxiety in my stomach as I remembered how Dolores had described Vita: a cursed heirloom.

"Not with Isabelle, no. But for centuries, the trouble was believed to begin with her." Basil flicked the stick all the way across the ceiling, to point to another branch of the family tree. "But because of the misogyny of the times, when a tragedy of nature occurred, it was always the mother's fault."

Basil went back to Eleanor's book and read:

> With the marriage of Isabelle and Frederick began the House of Montebianco, whose progeny would dominate Nevenero for hundreds of years. Over time, the family would prosper, and the Montebianco influence would stretch from the mountains clear to the sea in a honeycomb of castles, fortresses, and forested estates. By the eighteenth century, it was said that a traveler on horseback could not ride a full day without hitting one of the family's properties. They were rich; they were connected; and they, despite their noble breeding, or perhaps because of it, carried the seed of a monstrous nature that bloomed in Vittoria.

Vittoria. A heavy silence descended between us.

"This is the Vittoria born in 1915, the mother of Guillaume and Giovanni?" I asked, remembering the cartouche in the mausoleum. "My great-grandmother. Not some other ancestor?"

"That's right," Basil said, pointing the cane back at the ceiling and locating a name: *Vittoria Isabelle Alberta Eleanor Montebianco, 1915– .* No date of death.

"There is a Vittoria Montebianco buried in the mausoleum," I said. "A plaque shows that she died in 1920."

"Ah, you found that, did you?" Basil said, smiling slightly. "It was just a ruse. When it became clear that Vittoria would be an embarrassment, the family staged her death. They spread the word that she was ill. They had a funeral. They hid her existence from the world thereafter."

"There was *one* Vittoria, then," I said, sounding him out. "And this Vita had medical problems?"

"You could say that," Basil said. "Others certainly did."

"But you think there was something else going on?" The altar with the list of unbaptized babies, the death certificates of stillbirths in Milton, my own difficulties having a child— perhaps they were all connected. "Something hereditary?"

Pursing his lips, Basil pushed Eleanor's book toward me. His thumb marked a paragraph:

No one, not even the other members of the Montebianco family, was allowed to see Vita. She was so hideous, so lacking in human refinements, that she remained locked away in the northeast tower, as if she were a devil in our midst. It was necessary to hide her. She could not, under any circumstance, be allowed to roam freely. I could only imagine what she would do with such liberty. No doubt she would feast on the village babies and dance naked in the moonlight.

I closed it quickly, as if the words might infect me. "That's pretty strong stuff," I said.

"One must remember," Basil said, "that then, before modern medicine, diseases and physical problems were considered demonic manifestations or curses. And this part of the world modernized much, much later than other places."

"Still, it seems so dramatic, don't you think? Feasting on the village babies and dancing naked in the moonlight?"

"Quite right. Vita certainly never did any of that."

I opened the book again and reread the passage. *She was so hideous, so lacking in human refinements, that she remained locked away in the northeast tower, as if she were a devil in our midst.*

"Eleanor must have really hated Vita to write this about her."

Basil sighed. "I think her feelings were more complicated than hatred," he said, as he pushed Eleanor's memoir to me, urging me to read it. "You see, Eleanor was Vita's mother."

"And Eleanor's memoir describes Vita's illness?"

"It contains everything we know about it," Basil said, closing the cover and putting the book in my hands.

Anticipation rising through me, I tucked Eleanor's memoir under my arm and hurried back to my rooms to read it.

November 1915

The northeast tower is awash with tears and prayers.

It has been months since her arrival and yet it seems that I have been her mother an eternity, holding her in my arms as the doctors and priests arrive and depart, ordering the servants to take the bloody dressings away after cleaning her wounds, examining her bizarre features, staring into her large eyes searching, forever searching, for some sign of God.

We named her Vittoria, but I call her Vita, denoting life. Vitality. Yet, surely, Vita is not meant to persist in this world much longer. God will repossess His creation and cleanse it of the spirits that have taken hold of her soul. Is it wrong to question such a creation? It seems to me that such a child was not meant to be born. It shames me to admit that I wish Vita dead.

"You received the child from God," the priest said, when I confessed this terrible hope to him. "And He may see it right to call her back to Him. But she is yours to guard until that day comes."

I endeavor to keep his words with me. But even this morning, when I heard her strange, garbled cry—a sound unlike any I have heard before, as if she is choking on her tongue—I slipped my fingers around her tiny throat and pressed until the baby turned red, then blue under my white knuckles.

Am I capable of murdering my own child? I believe I am. If one is capable of creating such a creature, one must be capable of destroying it as well.

Yet, I submitted to the priest. I promised the Lord that I would keep the child as best I could. I would shield her from those who would harm her, which, if her existence becomes known to the villagers, will be many. But later, alone in my chapel, I begged the Lord to let Vita die peacefully in her sleep, to take her gently and easily, so that her disfigurements of body and soul might disappear from God's earth.

If Vita had come into the world in a violent storm of pain and suffering, I might better understand God's intention in sending this punishment to us. But she did not. Her birth was quick, almost painless. She was my fourth child, and the first to survive outside of my body. One would think that such an accouchement would bring forth a child full of strength. A blessed child. But I understood something was wrong immediately. The infant did not cry. There was no sound at all, save a horrified gasp from the nurse.

I looked at the nurse and saw she was white with fear.

"It is alive?" I demanded, for my first thought was that the child had arrived stillborn. When she did not reply, I asked again: "Does it live?"

"Yes, madame," she said, something odd in her voice, something fearful. "A girl. I believe."

And with that she swept the baby from the bed to a tub of water, to wash and swaddle my daughter. To examine her again.

I thought she would clean her and bring her to me immediately, but the room became quiet for many more minutes. When I heard the nurse sobbing, I knew something was frightfully wrong. I pushed myself up and looked across the room. The nurse stood over the child, looking down upon it, transfixed.

I was too weak to walk, but determined to see the infant. If she had died, I would hold her a moment before relinquishing her to the priests. If she lived, and was ailing, I would hold her to my breast until the doctor arrived.

I called my maid to help me stand. A rush of blood slid down my thighs as I walked across the room, leaving a trail at my feet. The last thing to catch my eye before I looked upon my daughter was a bright stain of blood blooming like a poppy over the stone floor, its vermillion hue a shock of beauty against the dull stone. I remember this stain clearly, as a sign of innocence, the way Eve may have looked at the fruit before biting it.

Then I gazed down upon the beast lying before me, and everything in the world changed.

My child was deformed. That much was clear immediately. Her head was too large, and her eyes enormous, so big that they appeared to comprise half of her face. Her features were not regular, but marred with what I have come to think of as an animal quality—her nose was flat, the nostrils open and exposed to view. The mouth was thin and wide, like that of a lizard, and, to my horror, there were rows of sharp teeth in her mouth, as if she were born to devour all that came near. The forehead was large, with a distinct ridge over the eyes, and her ears were shaped in a fashion most unnatural. While the head was overdeveloped, the body was shriveled and insubstantial, weak and small. The chest and stomach were covered in a coat of thick hair that, as the nurse washed the blood away, revealed itself to be white. The arms and legs were normal in appearance, and the sex clearly formed between her legs, but her feet were of a most strange shape. And her skin! It was so white, so thin, so unnatural. After the blood had been washed away, I could not help but trace my finger over the skin of her chest. Through it, I saw muscle and bone and veins.

I felt no desire to hold my child, but I reached out to take a small, bizarre foot in the palm of my hand. It was warm, soft, just as one would expect to find the flesh of a baby. My heart folded into a tight package, one that would never open. I could not love this creature.

Vita didn't cry or whimper. While her eyes were fixed upon me as I touched the deformed foot, she did not pull away. It seemed she was assessing me with the same scrutiny that I assessed her.

It was then that I turned to the midwife and asked a question I would often repeat: "Tell me, what in the name of God is it?"

"It is a monster," Ambrose pronounced, when he visited the northeast tower some days after the birth. I had dismissed the servants and led him to the baby. He looked her over, saw what I had seen, and said, "Leave it to the wolves now, before it grows bigger."

"Is it possible that you are so cruel as to kill your own child?" I asked.

"We would show mercy to kill it now, before it grows stronger. We cannot allow it to live. Can you imagine bringing this into the family? It is impossible."

I thought of Isabelle of Savoy, my husband's ancestor, and her reputation for crime and infamy. Perhaps such was the Montebianco blood. "God would not forgive us if we should murder this child."

"This is not a child," Ambrose said, looking at the fur, which had by that time spread over most of Vita's body, leaving only the head, the hands, and the feet fleshy. "This is a beast. If the villagers discover her existence, we will be burned out of Nevenero."

"But look. Do you see? She is little threat. She was born weak." I turned the baby over on its stomach to show Ambrose the spine. The creature's skin had not closed over the column of bones. At birth, there had been a milky trail of raw muscle. The midwife had sewn her closed, leaving a long line of black stitches from buttocks to neck. "She will not live long, being so malformed," I said. I believed this, as I believed in God's mercy.

"Let us pray that it dies soon," Ambrose said, looking away

from the child with disdain. "We cannot have the devil living here among us."

For the first time, I felt a flare of maternal feeling. This poor, wretched creature might be monstrous, but she had come from my body. She was, despite everything, a Montebianco. When my husband accused me of keeping a demon, I responded:

"If she is a devil, what does that make us?"

Ambrose settled his eyes upon me. He knew very well of what I spoke. We had always ignored the stories of madness and deformity that appeared in the Montebianco lineage after the time of Leopold. We believed the misfortunes of his ancestry to be inconsequential. Now, with this child, we could not deny them any longer. Vita had emerged as proof of his terrible heritage.

"She is sickly," he said at last. "Surely, she will expire soon."

"And if she survives," I whispered, turning her over on her back so that her large blue eyes fixed upon me, "I will keep her. I will protect her."

"And who will protect you?" Ambrose said. When I did not reply, he walked to the door. As he left, he turned and said, "As Lucifer came to curse his creator, this beast will turn against its maker."

July 1919

There are times when I almost believe she could become a normal child.

Yesterday, in a spasm of optimism, I dressed her in a blue silk dress and took her into the gardens to take the sun. The sky was clear, the pond glistened in the light, and the mountains were colored by wildflowers. It was as calm and pleasant a scene as one could imagine. The servants set up a chaise near the pond, not far from my precious grove of Mûrier blanc, and brought us our lunch,

*making sure no one was about to witness our strange, secret party.
We have learned to be careful in recent years. I allow no one in
the northeast tower save our priest, and he has sworn to remain
silent on the matter of my daughter. Half the servants have been
dismissed. The other half are kept far from the east wing of the
castle. The truth is: I fear them, fear they will gossip in the village,
fear their talk of the monster child of Eleanor Montebianco.*

*When I was certain we were alone, I instructed the nurse to
let Vita go free. She unharnessed the child, then placed her on her
extraordinary feet, and let her go. At first, she was timid. She
had never been allowed to play in such an open space before. Then
the child began to run. What speed she has! I could not match it,
nor could any in our household. It wasn't long before a* Papilio
machaon, *with its brilliant yellow butterfly wings, came flitting
down from the heavens, pausing on a bush of pink flowers. Vita,
her eye drawn to its quick, colorful movements, endeavored to catch
it. Of course, the butterfly lifted into the air, eluding her with
ease. As it flitted away, she watched it, her large blue eyes filled
with wonder, but also something more. Something intelligent and
calculating. I could see that she wanted to capture the creature. She
wanted to catch it and possess it.*

*Vita waited and watched for many minutes until the beautiful
thing flitted back to the bank of flowers. Slowly, quietly, Vita
closed in. Soon it was within her reach. With a ruthlessness that
one might find in a mantis, Vita snapped the butterfly in her teeth.
I gasped in horror. There it was, her true nature, plain as the
sunlight on her white-blond hair. One minute, she was a child at
play. The next, an animal.*

*The moment has stayed with me, bolstering my resolve to keep
her from contact with the exterior world. If others see her instincts
at work, she will not survive long.*

Aside from physical dexterity, and a sharpness of eye, the incident showed me that there is more to this small unfortunate creature than the ruins of a human being. No, there is more to my child than monstrous deformities. God has not abandoned her, as Ambrose claims. Rather, He has blessed her with unseen gifts, given her a richness of physical gifts that, because they are not like ours, we call demonic. But she is not a devil. She is not a curse. She is special. We must only wait and allow her nature to unfold so that we might see her for what she truly is.

Against the wishes of Ambrose, and the warnings of the priest, I brought the child to Pré Saint Didier to take the waters. Ambrose planned to make the journey, and as the carriage had been prepared and he would have our usual rooms at the hotel, I insisted he bring us along. The waters are miraculous, rich with iron and arsenic, their curative powers discovered by the Romans and known to one and all in these mountains. How could I, who has tried every other method, deny my child the benefit of this source of health?

"But my cousins," Ambrose objected, when he understood that I would not be dissuaded. His fear wasn't without reason. The House of Savoy knows nothing of our misfortune. And yet I insisted, promising that the child would be treated privately, in the presence only of our doctor, and that not a soul from the House of Savoy would see her. It was a promise that I should not have made, for, as anyone who has taken the waters at the source knows, privacy is an illusion. Those of our milieu mingle in the waters freely. I would have to invent new means of discretion. I would have to find a way to hide Vittoria from them.

The hotel sits at the base of Mont Blanc, some distance from Montebianco Castle, in the flats of the Val d'Ayas, near a wide, cobblestone road. The hotel is large and modern, with many rooms, a restaurant, and a casino, where Ambrose plays vingt-et-un until early in the morning, winning and losing as the Lord should have *it. The thermal baths are below the hotel, sunk into the rock of the mountain, the clear water bubbling up into pools. One can float for hours there, the warm water filling one with vitality. Attendants bring refreshments to the pools, and there is a room with a wood-burning stove. The heat causes the blood to rush through the limbs with such force that one can hardly move afterward. There is sorbet in glass bowls, champagne, berries, cakes. How civilized it all is compared to our corner of the mountains!*

Before Vita's birth, we took the waters at Pré Saint Didier often, and had formed the habit of spending our evenings with certain families. They will expect the old routines. Champagne on the veranda. Dinner. Walks by the fountain. Surely, they will inquire about our child—the only one the Lord has granted us. But perhaps not. Nothing is quite so boring as discussions of children. I will tell them that Vittoria is with the nurse, ill, in bed with fever. They will forget Vita exists.

We arrived, and the nurse carried Vita directly to the rooms as instructed. I met with the doctors and explained that my child was ill, with malformations of the bone. They believe the water will help relieve her swollen joints. When I requested a private bath, they complied. There is a small bathhouse away from the main source, where I can take her undisturbed. And so, the next morning, I wrapped her in linen sheets and brought her to the pools early, before the sun rose.

What a success it was, Vita's first bath! At first, she merely sat in the bubbling pool, looking about with her enormous eyes. After some minutes, she began to smile. She began to splash and play, then to sing. The warmth soothed her, producing a wonderful calmness. It was as if the heat from the center of the earth settled her spirit.

But what gave me the most pleasure was the transformation that I saw in my child. Vittoria appeared, suddenly and inexplicably, beautiful. In that pool of Alpine waters, in the lemony light of morning, her abnormal features were radiant. Her pale white skin took on the quality of ice, giving her a regal bearing. I saw it. My daughter has the makings of a noblewoman.

I took Vita to the bath every morning for a week, and each morning she grew more confident in the water. Perhaps this triumph left me blind to reality, because I stayed later and later at the bath, until one day I remained too long and a very fine, very fat lady waded into the pool. I felt myself freeze as she approached, my body stiffening like a statue as she looked Vita over, her eyes showing first confusion, then horror. She screamed in fright, pointing at Vita, her voice rising to such a level that soon the attendants arrived. This unfortunate woman was so undone that they carried her away. And while I cared nothing about the state of this woman's nerves, I did care about my poor Vita. She understood, with brutal clarity, how very monstrous she is.

In the four and a half years since her birth, she has grown into a stout and strong little thing. The wound along her spine has healed entirely, and as her back is covered in fine white hair, the scar is not visible. Her head is still unnaturally large; often it seems that she will fall over from its weight. But her shoulders and back are beginning to grow sturdy, and she has, in the past months, grown an abundance of lovely blond hair, which her nurse brushes and styles to cover her ears. Indeed, strange as she is, her body is taking on a more normal shape. Her arms and legs grow longer each month. And her eyes, while large and strange, have become intelligent. She sees and understands the world around her.

She has, of late, been learning the rudiments of the alphabet, and it pleases me to know that she has made progress. Victories come slowly with Vita, but it was recently brought to my attention that she has succeeded in writing letters, and these efforts have led to simple words: "oui," "non," "maman." This leads me to believe that one day she will begin to understand complex language. We are introducing words in numerous languages, to gauge if one might be better suited to her abilities. The introduction of English has yielded the most words thus far. I have written to my cousin in London, asking her to send us an English tutor.

We had a British naturalist at our gate the other day. He had heard, on his travels through our mountains, of a noble-born, malformed child and, after making inquiries, was directed to the castle. I was enraged upon learning that our secret, so carefully guarded, could be discovered so easily as this! If that is the case, anyone throwing about questions and a few gold coins is able to discover Vita. I have spoken to Ambrose about this, and he agreed with me. We must suppress all talk of Vita among the peasants. We must hide her existence. We will announce that Vita has died, hold a funeral, and be done with it. We will hide her away. She must live in secret.

There is, as Ambrose warned, something devilish in her.

Sometimes she studies the world with a cold, calculating regard, one devoid of gentleness. It is an expression that chills the senses, it is so devoid of emotion, so outside the realm of human interaction. I wonder then if the defects of her body do not reflect the defects of the soul.

When I try to give the child affection, which I admit is rare and unnatural for me—frankly, my heart closes when I see her; I reject this imperfect copy of myself—she stiffens, as if I have shown her violence. Perhaps she senses that I have no love for her, only compassion, tolerance, and duty. And, more and more of late, horror.

The other evening, for example, I went to her rooms in the northeast tower to wish her a good evening. Vita was with her nurse when I arrived, a collection of rag dolls scattered about her. I was pleased by this simple scene, as I thought she might be playing the kind of domestic games I played as a girl. Indeed, the doll had come from my own collection. But when I bent to see her, I found that every one of the dolls had been ripped and torn, violently denuded and decapitated. The child had gnawed through the dolls with her sharp, strong teeth. In the process, she had bitten her own flesh, and blood had dripped over the wreckage, drying brown and hard on their mangled bodies. When I asked the nurse about this state of affairs, she informed me that Vita had eaten every one of the dolls' heads whole.

"Eaten?" I said, perplexed. "Surely, she could not have eaten rags. She would be ill."

The nurse assured me that Vita had, in fact, devoured them.

Suddenly, there was a scratching in the corner of the room, a cacophony of claws, as a rat scrambled across the nursery. A look of fascination passed over Vita's face, and she stood and darted about the room, following the noise. Her gait was uneven, her weight shifting from leg to leg as she moved, as if her hips were not joined to her body. Then, without a word of warning, she lurched at the rat, grabbed it by the tail, and bit into it. She struck so fast, and there was such elegant ferocity to her movements, that I wouldn't have understood what had happened had it not been for the burst of blood spattered across the stone floor. As I watched, Vita devoured the rat, dropped the tail on the floor, and wiped the blood from her lips with her sleeve. She must have seen my astonishment, because she began to laugh.

"I believe," the nurse said, her voice dropping to a whisper, "that she is catching more mice than the courtyard cats, madame."

I stifled a sob in my throat and turned to hide my pain from the nurse. I thought of the butterfly Vita had killed some time before,

*the pleasure she had taken in the kill, how she had crushed its
wings in her jaws.*

December 1928

My child is possessed.

*Satan has rooted himself into her body, and through his
nefarious means—so cruel and various in their tortures—has
created a vessel in the body of my girl. Priests from as far away as
Turin have come to examine her and are in universal agreement:
Vita houses the devil. She is a succubus. Her soul has arrived here
from hell.*

*The incident occurred last week, in the gardens outside the
northeast tower. These tranquil grounds around the lake have become
the site, these past years, of Vita's promenades outside the castle. She
adores nature, and although she has been forbidden to venture out of
the northeast tower without supervision, I occasionally allow her the
freedom to ramble unattended. I have found that after she has been
climbing in the foothills of the mountain, or when she has ventured
into the great pines near the castle wall, she is almost content. I
know that she is not to be punished for her monstrous form. I must
help her to live inside the prison of her body. If she must run in
the snow to soothe her distressed mind, so be it. If she must climb
in the mountains to tire her limbs, I will allow it. I can offer these
comforts, at least.*

*Such was my intention when I unfastened the lock on her door
and let her go free. It was the feast of Saint Nicholas, and the
village houses were illuminated with candles. We could see them
glowing in the distance, pricks of light in the darkness below the
castle. Snow fell softly, creating a powder over the evergreens. Vita
wanted to ramble in the garden. It was a small indulgence, or so I
thought at the time.*

*Later that night, a party from the village came to the castle.
They demanded to speak with Ambrose, and when my husband
opened the windows of the west tower, I saw twenty or so men
gathered below. They held torches and screamed our name:
"Montebianco! Montebianco!"*

*Looking down upon the crowd, my husband demanded to know
why they had come at such an hour.*

*The crowd responded with shouts of rage and anger. "Beast,"
they cried. "Beast!"*

*I knew at once that they were referring to Vita. Vita was being
held in the home of the village magistrate. The men had come to
inform us that she was being held on charges of grave wrongdoing.*

"What has she done?" Ambrose demanded.

"She has committed murder," came the response.

*Murder! Vita's fits of violence were well known among us,
and I had observed that the instinct to hunt had grown more
pronounced; the butterflies and rats had led to other, larger
kills—marmots and rabbits and mouflon. But the murder of a
human being? Vita had never shown such an inclination. I could
not bring myself to believe it.*

*"They are wrong," I whispered to Ambrose. "Vita isn't capable.
Demand proof."*

"What proof do you have?" Ambrose called down.

"I myself saw the act," a man said, stepping forward.

*"I, too, witnessed the violence," said another man, as he stepped
forward to join the first.*

*"And I, with the help of these others, endeavored to restrain the
beast," said a third.*

*Beast. The word echoed through our room, silencing Ambrose
and myself.*

*Ambrose told them to go home, and he would come to Nevenero
at once. He ordered the carriage be made ready and began to dress.*

When I saw that he would go immediately, I ran to my boudoir, dressed, and hurried to the courtyard, arriving before my husband, and I climbed into the carriage and covered myself in blankets. I knew he would order me to stay, but I would not abide being left behind. I would see for myself the crime for which my child was accused.

We found Vittoria bound with rope in a stable.

Covered in blood, her clothes ripped from her body, her feet unshod—she looked every bit the murderess the villagers had described. Ambrose, who could never stand to look at his daughter, even when I combed her hair and dressed her in fine clothes, turned away, his expression filled with disgust, and demanded to see what Vittoria had done.

They took us to a stone village house, one of the many that clustered around the center of Nevenero. As we walked through the door, we found a scene so shocking, so unlike anything I could have imagined. I surveyed the atrocities as if they were something apart from me, a pièce de théâtre *being played out on a stage. Not even the nightmares of Dante could compare with the scene that unfolded before my eyes.*

Two men, brothers, had lived. And two were now dead. That is the simple calculation of the damages wrought by my daughter. But the actual accounting of what Vita had done is harder to tally, as the amount of destruction—and the amount of blood—gave the illusion of a massacre. The bodies of those slain had been hideously disfigured. A limb torn from one body lay near another. A foot ripped from its ankle stood upright in a shoe. Hands, heads, arms, legs—incongruous pieces of the human form were strewn about the room.

A sensation of numbness fell over me as I took it all in. I believe I may have fainted, for the next thing I recall is the hand of my husband gripping my arm to help me stand. Blood stained the floorboards black. It was so thick that, as we left the room, the hem of my petticoat grew crimson.

As Ambrose led me back to the carriage, I saw that a small crowd had gathered outside the stable. Some held torches. Others carried axes and cudgels. I gripped the arm of my husband, terrified.

"They will kill her, Ambrose," I whispered, so the peasants would not hear me. "They will burn her alive."

"That would be the answer to my prayers," my husband said.

"Please," I said, knowing he was more concerned about what the incident would do to the Montebianco name than what would happen to Vittoria. "For the children we might have one day. They will kill first one, then all of the Montebiancos."

Ambrose sighed, considering what he must do. Sacrificing Vittoria did not harm him, but the idea of losing our future children was not easy to bear.

"These are peasants," he said, grabbing some coins. "I know how to placate them." He put me in the carriage and secured the door. I collapsed into the cushions, covering myself with a rug. My whole body shook with fear. Although I had insisted upon coming to the village, I wished that I had spared myself. The mind is like warm wax, the world like a brass seal pressed into it. Such imprints are forever stamped into us. I am eternally marred.

Finally, Ambrose returned to the carriage, pulling Vita with him. As we climbed the road back to the castle, I took her hands in mine. Tears were streaming down my cheeks. I was ill with horror, but I found my will to speak stronger than my disgust.

"Did you kill those people, Vittoria? Tell me the truth. Was it you?"

My child answered in quiet, respectful French.

Ambrose's face hardened. He looked at his daughter, hatred in his eyes. "Why?" he said. "Why would you do such a beastly, murderous deed? Are you a human being? Or a monster?"

They startled Vita, her father's words. They were the first and last sentiments Ambrose addressed to his daughter. Vita's large blue eyes were wet with tears, but she couldn't speak to him. Instead, she came to me and whispered her response in my ear.

"What reason did she give?" he asked.

I lay back in the seat of the calèche, my heart pounding in my chest. "They attacked her," I said. "She came upon them when she was walking. They attacked her and she defended herself. They struck first, Ambrose."

Father Francisco, who came to Nevenero to christen Vittoria after her birth, and who has followed her strange development with such loyalty these past years, will perform the exorcism.

He took me aside late last night, after we brought Vita home from the terrible ordeal in the village, to tell me he believes the devil lives in the girl.

"You are not alone," I told him. "The villagers believe so as well, and they would have killed her had Ambrose not intervened."

Father Francisco promised that everything would soon change. He would make the devil confess to what happened in Nevenero. "An exorcism will liberate the child," Father Francisco said. "It will free her from the spirits that have so twisted her soul. And it will, Countess, liberate you."

I acquiesced, but insisted that I be present during the ritual. I wanted to hold Vittoria's hand in mine when they tied her down. I wanted to speak to her as they subjected her to their holy oils, their golden crosses, their prayers. I would stifle her cries when they branded her with hot irons. In my desperation, I thought I might *offer her some of my strength. But it is not strength she needs. She is thirteen, no longer a child. After what I saw in Nevenero, I know she is strong, so very strong.*

Vittoria needs God to help her survive. I hoped that I could be part of His presence, a ministering angel to help her through the worst.

But when it came time for the ritual to begin, I couldn't go into the northeast tower. It was too much for me to bear, knowing that I created such suffering. Or perhaps I was afraid that the priests would make me confess my sins. I would have no choice but to tell them the truth: I want to kill my daughter. I have protected her, and yet, in my weakest moments, I question the goodness of such protection. It is as Ambrose said: Vittoria should die. If God, in all His benevolence, does not take her life, it is time that I, who gave her life, take it away. God will forgive. Who is He to judge me? He in all His wisdom and glory has created a monster.

The priests want a confession from the devil, but it is we, the Montebiancos, who must confess.

September 1930

The British naturalist returned to the castle this morning. It has been years since he first came to us. Years since I made it understood that he would not be allowed access to Vita. And yet, here he was again.

Ambrose has been dead a year, and still, I felt afraid of what he might say to find me alone with such a person. We do not receive visitors, even if they are known to us, especially foreign ones. I told the groundskeeper to ask the naturalist to leave, but the man was persistent. The groundskeeper returned with a stack of letters of introduction. His name is James Pringle, and he is apparently very well connected among the men of science in Germany and was a student of Dr. Huxley in London.

I invited him to sit with me in the salon for tea, fully intending to send him on his way back to Switzerland. But he was a charming man, and it was pleasant to speak English again; it has been so long. And so I invited him to join me for lunch in the grand hall. I ordered that a chicken be roasted and sent for a bottle of wine from the cellar. When we ate, I asked why he should be interested in my child, and he confessed that it was his specialty to document and study the irregularities of the human race. He apologized profusely, but was nonetheless bold enough to ask of the particulars of her affliction—from what did she suffer? How did it come about? Can she express herself with language? What is her diet? Could he sketch her? And, if he could be so bold, could he offer his learned opinion of a method of treatment for Vita's ailments?

By the end of our lunch, he had charmed me. I trusted him and gave him permission to visit Vita.

In the northeast tower, we entered to find Vita bound to her bed. It had been a difficult morning, apparently, and the nurse had called for help in securing Vita's hands and feet in restraints. She was quite wild when we arrived, screaming, uncontrollable. She made no sense whatsoever, and I blushed in shame at the exposure of her inferior mind.

It had little effect upon the good naturalist. In fact, this spectacle pleased him immensely. Upon seeing her, he went to the side of the bed, where he stared at her as if she were a rare jewel. He pulled up a stool and began to draw her. One hour turned into two, then three, and at the end of the afternoon, the naturalist had a book of sketches. He seemed overwhelmed by the experience and was in a hurry to go, presumably to show his sketches to colleagues. Of course, if he had known that my groundsman waited outside the castle gates to confiscate the drawings, he would not have been in such a hurry.

"Don't let anyone tell you she is deformed," he said, as he packed *his pencils and brushes into a leather case. "She is not deformed. She is special. She has simply arrived here from another time."*

Arrived here from another time! Those words have perplexed and sustained me. She is not deformed; she is special, my Vita. I did not have the heart to tell him that my child has killed a human being.

Despite the seizure of his drawings, James Pringle returned the next month with books for our library. Jean-Baptiste Lamarck, Alfred Russel Wallace, Charles Darwin, and other, more obscure authors whose names I came to know only after I began to study them in earnest. I found books on morphology and embryology from the nineteenth century, texts by Aristotle and Empedocles and Lucretius. At the suggestion of the naturalist, I read about how the natural world came to be populated so wonderfully, with such variety. But also about how the forsaken creatures fall to those more adapted, stronger and more aggressive than they. I told him it is a Godless theory, evolution, and he only smiled and pressed me to continue with my reading.

One day, we stood in the library together—James, Vita, and me—and he showed me a large folio of watercolors that illustrated Gregor Mendel's famous experiments with peas. I studied these watercolors, taking in the combinations. They showed an explosion of varieties—short-stemmed peas with purple flowers, long-stemmed peas with yellow flowers, purple flowers with constricted pods, and so on.

The variety of Mendel's peas interested the naturalist. In nature, he said, inheritance was a matter of endless mixing, new traits showing up with each generation. They were distributed and various, leaving no single trait to dominate a family indefinitely.

What he meant to say, I believe, is that Vita's affliction may

*resurface, should she reproduce. Thank heaven that will never come
to pass.*

*Rumors have come to Nevenero that avalanches are to blame for the
loss of a hundred or more soldiers training in our region.*

*It is also said that the surviving men have passed along the
edge of our domain, some distance from Nevenero village, and that
they stopped to seek shelter. I hope they will leave us in peace. The
billeting of soldiers is not a Montebianco tradition, by any stretch of
the imagination, and Ambrose would have forbidden me to harbor
our enemies in any case.*

*I cannot help but imagine avalanches. The great cracking of
ice and the thunderous tumult of snow falling, crushing, killing.
One hundred men buried in snow! Such devastation, and yet, they
fight on. What strength they have, these men. What dedication.
Endurance of this kind inspires resolve in me. It helps me bear my
own avalanches. Vita tests my strength, and yet I battle her. Battle
her hungers, battle her rages, battle the strangeness and shame until
I am little more than a husk. The truth is that I am old and tired.
I cannot fight much longer. Ambrose used to say I was ashamed of
Vita, that my vanity was offended by her existence, but it is not out
of pride that I have locked her away. I used to believe that terror
would kill me, but it is not so. Exhaustion erodes the body more
than fear. Vita will kill me, as I expected, not with her savage
teeth, but with her relentless vitality.*

*There are times I observe her, as if watching an exotic animal
in a zoo. She has become that to me, my daughter, a strange and
unknowable thing. Something of the animal kingdom. Something
studied by the likes of naturalists like James Pringle. I try to see her
for what she has become. She is nearly fifteen years old, and has all*

the attributes of a woman. Sometimes, when I see her from a certain angle, she is almost pretty. And then she turns to me, baring her yellowed teeth, and I know her not at all. I see a monster. I look away in disgust. She understands that I am revolted. And again, we are at battle.

Perhaps the time has come for me to lay down the sword and surrender. Now that Ambrose has died, and I am alone to care for our child, I must accept that there are limits to my power. The Lord knows that I can't do anything to change Vita. I have accomplished what I can. The greatest evils of her childhood have been subdued. The priests did much to alter her proclivities toward violence and their instruction has allowed her to read the Bible. She does not attack when we are nearby, but only surreptitiously, when she believes she is unwatched. As Ambrose used to say: the child has been trained like a dog—to be quiet, docile, tame. She follows commands without understanding them. Not that she could ever integrate into the world outside the castle. Even now, almost two years after the incident in Nevenero, the villagers have not forgotten her. They would kill her on sight if she were to go there. Instead, she has created her own solitary habits. She sits on the east lawn, by the pond. Sometimes, she disappears into the mountains. What she does there, alone in the snow and ice, I cannot imagine, but when she leaves, she is gone for many days at a time. She returns calm, almost at peace. This alone is enough for me to be thankful.

I passed an hour with Vita today before leaving her to the surgeon.

She was found in the mews in a terrible state. The groundsman came to me in the library, his face white and twisted with fear. "Mademoiselle is unwell" is all he said, averting his eyes in the way they all do when speaking of Vita: with shame and confusion. I put my book aside and followed him through the courtyard to the mews.

"She is in the northeast tower?" I asked.

"In the mews, madame," the servant said. "Where the soldiers were sleeping."

The soldiers may have left, but the smell of them remained, the scent of sweat and wine, and the mineral odor of blood and festering wounds.

Vita stood in the shadows, beyond the hay piles, her eyes wide. It was a look I had never seen before, one of confusion mixed with shock.

"Vita, come," I said. "You shouldn't be here."

She stepped closer. The dead of winter, and she was without shoes—that was the first thing I noticed. The second was the blood on her hands and on her dress. On her legs and her feet. Blood everywhere.

"What has happened here?" I asked, beginning to fear that she had raided the barns again. The goats were always in danger when Vita was unattended. We relied on them for cheese and milk and meat all winter. We could not afford Vita's plunder.

But as she came closer, I understood that this was not one of her usual episodes. My child was in pain. For the first time in many years, I felt something close to the sentiments I had felt at her birth: awe at what I had created. Compassion.

Vita threw her hands in the air, to show me the blood, waving her arms in a crazed fashion. She was not in her right mind. She howled and howled and howled, and the pain in that howl alerted me that something terrible had happened, some new violence. Finally, I understood that Vita had been violated.

I dismissed the groundsman, telling him to go to Nevenero to fetch the village doctor. Then I asked Vita to explain. In a number of gestures she made me understand that the soldiers had tied her hands to a post and covered her head with a sack. I could see that she didn't understand what had happened. There being no hope that she should marry, I had never thought to explain the nature of men and women's relations. She must have been utterly unaware of what the soldiers wanted from her when she came to the mews. She had wandered into a trap without knowing how to defend herself.

Later, in the tower, the doctor examined her, but his concern was less for mending Vita's wounds than for discerning what variety of creature Vita was to begin with. He brought the candle close to her, illuminating the pallid skin of her cheeks and neck, the white hair that grew over arms and chest, the unnatural feet. He looked at her as if she were a demon.

"What kind of beast is this, madame?" he asked.

"She is a Montebianco," I said. "And you will treat her with respect."

What a look he had as he put the candle on the table! How his hands trembled as he took up the scissors and thread! I thought he would turn and flee the tower. I took out my purse and gave him an enormous sum so that he would stay and tend to her. Pocketing the bills, he lowered his eyes and did not raise them again. He sutured the wounds and promised to return with medicine from the village. "Do not speak of this to anyone," I said as he left.

All that night, I sat at Vita's bedside. She was asleep, spots of blood staining the sheets, and it seemed to me that, in her weakness, she was more my daughter than ever before.

The perfume pleases Vita. It came today with the shipments from Paris, a crystal bottle wrapped in cloth. I unwrapped it and the air filled with the scent of oakmoss and bergamot. I knew she would like this gift. Fragrance has always soothed Vita, her sense of smell being extraordinarily acute, and perfume has had the added benefit of brightening the atmosphere around her, which is often tainted by an unsavory odor. While I have given her vials of eau de toilette *and some bottles of cologne, this is her first real perfume. It is called Mitsouko, by the French perfumer Guerlain, and is rather strong in character, which, I believe, suits Vita very well. After all that she has suffered, I hope the gift will give her some happiness. Indeed, she smiled for the first time since the incident after smelling it.*

June 1930

The doctor returned today to see Vita. Her recovery has been remarkable, he told me, much faster than expected. He watched her feed—one can hardly call it eating—in the chamber outside her rooms. We gave her a chamois, fat and old, with thick, curved horns, and it was reduced to bones in a matter of minutes. Our good doctor was astonished at this but said nothing. Money has made him discreet. The chamois will hold Vita for nearly a week.

Now that the village doctor is accustomed to Vita's abnormalities, he has become a kind of guardian to her. He has taken to teaching her about the medicinal mushrooms he used to cure her—varieties that grow in the shady, moss-heavy crevices under the spruce trees. He explains how to find them and how they heal the body. One afternoon, after rambling in the mountains, Vita and the doctor made a list of the mushrooms they had collected:

—Boletus
—Lentinula edodes
—Trametes versicolor
—Inonotus obliquus
—Grifola frondosa

Vita is happy—this child who grew up without a father's love—to have a teacher. When they returned from their excursion, she placed the mushrooms in a line on her table and studied them, lifting the delicate caps, brushing her fingernails over the fibrous stems. Then she ate them and asked for more. The doctor asked if he might take her to the forest regularly, to show her where the mushrooms grow. "She might find pleasure in the hunt," he said.

"But, Doctor," I said, making sure we were alone. "You have heard of her violence. Aren't you afraid for your life?"

He looked at me for a moment, as if weighing his response. Finally, he said, "No, madame. She is violent only when violence is acted upon her first. When shown kindness, she is kind. That is the way of animals and humans alike."

I wanted to cry at this simple wisdom. He understood my child the way her father never had.

Promising to come back the next month, the doctor tipped his hat and left.

He kept his promise and returned some weeks later. He wore thick-soled boots made for climbing the foothills of the valley. But Vita was too ill to search for mushrooms. A malady had come over her suddenly, leaving her lethargic. She couldn't eat or leave her bed. She stared out the window of the northeast tower, gazing past the pond to the mountains beyond.

I had brought in a priest, believing it a spiritual malady. The spring in Nevenero is a trying season, with its bursts of brilliant warmth obliterated by snow and ice. But it wasn't melancholia that had got ahold of Vita. After the doctor examined her, he informed me that Vita would have a child.

There are many ways we could kill the child. The nurse could feed it poison. Or drop it from the window of the tower. Or bring it to the kitchen, where it would be quietly strangled. The only certainty is that it must be done. I must redeem myself for the weakness I showed with Vita. The legacy of the Montebianco family must dissolve into the mountain air, disappearing from the earth like the fog at sunrise.

It would be best if it were to die before it lives, its heart stopping in the womb, before it sees the world at all. I lost three children in this fashion. Stillborn, marbled in blood, they were taken away and buried before I could love them.

But Vita's child is healthy. If one watches the strength of its movements in her belly, the thumping of its feet against her body, it becomes clear that there is little hope for a miscarriage. It is strong. It grows. And thus I must be resolute. I must become as hard-hearted as Ambrose.

The doctor comes every week to examine Vita. He has agreed to help me. He has promised to tell no one. And in return, I will give him land outside of Nevenero. A house for his son. Some goats. He will help me destroy this terrible legacy.

Each week he expects to deliver the child, and each week he returns to Nevenero. Lately, his manner has changed.

"It is very strange," he said, swallowing back the words as if they were too angular. "The child should have been born many months ago. It is long overdue."

"How long?" I asked, trying to count out the weeks, but I have no sense of time any longer. There are only the seasons. It was the beginning of the winter. November.

"Eighteen months have passed since the soldiers left," he said. "And when I examine your daughter, I see no change. She fattens. C'est tout."

It was true: Vita had become enormous, so large that she could not leave her room. She slept most of the time, her body round and ripe.

"It should have been born by now," I said.

"In fact, we don't know," he said, without meeting my eyes. "A

human infant remains three-quarters of a year in the womb. But a creature like Vita . . . We don't know, madame."

November 1931

The twin boys, Giovanni and Guillaume, were born on Toussaint, a sign, I believe, that we have been given a reprieve. After all I had feared, and all that might have been, we have avoided the worst.

Giovanni arrived first, claiming the title of his ancestors, but Guillaume was not inferior. He is a fine child, heavier than his brother, more alert. They are identical twins, not les faux jumeaux, *but their behavior is nothing alike: as Giovanni cried, Guillaume looked about the chamber, astonished by the world. Not a sound. Not a cry. Simple acceptance that God has placed him here among us.*

The doctor met my eyes after the boys were cleaned and wrapped in linen. We had an agreement. If the baby was like Vita, he would slit its throat and dispose of the body. If the baby was free of Vita's deformities, we would allow it to live. Both boys are healthy. Both free from Vita's afflictions. They will live, and with God's blessing, Vita will pass away, giving over the future of Montebianco Castle to them.

FIFTEEN

✦

FOR DAYS AFTER finishing Eleanor's memoir, I could think of little other than the terrible history I had discovered. The strange scenes of Vita's childhood—the crushed butterfly, the exorcism, her encounter in the village—haunted me, filling me with an immense sense of sadness, not only for the little girl born into an era of ignorance, to parents who could not comprehend her mental and physical challenges, but for the teenaged girl who had been the victim of sexual violence. That my grandfather had grown up in the shadow of this violence, the child of rape, the child of a mother incapable of caring for him, explained a lot, as did the fact that Vita had clearly suffered from a serious genetic disorder.

And yet, discovering that my family carried a congenital illness lifted a heavy weight from my shoulders. Giovanni and Marta's stillborn babies, my dead brother and sister, my own series of miscarriages—they were all the result of some error in our genetic code. For the first time in months, I felt free. I wasn't to blame for my inability to have a child. I, like Vita, was a victim of inheritance.

READING ELEANOR'S MEMOIR made me want to meet my great-grandmother more than ever. If only I could see her, I believed, I could reconcile Eleanor's exaggerated and emotional account with my own. All that week, I waited to see Dolores, but after our talk in the portrait gallery, she had taken ill and had not left her rooms. I was alone for much of the time, left to wander the castle and the courtyard, which left me edgy and ill at ease.

But I didn't truly begin to panic until the end of the week, when Zimmer did not show up. No one at the castle appeared to place any importance on the day of the week, but after I had counted seven days, and Zimmer had not returned, I knew that Basil had been telling the truth: Zimmer was not coming back for me.

DOWN THE CORRIDOR from the grand hall, tucked in a nook, sat the single connection to the outside world: a rotary telephone.

The castle was isolated, but if the telephone worked—and Basil had said that he was constantly making calls for Dolores, so it must—then we were not entirely cut off from the world. I could get in touch with someone in the nearby villages of Pré Saint Didier or Palézieux. I could try to call Luca. I could try to get ahold of Enzo. It didn't matter who I called. As long as I made contact with someone outside of Nevenero, they would surely get me a helicopter.

The trick was getting to the phone without anyone finding out. Dolores was aware that I wanted to leave, and there was no objective reason I should hide the call, but I felt an instinctive fear of being overheard, as if Greta or Sal would stop me. And so I waited until the middle of the night before slipping from my room. I didn't turn on the lights, and I felt my way into the corridor, fingering my way along the rough stone walls, inching forward through the darkness. The stone steps of the stairwell had been worn down over the centuries and were so slippery that one misstep would send me tumbling headfirst into a deep, twisting abyss. Finally, I sat and slid the rest of the way down on my butt, like a child sneaking downstairs after bedtime.

I was just feet from the telephone nook when I heard the muffled sound of footsteps. Fearing that Sal had come in from the mews, I ducked behind a curtain, pressing myself against the window. Holding my breath, I looked outside. The world appeared fractured, distorted by the honeycomb pattern of blown glass. The shuffling came closer, then closer still. What would Sal do, I wondered, if he found me? What could he do? I was free to walk through the castle. There was nothing to stop me. Yet, I was sure that if he discovered me hiding behind the curtain, there would be trouble.

When the sound passed, I peeked out from behind the curtain and found not Sal but Greta shuffling slowly away. What she was doing there in the middle of the night was beyond me, but I had more urgent business to worry about, and I hurried into the alcove, where I fell into a velvet chair next to an old-fashioned rotary telephone perched on a wooden table. That there was a working landline telephone at all was a testament to the Montebianco wealth. Even if the village had been populated, and the service was paid for by more than a single family, it would have been a technical feat to get the wires all the way up to Nevenero, let alone to keep service in repair through the winter. However they had managed it, the important thing was that it was there. And it worked.

I picked up the receiver and listened. The tone beeped in intervals, insistent, waiting for me to dial a number. The only number I knew was for the Miltonian; I had called Luca there every day for years. A clicking tapped in my ear as the number registered, but I couldn't get through. I was met with nothing but an incomprehensible recording in rapid Italian. Finally, I managed to reach an operator, and in a matter of seconds, I heard the jarring sound of country music under Luca's sweet, somewhat querulous voice.

"Luca," I said, feeling suddenly panicked, breathless. "Hello? It's me. Bert. Can you hear me?" I glanced at the cuckoo clock in the hall. It was four a.m. in Italy. That meant it was about ten at night in Milton. I had no idea what day of the week it was, but from the sound of it, I guessed Friday.

"Bert?" Luca said. It was more a statement of disbelief than a question. "Where are you? Is everything okay?"

"Yes—I mean no," I said, standing and walking into the hall to make sure I was still alone. "I need your help."

I could hear Luca picking up the base of the phone and walking to the far end of the bar. I could picture it all perfectly—the whiskey shots with beer chasers all lined up on the bar.

"Where are you? You were supposed to be back by now. I've been so worried," he said. "I've been calling that Enzo guy, but he's not responding. Are you back home? Why would you just disappear like that?"

I felt a wave of love and gratitude wash over me. Even though I had caused him so much trouble, he hadn't forgotten about me. He had been worried. He had called Enzo. There was one person in the world who had been looking for me.

I heard Luca's father in the background, laughing and talking to one of the regulars. It was definitely Friday, everyone out spending their paycheck. Nothing ever changed in Milton.

Suddenly, the phone went silent. "Luca?" I said, afraid I'd lost him. I heard the panic in my voice. "Are you there?"

"I'm here," he said. "Just moving to a quieter spot. So where are you? What's going on?"

"I'm in Nevenero," I said. "The estate told me that I needed to come here to meet my great-aunt Dolores, but there is way more going on here than they told me. Dolores is sick, and there is this crazy tower, the northeast tower, it's called, where my great-grandmother—who is alive, it turns out, and has some kind of genetic disorder—is being held. Luca, things are totally fucked up here. I need to come home."

"Hold on, hold on," he said, his voice calm in an effort to bring me down a notch. "Are you hurt?"

"No, I'm okay," I said. "But I need to get out of here. This guy Zimmer was supposed to get me, but he hasn't come back, and it's been . . . What's the date?"

"Friday, January nineteenth," he said.

"I've been here three weeks? Do you understand that I am trapped? We're snowed in. There are no roads open. Nothing."

"I understand," he said. "I'm going to find a way to get you out of there. I'll get in touch with Enzo somehow. If he doesn't respond, I'll come get you myself. But I need to ask you something first. What's going to happen when you're back home?"

Of all the questions he might have asked, it was one I hadn't expected. And the one that hit me hardest. "What do you mean?"

"After what happened in Turin . . ." he continued. "Not the fight, but everything else. After that, I thought things would change for us."

"I thought that, too," I said, tears blurring my vision. I had hoped that we'd passed through the darkest part of our marriage and could start again.

His voice was soft, more tender than angry. "I'm sorry for what I said to you. I should have told you earlier about what Nonna said. I just need to know if we're going to make this work."

I wiped tears away with the back of my hand. "I'm sick of hurting you," I said. "It's all I've done for years now."

"You know I'd do anything for you."

My heart fell. Of course I knew that. He had proven it time and time again, sacrificing himself for me. I listened to the bar—the song on the jukebox, the voices in the background—and felt a deep, painful longing to be back home with him.

"I want to start over," I said. "I know we can make things work."

"We can adopt," he said.

"I want that, too," I said. "But there's one thing I need to know." I took a deep breath, finding the courage to ask. "After the baby was born, was there paperwork you filled out?"

"Just what the nurses gave me."

"Did you have to write down a name?"

There was a long, tense pause, and I could feel the pain, months and months of mourning, collecting. "I called him Robert," he said, his voice cracking. "After my dad."

My eyes filled with tears. "That was a good choice, I think."

We sat in silence for a moment, loss settling between us. Finally, Luca cleared his throat and said, "I'm going to talk to my dad. We'll get you out of there."

"I love you," I said. "I can't wait to see you."

"I love you, too. I'll be there soon."

I hung up the phone and walked into the hallway, trembling with emotion, fear and relief and dread, all the feelings I hadn't expressed to Luca. Now that he knew what had happened, everything would change. He would get in touch with Enzo, and Enzo would make Zimmer send a helicopter, and I would be on my way out of there. Soon, I would be thousands of miles away from the Alps, safe at home with Luca. We would be starting the next chapter of our lives.

These thoughts were going through my mind when I looked up and found Greta staring at me, her eyes huge with astonishment. Before I could utter a word, she turned and hurried down the corridor as if chased.

AFTER MY CALL with Luca, a desperate restlessness overtook me. I walked through the castle at all times of the day and night, searching for the helicopter from various angles, catching the sun from the salon and the moon from the grand hall and the snow-topped mountains from the library turret. I checked the sky from my bedroom every evening, opening the window wide and searching the crepuscular light for a helicopter on the horizon. Each morning, I prayed that Greta would arrive with news that I would be returning to Turin that afternoon.

One evening, as I was reading family records in the library, I wandered to the window. It was early, perhaps four o'clock, the sky darkening as the sun set. There was no helicopter on the horizon but, as I turned back to my reading, I saw a smudge of dark smoke drift across the sky. At first I thought it was a distortion created by the ice on the glass, or a low dark cloud, but when I opened the window to get a clear view, I knew for certain: there was smoke rising from the village below.

I ran downstairs, thinking of how I could get to Nevenero. Sal had said it was too far to walk, but that was ridiculous: it was ten minutes away, maximum, even walking against the wind. If I could only get there, I would find whoever had lit that fire. With their help, I would be out of the Alps that very night.

I grabbed the mink from the cloakroom and ran out to the courtyard. It had snowed all afternoon, and while Sal had plowed the courtyard, pushing the snow up into piles along the perimeter, the flagstones were icy. I slipped, steadied myself, and, while regaining my balance, saw it: the enormous iron gate blocking my way. I walked to it and gave it a hard push. It didn't budge.

While Greta and Basil (and Bernadette, I supposed, although I had still not met the cook) had rooms in the castle, Sal lived in a modern apartment in the mews. As I ventured through the open door, I saw that the ground floor was unfinished, unheated, and overflowing with equipment. To one side, a snowcat sat high on its wheels and belts like a miniature tank. Sal used the snowcat to groom the snow beyond the moat, including the east lawn, packing the surface to the texture of a ski run. The other side of the mews was cluttered with tools, boxes of trash bags, stacks of slate shingles, and plastic bins filled with dog food. There was a metal pen in one corner where the dogs slept—Fredericka and three other Bergamasco shepherds. A wooden staircase led up to Sal's apartment, and just behind this staircase hung a corkboard filled with hundreds of hooks.

The dogs went crazy the second I stepped into the mews. They jumped up, scratching and clawing at their cage, barking and growling, desperate to get at me. I froze at the sight of them, and I wanted to turn and run, but I saw that the keys—the ring with the big, old-fashioned gate key—were there, not far away, hanging on the corkboard.

Suddenly, the door opened upstairs. I pulled back. Above a burst of Italian opera, Sal shouted for the dogs to shut up and then, without so much as looking in my direction, he slammed the door closed. Giving Fredericka a smile of triumph, I walked behind the staircase and grabbed the keys. But as I opened the gate, and pushed back the heavy door, my heart fell: the smoke was gone, blown away by the wind.

I was positive that I had seen smoke, but the only way to be sure was to go to the highest point of the grounds, where I could see the village clearly. Pushing the gate closed, I took the footpath around the exterior of the castle, relieved to find that Sal had shoveled. It was hard enough to fight the wind without wading through snow in my running shoes.

Nevertheless, my feet were soaked by the time I reached the east lawn. A full moon had risen into the clear, dark sky so that the snow glistened and the hedges fattened with shadow. I climbed past the pond, past the white mulberry trees, to the mausoleum, where I stood high above the village of Nevenero.

The village was tucked into a ravine below the castle, and I would have missed it entirely without the light of the moon. There were clots of houses, twenty, perhaps more. Between the castle and the village lay a smooth sweep of snow. The roads were buried. The houses were dark. There was nothing but gales of wind blowing down from the mountain, whistling. Nobody could possibly be down there. I could brave the wind and snow, but it would do me no good. Nevenero was empty.

I had turned to go when a sound came from somewhere beyond the mausoleum. I stopped to listen. There it was again: snow crunching as something moved over the east lawn. An animal, most likely, I thought as I walked past the white mulberry trees, straining to see across the lawn. At the edge of my vision, a flicker: someone walking near the greenhouse. There was a flash of white in the darkness as the figure paused, then disappeared behind the greenhouse.

My first thought was that Sal must be collecting herbs again, but I dismissed it: Sal was listening to opera in the mews. Then I wondered if it could be a large animal—perhaps a bear that had wandered down from the mountain. Or maybe I'd been tricked by fog settling over the pond. On cold, wet nights, sheets of mist collected over the valley, layering the lawn with a milky film. But while it might have been possible that a low cloud had twisted over the lawn, it was not the case on that particular night. The sky was clear, with a full moon and stars blazing overhead. No, it wasn't fog. It could not have been anything other than what I saw: a person walking across the east lawn.

Whoever it was, I wanted to get as far away from it as possible. I hurried down the path to the pond, heading toward the gate in the hedge, the chill air sweeping over my skin. The temperature had dropped, and the air was so cold it caught in my chest and compressed, settling heavy in my lungs, making it difficult to breathe. The mink wasn't enough to keep me warm, and my shoes were soaking wet, but it didn't matter—I was too numb with fear to care.

I jogged past the pond and was almost at the gate in the hedge when I saw a figure standing in the distance, beyond the greenhouse by the castle wall. It was tall, with long hair, which made me believe it to be a woman, yet, as I strained to see more clearly, I couldn't be sure.

Whatever it was, it seemed as surprised as I was. In that moment, the two of us frozen with fear, I became paralyzed, unable to breathe, unable to even blink. It stared at me, and I stared at it, stunned. My heart beat hard, the sound thrumming in my ears. Finally, I turned away, breaking the moment, and the figure ran.

SIXTEEN

✣

WHAT HAPPENED ON the east lawn left me too un-nerved to sleep. I lay in bed, my mind circling what I had experienced, dissecting the encounter in the way one might track the memory of a car accident, desperate to create a logical sequence out of a chaotic tragedy. After the person ran, I had stood there for what seemed a very long time, too afraid and disoriented to move. I almost believed I'd imag-ined the whole thing, but it had left several clusters of foot-prints in the snow. I'd squatted down to get a better look and found there, illuminated in the moonlight, the impression of a large, flat foot. The snow was powdery, the print imprecise, but it was clear enough to see that it had not been an animal.

Back in the courtyard, I leaned against the gate, breathing so hard the world seemed to drain away. There was only the cold metal against my back, the flash of stars overhead, and the realization that whomever I saw on the east lawn, that strange pale creature, was not something in my head. It was real.

BY THE TIME the sun rose, I had managed to convince my-self that everything I had experienced on the east lawn—the strange apparition of what could only have been a woman, the footprints in the snow, all of it—could be explained in a logi-cal fashion. Obviously, there was someone living in the castle

I hadn't met yet. It couldn't have been my great-grandmother—the woman had been too young—but perhaps it had been the cook, Bernadette, collecting herbs for her medicines from the greenhouse. Basil had warned me that Bernadette's appearance was peculiar, and the woman I had discovered was definitely that. It had been a dark, windy night; she had taken me by surprise, and I had simply overreacted.

Greta brought a tray to my room and put it on my desk. I got up and poured myself coffee. I hadn't slept at all and needed caffeine. As I stirred in some cream, something in the distance caught my eye: smoke rising from Nevenero village. I almost dropped my cup. "Do you see that?" I asked Greta, stepping closer to the window and pushing back the curtains to see more clearly. There *was* smoke rising from the village. Someone was burning a fire in one of the houses. Nevenero wasn't empty after all.

But Greta wasn't interested in the smoke, and she didn't look out the window. Instead, she stared at me, her large, unblinking eyes filled with worry.

"Greta," I said. "Is there something wrong?"

She nodded her head: Yes, something was wrong.

"What is it?"

She fixed her gaze upon my desk, staring at Sal's ring of keys. "He has been looking everywhere for these," she said, her voice little more than a whisper.

In my terrified state, I hadn't thought to put Sal's keys back. In fact, I couldn't remember if I had locked the gate when I came back from the east lawn.

"Would you put them back for me?" I pleaded. "Please?"

She shook her head: No, she wasn't going to take them back.

"But you could hang them in the mews and he would never notice," I said.

Tears welled in her eyes, and she shook her head again. "I can't, madame."

"Please, Greta," I said. "He would never know."

"You don't know why Sal is here, do you?" she whispered.

It hadn't struck me until that moment, but I had no idea why Sal, a healthy, decent-looking man in his early forties, would live as he did, so far away from the world. "He needs the work?" I ventured.

She shook her head, her eyes wide with feeling. "He killed his brother," she said. "He didn't mean to. He shot him. It happened during an argument."

While this news was unexpected, something about it matched up with the image I had of Sal. "Why isn't he in jail?"

"Mr. Zimmer," she whispered. "Mr. Zimmer helped him. And now he helps Madame Dolores to repay his debt."

I was furious. Zimmer had lied to me about everything—Dolores's reasons for wanting to see me, Vita's existence, and even Nevenero, which was clearly populated. The estate had manipulated me and had sent me off to the middle of nowhere, where a murderer held the keys to the gate. As soon as I got back to the real world, I would make sure they understood how angry I was.

"Mr. Zimmer is going to be answering to me about that," I said at last. "As is Dolores."

Greta gave me a terrified look as she picked up the tray with my breakfast.

I grabbed the keys from the desk and held them out to her. "Take them," I said. "Please. If you help me now, I will do everything I can to help you find out what happened to your son."

She looked at me for a long, somber moment before taking the keys and slipping them into her pocket.

DOLORES HAD NOT left her rooms in weeks, and although I knew that her health had deteriorated and she was not well enough to see me, I was so upset by that point, so frustrated and confused about what was going on, that I didn't care. Debilitated or not, Dolores was going to call Zimmer and tell him to come get me. At the very least, she would instruct Sal to take me down to the village in the Range Rover. It didn't matter how it happened, but I would be leaving Montebianco Castle by nightfall.

I hurried from my rooms and headed to the first-floor salon, where Dolores took tea in the mornings when she felt well. It was empty, the damask drapes closed over the window, so I walked the cold, drafty hallways to the west wing, trying to find Dolores's rooms. It had been weeks since I wheeled her there after our talk in the portrait gallery, and I had forgotten the way. I must have taken a wrong turn near the ballroom, because I walked in circles for another half an hour or so before I came to a set of double doors, open, light flooding the corridor.

I stepped into an enormous wood-paneled hall filled with rows of animal heads—bear, mouflon, chamois, and stag—mounted on the walls from floor to ceiling. The beasts were so lifelike that they seemed to follow me as I moved, their glass eyes tracking me.

"Pretty impressive taxidermy, wouldn't you say?" Basil said.

I turned to find him sitting at a table, his ledger spread out before him. He stood, closed the ledger, and joined me.

"But the really impressive trophies are the ibex, over here." He led me to a wall of mounted horns, each pair sharp and erect as sabers. "The family has over a thousand pairs of ibex horns mounted in this trophy room. It used to be a sign of virility to capture an ibex, and the Montebiancos were nothing if not virile. They only stopped trapping the poor things when they became endangered in the nineteenth century."

I felt, suddenly, a kinship with the ibex: captured, trapped, on the verge of extinction. "Basil, I need your help," I said. "I've had enough. It's time to call Zimmer and tell him to come get me."

"I see." I must have sounded as desperate as I felt, because Basil gave me a look of concern. "I know Dolores has been unwell, but perhaps I can speak with her."

"You know his number," I said. "Why don't you call him for me? I can't stay here any longer."

"Understood," Basil said, going back to the table and collecting his ledger. "I would be very happy to communicate with Mr. Zimmer on your behalf, but I will need permission to do so."

"You don't have to call yourself. You can just give me his number," I pleaded. "Please, Basil."

But Basil didn't reply. He had walked to the far end of the trophy room, where he was returning something to a glass cabinet. I followed him and found a case filled with exotic objects—fossilized ammonites, butterflies pressed between sheets of glass, chunks of quartz, dozens of amethyst geodes, a stuffed hummingbird, and a string of sharp yellow teeth, perhaps fifty, bound together with twine.

"What is that?" I asked, walking to the cabinet.

"Trophies of another sort," Basil said. "I have been cataloging the collection of rock crystals. They are extraordinary and should really be in a natural history museum rather than locked up in a dusty trophy room."

I reached into the cabinet and took the string of teeth between my fingers.

"Wolves' teeth," Basil said. "Quite old, I believe. Collected for good luck and worn by generations of Montebiancos during the hunt."

As I returned the teeth, something else caught my eye: a glossy white coil at the back of the shelf. "May I?"

Basil nodded in assent, and I lifted a long, thick braid of white hair from the cabinet. It was course, like horse's hair, and thick as a rope. "What on earth . . . ?"

"Hair," Basil said. "Quite a lot of it."

I unfurled the coil. It slithered over the floor like a bull-whip. "Hair from what?"

"I cannot verify the story," Basil said. "And it is, in all likelihood, apocryphal, but Guillaume told me that his grandfather Ambrose Montebianco, the twenty-sixth Count of Montebianco, your great-great-grandfather, killed the owner of that hair in the early nineteenth century."

I turned back to him, fascinated. "Really?"

"The story goes that he came across a man while hunting. He shot him, then cut and braided his hair as a kind of trophy."

"There's so much of it," I said, running the braid through my fingers as I wound it back into a coil and placed it on the shelf.

Basil lifted a photograph, tucked between two crystals, and showed it to me. "That is probably what the man looked like."

I recognized the photo immediately as the one I had seen in Turin: the Beast of Nevenero.

"This fellow is not the owner of the hair, as this photograph was taken in the early twentieth century, but, from the account I heard from Guillaume, this man in the picture and the owner of the hair seem to be of the same breed."

"How strange," I said, examining the photo more closely. "I saw this photo before."

"Let me guess: *The Monsters of the Alps*," Basil said, shaking his head. "That book has done quite a lot of damage to this region. Look." Basil turned the photograph over. Written in faint pencil was the word: *Iceman*.

"Iceman?" I asked, perplexed.

"That's what the family called it," Basil said. "Not very tasteful, if you ask me, to keep human trophies, but . . ." Basil returned the photograph to the cabinet and closed the door. "No one has asked me, so I leave it alone."

WITH BASIL'S HELP, I found Dolores's rooms. She sat in her wheelchair near the fire and, hearing me at the door, asked Greta to show me in. I stepped into a huge, ornately decorated space, all silks and velvets, the colors bright and clashing. The decor was so different from the dour atmosphere of my rooms, so unexpected, that it felt like finding flowers and lemons in the greenhouse: a bright living thing in the dead of winter.

"Come in, child," Dolores said, her green eyes fixed upon me. "Come in."

Greta gave me a strange look, half frightened, half conspiratorial, and I realized she was trying to tell me that she had done it: the keys were back in the mews.

"That will be enough for now, Greta," Dolores said, dismissing her and turning to me. "It is nearly time for my nap. Would you be so kind? My bed is there, beyond the chinoiserie."

I steered Dolores between a pair of large oriental vases painted in jeweled colors and into a bedroom that was as Victorian as the salon: heavy brocade silk drapes, the floor covered with oriental carpets, every inch of the walls occupied by oil paintings of flowers. A cut crystal vase near the bed bloomed with pink peonies cut from the greenhouse.

"You look as strong as Greta," Dolores said, eyeing me from her wheelchair. "Can you manage?"

"I think so," I said, and after turning back the bed sheets, I slid my arms beneath her—one arm against her back, the other under her butt—and lifted. She was skin and bones against my chest, light as my suitcase, and I deposited her in her bed with ease.

"Would you mind putting some wood onto the fire?" she asked. "The cold creeps in so quickly."

I took birch logs from a basket and lay them on the dying fire of the *kachelofen*.

"I've come to ask for your help," I said, all my anger dissolving as I stood before Dolores. She seemed so frail and helpless. "Zimmer was supposed to return, but he hasn't. Could you authorize Basil to call him?"

"Of course, I would love to help you," Dolores said. "But it was not *I* who told Zimmer to stay away."

"You didn't?" I asked, perplexed.

Dolores shook her head, fixing me with a dark look. "You will have to speak to Vita. The servants answer to her."

"But I thought she was . . ." I searched for the right word. "Disabled."

"Her disabilities have never kept her from controlling the

family," Dolores said. "Her mother, Eleanor, was the only one who kept Vita in check, and while Eleanor died in nineteen forty-two, leaving the estate to her grandson Giovanni, Vita did her best to control things from behind the scenes."

"But Giovanni was only"—I did the calculation with my grandfather's year of birth, 1931—"eleven years old in nineteen forty-two."

"There was a legal guardian installed, a version of Zimmer who managed everything until Giovanni and Guillaume were of age. When I met Guillaume in nineteen seventy-one, Giovanni was long gone and Guillaume ran the estate himself." Her eyes filled with tears. "I loved Guillaume, but I admit, I didn't have the clearest picture of his situation. My family had known the Montebiancos for generations—I am a descendant of the English Crawfords—and I was introduced to Guillaume on one of our skiing holidays. I married him before I understood what I was getting into, I daresay, and although we made the best of it, Vita made our lives impossible. We couldn't invite friends to Nevenero. It was too difficult. We rarely traveled. Guillaume could never leave his mother. Not after Giovanni abandoned her. You know, Vita is a monster, but she suffered greatly after Giovanni left. She loved her sons to the point of obsession. Do you know that Giovanni didn't even tell them—Vita and Guillaume—that he was leaving? He just took off in the middle of the night with one of the village girls."

"My grandmother," I said. "Marta."

"*Marta*," Dolores said. The name sounded ugly, coarse. "Well, Miss Marta was lucky. I imagine she and Giovanni had a splendid life in the New World. My life, on the other hand, was hell. Vita hated me because Guillaume loved me. He loved me more than he loved her—at least I have that to hold on to."

Dolores glanced at me and, recovering her composure, said, "You might say that Vita and I have a long-standing feud. With time, it has become a kind of standoff. She has always had the upper hand—Guillaume protected her—but Guillaume is gone now. I just may win in the end. And if I do," she said, smiling with pleasure, "you, and all the Montebiancos after you, win, too."

The fire cracked and popped, the heat of it warming my back.

"I want to see her," I said, determined to speak to Vita myself about Zimmer. "Maybe she will listen to me."

"That can be arranged," Dolores said, her gaze settled on me, as if I had come around to the very subject she had been hoping to discuss. "I don't know if you've noticed, but we have a wonderful greenhouse here at the castle."

"Of course I've noticed," I said. "The citrus trees are amazing."

"The blood oranges are a great luxury in this climate," she said, her eyes flashing with a sudden complicity. "A great luxury to be sure. But I'm not interested in citrus trees, my dear. I am much more concerned with what Sal has been cultivating for us."

I remembered the rows of herbs Sal had harvested, the clipboard and the paper with the Latin words.

"Sal is quite an adept horticulturalist," Dolores continued. "He has been growing some treasures for me. They are fickle things, even in the best of conditions, and difficult to cultivate at this altitude, or so I am told. But Sal has managed it. Alone, the plants are more or less harmless. Ingest one, and there would be stomach problems and an extended stay in the water closet, perhaps. But together, they form a very powerful poison, one that can *eliminate* a person altogether, should that person drink it."

She met my gaze and held it. A tingling grew in my chest, a chilling and horrible sensation as I realized the purpose of the herbs Sal had collected in the greenhouse.

"The only question remaining," Dolores said, "is when."

SEVENTEEN

❧

I REMEMBER IT NOW, all these years later, as if I were still there, standing in the northeast tower. Everything I had heard said of Vita, all that I had imagined after seeing her portrait in the gallery, everything I had felt upon reading Eleanor's memoir—nothing prepared me for what I found that night.

She stood near the open window. The moon had risen, and the glow of its light fell over her severe features and white hair. She seemed to swim in her black dress, which was many sizes too big for her. I understood from Eleanor's memoir that she had no choice but to wear loose clothing—the abnormal formation of her spine and the wide bone structure of her hips made it difficult to wear anything else. The tight silk dress she had worn to sit for her portrait, with its row of shining buttons, must have been—like the beauty of her sixteen-year-old face—a fabrication.

Vita heard us come in, but she continued to stare out the window, her gaze fixed on the mountains, the bone-chilling cold of the Alpine air ruffling her hair. She seemed unaffected, even as I shivered. Greta had carried Dolores up the stairwell and was depositing her on a couch near the fireplace when Vita turned and scanned the room, her eyes sharp and intelligent. In the moonlight from the window, her skin seemed white as chalk, and the pearls around her neck gleamed. She wore large jeweled earrings, just visible through the streams of white hair that fell around her face and tumbled over her shoulders, thick as a shawl.

"Vita," Dolores said slowly, as if speaking to a child. "Vita, I have brought someone to meet you."

But Vita knew this already. She had been staring at me for a solid minute. "Please, come in," she said, gesturing for me to join Dolores near the fireplace. "Sit where it's warm." She closed the window and walked to the center of the room. "Will you have some wine?"

"Thank you," I said, feeling my voice catch in my throat. I don't know what I had expected, but Vita, with her haunting blue eyes, her frightening pale skin, and her misshapen features, was not it.

I sat across from Dolores on another couch. While Vita went to a cabinet and poured out two glasses of wine from a crystal decanter, I glanced around the room. There was a table stacked high with books, a four-poster bed, a vanity crowded with bottles of perfume, twenty at least, elaborate crystal spray bottles and vaporizers with French labels. There was nothing in her living space that pointed to Vita as the horrid, uncivilized fiend Dolores had described. Or the kind of person who left a dead goat in her antechamber. The most menacing presence in the room was the heavy, floral scent, thick and sickening, of her perfume.

"Alberta would like to ask a favor of you," Dolores said, giving me a look. "About her stay at the castle."

"Of course," Vita said, as she lumbered across the room, her gait uneven. She lowered herself slowly into a chair and stretched her legs, her large, flat feet proof—if I had needed it—of our blood relationship. She placed two glasses of wine on the table before us.

"No wine for me, Vita?" Dolores asked.

Vita gave her an amused look. "You are too ill for wine, Dolores."

"On the contrary," Dolores said, "I am too ill to abstain."

Vita laughed, her earrings sparkling in the firelight. "Then, of course, you must have a glass of wine. It is a rare one, too, from my mother's dowry collection. I asked Sal to bring it up for this very special occasion."

As Vita went to the cabinet and poured another glass, I stole a glance at my great-grandmother, endeavoring to reconcile the expectations I'd had of Vita with the reality before me. She was very strange looking, yes, but the portrait in the gallery had caught a certain truth: her magnetism. An intensity in her manner. Her power.

Vita returned to the fireplace, the glass of wine in her hand. Dolores reached for it, but Vita swept it out of reach. "Let it breathe," Vita said, as she placed the glass on the mantel. "It is an eighteen ninety-nine Chateau Margaux. It needs air. We will all drink a toast together in a moment."

By then, Greta had the fire going strong. The room had begun to warm. In the light of the fire, I looked more closely at my ancestor. Vita's skin was pale and deeply wrinkled, giving proof to her age. Her white hair was thick and glossy against her black dress. When she smiled, her teeth jutted this way and that, sharp and crooked and yellow. Yet, she was so filled with vitality that it was hard to believe she had been born a full century earlier.

"Alberta," Vita said. Her eyes lit up upon her saying my name. "*Alberta Montebianco.* Here you are. The granddaughter of Giovanni. *Alberta.*"

"She's not the first Alberta in the family, you know," Dolores said, glancing at the wine.

"The second child of Isabelle and Frederick was Alberta," Vita said. "Back in the Middle Ages."

"Correct. The name has been used many times since then," Dolores said. "The Montebianco family has a rather limited imagination when it comes to the naming of offspring. They just recycled names ad infinitum."

"True, very true," Vita said. "We are not artists, the Montebianco family. We are nobility. Now, come, let me have a look at you." Vita leaned close, so that her large blue eyes were level with mine. "I have waited so long to see you."

I averted my eyes as she examined me, feeling something ferocious in her gaze. Maybe she was as curious as I about our resemblance: the large blue eyes, the white-blond hair, the broad shoulders, the cleft chin. Our peculiar feet.

"Now," Vita said, smiling. Her mouth twisted, as if the jaw had been broken. "What was it you wanted to ask me?"

"She wants Zimmer to come with the helicopter," Dolores said, speaking before I had the chance. "She feels like a prisoner here and would like to leave."

Vita gave me a look of surprise. "Is it true that you feel like a prisoner here, Alberta?"

"Well," I said, feeling blood rush to my cheeks. "It's true that I would like to go back home."

"Then, of course, you must call Zimmer," she said. "Basil will assist you."

"Thank you," I said, embarrassed by how easy it had been to make my request, and reproaching myself for waiting so long.

Suddenly, Vita leaned to me and took my face between her hands. Slowly, she brought her eyes in line with mine. Closer. Closer she bent, so that the proximity became awkward, uncomfortable. Her perfume grew heavier; below this, the strong, animal smell of musk and sweat seeped from under her dress. Closer. Closer. So close, it felt as though she meant to kiss me. Then, closing her eyes, she took a long, slow inhalation.

"Come, Vita, now, really. *C'est impolit,*" Dolores said. "Ignore her nonsense, Alberta."

But I was too flustered to ignore Vita. The blood pulsed through my body as Vita pressed her lips to my ear. "You are one of us," she whispered. "I smell it in you."

"Smell what?" I asked, my heart pounding. My hands trembled. "What do you smell?"

"Please, Vita," Dolores said. "Leave the poor woman alone."

"What did you smell?" I insisted.

"Limestone and moss," Vita said, her eyes fixed on mine. "Quartz and granite. Charred cedar. And ice. In your veins, floating through your blood, there is ice."

"Vita believes she can *smell* a Montebianco," Dolores said, shaking her head. "And while her sense of smell is quite good for an old relic, I do think she is being a bit fanciful."

Vita turned to Dolores. "And you smell like generations of English peasants. Limitation and barley."

I sank back into the couch, my heart lodged in my throat, and my palms wet. I desperately wanted to drink my wine.

"Things do get a little *primitive* around here," Dolores said. "I daresay one gets used to it."

I met Dolores's eyes, and she flicked her gaze to a small vial that lay empty in her palm. I glanced at Vita's glass sitting on the table nearby. While Vita had been looking at me, and her back was turned, Dolores had poured the poison into her wine. Suddenly, I understood: Dolores had brought me to the northeast tower to distract Vita. I had been used as a decoy.

"Tell me," Vita said, sitting back in her chair. "How did you come to be here?"

As I told her of the letter that had arrived at my home and my meeting with the estate's lawyers, Vita listened, expressionless. When I'd finished, she stood and walked to the fireplace, where a portrait of a woman astride a black horse hung above the mantel. The woman had dark, serious eyes; a long, narrow face; and thin, terse lips.

"That is Eleanor," Dolores explained. "Vita's mother."

"I always thought my sons inherited her temperament," Vita said, giving me a long, searching look. "Did you know my son Giovanni well?"

"I was very young when he died."

Vita considered this. "And your parents? Are they still living?"

"They are gone, too," I said.

Vita sighed and sat back down in her chair. "You are alone in the world," she said. "Like me." She returned to the fireplace, took a leather-bound book from a pile on the mantel, *Emily Dickinson Poetical Works* stamped on the spine. She opened the book and read:

> *A LONG, long sleep, a famous sleep*
> *That makes no show for dawn*
> *By stretch of limb or stir of lid,—*
> *An independent one.*

There was sorrow in her voice as she read the words, grief softening her cold, hard features. "A long, long sleep," she whispered. "That is how I imagine my mother in the mausoleum. It is how I imagine my mother's mother. And her mother, too. They are all there, sleeping, waiting for me to join them. Just as I will wait for you, and you will wait for your children's children."

"It is all well and good to quote verse, Vita," Dolores said, shooting me a look. "But I can't imagine that Alberta cares about poetry just now. She's come a long way and suffered much inconvenience to learn about her family. Now, from what I know of Eleanor, she was a wonderful woman, well educated, and a poet in her own right."

"It is true," Vita said ironically. "My mother had a way with words."

"Indeed she did!" Dolores said. "She was adamant about documenting the history of the Montebianco family, including certain elements that others might have wished to forget. It was Eleanor who brought in a naturalist, if you recall. *Quel désastre.*"

"Mr. James Pringle was an expert," Vita said. "My mother had every reason to trust him. He believed our situation was extraordinary. Special. Worthy of study."

"You know as well as I do," Dolores said, "that the incident in the village nearly destroyed the entire family. Guillaume carried that burden his entire life. Giovanni left because of it."

Vita glared at Dolores, her expression tight. Greta, who had been watching from across the room, stepped in front of the fireplace, looking from Dolores to me, as if preparing for a fight. "Madame," she said, her voice filled with anxiety, "I think we should be going now."

But Dolores wasn't finished. "All my life I have cared for you, and I can tell you one thing: you have been nothing but a burden. And before I leave you to Alberta, whose existence you will ruin as surely as you have ruined mine, I want you to know that the Montebianco family will win in the end. They will survive you. You are an aberration, a freak of nature, one that will be overcome."

"Madame," Greta said, her voice cracking with anxiety. "Please."

Vita stood and gestured for Greta to be calm. "Don't worry, I am not angry, Greta," she said, her voice gentle, as if she were speaking to a child. "In fact, I would like to ask that we stop this silly bickering and take a moment to welcome my great-granddaughter properly. Do you mind?"

Greta took Dolores's glass from the mantel, then ours from the table, and distributed them.

"Come, my dear," Vita said. "Let's not fight in front of Alberta. Chateau Margaux heals all wounds."

"My feelings exactly," Dolores said, taking a glass in hand.

"A toast to Alberta," Vita said, raising her glass. "Welcome home."

"To Alberta," Dolores said. "May you survive this family better than I have."

We raised our glasses and drank the wine down. For a full minute, we sat by the crackling fire, silent. The tension between us was taut as a wire, as if we were all aware that a monumental act had taken place, yet no one dared acknowledge it. Adrenaline coursed through me as I glanced from Dolores to Vita. I couldn't be sure Dolores had poured the poison in Vita's wine—I had not actually seen her do it—but there was no other explanation for the empty vial. I struggled with what I should do. Confront Dolores? Warn Vita? But in the end, I didn't do either. There wasn't time. As I struggled to act, there was a great crash. Dolores had fallen to the floor.

As the poison took hold, I understood that Dolores's plan had backfired. The herbs Sal harvested served their purpose, but Dolores, not Vita, had drank the deadly wine. At first, I couldn't understand how Dolores could have made such a mistake, but then I saw Greta standing by, doing nothing at all to help Dolores, and I knew: Greta had distributed the glasses. She had exchanged Vita's glass, making Dolores a victim of her own scheme.

I watched in horror as Dolores's hands grasped at her throat. "Greta," I said, my voice a plea and a question, as Dolores gasped for air. "Do something." But Greta only watched as Dolores writhed before the fire. I knelt by her side, but there was nothing I could do: Dolores's face flamed red, then drained to a pale gray, and set at last into a deathly stillness. And while I witnessed it all, and knew that Dolores was unquestionably dead, I couldn't quite believe it. Not her horrid struggle, or the look of satisfaction on Vita's face as she watched her rival die. Not the workmanlike movements of Greta as she collected the shards of glass and wiped wine from the floor with a cloth. The shock of it all made Dolores's death unreal. But most horrible of all was the expression that had fixed upon Dolores's face in death, an expression of betrayal that would remain burned into my memory forever.

GRETA HELPED ME to my rooms, where she ran me a bath and left me alone to recover. I sank into the water, trying to wake from the nightmare playing through my mind. One second Dolores had been drinking wine; the next, she was dead. Pressing my cheek against the marble bathtub, I tried to soothe the throbbing in my head.

Vita stood over every memory, returning to me again and again, so that I could almost smell the heavy floral scent of her perfume. I understood why my grandfather had left. I understood why Dolores had wanted her dead. Taking a cake of goat milk soap, I washed my skin until it was raw, but scrub as I might, I couldn't remove the images from my mind. The crash of the wineglass as Dolores hit the floor. The desperate, dry bark of Dolores's choking. The smug look of triumph on Vita's face. And her voice as she said: *In your veins, floating through your blood, there is ice.*

By the time I got out of the bathtub, it was well after midnight. I put logs on the fire and opened the window wide, so that the night sky stretched before me. Rivers of freezing air filled the room, making the fire flicker and the candles snuff to black. I leaned against the window ledge, bathing in the bright moonlight, looking out over the mountains as Vita had only hours before. The air was sharp, like blades against my skin, and I wondered for a moment if Vita was right, and that I was, deep down, like her.

The cold air had the effect of shocking me out of my disordered state of mind. I began to see my situation with clarity. I couldn't stay there another day. The moon had begun to set over the mountains, and shades of sunrise hovered in the east, giving enough light to see smoke rising from a house in the village. There were people down there. If I made it to them, they would help me.

EIGHTEEN

❧

T HE MAGNIFICENT LANDSCAPE I had admired from
above—the pristine craggy peaks and luxurious crevices
observed from behind the thick Plexiglas of the helicopter
window—became a series of treacherous obstacles on the
ground. It was bitterly cold. I fought through knee-high snowdrifts, wind scraping my skin, ice crystals stiffening my hair. I
blinked and my eyelashes clung together, freezing and melting, freezing and melting again. I hadn't realized when I
slipped out of the courtyard that I would be throwing myself
into a glacial hell.

Within minutes, my hands had gone numb, and my
feet—buried in snow and protected by nothing more than my
running shoes—became wet, then frozen. I knew I could
withstand cold better than most people—my walks with my
grandfather had taught me that—yet I wanted to lie down,
curl up in the mink coat, and sleep. Thoughts of seeing Luca
again pushed me onward. I had the leather pouch Enzo had
given me in Turin and would use the money to hire a helicopter. Maybe, if I were lucky, my phone would have reception in
the village. If I could only get there, I would be on my way
home to him.

Just as I was beginning to lose hope, the spire of a church
rose into view. I pushed ahead, moving toward it, ignoring
the pain in my limbs as I entered the village. I knew that

Nevenero had been abandoned, but I wasn't prepared for the extent of the desolation. The buildings were in ruins, the windows broken, the doors unhinged. The houses were shuttered, some with boards nailed over the windows. Nevenero was a wasteland: deserted, lifeless, frozen. The smoke I had spotted at the castle was impossible to see from the ground. Storm clouds had rolled in, swallowing the smoke in a roiling, ashen sky. But there wasn't time to lose: the brittle air, the murderous wind—if I didn't find shelter soon, I would freeze to death.

Just when I was beginning to panic I saw, behind a row of stone houses, a light flicker in a window. A person moved behind the slats of a shutter and disappeared into the depths of a room. Without thinking, I rushed to the door and began knocking. The door swung back.

"Bonjour?"

The man was young and athletic, his features chiseled, his expression a mixture of amazement and suspicion. He wore a tight microfiber shirt, ski pants, and heavy socks. A woman in similar gear stood behind him, peering at me with astonishment. The air smelled of coffee and toasted bread. A fire—the very fire that had sent smoke signals to me at the castle—burned in a fireplace beyond.

I was shivering so hard my words came out in a jumble. "Do you mind if I come in? To warm up a second?" I stammered. "Please. I'm freezing to death."

The man blinked. He was so surprised he couldn't speak.

"I'm sorry, but I'm very cold." I stepped back and looked up the hill, toward the castle, its flags minuscule in the distance. "Could I come in for a just a minute? To use your phone?"

The woman stepped into the doorway, rescuing me. "Of course," she said. From her accent, I gathered that she, like her companion, was French. "Come in, you are looking like a *glaçon.*"

I stepped into a room filled with climbing gear: boots and heavy jackets; backpacks and ice axes and reams of rope scattered over the floor. A black harness with buckles and straps lay on the table. I must have looked confused, because the woman said, "Alpine body harness. For ice climbing."

I rubbed my hands together, trying to bring some feeling into my fingers. The woman said something in French, and the man brought me a steaming cup of coffee. *"Un café?"* he asked.

"Yes, yes, thank you," I said, falling into a wooden chair, its thrush seat hard under me. I wrapped my fingers around the ceramic cup, the heat stinging my hands.

The couple sat down and stared, waiting for me to collect myself. I looked more closely at them. The man was tall and athletic, with wide shoulders and a receding hairline. The woman was thin, with dark bangs that fell over penetrating brown eyes. They were young, in their thirties, sporty and very curious about me.

Finally, the woman said, "I'm Justine. And this is Pierre. He didn't mean to be rude, but you surprised him. There aren't people up here. Ever."

"I'm Bert," I said, relishing the sound of my name, my simple, familiar name. "Bert Monte."

"Here," Pierre said, his English heavily accented as he moved my chair to the fireplace. "You'll warm up much faster."

I sat, feeling the warmth of the fire against my skin. The caffeine spiked through my body, dispelling the cloud of disorientation that lingered from the cold. "Thank you. I didn't expect to be out in the snow for long. I thought I'd find someone who could take me down the mountain."

"Find someone?" Justine said, and by her tone I knew she thought I was utterly crazy. "Here? The village has been empty for fifty years, at least."

"But *you're* here," I said, glancing around at the boxes of canned food, tins of coffee, and crates of bottled water. "I saw the smoke from your fire."

"Only for the week," she said. "As you see, we like to climb. But I am also a journalist. I'm working on a book." She looked down at my sopping-wet tennis shoes. "I'm sorry to be blunt, but what in the name of God are you doing here? The nearest town from Nevenero is a hundred kilometers away. The ski resorts are even farther."

"I've been staying at Montebianco Castle, helping a sick relative," I said. "We scheduled a helicopter to take me to Turin, but it . . . didn't show, and I need to get home as soon as possible."

Justine looked at me, wide-eyed. *"Montebianco Castle?"* She turned to Pierre and spoke in rapid French, gesturing to me and then in the direction of the castle. Pierre regarded me with curiosity, then suspicion, as he asked Justine a few questions. Finally, she turned to me. "We don't understand how it's possible for you to be staying at Montebianco Castle. It is empty except for an old lady and her domestic employees. I went there to inquire about an investigative article I was writing. I was told that the owner had died."

"The Count of Montebianco did die," I said, considering my words with care. I could not reveal the truth about the Montebianco family to this stranger, or to anyone. "I was visiting his wife, my great-aunt Dolores, who was very ill. Cancer. She passed away last night."

"You are a member of the Montebianco family?" she said, incredulous. "An American?"

"My grandfather was Giovanni Montebianco. He left after the Second World War."

Justine stared at me, pale and somber. "My family comes from this village as well," she said. "This house has belonged to my family for hundreds of years. My grandparents fled Nevenero in 1952 and immigrated to France. They were some of the last to leave. But my grandparents loved this place. My family have been goat herders and mountaineers for generations, which may explain why I have been drawn to ice climbing. These mountains are in our blood. My grandparents never wanted to leave. This house was all they owned. But no one could stay here. It is a dangerous place, the castle." She fixed me with narrowed eyes. "I understand why you would want to leave."

"Then do you mind calling me a helicopter? Please? I will pay whatever is necessary."

"I can call the pilot who is supposed to come for us next week," Pierre said. "The storm has made it difficult to get through, but I will try."

Pierre stood, went to the fire and threw in a log. It began to crackle and pop behind the screen.

"Anything you can do would be great," I said. I glanced at the fireplace. The smoke from the fire was visible in the sky. If I had been able to see it, so would Vita.

"I grew up hearing about your family," Justine said. "But to be honest, for most of my life, I thought these stories were nothing but a bunch of legends my grandparents told about their old village. A way to cope with nostalgia and a way of keeping these mountains alive for me and my brothers."

"What kinds of stories?" I asked, turning closer to the fire.

"From the time I was very little, my grandparents would tell us about the monsters in these mountains. They had grown up hearing tales of demons, vampires, dragons, and devils. When a dog ran away, it had been eaten by a dragon. If the sheep's wool was too thin, a vampire had sucked its blood. When a child disappeared—which happened with some frequency—it was stolen by an evil beast. Or so the stories went." Justine shook her head, as if it were too outlandish to believe.

"Cretinism existed up here until the early twentieth century," Pierre added, as he collected the empty coffee cups and walked out of the room.

"Well," Justine said, turning to me, "cretinism is one thing. But there were so many old legends. My grandparents loved to scare us with tales of Krampus. Half devil, half goat, with twisting horns, with teeth like a wolf's. Each Christmas Eve, Krampus would sneak into the village to punish the children who had been naughty. While Saint Nicholas would reward the good children with toys, Krampus would capture and torture the bad ones, biting and beating them to death. When misfortune occurred in these mountains, it was convenient to blame these tragedies on the regional mythical creature. My parents grew up dismissive of their parents' tales. But now I believe there is something to the legends. Not Krampus. Not dwarfs. Something else. I am certain there is something monstrous living in these mountains. Something that has lived here for many, many generations."

"You seem so sure," I said.

"I have good reason to be sure," Justine said. "I saw it myself."

All the anxiety and fear I had felt the night before rose up in me again. "What do you mean?"

Justine leaned forward, looking me in the eyes as she spoke. "Two years ago, we were here in Nevenero climbing on the glacier. I'd drifted away from Pierre, to a great mass of ice hanging between screes of granite. I was frustrated. I had dropped my ice ax. It was my fault—I should have had it tethered—and this made it even worse. If you have no experience on the mountain, you probably don't realize what a handicap it is to be one hundred meters up a wall of ice with no ax, but I will tell you, it is a very uncomfortable feeling, like losing a shoe while running a marathon. Luckily, my ax had fallen within sight, onto the ledge of a granite plateau. I rappelled over, lowered myself down onto the plateau, and grabbed it.

"It was then that I saw them: footprints in the snow. At first, I was sure they were human. But then I realized that this meant a human being would have been up on the glacier *barefoot*. It was February in the Alps, and totally unthinkable to be barefoot in those conditions." She glanced at my flimsy shoes, as if to emphasize how crazy it was to be unprotected in the elements. "Also, there were drops of blood alongside the prints, which made me believe I'd come across a wounded animal of some sort. I got down and looked closer and saw that the prints were very wide. At least this big." Justine used her hands to demonstrate the size of the prints. "Incredible feet, really.

"I decided to follow the prints. It was snowing, and they would be covered soon, so I hurried along the granite ledge, my eyes trained on the prints. The path was narrow, only a meter wide, with an escarpment of rock to my left and a deep cavern to my right. I am used to heights, of course, but usually

I'm clipped in to ropes. Yet, I was so focused on the prints that I paid little attention to the danger. I ran over the icy ledge, heedless of the fact I might slip. The prints went on for a kilometer or so when, all at once, they veered into a gaping passage in the rock.

"I paused, listening. There was a struggle inside. I heard a cry of terror. It sounded human, so I ventured inside. I hoped to take a few pictures to show Pierre and hurry away to safety. But what I found was not at all what I expected. There, at the center of the passage, stood a kind of human being. It was tall and thin, with wide shoulders, long, strong arms, and white hair. It wore a leather vest and some trousers but no shoes, and it stood on two legs, as the prints had shown. The skin was pale, so pale that it blended in with the snow."

Justine brushed her bangs from her eyes.

"But most terrible of all, it was carrying a human child. A little boy."

As Justine said these words, a feeling of horror welled up in me. *Joseph.* It must have been Greta's son. I wanted to ask her to describe the boy, but I knew if I spoke I would show how deeply her story affected me. I would give everything away. "What did you do?" I managed.

"Everything in my body and soul revolted. I sobbed, or screamed, something between the two. The noise caught the creature's attention. It turned and looked at me. Our eyes locked for a moment. I wanted to turn and run, but I couldn't move. I was paralyzed by fear, and by something else, too, something closer to fascination. I stared at it, this tall, white-skinned, blue-eyed beast, and odd as it may sound, I felt that I was in the presence of something marvelous. Some part of nature we rarely experience. I found there was something *in-telligent* about it, something I recognized as human, not only in the shape of the face but the expression. And so I spoke to it, hoping that it would understand. 'I'm Justine,' I said. 'Justine.'"

Justine glanced at me, perhaps worried that I would think she was out of her mind. But I knew the exact feelings she described.

"The creature turned to me," Justine said. "And I was sure, from its expression, that it had understood, if not the words I spoke, then my intention. It came closer, so close I saw its glassy blue eyes. I wanted to help the child, I wanted to take him in my arms and carry him down the mountain, but I couldn't. I was too afraid. Instead, I ran."

Justine looked at me, and I saw that her eyes had filled with regret.

"I was some distance away when I heard its voice. Although the sound was muffled by the wind, it seemed to me that it had called for me to come back. *Justine,* I heard. *Justine.* The monster had said my name."

NINETEEN

❧

I 'VE UPSET YOU," Justine said, leaning to me and touching
my hand. "I'm sorry. I shouldn't tell that story, especially to
someone I've only just met. Come, I'll make it up to you.
Pierre has made lunch."

I followed Justine past the fireplace to an old-fashioned
kitchen with an iron potbellied stove and a stone sink. Pierre
had been cooking. The air was warm and smelled of roasting
meat. Pierre opened a bottle of red wine and filled three plastic cups. Justine lifted a stack of plates from a shelf and set the
table. The kitchen window was covered with a crust of ice,
giving the world outside a watery, insubstantial look, as if
everything beyond was melting. Wind whistled in the chim-
ney. The storm was nowhere near over. I glanced at Pierre,
wondering if he had tried to call the helicopter.

As we sat, Pierre placed a metal roaster on the table. Justine added a bowl of mashed potatoes. The meat smelled rich,
gamey. Pierre cut a piece of meat and put it on my plate. "I
hope you like lapin," he said.

"Wild rabbit," Justine translated. "Try it with mustard. It
is delicious. Pierre shot it yesterday."

Pierre poured more wine into his plastic glass and raised it.
"Bon appétit."

As we ate, they talked about ice-climbing gear, the top-
ranked competitive climbers—a number of Koreans were

ranked highly that year—and their intention to get back on the mountain as soon as the weather cleared.

But even as we talked, I felt Justine's story weighing on me. I couldn't help but think of the boy she had wanted to save and the creature she had fled. Finally, when there was a pause in the conversation, I said, "I'm sorry, but I can't forget what you told me by the fire."

"I can see that," Justine said, refilling my glass. "You look like you've seen the monster yourself."

I tried to smile and took a drink of the wine. "Do you remember what it looked like?"

"I will never forget it," she said. "There was a human cast to its features—big blue eyes, a large skull, a wide mouth—but it was not human, I was sure of that. And yet, it wasn't an animal either, or at least not an animal I could identify."

"What was it, then?" I asked, my heart racing. The description matched the photo of the Iceman so precisely that I could hardly breathe.

"For a long time, I wasn't sure," Justine said. "And so I began to research the legends and myths of this region, hoping to find something more substantial than the old fireside stories. It became a kind of obsession for me, to be honest. I went to natural history museums in London, Paris, Switzerland, and Germany. I spoke with professors who have studied the history of the Alps. I went to archives and read all the personal accounts I could find.

"There was a remarkable conference on cryptozoology last year in Lausanne. Cryptozoology is not only about sensational creatures like the Loch Ness Monster and Bigfoot. You may read about those kinds of monsters in the tabloids, but there are more ordinary discoveries all the time. For example, a new variety of jellyfish, one that had never been documented before, was recently discovered in the Mariana Trench, thirty-seven hundred meters underwater. Antarctica and Africa are full of undocumented life-forms. Cryptozoologists estimate that fifteen to twenty percent of the animals in the world are unknown to us. There is so much in nature we haven't seen yet."

She stood and went into the other room and returned with a backpack. She opened it and pulled out a worn paperback book, *Sur la piste des animaux inconnues,* by Bernard Heuvelmans. "Bernard Heuvelmans was the founding father of cryptozoology, the science of studying and identifying animals of more or less unverifiable existence."

"You mean extinct?"

"Sometimes," she said. "But more often they are animals that have not been documented by science." She pulled a second book from her backpack. "This was published by Oxford University Press just this year. It is a scholarly investigation into Yeti, Sasquatch, Almasty, and Bigfoot accounts. It examines the eyewitness reports, the videos, the DNA analysis done on hair samples, and, to my mind, the most interesting part of this variety of scholarship: Eric Shipton's famous nineteen fifty-one photographs of Yeti footprints."

"I didn't know such scholarship even existed," I said.

"Not many people do," she said. "The Yeti is a topic most often associated with crackpots and B-movies. Not serious scholarship."

I picked up Justine's book and paged through it, skimming over pictures, graphs and charts, and story after story of Yeti sightings. There were the photographs from Sir Edmund Hillary's expedition to the Himalayas and an essay about Sasquatch sightings in Oregon. As I paged through it, nothing in the book seemed to offer definitive proof. Footprints could be faked, photographs doctored, blood samples altered. If I hadn't seen Vita myself, I would have tossed the book aside without giving it a second thought.

As I handed the book back to Justine, a business card fell to the floor. I picked it up and read:

LUDWIG JACOB FEIST
Cryptozoologist
Museum of Zoology
Lausanne, Switzerland

Justine plucked the card from my fingers and tucked it into her pocket. Then she turned to a series of photographs in the book. "Here they are," she said. "These were taken at Menlung Glacier in Nepal. They changed the way the world thinks about the legend of the Yeti."

I looked at a series of exceptionally clear photographs of footprints in snow. They showed a large, wide foot with two big toes and three small ones.

"Shipton's pictures are so clear, and so perfectly composed, that there could be no doubt about their authenticity. Some later scholars have tried to argue that ice melt caused the enlargement of the heel, but that has been effectively dismissed. In fact, it is hard to argue with Shipton's evidence. There were a number of witnesses at the site—the prints were actually discovered by Michael Ward and their authenticity verified by Sir Edmund Hillary, who led the expedition. There were many Englishmen as well as native Sherpas who saw the prints and verified Shipton's account. The scientific community accepted the Shipton photographs, and they are now the most concrete evidence that a species of simian–Homo sapiens still exists."

"At least in nineteen fifty-one," Pierre added.

"After thinking it through," Justine said, "I have come to the conclusion that the creature I followed, the creature my grandparents had always warned us about—the Beast of Nevenero—is related to the Yeti, or a similar creature. The Sasquatch in North America, the Almasty in Russia—they all have similar traits, leave similar prints, have been described to have similar behaviors. Which leads me to believe that they are one species that has spread over numerous continents and evolved in different ways. Although, in fairness, the beast that I found diverged in very significant ways from traditional descriptions."

"How so?"

"There were physical differences. Descriptions of the Yeti are more or less uniform—the monster is gigantesque, for example. But the creature I saw was no giant. It was large, yes, and clearly very strong, but it was of a more or less human scale. Also, the Yeti is always described as being covered with fur. The original name for the Yeti came from the Tibetan *Miche,* which means 'man-bear,' and there is even speculation that the original Himalayan sightings were of a species of polar bear. But the creature I saw wasn't covered in fur. There was hair over its chest, its back and legs, but *hair,* not fur. In fact, it appeared to be similar to human hair. And its arms and legs were human flesh."

Images of Vita came rushing over me. I saw her pale skin, her large blue eyes. I remembered the description of her at birth, with her rows of sharp teeth. I turned to Pierre. "What do you think of all this?"

"After Justine told me what she saw, I was doubtful," Pierre said. "Her story was, frankly, very difficult to believe. But she was so shaken that I knew something had happened. Then I read Heuvelmans's books. And went to the lectures in Lausanne. Cryptozoologists take their work very seriously. And their theories are backed by facts."

"So you are a believer?"

He put his hand over Justine's and squeezed. "I guess you could say that."

Justine gave him a weak smile. "I admit, I have become the Don Quixote of the Alps. Pierre is kind. He doesn't want me to feel alone. But every time we train, and we are up there on the glacier, I am looking to see another one."

Pierre refilled Justine's glass. Her cheeks were flushed from the wine, or perhaps from the excitement of the topic.

"But the Alps are so vast," I said, eating the last bite of my rabbit and washing it down with wine. "It seems unlikely that you will ever have another encounter like that."

"The odds are not so great as one would imagine," Justine objected. "You should read about the Gigantopithecus, the species of ape dating from the Pleistocene period that Heuvelmans identified as the Abominable Snowman. It was a kind of orangutan, supposedly extinct. But it was not extinct at all. It lived in the Himalayas, undisturbed by human beings, and the species survived, perhaps for millions of years. The same could be true here, in the Alps, especially in this part of the mountains. It is so remote, so uninhabitable, that there could be any number of so-called extinct life-forms thriving here. The Yeti could be here, and humanity would never know."

"And besides," Pierre said, "the reward for a live Yeti is enormous."

I looked from Justine to Pierre. "There is a reward?"

"Yes, the International Society of Cryptozoology has offered a generous reward," Pierre said. "Any information that would lead to the capture of a Yeti brings one hundred thousand euros."

"It isn't the motivation for our search," Justine added. "But it doesn't hurt."

"The Montebiancos know the secrets of these mountains better than anyone," Pierre said, pouring the last of the wine. "We could split the reward three ways."

"Sorry to disappoint you," I said. "But the only thing I know about these mountains is that it is incredibly difficult to get a helicopter out."

Pierre was watching me carefully, too carefully, and I felt that he must suspect something. Maybe he'd guessed that I had been hiding information. It seemed, for a moment, that he could see into my soul—or, rather, into my genetic code— and glean the truth of my heritage. And while I shrugged off this feeling and finished my glass of wine, there was some truth to it all. I was hiding something, something my body carried deep inside it, wrapped up safe like a seed at the center of an apple.

LUNCH, COMBINED WITH my sleepless night at the castle, left me exhausted. By the end of the meal, I could hardly stay awake. Seeing my beleaguered state, Justine made up a bed on the couch and insisted that I take a nap. I fell into a deep, dreamless sleep, the kind of sleep that leaves one, upon waking, unsettled and disoriented. When I woke, night had fallen, leaving the room completely dark except for the flickering light from the fire. I had slept the entire day away. The storm wasn't over yet—snowflakes swirled outside the window. There was no way around it: I would be in Nevenero for the night.

Pierre and Justine were in the kitchen speaking quietly in French. I strained to understand them. *Ç'est fini. Elle dors? Oui, c'est bon.* They weren't far away, but it seemed a great distance to me, as if I were listening to a conversation from the bottom of a deep well.

My mind returned to what Justine had seen in the mountains two years before. I saw the tracks, the cave, the beast carrying the child. As the scene played through my mind, my blood went cold. The description of the creature was so similar to the photograph in the trophy room, so similar to Vita, that it could only mean there were others like her out there, alive somewhere in the mountains. The braid of long white hair in the trophy room seemed to back this up. And yet, I struggled to understand how it could be true.

It was then, as I stretched my legs, that I felt a draft of cool air brush over my feet. I had gone to sleep with my shoes tied tight. They had been soggy from the snow, so I had let them hang off the edge of the couch, hoping the fire would dry them. Now my feet were bare and exposed. The wide, flat bridge; the thick, meaty pink pads that protected the heel and ball; the second toe, with its long, hooked nail glinting in the firelight—everything that I had hoped to hide had been revealed.

I tried to sit upright, but a hard, tight tug cinched my body, holding me down. I couldn't move more than a few centimeters in any direction. I struggled, trying to get out, but there was no give. Looking down, I found a row of bright-colored straps locked over my chest, my waist, my legs, even my ankles. Pierre and Justine had used their climbing ropes to belt me to the couch.

I looked around the room the best I could, trying to stay calm, but it was easier said than done. I was terrified. Thoughts of every horrific thing that could happen to me—murder and rape and torture—rushed through my mind. Instinctually, I revolted against the restraints, pushing against the straps, twisting and turning as I tried to break free.

The noise brought Pierre and Justine. Pierre held a hunting rifle in his hands, and Justine stayed behind him, her eyes wide with fascination. "There's no need to be afraid," Justine said.

"They're too tight," I said, panic making my voice strange. "I can't breathe."

"They have to be tight," Pierre said. "Or you will run."

With that, Pierre took Justine by the arm and led her out of the room. I stifled a sob, feeling my cheeks grow wet with tears of fear and frustration. I called after them, trying to convince them to let me go, begging them to tell me why they'd restrained me, promising them money if they would untie me. I could hear them talking in the kitchen, and while they spoke in French and I couldn't understand a word they said, I clung to the hope that they would realize their mistake and free me. Soon, I would be back home, safe with Luca, telling him the story of my captivity as if it were nothing more than a dark fairy tale.

TWENTY

⚜

I WOKE AT THE first light of day to the creeping sensation of fingers on my feet. I jerked back, a reaction that was pure animal instinct.

"There, there," a male voice said. "No need to get upset. I'm just taking a look at your beautiful hallux."

The owner of the voice sat on a chair at the end of the couch. He was an older man, perhaps sixty, with a trimmed white beard and wire-rimmed glasses. He wore a ski jacket, unzipped to reveal a bow tie. A notebook, tape measure, and camera sat on the table nearby. Pierre and Justine hung back behind him.

I glanced toward the window. The snow had stopped falling at last, and bright light drifted through the shutters. Had this man come in a helicopter overnight? Had I really slept through helicopter noise? Maybe Pierre and Justine had given me something to make me sleep.

"Are you aware that twenty-five percent of the bones in the human body are located in the feet?" the man said. "One-quarter. Exactly twenty-six bones in each foot. Quite a *feat* of engineering, wouldn't you say?" He laughed a high-pitched, childlike laugh at his facile pun. "But that is in the *human* foot. I can't say what we'll find when we X-ray your feet. Your feet are quite unusual. Not at all like human feet. More like the feet of the Gigantopithecus, wouldn't you say?"

I met Justine's eyes and she looked away. She felt guilty for doing this to me. I could see it.

"My name is Ludwig," the man said. "And you are Alberta Montebianco."

"Dr. Ludwig Jacob Feist," I said, remembering the card that had fallen from Justine's book. "The cryptozoologist."

That I should know his name and profession startled him. "Why, yes, that is correct. But do call me Ludwig. And I am here today in the capacity of a civilian, a gentleman scientist if you will."

I must have sneered, because he looked hurt.

"You don't believe me?" he asked. "When Justine spoke with me last night and informed me she had a live specimen in her care, it wasn't professional duty that compelled me to be dropped in by helicopter on a moment's notice. If this were an official collection, I would have needed clearance from Lausanne, which takes twenty-four hours minimum, and I would have needed another scientist to accompany me to document everything. No, this is personal." He shifted in his chair. "My professional life has grown around the search for exotic, undocumented life-forms, but you, *you* are something else. You are an impossibility. A wonder of evolution."

He placed his hot hands on my feet and I flinched. But as I pulled away, he only gripped my ankles harder.

"Do you mind, monsieur?" he said, glancing back toward Pierre. Pierre walked over and placed one hand on each ankle, pinning my feet to the couch.

"Very good. Much better," Dr. Feist said, smiling at me like a dentist about to extract a tooth. "I need you to be still while I get a proper look." He bent over my feet and looked at them. For two, three, four minutes he stared. Finally, he said, "Come, Justine. Look what you've discovered."

Justine joined him at the end of the couch. Dr. Feist traced a line across the bottom of my foot with his finger as he spoke. "The width is similar to that of the Almasty, as it was documented in the Russian steppes. There is no arch to speak of. The padding is more pronounced than a human foot, fuller, more rounded. And, of course, the secondary hallux next to the primary is a classic trait. But what I find extraordinary, what I didn't expect when you called, my dear Justine, is that except for her feet, she appears to be totally and completely Homo sapiens."

"That is why we didn't know," Justine said. "It wasn't until I removed her shoes that I saw she was . . . *different.*"

"No doubt this is how she has managed to live as she has for so long," Dr. Feist said. "She looks like us, behaves like us."

"Her features are totally human," Justine said.

"And yet, who knows what is hiding under the surface. As you surely know, the composition of our genomes is ninety-nine point nine five percent the same. That leaves point-oh-five percent variation that accounts for the differences in eye color, hair color, skin color, inherited diseases, and so on. What would the world be like, I sometimes ask myself, if we relied on this truth—that we Homo sapiens are one group with large patterns of kinship—rather than holding fast to the superficial differences that have caused our species so much suffering?"

Dr. Feist looked at me, tears in his eyes. The man was insane, I realized, laughing one minute, crying the next.

Collecting himself, he said, "But I digress. Clearly, she is more than she appears to be. Looking only at phenotype can obscure what is really going on underneath the surface. Please forgive me for prying, Alberta, but I am so curious: Has anyone else in your family displayed such traits?"

I stared at him, refusing to answer.

"She mentioned she is related to the Montebianco family," Justine said. "An old family from this area."

"Until we run tests," Dr. Feist said, "we won't know if it has been inherited or not. If others in her family show this trait, she may carry the genetic material for this strange characteristic." He turned back to Justine. "You said she spoke to you at length?"

"We had a long conversation," Justine said. "She's quite articulate."

"Therefore no anomalies of the temporomandibular joint. Both humans and apes—and the creatures we call Bigfoot or Yeti, one might suppose—have thirty-two teeth. Humans, however, have a parabolic-shaped jaw, while apes have rectangular jaws. The reason apes don't speak—other than the cognitive reasons—is because of this primary structural difference. But," he said, looking at me with a mesmeric fascination, "we know very well that the smallest difference means everything for the survival of a species. What is it that Charles Darwin said? 'A grain in the balance will determine which individual shall live and which shall die—which variety or species shall increase in number . . .'"

"'And which shall decrease or finally become extinct,'" Justine said, finishing Dr. Feist's sentence. It was a religion, I realized, this worship of Darwin. A cult.

"Yes, precisely," Dr. Feist said. "She's been hiding in plain sight." He looked down at me, his eyes narrowing. "Perhaps she didn't even know herself what she was. What do you have to say, Alberta? Were you aware of how special you are? Of your function as a transitional form?"

I stared at him, angry and humiliated, but the truth was his words hit me with particular force. I had known that I wasn't like everyone else. My wide, flat feet were abnormal. The secondary hallux, as Dr. Feist had called it, was a constant embarrassment. But I had found a way to live with it and never considered it to be anything but a superficial defect, a weird flaw, like being double-jointed.

"She is what you have been looking for, then?" Justine asked.

"Oh, yes. Oh, yes, indeed. She is of great interest to crypto-zoology."

"What do you think she is, exactly?"

"I will know more once I get her to our facility in Lausanne," Dr. Feist said. "I'd like to do some genetic tests. But I would wager that we will find her to be Homo sapiens expressing long-dormant genes of a pre–Homo sapiens hominid. A throwback, if you will."

"There were many kinds of pre–Homo sapiens hominids," Justine said. "Dozens."

"True," Dr. Feist said. "The earth was once filled with earlier varieties of human beings. We—the last and only survivors of these ancestors—inherited everything." He stared at me intently, studying my features. "I would guess she carries a large number of Neanderthal variants."

The words stung. I imagined a hairy, inarticulate thing, ugly and ungainly. Did I really have the features of a Neanderthal?

"Surely not," Justine said. "She is much too . . . *human* to be a Neanderthal."

"Ah, that is where you are wrong! In the past fifteen years, we have proven the hominids we call Homo neanderthalensis to be much more like us Homo sapiens than previously believed. They were not hairy, apelike creatures that jumped around in caves, as they have so often been depicted. They were elegant, even beautiful archaic human beings with language, developed societies, family structures, and even artwork. Recent technology in dating cave paintings has shown that Neanderthals actually created pictures and symbols in their dwellings, which proves they had the capacity for higher thought processes. Fossils reveal that their vocal cords were swollen, suggesting complex language. They evolved during the European ice age and could withstand conditions that Homo sapiens would never have been able to live through, although it is clear that Neanderthals and Homo sapiens coexisted for a period of time. Some theories suggested that Homo sapiens waged war on the Neanderthals and killed them off. I don't believe that to be the case. I believe Homo neanderthalensis and Homo sapiens were friends and partners. Genetic material taken from a finger bone of a fifty-thousand-year-old Neanderthal male has recently yielded models of a hominid with blond hair, pale skin, and blue eyes. The Neanderthals may account for what we now recognize as Northern European coloring. They may have looked a lot like"—Dr. Feist looked at me, his eyes glistening—"Alberta."

"She is a missing piece to the puzzle of evolution," Justine said, looking at me as if I were a prize she had won.

"And the reward?" Pierre asked.

Dr. Feist looked a bit lost for a moment. "Oh, yes, that," he said. "The reward is yours. Every cent."

Turning his attention back to me, he lifted the tape measure and began taking measurements, scribbling them down in his notebook as he went. Balancing his notebook on his knees, he lifted the camera and snapped a series of photographs. Sweat soaked my clothes. No matter how I struggled, I couldn't break free from Pierre's grip. I was trapped. The helplessness and rage I felt at this moment is hard to relive, let alone describe. The most secret, hidden part of myself was be-

ing exposed, documented, recorded. Knowing there was no
way to stop him, I closed my eyes in horror and shame and
resigned myself to his touch.

A LOUD NOISE cracked in the room. From my tied-down
position on the couch, I couldn't see what was happening, but
I heard the heavy wooden door fling open and felt a burst of
cold as air rushed into the room. I heard Sal's voice shouting
my name; I saw Pierre step away from the couch to go for his
rifle. There was the sound of gunfire and Justine's sharp, high
scream as a second shot was fired, then a third. The quick suc-
cession of sound and movement in those seconds seems as
much a blur to me now as it did then. I don't know who fired
the first shot—Pierre or Sal—or who died first—Pierre or
Justine—but I was left with the impression that it had all
happened just the way Sal had planned—quick, cold, and efficient.

The one thing that has remained clear in my memory is
Ludwig Jacob Feist. He had been so entirely absorbed in his
examination of me, his concentration so fixed, that even Sal's
explosive entrance didn't tear him from my side. At first he
simply froze. His pale eyes went wide behind his glasses, reg-
istering that he was conscious of a disturbance. And then he
calmly slipped his notebook full of measurements and his
camera filled with photographs into a pocket of his ski jacket,
stood, and ran.

The next thing I knew, Sal had Feist by the arm and was
pulling him out of the house. There was the slam of a door
and then Sal returned and unbuckled me, strap by strap, until
the blood returned to my arms and legs. I sat up and scanned
the house. Everything looked different in the harsh sunlight—
exposed and diminished. As I walked out of the house, I

paused at the bodies of Pierre and Justine. They had fallen side by side, their blood pooling together over the stone floor.

Outside, the sky was a clear, pale blue, filled with a rare show of sunlight that gilded the mountains gold. The only sign of the storm lay on the ground—high snowdrifts licked at the buildings, covering doorways and windowsills. The snowcat had plowed a path through the snow and sat idling in front of the house, sending clouds of exhaust into the air. Dr. Feist shouted for help from inside the cab, his voice dampened behind the thick plastic windows.

Sal walked out of the house carrying the mink coat I had worn on my trek down the mountain. He must have searched through Justine's and Pierre's belongings, because he carried the books on cryptozoology under one arm. The backpack hung over his shoulder. My tennis shoes were in his hand.

"Madame," Sal said, pausing to look me over. "We had best get going. Vita would like you at the castle." He walked to the door of the snowcat and opened it. "Come, madame. Get in."

Right then and there something inside me broke. All that had lain dormant for weeks and weeks exploded in my mind. For the first time, I understood the truth: Vita was not suffering from a genetic disorder. She was not physically disabled. She was a mutation. She was, as Justine had said, a missing piece of the evolutionary puzzle. But she was foremost my puzzle, the mystery that explained me, the ancestor whose defects defined mine. I couldn't go back to the castle. I couldn't return to Vita and all that she represented. And so I did the only thing I could: I turned and ran.

Through the abandoned village I went, pushing through the snow. I was barefoot, but I didn't feel the cold. As I ran, I felt a new power take hold. I was stronger than before. My lungs were bigger, my legs faster, my eyes sharper. These mountains were my habitat. I could run forever and never stop.

I heard the engine of the snowcat grinding behind me. I dove into a narrow passage between two houses, climbed past an old shed, running and running, until I came to the base of the mountain. An enormous ledge of rock loomed above, heavy slabs of granite frosted with snow. But now everything was different. I hoisted myself up, clutching at the rock face, and began to climb. As the snow crunched under my feet, I remembered my grandfather taking me barefoot in the snow. I understood now that he had wanted to teach me something. I understood that this terrain was part of my nature: the snowy rise of the mountain, the ice-covered rocks, the rows of evergreen trees just ahead. With my strong arms, my wide feet—I had been made for these mountains.

When I reached the top of a ridge, I turned to see how far I had come. Nevenero was below, abandoned, a single stream of smoke rising from a single stone house. The castle, tucked into the valley, lay like a cold tile against the snow. The whole world was at my feet. I didn't know how I would get out of there, but it didn't matter anymore. I was free of them— Dr. Ludwig Feist, Justine and Pierre, Sal, Vita. My childhood isolation and my failing marriage and the miscarriages. *Free.* And I knew, as I stood there, looking over the vast mountain ranges, something that I had never known before: I was powerful. Strong enough to survive in the mountains. Strong enough to survive in ice and wind. Strong like my ancestors.

I turned back toward the mountains, ready to climb even higher, when suddenly the *crack* of a rifle rang through the air. A burst of heat rushed through my thigh, sending waves of fire up my spine. I staggered forward, the hard, cold granite breaking my fall. As I tried to pull myself up, I knew: I had been shot.

SAL CARRIED ME down the slope and put me in the snow-cat, where he bound my leg with dish towels from Justine's kitchen, creating a tourniquet to stanch the blood. It didn't work. I lay across the seat bleeding, the pain of the wound shooting through me. The bullet had torn a hole through my jeans and into my flesh, creating a mess of blood and skin and muscle and bone. Nausea overcame me, and I buried my head in the seat, closed my eyes, and tried to make it all go away.

From the sound of it, one would think Dr. Feist had been shot. He whimpered and pleaded from the back where he had been tied up with Justine and Pierre's hiking ropes. The pain in my leg was too much to bear, and his whining only made it worse.

"Shut up," I said. I glanced back and saw that his glasses were gone, and a line of blood dripped from a cut above his eye. Gone, too, was the clinical assurance of his position. Now that the roles were reversed, he wasn't so calm. He looked at me with pure terror. "Please, Madame Montebianco," he whimpered. "Please."

Sal drove up the hill, toward the castle. "Is he bothering you, madame?" His voice was kind, deferential. "I can shut him up, if you want."

Hearing this, Dr. Feist's terror grew. *"Take my camera. Destroy it. I will have no proof of anything. I will never breathe a word of this to anyone. No one would believe me anyway. Just let me go. Please."*

"Yes, Sal," I said. "Shut him up."

Sal jerked the snowcat to a halt and pulled Dr. Feist into the snow. "She told you to stop talking," Sal said. He shot Dr. Feist once, twice, the sound of the shots echoing through the mountains as he climbed behind the wheel and drove up to Montebianco Castle.

TWENTY-ONE

✦

B ERNADETTE IS GOOD with knives," Sal said by way of introduction.

I looked up to see the cook looking down upon me. She had a plump, cheerful face with round, rosy cheeks, huge eyes, and a double chin, giving her the appearance of a ghoulish child. She stood next to Sal, her skin glistening with candle-light.

"Ready?" Sal asked Bernadette.

Bernadette nodded and held up a short, sharp kitchen knife.

I gasped and pulled away, but Sal held me down. Pinned, I took in my surroundings. I was on a mattress in the mews, near the dog cage. It was dark except for candles burning nearby. Greta stood by Bernadette's side, a bottle of Genepy des Alpes in one hand and a shot glass in the other. She filled the glass and gave it to me. "Drink," she said, pushing it to my lips. "Now. Before Bernadette begins."

I later learned that Genepy des Alpes is distilled from the herb genepy, or artemisia, known in English as wormwood— the primary ingredient in absinthe—and was used in the Alps to cure any number of maladies—altitude sickness, wound disinfection—and as a digestive aid. But unlike commercial Genepy des Alpes, with its regulated quantities of the psycho-active element of wormwood, thujone, Bernadette's homemade version caused hallucinations and had the power to put me out cold.

Greta fed me shot after shot, creating a fire in my throat and a sickening warmth through my limbs. When I tried to sit up, everything fell away. I drank a good half bottle of the stuff and descended into a strange, surreal darkness that I have not experienced before or since.

I don't remember much of the operation itself, but Greta told me later that I lost a lot of blood. From the look of the scar on my thigh—oblong and uneven, shiny and pink as pulled taffy—I know that Bernadette, with all her expertise with knives, didn't perform the most elegant of surgeries. She removed the bullet the way one might have done during the Napoleonic wars—with a sharp blade and lots of liquor.

While my body lay in a state of profound trauma—opened and bleeding under Bernadette's knife—my mind sank to a deep, fortified place of protection, a faraway bunker where it carried on untouched by pain. I was, suddenly, transported to the trophy room, where I stood before animal heads mounted across the wall. The bear, the mouflon, the deer, the thousands of ibex horns—everything twisted around me like branches in a forest. All was as it existed in real life. But it was the Iceman that I saw most clearly. In the workings of my hallucination, the man in the photograph lived. It stood upright before me, its eyes gleaming with vitality, its long hair cascading over its shoulders, no longer just a trophy in a cabinet but a living being. It spoke to me in a language I couldn't understand, and yet, somehow, every word made sense: *A long, long sleep. A famous sleep.* I backed away from the creature, terrified, screaming.

I woke, startled, gasping. I had never felt anything like it, that pain mixed with the disorientation of my hallucination. I cried out as the knife dug into muscle, prying the bullet from my tissues. Leaning over the side of the mattress, I threw up.

Greta poured a shot and brought it to my lips. I drank it down and lay back again. My mind was bombarded with strange images, so vivid, so *real,* that I couldn't distinguish between fantasy and reality. Where had I been? Where was I now? The pain paralyzed me, but so did the genepy. The whole world seemed twisted and unreal. Bernadette, standing over me with her bloody knife. Greta, holding a blood-soaked cloth. I fought to sit up, struggling to get off the mattress, but Sal pressed his forearm against my windpipe, pushing me back down onto the table. "Stay still, madame," he said, as my consciousness slipped away again.

Back in the trophy room of my hallucination, the Iceman was gone. Instead, I found another creature, a female, her face an echo of the Iceman's face, a pallid, pitiful thing, her skin tight against her cheekbones, her nose flat, the jawline hard and exposed. A single blue blood vessel, thick as a garden snake, pulsed across her forehead, throbbing and twitching over her scarred cheek and cleft chin. The image seemed to waver, the edges bend away, as if melting. I tried to touch her, but my hand hit a hard, reflective surface. It was my own image, reflected in a gilded mirror, my own pallid face, myself asking: *What are you?*

I screamed and felt a hard whack across my back. I had vomited in my sleep. Once, then again, a hand slapped me. Suddenly, a shot of air rushed into my lungs. The jarring experience of coming back to reality left me dizzy. I gasped for breath, inhaling with all the force I could muster, shivering with sweat and agony.

"Breathe," Greta said as she helped me sit up. I felt nauseated, beaten. "That's right. Breathe. You are fine, madame."

As I woke, the world seemed to swirl and buckle. I heard the dogs barking in their pen, and above, in the rafters of the mews, a row of crows sat watching, silent witnesses to my suffering.

My wound sutured, Bernadette said something I couldn't understand—I later learned she spoke Franco-Provençal—and jumped off a chair onto the floor, like a child escaping from the dinner table. I blinked, trying to see clearly through the thick miasma of my stupor. Bernadette was half the size of Sal but wearing the same burlap trousers and boots. I watched her walk across the room, sure that I was hallucinating. But it was no hallucination. Bernadette the cook was a cretin.

WHEN I WOKE—TREACHEROUSLY hungover, everything throbbing with pain—I lay behind the curtains of my four-poster bed. A fire burned in the *kachelofen,* and a makeshift nursing station had been set up nearby—bandages, scissors, a glass bottle of disinfectant, and the bottle of Bernadette's homemade genepy. The bed was made up with clean white sheets. Pulling back the covers, I saw that Greta had dressed the wound, but my thigh was as swollen as a tree trunk. When I tried to get up, an explosion of pain shot through my body. The very thought of drinking more made me ill—the gin hangovers of my previous life were nothing in comparison to what the genepy did to me—but the pain was so strong that I poured myself a shot and drank it down.

The next days passed in a blur of sleep and misery. The wound became infected, and I could do nothing but stay in bed, suffering. I slept and woke and slept more and woke again. I swallowed more genepy, trying to stop the pain. The images in my mind bled into the reality around me until everything took on the hue of a dreadful hallucination. Soon there was little to separate the dream world from the waking one.

Greta fed me my meals, sitting by my bed and spooning Valpelline soup—hearty fare made of cabbage and meat—into my mouth. She changed my bandages, put logs on the fire, dusted and swept, replaced empty bottles of genepy, and left. She emptied a porcelain bedpan that, she informed me with pride, had been in the family for three hundred years.

Some days after my surgery, when I was strong enough to sit up in bed and eat alone, Greta arrived one morning with a tray of coffee, slices of black bread, and a jar of strawberry preserves. A luxury, she said of the preserves, dropped with that month's helicopter delivery and sent up by Bernadette.

"When was the helicopter here?" I asked, a rush of disappointment hitting me. The helicopter had come and gone without me.

Greta shrugged, then went on to explain the arrangements being made for Dolores's funeral, describing the bouquets of flowers they had taken from the greenhouse, and the prayers they had chosen to say in the chapel, and the dinner Bernadette would prepare after the internment in the mausoleum. I stared at her in amazement. Greta behaved as if she were innocent, as if she had not colluded with Sal and Vita, and Dolores had died of natural causes.

Later that day, I woke from a nap to hear a flute playing in the courtyard of the castle. I pulled myself out of bed and dragged myself to the window, pain shivering through me each time I put pressure on my leg. Pushing back the heavy curtains, I found a small, morbid party below, dressed all in black and walking together to the chapel: Basil and Greta, Bernadette and the dogs, led by Sal playing the flute. At the tail end of this party came a large, limping figure wearing a black veil. Vita. The matriarch. The family secret.

THAT NIGHT, AFTER Dolores's funeral, when the castle was quiet and dark, I woke to a presence in my room. I strained to see, but the sky was cloudy and moonless outside my window, and the fire had gone to ashes hours before. And yet, I could feel the hot gaze of a living creature standing nearby. I heard the slow intake of breath, and the slow exhale of it. Fumbling with the matches at my bedside table, I lit a candle. The room popped into clarity, revealing Vita.

She stood at the side of my bed, gazing at me through the curtains, her fingers wrapped around the bedpost. She wore her funeral clothes, a black velvet coat and a black silk dress, the bodice dotted with dark embroidery, the skirt stiff with crinoline. She came closer, and I saw that the dark markings on her dress were not the silk of embroidery at all, but moth holes, large and frayed. Light from the candle fell over her pale face, illuminating the deep lines and wrinkles in her skin. Perhaps it was the weak light, but it seemed to me that Dolores's death had brought her closer to her own. Her eyes seemed hollow, skeletal.

"What is it?" I whispered, hearing the tremor in my voice. I did not want her near me, let alone hovering over me like that.

"I came to help you." She glanced at my bedside table, filled with bandages and bottles. She put her hand on my leg. I flinched.

"This is your fault," I said, struggling to pull myself up in bed so that I could face her. "You sent Sal after me."

"It wasn't time for you to leave," she said. Her voice was so low I could hardly hear her. "There is too much left to do. You haven't the slightest idea of your responsibilities or how important you are. It is time for you to learn what must be done. I may not be here much longer to show you."

"I want to know what we are," I asked. "What happened to make us . . . like this?"

Vita sat on the bed at my side, her face filled with emotion. "That is not something I can tell you," she said. "You won't understand unless I show you. And in order for you to see it, you must be strong. You must heal." She pulled the covers back from my leg and unwrapped the bandage. "Now, let me see the damage."

The swelling hadn't gone down. My thigh was thick, the muscle bursting the skin like cooked sausage. Green pus had seeped everywhere, suppurating at the suture, hardening to a yellow crust beyond.

Vita shook her head, dismayed. "There is something wrong here," she said. "You aren't healing as you should. I don't understand. You are young and strong." Her eyes fell on the bottle of genepy on the bedside table. Her expression soured. "Did Sal give you this to drink?"

"Greta," I said. "To help with the pain."

"Of course. When it comes to ignorance and superstition, you can always rely on Greta and Sal. This," she said, taking the bottle in hand, "is as toxic as the wine I gave Dolores." She turned, opened the window, and flung the bottle out. There was a crash of glass as it hit the flagstones of the courtyard below. Vita returned to my bedside, smiling, satisfied. "That takes care of that."

Cold air had chilled the room. The image of Dolores, poisoned, her face twisted in pain, appeared in my mind.

"Here," Vita said. She pulled a cloth bag from the bedside and removed a foil of capsules. "These are antibiotics," she said. "Take them with food." She pulled out another pack of pills. "These will kill the pain more effectively than genepy," she said. "But they can be addictive as well, of course. You must only take enough to get you through this. Do not accept anything from Greta. Nothing. Do you understand?"

I took the pills and swallowed them with water.

"I know this is not easy," Vita said, placing her hand on mine. "But life is not easy for us Montebiancos."

"I read Eleanor's memoir," I said. "I know what you went through."

Vita's expression shifted, and she seemed to consider me with more care. "Do you?" Vita asked. "Do you really know what it is like to suffer?"

And in that moment, as we sat together in the candlelight, I almost confessed the one thing I had never told anyone, the secret I had carried with me every day since I lost the last baby. My child, born after many hours of labor, had not died immediately. When the nurse brought him to me, and I held him in my arms, he was alive. His body was small and his head large, and he was covered, as Vita had been, in fine white hair. His feet were wide and flat, with an elongated second hallux (as Dr. Feist had called it) clotted with blood. He stared up at me with large blue eyes, and in the seconds before he died, as he struggled to breathe, he opened his mouth, revealing rows and rows of tiny, sharp teeth.

TWENTY-TWO

✦

M Y RECOVERY WAS slow and painful, the days stretching around me, elastic. Basil came to my room bearing
books, bags full of leather-bound classics he chose from the
library. Stories became a place of respite, a refuge from the
thoughts that swirled through my mind like acid in a stomach. I clung to these books with the same obsessive need I had
felt for the genepy, reading them with an addictive greed.
George Eliot, Wilkie Collins, the Brontës. I became lost in
these stories the way one might get lost in the hallways of the
castle: one minute I knew my way, the next I was subsumed in
a cataclysm of darkness. I read *Frankenstein* many times that
winter, enthralled by the tortured monster who climbed
through the very Alps that rose outside my window, a creature
betrayed and despairing, a wounded son and murderer, a thing
wanting love but finding only death and despair. In this regard,
I should be grateful for my injury. Had it not been for my time
in bed, I might never have come to love books as I have, or
developed the desire to write about my own tragic life.

A week or so after I began taking antibiotics, Greta removed my bandage to find the swelling had gone down.

"Good," she said, as she changed the dressing. "Very good."
She brought me a crutch and placed it near my bed. "This is
not necessary," she said, sweeping away the porcelain bedpan.
"Now you will walk to the toilet."

At first, I used the crutch only to get to the green silk screen of my bathroom. Then, I began making small trips around my room, from the bed to the window, from the window to the fireplace, from the fireplace to the toilet, pushing myself a little farther each time. I began to venture out into the hallway, where there hung the portrait of my third great-grandmother—Flora Montebianco, 1819–1858—who was married first to Cosimo Montebianco and then his younger brother, Vittorio, making her my third great-aunt as well. Flora, Basil explained, had died giving birth to Vita's father, Ambrose, a fate that seemed to mark her with a jealousy of the living. Flora stared out from her portrait with such bold intensity that I felt she was recording all my actions, slyly assessing me from the cage of her gilded frame.

DURING THOSE PAINFUL weeks of convalescence, I longed for Luca to arrive, although in truth, I was beginning to accept that he might not come for me. My husband was not the kind of man to make false promises, but then again, our relationship had been so broken for so long that I couldn't blame him for backing away. Still, I wanted to see him and to tell him I was sorry for everything. Sorry that my depression and anxiety had separated us. Sorry that I had not understood how much I needed him. But most of all, I longed to tell Luca that his love and acceptance had saved me from more than loneliness, more than being shunned by our community—his love had made me feel alive.

And then, one afternoon, it seemed Luca had finally arrived. I lay in bed when an abrasive whirring came rattling through the windows. I sat up just in time to see the dragonfly body of a Eurocopter descend. I grabbed my crutch and hobbled into the hallway, trying to stay upright. It was a slow and painful trip. I made my way down the corridor and to the central staircase, and was able to hop from step to step, clutching at the balustrade for support, all the while keeping my mind on my goal: the courtyard, the helicopter, my husband, home.

I had just made it to the landing and was about to embark upon my final descent when, from out of nowhere, an animal blasted past me, knocking me down. Fredericka, the Bergamasco shepherd, was loose in the house. I fell, shielding my head with my crutch. Fredericka's teeth bit into the wood, gouging it. I had pushed her away with the crutch, and was trying to fend her off, when I heard a flurry of footfall on the stairs. There was a click of a leash, and Greta yanked the dog away. She wrestled her down the steps and tied the leash to a wooden finial.

"Jesus Christ!" I said, trying to catch my breath.

Greta shrugged, as if to say that it wasn't Fredericka's fault, that it merely was her nature to attack, and that I should know better. But I wasn't swearing at the dog: through the thick, handblown glass of the bay windows, the helicopter lifted off and flew away.

"The monthly supplies," Greta said, seeing my disappointment. It hadn't been Luca after all.

I stood and began dragging myself away, but Greta grabbed Dolores's wheelchair, stationed nearby, and pushed it to the bottom of the stairs.

"Sit," she said, gesturing for me to get in. "I want to show you something."

I had hardly sat down when Greta walked down the hall, pushing me fast, the wheels of the old chair wobbling as if they might fall off. We spun around the edge of the west wing, toward the north side of the castle. There was no electricity in that ruined part of the structure, as I'd learned in my early explorations, and so Greta stopped to grab a lantern. I gripped the handles of the wheelchair until my knuckles went white.

Finally, we stopped at a set of double doors. Greta opened them and pushed me inside. I lifted the lamp and put it on a table, so that it cast a flickering light over a large room. Looking around, I found a nursery. Or, at least, it had once been a nursery. It was as abandoned as the second-floor ballroom. Cobwebs hung in the corners and a thick layer of dust coated everything.

And yet, from the doorway, I could see that it had been used in the not-so-distant past. The walls were covered with colorful drawings, the kind you see in a kindergarten classroom, only the large sheets were curled at the edges and mottled with mildew, some ripped, others hanging from one corner. Old-fashioned toys—rocking horses and Lincoln Logs and wooden blocks—were mixed up with modern ones: a doll house, its rooms fitted with miniature furniture; puzzles and picture books; a Playmobil village with hundreds of figurines; stuffed animals—monkeys and puppies and kittens with glass eyes. Along one wall, a muddle of dolls lay in disarray, abandoned babies waiting for their mothers to return.

I turned to Greta, who was watching me carefully. "Was this Joseph's room?"

"Vita let him play here," Greta said. "This was her nursery when she was a child, then her sons came here, too." She bent down and picked up a wooden train. "Joseph loved this! He played with it for hours."

I used the crutch to hobble to an enormous table filled with LEGO pieces. At the center of the table sat a castle, its towers tall and sturdy, its drawbridge raised. Nearby, small houses clustered together into a village. It was a reproduction of Montebianco Castle, with the village of Nevenero below.

Greta walked to the wall and pulled down a drawing. "This was his," she said. "He liked blue. I don't know why, but it was his favorite color. He always drew everything in blue."

I took the drawing. A blue man with long hair and enormous eyes stood alone, surrounded by rocks. The hands were large and the feet enormous, out of proportion to his body. Below the picture, Joseph had written the word "Simi."

"Do you know what this is?"

Greta shrugged. "Something he made."

I walked to the wall of drawings. There were more creatures like the first, all drawn in blue crayon. Some climbed rocks. Others stood in trees. There were men and women and children, all with the same characteristics of the Icemen. The wall was full of Joseph's drawings.

"Did he have a story about these drawings?" I asked. "They all have the word 'Simi.' Do you know why?"

"He was always making up stories," she said, looking at the pictures with care. "And Vita did tell him many things that happened in these mountains. The local legends and myths and such. Some of these might be drawings of those stories." She turned back to me, tears streaming down her cheeks. "Sometimes he liked a toy and played only with it for months. It was like that with the blue men."

"Was he ever afraid?" I asked. "Afraid of Vita or . . . anything else?"

"Madame Vita is not all bad. She loves children," Greta said. "She loved Joseph. She helped me. She hired me when I needed to leave Germany and let me bring a child. Not everyone would do that, you know. She was kind to my son."

"Is this why you stay here?" I said, gesturing to the wall of Joseph's drawings, to the abandoned toys. "In case he returns?"

"My son is coming back," she said, and for a moment, hope burned in her eyes, giving her a look of a woman who believed with all her heart in a miracle. "You promised to help me find him. I know you didn't lie to me, madame. I know you'll bring him home."

As we left, I stepped over a rag doll, ripped and stained, its arms torn off, its dress frayed. The cloth was so old it had begun to disintegrate at the seams, and I wondered if it could be the same doll Eleanor had given her daughter, Vita's first friend. When I picked it up, I saw gashes in the face, the smooth skin deformed by Vita's sharp teeth. The linen was stained with brown drops of dried blood. The eyes stared blankly, devoid of life.

TWENTY-THREE

⚜

T HE NEXT EVENING I was sitting in my rooms near the
fire when Basil came to visit. I had sent a message to him
through Greta, asking him to come see me. He must have
thought I needed some cheering up, because he had a folio of
Ernst Haeckel's etchings of jellyfish and squid in one hand
and a bottle of bourbon in the other. While Vita had forbidden genepy, there was no restriction on bourbon. Basil threw
a log on the fire, poured out two glasses, and sat down across
from me.

"I saw the nursery," I said, raising my glass to him.

"Ah, I haven't had the heart to go there since . . ."

"Joseph made drawings of blue men," I said, sipping the
bourbon. "Dozens of them."

Basil considered this, and then said, "Greta brought one to
me after he disappeared. They are very evocative."

"There is this word, 'Simi.'" I showed him the page. "Do
you know what it means?"

Basil shook his head. He had no idea.

"Do you think there's some connection?"

"Between blue men and a child's disappearance?"

"It sounds ridiculous, I know," I said. "But maybe Joseph
was trying to express something that frightened him. Some
kind of abuse."

"Are you suggesting that Vita hurt Joseph?"

I remembered the incident in Eleanor's memoir in which Vita killed the men in Nevenero. I remembered the look of triumph on Vita's face as Dolores lay dying. Vita was capable of hurting people. But was she capable of hurting a child?

Basil finished his glass of bourbon, poured another, and went to the fire, where he poked the logs with a fire iron.

"Vita had an extraordinarily difficult childhood," I said. "Was she ever treated for trauma?"

"Psychological care was simply not done for most of Vita's lifetime," Basil said. "In Eleanor's time, Vita was considered a vessel of the devil. The cure for that was exorcism, prayers, fasting—all to rid Vita of evil spirits. As time passed, so did the approaches. If you look in the family archives, you'll find all varieties of reports. There is one account of a Jungian therapist brought in to explore the archetypal origins of Vita's behavior. There was discussion of shock therapy, which did not happen, thank goodness. She endured every kind of diet and physical regimen.

"Guillaume and Dolores were quite anxious to understand the real danger her existence posed to them . . . *genetically,* but to get a definitive answer to that question meant bringing in doctors, and while the question of what was actually wrong with Vita might have been answered through testing, Guillaume refused to allow her to be seen by anyone who might expose the family's past."

Basil left the fire iron against the wall and returned to the seat across from me. I could see, in the brightening of the flames, the creases lining his brow. "After Guillaume died, Dolores hired more researchers, authorized genetic samples to be taken from Guillaume's corpse, and paid a small fortune to find you. She made mistakes, I agree. The latest pharmacology had made its way here, and Dolores had been dosing Vita with powerful sedatives, which left Vita disoriented and angry. She also gave Vita SSRIs of various types—Paxil, Prozac, Celexa. She had a terrible reaction to these medications. They drove her into indescribable rages. She would become wild, confused, violent." Basil paused, met my eyes, and continued. "I'm not saying that Dolores had it coming, but . . . at times, she could be quite cruel."

As I took this in, I felt a new sympathy for what Vita had endured. And yet, I couldn't dispel the suspicion I felt. "Do you think Vita could have hurt Joseph?"

"Impossible," he said. "She is far too weak. She cannot even get down the stairs of the northeast tower without Greta or Sal to help her."

I took the drawing of the blue man in hand and looked at it again. The large hands and feet, the enormous eyes: I couldn't help but believe it was a clue to something.

"Have you heard of the Beast of Nevenero?" I asked.

Basil looked at me with surprise. "Yes, of course. It is one of the local monsters," he said. "A legend of sorts. It is quite well-known."

"Does this legend have anything to do with Vita?"

"If you are asking if Vita is that creature," Basil said, giving a strained laugh, "the answer is no. She is not the Beast of Nevenero. I know there were such rumors in the village, but they do not reflect reality."

"What *is* she, then?"

"It is a question I have asked myself many times," Basil said. "You read Eleanor's memoir. You know that Vita's condition has been the central question of the Montebianco family for generations. I myself have tried to look into it. There is a clue in Eleanor's memoir, when Eleanor writes about the grandfather of Ambrose, Leopold Montebianco. Do you recall it?

She wrote that madness and deformity began to appear in the Montebianco lineage *after the time of Leopold."*

Leopold? I thought, taking a deep breath. *Which ancestor was Leopold?* I tried to recall the family tree, painted on the ceiling of the library. Vita's parents, Ambrose and Eleanor. Vita's grandparents, Vittorio and Flora, the woman whose portrait hung outside my room who had died in childbirth. And then Alberta and Amadeo, the prince of Savoy, parents of Leopold. Counting the generations, I calculated that Leopold was my fourth great-grandfather. "What did Leopold do?" I asked.

"It is hard to say, as he didn't leave much behind. He has been mentioned in various documents in the archives as an amateur naturalist, an eccentric man who made discoveries of some significance in these mountains, but he has largely disappeared from the family records. There is a reference in one of the family catalogs to a field notebook, which I've been trying to get my hands on. But that notebook is gone. I have looked through every nook and cranny of this castle for it."

"What do you think he discovered?" I asked.

"Something extraordinary, from the sound of it," Basil said.

I REMEMBER THAT evening—Basil and I warm and tipsy near the fire—with a kind of longing, the variety of nostalgia one feels about a singular point in one's life before everything shifts. Those last moments of ignorance before the telephone rings with bad news, the hour before the baby is born dead, the endless frozen swerve before the car crashes. When I reflected about that night later, it seemed an instance of innocence so pure as to be sacred.

The next morning, I was drinking coffee near the window when I heard the commotion in the courtyard. The dogs were going crazy, their barking high-pitched with panic. I heard Sal call out for Greta, and saw her scurry across the courtyard, joining him at the gate. They were looking at something just beyond, while holding back the dogs.

Luca! I thought. Finally, Luca had come. I had been wrong. He had come for me after all.

I opened the window and shouted at Greta that I was coming down. My biggest fear was that Sal would hurt him. He had shot Dr. Feist, after all, and he had shot me. There was nothing stopping him from shooting Luca, too.

I threw on some clothes and hurried to the corridor, scrambling down the steps as best I could. My leg had healed considerably, but it took nearly five minutes to join them in the courtyard. Everything was a jumble in my mind as I rushed to the gates—all that I had learned about the Montebianco family, my new commitment to adopt a child, our plans to start over. Now that Luca had arrived, all the difficulties that had happened would take on a different meaning—they were the backstory of a new and better future. My strange ancestry would be a puzzle we would solve together, our failing marriage the preamble to a new life. Whatever genetic problems I carried could be studied and overcome. That day would be a new beginning. We would start again, together.

By the time I arrived in the courtyard, however, I knew that these dreams could never happen. The first thing I saw was a pair of leather boots, the laces caked in ice, splayed open over the icy flagstones, followed by a hand, blue gray and mottled with black from frostbite. At last I forced myself to look at Luca's face, which stared up at me, deformed, stiff and inexpressive. The dogs hadn't been barking at Luca's intrusion into the courtyard. They were barking at his corpse.

I threw my crutch aside and fell onto my knees next to him. He had been battered by the elements. His face was swollen, the skin distorted and hard, as if a plastic mask had been laid over his features. I grasped his hand. It was ice-cold, stiff, the fingers frozen through. A swath of skin on his chin was gone entirely, as if ripped away, and his eyelids had frozen open. I stifled a sob. This was my oldest and best friend, my husband, the person who had loved me despite everything. I blinked away tears, fighting the scream that rose in my throat. "No," I sobbed. It was the only word that came. "No. No. No."

"You know this man?" Sal asked, a morbid curiosity in his eyes.

"He's my husband," I said. I couldn't say his name. Not to Sal.

"Oh, madame," Greta said, her voice filled with alarm. "Come with me. Sal will carry him to the mews." She came to my side and helped me stand. I must have collapsed again, because I remember holding on to Luca, holding tight, as if he might come back to life if only I held on hard enough.

When at last Greta helped me up, Sal said, "The dogs found him. Lord knows how long he's been out here. From the look of it, I'd say weeks, even a month. I'm guessing they tried to hike here from one of the ski towns."

"They?" I asked, looking past Luca at the snowy wilderness beyond the gate.

Sal led me past Luca, to a body lying beyond the gate. It was Bob, Luca's father.

THE SKY WAS dark, the clouds shrouding the courtyard in a mist so thick that the chapel doors seemed, as I approached, to materialize from a cloud. Inside, the haze cleared, burned away by candles lit throughout the nave. The warm, flickering light made the stained glass scintillate and the rows of wooden benches glow, even as Luca and Bob's bodies—laid out on blankets near the altar—remained covered in shadow.

In the spring, when the roads cleared, Sal would transport my husband and his father down the mountain, and they would be shipped back to Milton for burial. But for the rest of the winter, they would lie frozen in the chapel. I would visit them every afternoon, sitting in the freezing cold, grappling with all I had lost.

On my first visit, I sat on a bench and looked at Luca. There he was, the man I had loved, the lips I had kissed, the hands that I had held. For years, he had been the entirety of my family. All hope of starting over had slipped away with his life. I understood then what I had not been able to fully grasp during our separation: my future was so entwined with his that I didn't know how to go on without him.

I knelt over my husband, looking at him, trying to remember what he had looked like before. It wasn't his face, that still mask, not his eyes frozen open in a horrid gaze. Not his hands stiffened to claws. Everything that had made me love this man had been siphoned away, and yet, it comforted me to be there next to his familiar body. I lowered my head to his chest, half expecting to hear the faint thrum of his heart. A wave of longing overtook me as I pictured him next to me in the enormous bed in Turin, the luxurious sheets wrapped around us, his eyes alight with the possibilities of what lay ahead. It had been many years since I had prayed, but I whispered a prayer then for Luca.

As I turned to leave, I saw a book on the altar. Making my way around the baptismal font, I found a thick Bible covered in dust and spiderwebs, the name "Montebianco" stamped in gold into the leather. The pages were thin and covered in tiny foreign words, but at the back of the Bible, folded into the binding, I discovered a registry of baptisms and marriages and funerals. Glancing down the list, I read names and dates matching those in the mausoleum—all my ancestors who had lived and died before me—but what interested me more than the Montebianco deaths were the dates written in the column under *Marriage*.

In the past century, there had been only a handful of additions: Eleanor and Ambrose, August 14, 1909; Giovanni and Marta, June 9, 1949; Guillaume and Dolores on September 3, 1971. The mostly empty page seemed too empty, like some great reproach to my grief. I searched my pockets for a pen and, steadying my hand, wrote out our names and the date of our marriage in the family Bible.

TWENTY-FOUR

✦

LUCA'S DEATH HAD opened a wound, one that throbbed with the sharpness of Bernadette's knife. I took the pain-killers Vita had given me and slept for days at a time. When I woke, I'd watch the world from the recesses of a trance. The sun fell softly over the stone floor of my rooms, settling on the flakes of ash from the hearth, filling the air with light and warmth—and still, I saw only the endless darkness of the truth: I would spend my life alone. Never would I find love or have a child. Never again could I pretend to be like other people. A normal life could not be for me; it wasn't written in my genetic code.

One night, a banging at my door woke me. I pulled myself out of bed and, with the help of my crutch, hobbled to the door and unbolted the lock. Sal stood in the hallway, Dolores's wheelchair parked before him.

"Get in," he said, gesturing to the wheelchair.

"Where are we going?" I asked, half asleep.

Sal gestured again to the wheelchair, with its shining cop-per armrests, Dolores's pillows on the seat. "Now."

I lowered myself into the wheelchair, adjusting the pillows to cushion my wound. Sal pushed me down the corridor and steered me through a series of narrow connecting hallways, before stopping abruptly at a door on the east side of the castle. He opened the door directly onto the east lawn, where I could see—standing in the snow—Vita.

Sal parked the wheelchair, lifted me out of it, and carried me over the east lawn, his boots crunching through the snow.

"Sal, put me down," I said. "I want to walk."

To my surprise, Sal released me. I limped behind him, the snow soft under my feet. Perhaps spring was coming. I didn't know the month, but the harsh bite of winter had left the air. Vita stood on a flat of snow before the high, dark mountains. I limped past the frozen pond, past a dead animal lying in the snow, blood staining an ellipse of color around its body. It was a rabbit, I saw, half-eaten by some wild creature, its long furry foot jutting into the air. Something about the position of the body, and the bloodstained snow, reminded me of Dr. Ludwig Jacob Feist.

At last, I made it to the top of the east lawn, where the castle grounds met the mountain. Sal greeted Vita, nodding at me as if he had delivered a trophy.

"I brought this, like you wanted," Sal said, and took a leather pack from his shoulder. "Bernadette says she's low on some things."

"Thank you," Vita said, taking the pack. She opened it, examined the contents, then nodded to Sal. "Tell Bernadette to send me a list of what we need."

Sal nodded in return and turned back to the castle, leaving Vita and me in the dark, windy night. It was moonless, without a cloud in the sky. Stars filled the darkness, an uncountable explosion of brilliance, proof that we were just one small piece of an immense, burning universe.

A gust of glacial wind blew down over the east lawn, cutting through me. My teeth began to chatter. Vita shot me an assessing look, one part pride, another part exasperation. "Surely you're not so sensitive to the cold as that?"

"My grandfather would have said exactly the same thing," I said. "He was always taking me out in the snow under-dressed."

Vita nodded, as if she knew exactly what I meant, and then, sliding out of her coat, she handed it to me. The warmth of her body lingered in the silk lining, as delicate as an embrace.

"Tell me. What was the date upon which my son killed himself?"

I gave her a sidelong glance, wondering why she had decided to ask this now. "I believe the death certificate said July 1993."

"And he left no note?" she asked. "No explanation?"

I shrugged. "Not that I know about."

"It is so . . . unlike my son," she said. "He was a very strong-willed man, with great moral conviction. I can't imagine that he would harm himself."

"My grandmother Marta had died that year. Maybe he missed her."

Vita thought this over for a minute. Then she shook her head. "I don't doubt that they were extremely in love and that my son missed his wife when she was gone. But that wasn't the reason."

"Then what?"

Just then, as if in answer to my question, I saw it—something moving at the edge of a cove of evergreen trees. An ibex, I thought. A wild animal feeding on rabbits. I couldn't see more than a shift of movement in the shadows, a presence obscured by spruce and cedar branches.

"These are the Icemen," Vita said and walked quickly up to the trees, leaving me to struggle behind. I dragged myself through the snow, my leg throbbing with pain, until I saw them clearly.

There were two of them, both men, both tall and skeletal with broad shoulders and long white hair that tangled to their chests. They wore cotton pants and leather vests that exposed their arms to the cold. Their eyes were large and blue below heavy brows, but most startling of all was the luminous, almost phosphorescent quality of their skin. Standing in the pocket of the east lawn, they seemed to glow.

I should have felt afraid, but instead an overwhelming sensation of relief flooded over me. Here was the monster Justine had followed in the mountains. The archaic hominid of Dr. Feist. The beast of Nonna Sophia. The missing link of James Pringle. I remembered Joseph's drawings, the word "Simi" written in childish blue script. Here, before me, stood the Icemen.

Vita was with them in the hollow of the trees. She gave one of the men the leather pack. He opened it, checking the contents, then closed it again.

"Come closer, Alberta," Vita said, turning to me. "It is time for you to meet them."

A wave of dizziness sent me off-balance. I stepped back, away from Vita, and leaned against the trunk of a spruce tree.

Vita walked to me and put her hand on my shoulder, as if to steady me. "Don't be afraid," she said.

"What are they?" I whispered.

"They are our elders," she said. "The native people of these mountains. They were here before any of us."

I glanced over at the men. They stared at me, their eyes glistening in the moonlight.

Vita smiled. "You will understand them better soon. For now, trust me."

She took me by the arm and led me to them. She told me their names: Jabi, with his heavy brow and thick white beard, and Aki, taller than Jabi, thin, beardless, the skin of his cheeks smooth and white. The light was dim, and it was hard to see him fully, but his features were strangely beautiful, rough-hewn. He seemed younger than Jabi, perhaps twenty-five or so. The men's clothes and leather boots were all store-bought.

Jabi spoke first, expressing himself with a series of sounds that I would one day, after I came to know the speech of his tribe, understand to mean: "Who is this foreigner?"

Vita spoke to him in his language, answering his question. Then she opened the leather sack and showed me the contents—boxes of bandages, bottles of pills, tubes of ointment, a pack of antibiotics. "They came for these," she said, closing the sack and giving it to Jabi, and he turned to go.

The man called Aki didn't leave, however. He stared at me in wonder, unblinking, his pale blue eyes filled with curiosity. Then, without warning, he leaned over and touched my cheek.

The gesture startled me. I pulled away, afraid. His cold hand against my cheek sent a rush of feeling through me—fear, yes, but also something else, something familiar yet painful, like the feeling of walking barefoot on ice with my grandfather.

"Simi," Aki said.

"Don't be afraid," Vita said. "That is his way of greeting you."

Stepping to him, I took his large, cold, rough hand in mine and shook it.

"Tell him it is my way of greeting him," I said.

He watched me with astonishment but didn't pull away. He glanced at Vita, as if she could explain my odd behavior.

She said something to him in his language, and he looked back at me and smiled.

Jabi glowered at me from the shadows, his expression both curious and disdainful. Finally, he hoisted the leather sack over his shoulder and, with a nod in Vita's direction, climbed back into the trees. As Aki turned to follow, I felt a strange urge to call him back, to bring his hand into mine again, if only to hold fast to the sensation of ice on my skin.

TWENTY-FIVE

❧

T HE ENCOUNTER WITH the Icemen had set something going inside of me, a gravity relentless in its forward momentum. For days, I could think of nothing but Aki and Jabi standing in the shadows of the evergreens, their pale white skin, their enormous height, their large rough hands. I felt the strange sensation of Aki's hand in mine. I had never experienced such intensely opposite emotions, curiosity and terror all mixed up together.

I was so turned around by the experience, so unsure of just what it all meant, that the only reaction I could manage was to stay in my rooms and think. I spent the entire week after the encounter sitting by the fire, struggling to make sense of it all. These days of paralysis gave me time to sort out what was happening to me and formulate my response. There was no point in looking to the sky for a helicopter to appear, or to imagine that I would be rescued or that I could run away from the truth. A transformation was taking place inside of me, I knew; I could feel it on a cellular level. I was becoming a new person, one who would have the strength to face my inheritance.

IT TOOK SOME weeks before I gathered the courage to go to the northeast tower again. I stood outside Vita's door, expecting to hear her shuffling around her room, but there was nothing but silence. When I knocked, she did not answer. Finally, I pushed back the door to find the room as dark and stifling as the mausoleum. The air was unusually muggy, the window shut and a fire burning in the fireplace. Greta sat by Vita's bedside, wiping her forehead with a wet cloth.

"What happened?" I asked, startled by the sight of Vita. An extraordinary change had come over her. She was very thin, her skin pink with fever.

"Come in, madame," Greta whispered. "See for yourself."

Greta stood, giving me the chair, and left the room. I sat down at Vita's bedside, near the table covered with perfume bottles. There were fifty, perhaps more, each crystal bottle filled with colored liquid. I picked up a square bottle tied with a silk braid, weighing it in the palm of my hand as I read the label—*Mitsouko.* I worked off the glass stopper, and a dark, oriental, musky smell filled the air.

When I looked back at Vita, her pale eyes were fixed upon me. "I hate that perfume," she whispered, smiling slightly. "It was my mother's favorite. I only keep the bottle to remember her. Let in some air. Greta is trying to suffocate me."

I went to the window and opened it. I stood there, glancing at the mountain, its ridges and crevices capped with fog.

"Come," Vita said, gesturing for me to return to the chair. "You came here to speak to me."

I left the window open and sat at her side. I had been trying to work out how to speak about the creatures to Vita, but in the end, I simply blurted out the most pressing question. "What are they?"

"What are they?" Vita said slowly. "You might as well ask: *What are we?*"

"Don't avoid my question," I said.

"They are our legacy. They are *your* legacy. When you are

ready, you will go to them and see for yourself how beautiful they are!" Vita's eyes were sparkling, and for a moment, I believed the fever had made her mad. She leaned to me and took my hand. "They are rare and precious creatures," she said, growing calm. "Somehow, through the millennia, they have survived. But the world is encroaching. This pocket of mountain has remained untouched, but for how long? Satellites, airplanes, helicopters—there is always danger for them. But now you are here. You are here, and you are strong enough to help them."

"I don't understand," I said, and I saw that my hands trembled in hers. "Why has this fallen to me?"

"We don't choose our birthright," she said. "It comes to us whether we like it or not."

The portrait of Eleanor on her horse looked down upon us. As I gazed up at her, the cadence of her voice came strong in my mind: *I have protected Vita, and yet, in my weakest moments, I question the goodness of such protection.*

Vita followed my gaze up to Eleanor's portrait. "They terrified her. She wouldn't even meet them. But she knew they existed. She understood the choice I made."

"What choice was that?"

"To protect them," Vita said, her voice weak. "I vowed to help our ancestors survive."

With that, she reached over to the bedside table and pulled out a fat leather notebook from a drawer. Struggling, she handed it to me and gestured that I should take it. I opened the leather cover, and the binding cracked with age. Inside, I found a sheaf of papers that, when unfolded, revealed themselves to be pages ripped from Eleanor's memoir.

December 1933

With Ambrose gone, the truth belongs to me. It is mine and I can keep it hidden, as Ambrose did, or I can make it known. The greater part of me wishes to fold it up in a box and throw it into the oubliette in the northwest tower, where it will live in darkness, unknown. Another part, however, wonders if this is not something that must be seen by the world. As the naturalist who examined my daughter once said—Vita is an unknown treasure of our planet. Special. A creature from another time.

Ambrose held his secret as strongly as the oubliette holds prisoners. In all the years we were together, he said nothing. He waited until the very end of his life to tell me the truth of how Vita came to be.

Do I dare to write it down? I am superstitious. The British naturalist would laugh to hear me, but I fear bringing something terrible down upon us. I am uneducated in the ways of Mr. Pringle and fear the power of the pen to bring truths into being that might have remained unformed. And yet, if I do not write down what I have witnessed, the truth will disappear forever.

I remember it as though it were only last night when Ambrose asked for his confessor. The priest arrived from the village and went to Ambrose's bedside, while I stood, listening from behind the door. He had been sick for some months, and I believed he would recover if he could survive until spring. But the sickness took hold of his lungs, gripping with such ferocity that Ambrose spoke with a faltering voice, spending each word as if it were a golden coin. The weight and value of his words were not lost upon me.

"Heavenly Father, hear me . . . I must confess . . . something I have kept from everyone . . . the truth . . . Vita is my fault."

I heard him say it: Vita is my fault. His fault. A rush of relief swelled through me. I began to weep. This confession relieved me of a terrible burden. Always, they had blamed me. Surely I, the mother, was at fault for bringing such a creature into the world. But Ambrose's confession confirmed what I had long suspected: I had not caused Vita's troubles. He was responsible for Vita. The Montebianco family was responsible.

The priest was our confidant, having relieved Vita of spiritual burdens, and he knew enough to remain silent as Ambrose spoke. Ambrose asked the Lord's forgiveness. He said he should never have married me, that he had known even before we met that he was from a cursed lineage. His parents—who had arranged our marriage—had been foolish. He had been selfish. He had loved me and hoped that we would be spared. Now that Vita existed, he prayed she would bring no further suffering to others.

I listened to this strange talk, trying to understand it. But as soon as the priest left, I went to my husband's side and demanded he tell me everything. What did Ambrose know about Vita's origins? What had he hidden from me? What is our child? How did she come into being?

My dear Ambrose, who was once so beautiful and strong,

looked at me weakly. How time makes us wretched! How it deforms and destroys us! I put a wet towel against his neck and gave him spoonfuls of water from a cup. I had always thought death was like falling asleep, but his was a form of wrestling, as if the material and ethereal worlds were pulling him this way and that, both wanting him, both unwilling to let go.

"Why would you have me tell you?" he asked. "When it will only terrify you, my love?"

"I am an old woman now. You will soon be gone. What is left but honesty?"

It was then that Ambrose told me the horrible truth.

"I saw the creature with my father," he began, gripping my hand. "We were hunting wild boar in the caves above Nevenero. Do you remember, Eleanor, when I took you there?"

I nodded. One summer afternoon, when we walked together in the mountains, he stopped at an arcade of caverns, bent his knee, and gave me the bouquet of wildflowers he had collected. We were married already, our union having been arranged years before by our families, but it was only then I knew he loved me.

"I was fifteen years old when my father took me hunting," Ambrose continued. "I was inexperienced and worried that a boar would maul me. I carried my flintlock ready, clutching at its wooden handle so hard it was slippery with sweat. Wild boar shelter in those caves all winter. My father knew this and came to that same spot each year. I stayed close to my father, following in the deep tracks he made in the snow.

"We climbed and climbed until we came to the caves. My father bent and picked up part of a chestnut left with the

boar's droppings in the snow. 'There's one close by,' he said, and made his way to the mouth of a cave. I held back, watching him, listening. I wanted to see how he aimed, how he shot. I wanted to see if he flinched when the boar charged.

"It was then that I saw a movement in the trees. I flipped my rifle onto my shoulder and steadied it, taking aim. And there it was, staring at me. Its eyes enormous, blue, so big I couldn't look away. The brow was low, heavy, and the nose large and flat. White fur covered it from head to toe, so that it seemed to emerge from the snow."

"What was it?" I asked.

"It was an ape," he said. "But a man, too. An Iceman, whose eyes were blue as crystal. It was very big, so large that I had to raise the muzzle of the rifle to take aim at its heart. I only heard my father cry for me to stop after I pulled the trigger."

I stared at him, trying to understand what he was saying. There are many wild animals in our region, but no apes. The creature he described could not exist. It was impossible, his story. Impossible.

"The beast has been known in these mountains for generations, my father told me. They were here before us, even before mankind. They are from an earlier time, perhaps before the Flood. These are their mountains." A wave of pain washed over him. He clenched his teeth together until it passed. "There is a village of them somewhere above Nevenero. I have not seen it myself, but there were men in my family who have been there." He paused. "And once, very long ago, there was an instance of . . . crossing."

Ambrose glanced at me, to be sure I understood.

I stared at him, aghast. Could he possibly be telling me

that some part of his noble family—the fine and ancient line of Montebianco—was infected with the blood of this strange creature? That our child, our poor deformed Vita, was the product of such beastly stock? I could not believe it.

"That is not possible," I said at last.

"It has long been talked about in the village," he said quietly.

"But it is a legend," I said. I wanted to dismiss what he was telling me. I wanted him to die rather than continue. "A village legend."

"My grandfather, Leopold Montebianco, the youngest son of Alberta and Amadeo, and described by my father as a strange and eccentric man, discovered the village of Icemen in the mountains in 1812. He lived with the creatures for two years, studying them, making notes of his experiences, and when he returned to Nevenero, he brought with him a child, a son named Vittorio. This Vittorio was my father."

"Your father was like our Vittoria?" I asked, anger rising in me like mercury in a tube, hot and quick. Why had he not told me before? Why let me torture myself all these years?

"No," he said, grasping my hand. "There was nothing unusual about my father, Vittorio. And nothing, as you well know, in my nature resembles these creatures. But I knew the taint existed in our blood. I never wanted to continue the curse. And yet, I loved you. I could not keep myself from marrying you. Our child, however, has unmasked the truth: with Leopold, the Montebianco lineage became intertwined with these Icemen. Vita's forebears were creatures of the mountains. She carries the traits of this ancient race of beasts."

"Vita is one of them?" I asked, my cheeks stinging with

shame, although some deep part of my being was joyous to have this explanation of Vita at last.

"Yes," he said, raising his eyes to meet mine. They were filled with terror. "She is one of them. But she is also human."

As I finished reading Eleanor's memoir, I took a deep breath, folded the pages, and put them back into the book. There was a tension pulsing through my chest, a pressure so constricting, so tight, that I stood and walked back to the window to get some air.

I gazed out the window, at the immense vista of mountains, the peaks pale against the pinks and purples of the setting sun, struggling to take in the meaning of Eleanor's memoir. If what Eleanor wrote was true, Vita was not the only one afflicted with this legacy. A creeping sensation of horror fell over me as I understood: this was who we were. Not just Vita, but the Montebianco family, all born after Leopold. At last I understood all the terror and secrecy around Vita. My grandfather Giovanni's shame. The desperate measures Ambrose had taken to hide his child. The estate's requirement that I stay in Nevenero. It all made sense. Vita was the expression of our darkest secret, her existence proof of the taint in our blood. She was part of me, her genetic code twisted into mine, a legacy that I would carry with me and—if a child were to ever arrive—pass down. I was descended from these creatures. The Icemen were my ancestors.

TWENTY-SIX

✤

I RUSHED THROUGH THE hallways of the second floor, Eleanor's revelations thrumming in my mind. I pushed open the heavy doors, and walked into the long, narrow portrait gallery. It was afternoon, and a gray light fell over the room, giving the portraits a diaphanous, otherworldly appearance, as if they were not reproductions in oil, but the souls of my ancestors shimmering through the fabric of time.

The last time I had looked at the portraits had been the day I had pushed Dolores over the polished parquet floors in her wheelchair. I was startled by how much had changed. Then, I had been overwhelmed by the faces looking down at me, the luminous eyes, the traits that were so much like my own. I had gazed at each of these portraits, read the small brass tags, taking in their commanding presence, but I had never really known these people. Not their faces. Not their stories. Now I knew the murderess Isabelle of the House of Savoy and her goat herder husband, Frederick. I knew the strong, persistent voice of Vita's mother, Eleanor. I knew that Ambrose had loved Eleanor so much that he had married her despite his fear of having children. I felt Eleanor's feelings of repugnance at the sight of her daughter, Vittoria. I felt the tragedy of Vita's education, the horror of her rape, the victory Eleanor had felt at seeing that her grandchildren—Giovanni and Guillaume—had been born with normal human features. I felt the loneliness of Giovanni and Guillaume growing up under the tutelage of Vita's doctor. I understood what my ancestors had suffered, what they had lost. The Montebianco family stories were my stories now. For the first time, these people were really my family.

What would they do, if they were to peel from the walls and stand around me, these ghosts of the past? Would they be benevolent spirits, wrapping around me in a circle of protection? Or would they, like Ambrose, feel it their duty to stop the continuation of the Montebianco line? To kill me, the last living descendant of Leopold Montebianco, and be done with the family's cursed legacy forever.

I searched the plates affixed to the gilded frames until I found Leopold. In the portrait, he looked every bit as strange and eccentric as Ambrose had described. Tall, lanky, and pale, he had a white cravat at his neck and a book in his hands. He had been painted in the library, and the vaulted ceilings rose behind him, showing the family tree with all the Montebiancos who had come before. Leopold was the opposite of every other man in the room, dreamy as a romantic poet, a Byron or Shelley, his large dark eyes liquid with emotion. The portrait was darker than the others, the paints thicker, as if straining to express the extent of Leopold's saturnalia.

Vittorio, whose portrait was next in line, could not have been more different in appearance from his father, Leopold. While his father had been thin and introspective, Vittorio was hale, wide-shouldered, exuding power. With Vittorio came the beginning of the extreme whiteness of the Montebianco skin, the bright blue eyes, the hair rinsed of color. The traits—I now understood—that we had inherited from the Icemen. Then there was Ambrose, who was not quite as magnificent as his father, Vittorio, but not too shabby either, rugged from mountaineering, brow wide and tempered as a ram. Finally, I stopped before my grandfather's portrait. He looked down upon me from his horse. His appearance sent a shiver through me—it no longer reminded me of my own, as it had the first time I saw that painting. He reminded me of the Icemen.

I hurried to the very far end of the gallery where the portrait of Vita hung. Pushing aside the curtain, I stepped into the room. Someone had lit the candles, and the nook glowed with light. It was then, as I sat before the portrait of Vita, that I finally examined the book in my hands, the leather-bound journal that had contained the pages of Eleanor's memoir. It was a thick book, fat with a thousand onionskin pages, and filled—I saw as I pressed open the cover—with handwritten text, sketches of caves, a makeshift map. The cover was battered and the spine warped, as if it had been exposed to the elements. Some of the pages had been damaged by water, leaving washes of streaked and unreadable words. A braid of long, white hair—a shorter version of the braid in the trophy room—had been attached to the back cover with a string. I sifted through the pages, trying to read the barbed cursive, but it was written entirely in French. I could understand three large, bold words on the first page of the book:

NOTES DE TERRAIN

Under these words I found the florid signature of Leopold Montebianco. These were Leopold's field notes from his years living with the Icemen, the notes that Basil had been searching for.

IN ALL THE months I had known Basil, I had never seen his living quarters and didn't know exactly where they were. I walked through the hallways of the west wing, tapping on doors, hoping to find him. I had almost given up when I heard a record playing—the low call of a trumpet.

I knocked on the door. There was a shuffling, some coughing, and then the door flung open. Basil wore a silk robe and house slippers and a pair of striped pajamas.

"Oh, hello, Countess," he said, blinking with surprise. "Come in, please, don't mind the mess. Right this way."

He led me into his rooms—which were as big as mine—and I found myself pushing through a tidal wave of objects: flowerpots and empty wine bottles, paintings, old curtains. Books, hundreds and hundreds of books. A narrow passage had been made through the debris, winding through records and stacks of cookie boxes and crates of empty glass bottles and tins of prunes and newspapers, everywhere, stacks and stacks of newspapers. From floor to ceiling, everywhere I looked, was junk.

I squeezed my way into the room, pushing aside a steamer trunk to the small cleared space by the fire. Something in my memory clicked: the trunk was the twin of my grandfather Giovanni's trunk, the one from the newspaper photograph Nonna had shown me. The fact that he had lived here as a young man struck me with renewed force. Everywhere I went, Giovanni had been before me.

Basil whisked a stack of records off a chair and waved for me to sit. The records were all jazz. The album on the record player: Miles Davis's *Blue Haze*.

"I know what you are going to say," Basil said, pushing a pile of papers off another chair so he could sit. "I need to make a wider path from the doorway." He bit his lip, looking embarrassed and defiant at once. "And I plan to do that, as soon as I organize that . . ."

He pointed to a stack of leather boots in a corner. They were worn, with holes in the soles and mud on the laces. "Are those Sal's boots?" I asked.

"And Bernadette's and Greta's as well," he said. "They go through them faster than you'd imagine."

I glanced back to Basil, who was fiddling with his mustache. I understood, suddenly, why Basil had not left the castle. He had hoarded piles and piles of objects and now he couldn't bear to abandon them. He was a prisoner of his compulsions. No one was keeping him there but himself.

I gave him the pages from Eleanor's journal. "I wanted to show you this."

Basil took the pages, a look of astonishment growing as he read them. "This would certainly explain a few things." He gave me back the pages. "If, that is, this account is true."

"You think Eleanor could have made all of this up?"

Basil shrugged. "Well, clearly Eleanor believed it. But this account is not exactly firsthand knowledge. Her husband, Ambrose, told her the story of Leopold and the Icemen. Ambrose was dying. He could have been delusional, deranged. One cannot be certain. He could have been repeating his take on the local legends. These mountains bring out the imagination like nowhere else on earth. Just last month, not long after you asked me about the Beast of Nevenero, as a matter of fact, this came with our monthly book drop . . ."

He stood and walked to the far side of the room, where he dug through a wardrobe stuffed with newspapers and magazines. I hadn't believed that he had created a system in all that chaos, and yet he went directly to a particular pile of newspapers, lifted a magazine from the stack, and sat down again.

"This is one of the more interesting pieces I have read about the crazy legends up here," he said, opening the glossy pages of a magazine called *New Animal* on his lap. There was a re-production of the James Pringle photograph, a map of the Aosta Valley, a large color photograph of Montebianco Castle, and reproductions of the Shipton Bigfoot pictures. The head-line of the article read: "The Search for the Yeti in the Alps." The byline was Justine Jeanneau.

"This was the woman I met in the village," I said, aston-ished, my heart skipping a beat as I read over the article. I didn't know what startled me more—Justine's name on the article or the word "Yeti" in bold type. I scanned the pages, finding information about the Montebianco family, the history of the Yeti and Bigfoot legends in the Alps, and her experi-ence watching a Yeti-like creature steal a child. "She showed me these pictures before she called Dr. Feist. Before Sal shot me," I said. "Before he shot her."

"Hmm," he said, shaking his head. "It is unfortunate for her that she was still poking around here. She came to the castle to interview Dolores for the article. Dolores nearly had a nervous breakdown. Sal told the journalist in no uncertain terms that she better not come back."

"Dr. Feist had the same theory of archaic hominids," I said, going back to the magazine and scanning it, comparing what I saw with what I had witnessed myself. Aki and Jabi were nothing like the creatures in the article, but I had encoun-tered them only once, in the shadowy evergreens, and couldn't be sure. "He believed they were a missing link between Ne-anderthals and Homo sapiens."

"Well," Basil said, pointing to the photo by James Pringle, "so did Pringle, although he didn't use that language. He came up here over a hundred years ago and recorded them, but no one believed him." He closed the magazine and sat back in his chair. "But even this very convincing article doesn't prove that the Montebianco family has anything to do with the Beast of Nevenero, archaic hominids, or Yeti, or whatever it is one chooses to call them. That story is purely speculative. There is nothing in the family records to corroborate Eleanor's memoir. Believe me, I have looked. Not a shred of evidence about Leopold's time in the mountains, or his supposed affair with a creature."

"This article got some of it right," I said. "But there are mistakes, too."

The certainty in my voice caught Basil off guard. "How do you know?"

"Because I saw the creatures myself," I said. "They were here. Vita brought them."

"*Them?*" he said. "There was more than one?"

"There were two," I said. "Both men. But"—I removed Leopold's book of field notes and gave it to Basil—"I suspect this will give us more information."

Basil took the book in his hands and examined it. He bit his lip and furrowed his brow—the large mole above his eyebrow flexing—and opened the cover. "Oh!" he said. "Leopold's field notes. *Where was this?* How on earth did you get it?"

"It was in Vita's room," I replied. "She gave it to me."

"Devilish Vita," he said, as he paged through the book, taking in the sketches, reading the French. "I looked everywhere, even in her rooms, and couldn't find it." He turned the book so that he could examine the binding. "I believe I can rebind it," he said, stroking the book as if it were a pet. "Perhaps I can also save some of these water-damaged pages." Finally, he put the book down, a flicker of elation illuminating his eyes. "Do you know what this is? And what this means?"

Basil paged through the notebook. "There is so much information, one can hardly summarize. But I see that it mostly describes—in intricate detail—Leopold's years of living with *them*."

I pushed my chair close, taking in the pages of sketches, the charts, the endless stream of sentences.

"There appears to be two distinct sections," he said at last, after he had paged through the book. "One that is more personal—about his relationship with the female creature—and another that is more professional. Clearly, he meant to do something more with the field notes. Perhaps write a book or a scientific treatise, as that section is very well organized. The other parts are a bit haphazard. It may take some time for me to translate the personal bits, but the professional notes are quite easy to understand. I could read a few paragraphs to you now, if you like."

Sitting back in my chair, I was filled with anticipation for what Leopold's notes would reveal about the Icemen. As Basil began to read, I closed my eyes and listened as the village of the Icemen and its inhabitants came alive.

June 1814

THE FIELD NOTES of LEOPOLD MONTEBIANCO

"HIGH MOUNTAINS SUFFOCATE ME."—*Chateaubriand*

POPULATION:

The population of the iceman village is comprised of sixty-four individuals, fifteen males, thirty-two females, and seventeen children.

They live communally. I am reminded of the tribes of the South Seas, particularly those natives described by Captain James Cook on his voyage to New Holland. Namely, they are primitive creatures, but intelligent, with a system of communication, rituals, and family structures. Food, shelter, and clothing are shared among the tribe. Activities such as cooking and hunting are shared among the group. Tight couples are formed, although it is often the case that males have two or more female mates. Whether this is due to the lack of males in the current population—females outnumber males two to one—or mating preference is not certain. Children are raised communally, and no paternal identification appears to take place.

There is evidence that the population was once much larger, perhaps as recently as two generations ago, as is evidenced by cave art depicting large groups of males hunting game together. Great quantities of artifacts such as jewelry, spears, stone knives, and animal skins confirm that the population was once more populous than the sixty-four individuals now living in the community.

Fertility is robust, but child mortality is high. I witnessed the birth of six babies in the twenty-eight months I lived among the icemen. Five of these infants died within the first months of life. The length of gestation is longer than that of humankind, approximately fourteen months. Labor is shorter, and delivery less dangerous due to the anatomy of the female, namely a wide pelvis, which allows for fewer complications during delivery.

CONCLUSION: *While the birth rate is strong, the survival of infants is less certain. The iceman village is in decline. Isolation is crippling the icemen. If they mix their blood with the human population below, and bring hearty stock to their kind, strength and longevity would certainly ensue. I have instructed them to do so.*

LOCATION:

The icemen's caves are located approximately two kilometers northwest from Montebianco Castle, to the southeast of Mont Blanc. Although I have followed various routes, the least arduous, most direct trajectory from the valley of Nevenero can be found by following a path carved into the side of the mountain. It is my opinion that this path was created by the iceman himself, as the result of uncountable journeys to and from Nevenero over the course of centuries, perhaps to gain access to the rich hunting grounds of the valley. The path is marked by glacial ice formations and waterfalls of spectacular beauty.

PHYSIOLOGY:

The adult male iceman measures between 110 *centimeters and* 180 *centimeters at full height. The female is larger, measuring between* 115 *centimeters and* 190 *centimeters. Weight varies between the sexes, with female creatures being heavier. Among the sixty-four icemen of the village, I have observed that females carry larger supplies of fat and muscle. Such reserves of nutrition aid in fertility and ensure milk production for infants. But it may also explain the survival rate for females: females outnumber males and are, in general, more resilient.*

The flesh of the iceman is exceptionally white, without the variation in pigmentation one sees in human beings. No freckles, moles, or any other variety of coloration marks the surface of the skin. The eyes are uniformly blue and the hair is uniformly white. Hair covers much of the body of the male iceman and 60 *percent of the female. The feet of both male and female are wide and flat. The nails on fingers and toes are thick and yellow. The genitals are identical in size and shape as human beings.*

The physical features of the iceman in relation to humanity is striking. While the Creator has shaped them as He shaped our kind—in the mold of Himself and the first son Adam—there are marked differences that render the iceman wholly separate from humanity. The facial features are blunted. The chin shorn away. The brow wide and broad. These features beg to be compared to primates, but I resist such comparisons: the iceman is no animal. Indeed, in my observations, I have wondered if he is not more adept, more beautiful, indeed, more human, *than my kind.*

CONCLUSION: *The Lord has created the iceman with greater fortitude and resistance to the Alpine landscape than humankind.*

HABITAT & TECHNOLOGIES:

The iceman has survived in a narrow crevice between two high mountains. This land is protected by rock on all sides, with the center fertile, a seed pressed into a deep furrow.

The primary habitat of the iceman is composed of a series of low, wide caverns. Carved into the western side of the mountain, they number twenty-two in all, eleven on each side of a narrow arcade.

The iceman's caves are communal in nature. Cooking, eating, sleeping, production of clothing, food, and tools are the primary activities that occur in these spaces, although instances of storytelling, singing, familial interactions, and mating have been found to occur as well.

The caverns are barren, without even the most basic of furnishings, although I discovered a number of man-made objects in the large central cave, namely a ceramic jug and a handsaw, both of which were clearly fabricated by human beings. The icemen regard these objects as extremely valuable. Their existence among the icemen points to contact with human civilization. Indeed, it is my observation that they were acquainted with humankind when I arrived among them. They did not fear me, but rather examined the objects in my pack—a fountain pen, ink, this notebook, a snuffbox of tobacco, a pipe, a pocket watch, as well as other possessions. They considered these objects marvels of technology.

There is a great deal of importance placed upon a large central grotto located above the village. Decorative paint covers the walls and ceilings of this space. Primitive depictions of hunting, cooking, bathing, and so on were in evidence, proof that the iceman takes pleasure in the beautification of his environment. Animal skins, furs, and hides cover the floor near the fire pit, and it is the custom in winter to eat and sleep here.

No man-made structures exist in the village. Huts, tents, and teepees like those fabricated by the natives in America have not been detected. I have found no artificial barriers against the climate such as doors or shutters. The icemen live in the elements throughout the year and have the fortitude to withstand temperatures below freezing. I have endeavored to teach them to use their native elements—stone and wood—to construct huts, which would much improve their resistance to the cold.

Native tools include slabs of smooth granite for food preparation, knives carved of bone, and a number of wooden bowls shaped from the wood of birch trees. Clothing is primitive and made from the skins of animals. I have not observed the use of woven fibers of any kind. This, too, I will endeavor to teach them.

Food storage is basic, with meat and vegetables being dried in the open air or cooled by snow. Water is stored in a cistern outside of the cave.

CONCLUSION: The iceman uses and values advanced tools. Once in possession of more sophisticated technologies, he has the intellectual capacity to understand and use them. They are

*not creative in tool development, but intelligent in deploying
tools.*

MATING RITUALS:

*Sexual rituals are diverse and elaborate among the tribe of
the iceman.*

*Sexual attraction is shown in numerous ways, most often
by light physical contact, such as touching or patting. Bathing
is a communal practice that may lead to sexual engagement.
Oftentimes, mating rituals involve gifts such as food or
clothing. I have, on occasion, heard females sing to attract a
mate.*

*I have observed that sexual acts can be accompanied by
aggression—punching, hair pulling, spitting, and choking.
I have observed this behavior in young males in the weeks or
months after finding a mate. There is a fevered recognition of
attraction, a period of courtship, and a direct movement into
sexual relations. All three stages are marked by an abundance
of sexual desire, possessiveness, and so on. After fathering
a child, this behavior abates and a male will find a new
companion.*

*Sexual intercourse occurs without shame or privacy, often
in full view of the other members of the tribe.*

LIFESPAN:

*The icemen don't remember birth dates, and there is no
acknowledgment of time passing among them, but the elder
members of the tribe appear to be seven or eight decades old.
Elders are valued for their knowledge. There are distinct
funerary rights followed by all members of the community. The*

tribe buries their dead together. The burial site is located less than one kilometer from the village. Objects such as stone knives and furs are buried with the body. I observed six burials during my years in the village, five children and one elderly woman. There is elaborate and communal grieving over the dead. Upon seeing the tears and lamentations over the loss of life, I believe that the icemen are capable of the sentiments and deep feelings of human beings.

TWENTY-SEVEN

❧

S PRING DID NOT come gently to the mountains. May winds blew cold and fierce, slicing at the skin with the brutality of a blade. Freezing rain pounded the castle windows like fists, and temperatures fell below freezing at night, turning the rain to snow. But there were also moments of pristine clarity, when the sky was blue as far as I could see. Wild violets and tough, yellow-maned dandelions began to grow on the east lawn, giving the gray landscape patches of vibrant color. The white mulberry trees near the mausoleum began to bud, then blossom. One warm afternoon, the pond cracked open, leaving an island of ice floating at the center of dark water. Snow had begun to melt on the mountain as well. Water gushed through chiseled crags of the mountainside, streaming down in rivulets over the lawn. Sal had told me that the spring melt was essential to Montebianco Castle—the well filled from April to June, ensuring clean drinking water for the year—but the water came with such force that it seemed to me that we would all be swept away.

The day I saw an Iceman again, the sun had emerged for a full afternoon. Craving warmth and light, I left my rooms and walked the castle grounds, my running shoes squelching through the muddy grass, my feet soaked in cold, pure mountain water. I was just making my way from the greenhouse, a bouquet of pink dahlias in my hand, when Aki stepped out of the cove of spruce trees on the east lawn.

I stopped, startled.

Aki raised his hand, gesturing that I come closer. "Come," he called to me. He held up the leather sack Vita had given them the night we had met. "Please."

I walked to Aki, slipping behind the trees where the thick scent of pine needles and wet earth filled the air. With the pink dahlias in my hand, I squinted at Aki, taking him in. It had been a clear, moonless night when we met, the light so dim I had discerned only the most basic outline of his features. But it struck me then, upon seeing him that day in the sunlight, that he was beautiful, and that is how I would always think of him after. Beautiful, if such a word can be used to describe a man as rough as the mountains. He was taller than me by a full foot, broad-shouldered, his bare arms sinewy with strength, his white hair falling to his chest. His features were rough-hewn and craggy. His wide-set blue eyes met my gaze with cool intelligence. I understood the justice of the name Leopold had given them: Icemen. I felt certain that if I were to touch Aki, he would melt in my hands.

"I came for Vita," he said, eyeing the pink dahlias, their spikes so bright and strange. "But her window is closed. She leaves it open when we can approach."

I turned to look back at the northeast tower. Shutters blocked the windows. The windows had been closed since Vita fell sick.

"I need to see her," Aki said.

"That isn't possible," I said, surprised to hear him speak my language. "But I'll tell her you're here, if you want."

He furrowed his brow, looking at me intently, and it struck me that he wasn't sure if he could trust me.

"Yes," he said at last. "But no one else can know that I am here."

"Of course not," I said. "What do you want me to tell her?"

"We need more supplies. Antibiotics and bandages. Something for pain. A clean blanket. One of my people has been hurt. Hunting yesterday, he fell." Aki flinched as if he himself were injured. "We need food, too. The winter has been long this year. Vita's window has been closed for a long time."

"The window is closed because Vita is sick."

He looked alarmed. "Very sick?"

I nodded. "I don't think she will be able to bring you the things you need herself. But I can."

Aki examined me, his eyes boring into me, and it seemed he was capable of seeing below the layers of skin and muscle, through the cage of my ribs and into my heart.

"You will be able to find us?" he asked.

I looked up the mountainside, imagining the village as Leopold had described it, nestled into a crevice of the mountain.

"Follow this path," he said. He held back the branches of an enormous spruce tree to reveal a path beyond, worn deep into the stone of the mountain. "Straight up. I will wait for you."

But before I could ask him how far I should climb, or where, exactly, he would wait, Aki slipped away. The branches of the spruce tree sprang back as he left, obscuring him in a crush of green needles.

THERE WAS NO doubt that Vita's strength had deteriorated since the last time I visited her rooms. She lay in bed, her skin glistening with fever. She was gaunt, little more than skin and bones, giving her the appearance, in the flickering firelight, of a cadaver. The heavy scent of perfume was gone. Now there was nothing but the smell of a life reducing to primary elements—sweat and urine and infection and sour breath. Vita would soon be gone.

Greta had been there recently—the fire burned strong in the fireplace. A full pitcher of water sat on her bedside table next to a bottle of pills.

"Vita." I touched her hand and found her skin was cold and thin, dry as rice paper. "Vita, I need to speak with you."

She opened her eyes and glanced at me. I regretted waking her, but Aki was waiting.

"Aki came back," I said, holding up the leather sack.

"Already?" she asked, blinking her eyes, struggling to see.

"He says he needs more antibiotics and bandages."

Vita struggled to sit up. I helped adjust her pillows, poured her a glass of water, and brought it to her mouth. "Someone was hurt?" she asked.

"One of them had an accident while hunting."

"Who?"

I shook my head. "He didn't say."

She looked upset. "All of their supplies are in the pantry in the kitchen," she said. "Bernadette manages them for me and reorders when we are low. If they require something we don't have, a medication, for example, it can be ordered and dropped in. Just tell Bernadette."

"Have you been to their village?"

"Many times. In fact, when I was younger, I spent weeks at a time living with them."

"In their caves?" I asked, remembering Leopold's field notes.

Vita smiled weakly. "They haven't lived that way in my lifetime. They have stone houses now, well built and warmer than the caves. They build what they need—beds and furniture and so on. I have supplied them with what they cannot make—clothes, shoes, cookware, dishes, blankets, and so on. They know they can always come to me for help."

"Aki was worried when I told him you were sick."

"The Icemen need me to survive. If I die, they will most certainly suffer. There is a reason they are the last of their kind, you know. They cannot fend for themselves. That is why *you* are so important. You must help them when I'm gone."

Vita pushed herself up in bed.

"They have a word for us in their language: *kryschia.* It means protector and educator. It began with Leopold. Every generation since Leopold has protected them except my father, Ambrose the coward. He not only stopped offering supplies— which is our duty—but he shot and killed one of them."

I thought of the rope of hair in the trophy room, its thickness, its weight in my hands.

"Half of their population died during my father's lifetime. When I came to understand who they were, and what my place was in their community, I vowed to never let that happen again. I have kept my promise, even when it was difficult. With medicines, warm clothing, seeds and simple technologies, I have helped them become stronger, better, capable of fighting the elements and illness. I have made them understand their position in relation to our kind—they know that they are different from every other human being on the planet, that they are alone in the world, but that they are *human beings,* rare and special treasures whose lives must be respected." Vita met my eyes, to be sure I was listening. "The most valuable contribution I have provided has been security. I gave them the ability to protect themselves. The man you met, Aki, has a sister named Uma. At least, I believe Uma is his sister.

There is no real family structure among them. After a child is weaned, it is given to the village, and they all raise it together. In any case, I found them together in the village, and I brought the two of them here when they were young. I taught them skills they could use to survive."

"Is that why Aki speaks our language?"

She nodded. "They both do, Aki and Uma. I worked with them here in the northeast tower, teaching them to speak and to read. They learned very quickly. Uma, in particular, has tried to adapt to our ways. They have told me they shared their knowledge with the others, that Uma's medical skills have been invaluable, but I have not been to the village in many years, so I am unable to verify how their abilities have benefited the tribe."

I tried to imagine Vita with them in the village, but my mind kept going to the portrait of Leopold in the family gallery. His dark hair. His romantic expression and billowing silk cravat.

"How long has it been since you were there?"

"Nearly thirty years, now. It is a difficult climb, and I lost the strength to manage it decades ago. Aki and Uma still come regularly. They are like my own grandchildren, in many ways." A look of embarrassment passed over her face. "That dead goat you discovered when you first arrived was a gift from me. They brought it back to the village."

Vita gestured to the pitcher. I poured more water in her glass. As she drank, she glanced up at Eleanor's portrait. "It must have frightened you, and for that I am sorry, but there was no other way. I could not very well have them here openly. The servants would leave. They would tell outsiders. My poor mother could never abide them. They terrified Eleanor, *terrified* her. She would have gladly let them die out. She had a heart of steel, my mother. She insisted that we keep their existence a secret, and I agreed with her on that point. Can you imagine if they had been discovered? They would have been put in cages and displayed like animals in a zoo. James Pringle came the closest to exposing us. He photographed one of the elders, a friend of my grandfather's, and was planning to photograph the others, but Eleanor stopped him."

According to the information I had translated in Turin from *Mostri delle Alpi,* James Pringle had died in an avalanche while taking photographs in the mountains. I wondered what Eleanor had arranged to stop him.

"And Giovanni?" I asked. "Did he know about them?"

"They are why he left," Vita said, her voice so low I could hardly make her out. "We had terrible arguments about them. My son was very attached to me, you see. He was unhappy that they occupied so much of my life—I spent a lot of time with them when I was younger. He became so jealous that he began to tell outrageous stories about them."

"I've heard those stories," I said, and a shiver ran through me as I remembered Nonna Sophia's wide, terrified eyes, her warnings about Nevenero and the Montebianco family.

"Oh, I am sure you have," Vita said. "Giovanni said they were savages and that they were committing atrocities. And when I disagreed, he left."

I clenched and unclenched my hands in my lap, as if I were grasping at a fraying rope. "Was it true that they committed atrocities?"

"Of course not," Vita said, dismissing the idea with a wave of her hand. "It was that village girl Marta who gave him that idea. I admit, I have thought often of Greta's child . . ."

"Joseph," I said.

"Joseph saw Aki one afternoon when he came to the castle

to see me. The boy was quite affected by the encounter. But Aki would never do something like that without my knowledge. I'm sure that the child was taken by his father."

"You don't think there is even a small possibility that they are responsible?"

Vita turned back to me, her manner chilling. "I will not deny that there is something primitive in them," she said. "I know because I feel it, that wildness in my blood. It is something I have learned to . . . *overcome*. You read Eleanor's memoir. You know what I am capable of doing. My strength was quite a wonder, once. It was a gift I never understood fully until it left me. I am certain that this strength was passed down from the Icemen. Giovanni and Guillaume inherited it from me. And you, I would guess, have inherited it, too."

A fit of coughing overtook Vita. She sank into her pillows, her face sallow, her eyes filled with pain.

I stood to go. "You need to rest. I'll get the supplies from Bernadette and bring them to Aki."

"Wait," she said, grasping my hand and pulling me back into my seat. "There is something else. Something I must ask of you before you go to them. A request."

I sat at her side, feeling wary. What could I possibly do that she had not done already?

"As you know, Leopold lived among the Icemen for a number of years and returned with a child, my grandfather Vittorio. It was a secret, how Vittorio came to be born, even among the family. My father told Eleanor the truth because of the undeniable physical resemblance I have to them. What was not known to Eleanor, or to anyone else, were the details of Leopold's relationship with my grandmother. Her name was Zyana. In his field notebook, Leopold describes Zyana at length, the birth of my grandfather Vittorio, and their life together. What was unknown to everyone, even to Eleanor, was that Leopold and Zyana had a second child. A girl." Vita's eyes bore into me as she spoke. "Leopold left her behind, abandoned her, with the Icemen."

"But why would he do that?" I asked, feeling, for reasons I did not understand, deeply disturbed by the idea.

"It could have been that the girl had inherited her mother's traits and looked more like *them*. By all accounts, Vittorio appeared to be more or less normal and could pass for one of us. He was blond and pale and exceptionally strong, like the Icemen, but he displayed nothing that would frighten people." A look passed over Vita's features as she spoke, and I wondered if she felt the pain of her own childhood. "There is also the unfortunate reality that girls were of little value to the Montebiancos back then. If Leopold had to make a choice between his two children, he would have surely taken his son. In any case, the daughter's fate has plagued me for years. I assume that she, like so many of the tribe, died young. And even if Leopold's daughter did not die in childhood, there is no guarantee she lived long enough to have children. Or that these children had children. It is very likely that Leopold's descendants did not survive." Vita smiled, her glittering eyes and ravaged features giving her the look of an ancient creature, one who has survived a great battle. "But on the other hand, it is also possible that they did. That is what you must find out."

"But you went to the village," I said. "Why didn't you look then?"

"I did look," she said. "I found nothing definitive. That doesn't prove that Leopold's descendants do not exist. The Icemen tell stories about their origins, but they have no system for keeping information, and so nothing has ever been recorded. They think of life and death differently than we do, not as a beginning and ending, but as a contribution and re-payment to a life source. Death is a passage, one that is painful, but merely a movement to another realm. You will see, when you meet them, that their perceptions are very different from ours. They do not know how to classify or distinguish catego-ries in the ways we do. For example, when I showed Aki the mulberry trees by the mausoleum and a citrus tree from the greenhouse, he used the same word for both, which means, roughly, "plant." It is the same with human beings. When I ask if there is someone among them who is different, who has different features, perhaps, or maybe even a pigmentation to the skin that is different from theirs, they don't understand my question. They are a tribe, with all its strengths and all its flaws."

I felt suddenly overwhelmed by all that was being asked of me, not only by Vita, but by the entire Montebianco family, that chain of men and women stretching back hundreds of years. "How can I know, when even you couldn't find any-thing?"

"It is very simple, Alberta," Vita whispered, her strength gone. "Look carefully at the tribe. If a descendant of Leopold has survived, certain kinds of physical traits will be present. There may be pigmentation to the skin or hair—this would be a sure sign. Our kind is smaller. Our skulls are shaped dif-ferently. I looked for such traits years ago, when I went to the village. I found nothing then. But, as you know, inheritance is a trickster. One generation may hide its genetic treasures, while the next will put them fully on display."

TWENTY-EIGHT

✣

F ROM THE START, I struggled to climb the mountain. My leg was weak, still tender from the gunshot wound, my vitality swept away by months of lying in bed. My muscles had withered, taking with them the strength I'd had just months before, when I'd scaled the mountainside in Nevenero. I had felt then that I could climb to the top of the world. Now, after five minutes on the path up the mountain, I was on the verge of collapse.

Yet, I wasn't about to go back. I had the leather sack with the medical supplies Aki needed, and Vita's voice at the back of my mind urged me forward. *Promise me,* she had said, squeezing my hand as I stood to leave her. *Promise you will look for the descendants of Leopold. If you find one, bring him here.*

I climbed onward, pushing myself up the rocky trail. It wound higher and higher, switchbacking up rocky promontories, around deep, bottomless crevices, through thick groves of trees. The cold spring air tingled in my lungs. The scent of pine needles and limestone and wet earth hung heavily around me. I imagined the generations of men and women whose feet had worn down this rock, so many centuries of movement that had left the stone smooth and slippery.

Exhausted, my leg aching, I paused to catch my breath at the base of a waterfall. I dropped the leather pack. I took out a bottle of water, drinking it quickly and then filling it in a pool below the waterfall. Spring had melted the snow, sending water gushing down the mountain. It burst from a crack in the rocks, falling over a clutch of stones below, sending up swirls of mist. Sunlight churned in the air, splintered into a rainbow of colors that lifted, held form, and dissolved back into the mist again. In the winter, this free fall of water would freeze, coating the granite in clear, glistening ice. But for now, it gushed down to the valley below, soaking the earth.

By then, I had come to see that the true mysteries of the Alps had nothing to do with the legends of dragons and cretins and beasts, or any of the other stories passed down over the generations, but with the mountains themselves. The desolation of the peaks, the murderous indifference of black granite, the calamity of ice and snow—this was nature in its most indomitable and glorious expression. The feeling of vertigo as I stood before the waterfall was not so very different from what I had felt that first day at the castle, when I had gazed out the window over the peak of Mont Blanc: awe and wonder at the power of nature. An acute awareness that the mystery of creation and destruction existed here, in these mountains. Time, millions and millions of years of it, more than I could even imagine, had passed through these gorges, moving fast and treacherous as snow melt. The mountains had stood against it, strong and indifferent. The fierce beauty of it all made me tremble with humility and terror. What was I—what were any of us—compared to *this*?

I hoisted the pack on my back and pushed myself onward. I climbed for some time before I heard a noise ahead, a branch snapping, the scrape of feet over rock. I stopped, listening.

"Hello?" I called into the shadowy nothingness above me.

I reached into the pack and pulled out the knife I had taken from the kitchen. How well I could defend myself against a wild animal wasn't something I had considered. I steeled myself and continued on the path when, above, on a ledge of granite, I saw Aki.

For a long, tense moment, he stared at me, a look of surprise in his eyes. He seemed to be struggling with my presence there, and I realized that while he had asked me to come to him in the mountains, and had showed me the path to take, he hadn't ever really believed I would do it.

Aki climbed down the promontory of rock until he stood before me. I showed him the leather pack. He glanced at my offering and thanked me.

"Come," he said, motioning up the mountain. "The village isn't far."

My leg was aching, and I had no idea how I would climb another step, but I was determined to see the village. I braced myself and followed. Aki slipped behind a boulder and back onto the steep path. His pace was quick. I couldn't keep up.

Finally, he turned around, annoyed. I had fallen far behind.

"You must go faster," he said.

"I'll try. It's just that—"

He must have realized that I was in pain, because he asked, "You are hurt?"

I explained the gunshot wound, the botched surgery, my slow and incomplete recovery.

"But why?" he asked, confused.

"I was running away," I said. "Sal wanted to stop me."

This answer didn't make sense to Aki. He thought it over, his brow furrowed. "But this weapon," he said. "I have seen men use it to kill animals. Do you kill your own people with this weapon, too?"

"Sometimes," I said. "Sometimes we do."

"We do not," he said, looking at me. "Never. There are not

enough of us for that." He walked back to me. "Show me," he said.

I slipped my jeans over my hips, easing them down past the gunshot wound, revealing the pink scar on my thigh. Aki bent close to look at my leg, his gaze settling on my bare skin. He touched the scar, his thumb tracing the damaged skin, and a shiver went through me. When our eyes met, I could not look away, and for a moment, I thought something had passed between us, a moment of attraction and complicity.

It was a long way up and I wasn't going to make it without help. Sensing this, Aki squatted down and told me to climb on his back. I wrapped my arms around his neck and hoisted myself up. He glanced over his shoulder, asked if I was ready, and, with that, began to climb up the mountain.

Aki was strong and quick and adept. I held tight to him as he launched from rock to rock, his fingers pushing into cracks and crevices, his legs propelling us up. He moved with the energy and power of someone inured to the terrain, without hesitation, without reflection, pushing through banks of trees, scaling slopes, traversing the solid rise of each new plateau. I was so caught up in the sensation of weightlessness, the pure terror of clinging to him, I could hardly breathe. I buried my head in his neck, afraid to look, but when I got the courage to lift my eyes, I saw the mountain as I had never seen it before. The mineral-stained, striated surfaces, so close that I could have skimmed my nails against them as we passed. Fat rock crystal formations hung like opalescent beehives. Above, the mountain peaks rose like giants, their long, spiked ridges stretching as far as I could see. Snow glinted in the sun, too bright, too brilliant to look at without blinking. At the highest reach of my vision, a misty powder swirled in a solution of air, thick as yeast in beer. And below—pure vertigo. The earth fell away, dropping into a sheer, chiseled chasm of bottomless, formless space. This, I realized, was how a bird must feel riding the air to the top of the world.

At last, we reached a plateau. Aki dropped me to the ground and I fell onto a flat of granite. Although Aki had done all the work, I was out of breath, hot and trembling from fatigue. My leg burned from the effort of clinging to his body, the dull throb of pain pounding through my thigh. At that altitude, the air was cool and thin. I had lost all sense of equilibrium. I leaned against a boulder to get my balance and looked around.

There it was, the arcade of caves Justine had described, the very one she had discovered tracking footprints in the snow. Long and dark and crusted with ice, the passage had the appearance of a tunnel to another world. I hardly saw a thing as I walked inside. What light filtered down left only a weak, green haze that pooled over my feet like dirty water. The image of Joseph, Greta's son, being pulled through the crack in the mountain appeared in my mind, flickering as if projected on a screen. A child's desperate cry echoed in my ears. I shivered, and pulled my jacket close.

Aki walked off ahead. I steadied myself and hobbled after him, fear rising in my chest as he slipped through the narrow crack at the end of the arcade and disappeared. What lay beyond exhilarated and terrified me. I stood before this fissure, feeling my life collect into two parts, the life I had led before, and the life I would lead after I entered the village of the Icemen.

TWENTY-NINE

❧

I EMERGED INTO A tongue of land cut deep into a crevice of the mountain. Leopold had described the village as a seed pressed into a rocky furrow, and it seemed exactly that: a furtive garden in a fold of stone. The mountains angled up on all sides, shielding the village, protecting it. I understood then how the Icemen had survived. The only way in or out of the village was the narrow arcade of caves, that single crack in the wall. They were surrounded by a fortress of rock.

As Vita had told me, the village had grown since Leopold had described it in his field notes. Where once there were only caves, now there were stone huts. They were primitive shelters, cut from the mountain, the walls constructed of rough stone that appeared to be nothing more than the natural outcroppings of granite, the stone rooftops speckled with moss. This explained why the village hadn't been discovered from above—not by helicopter or airplane or satellite. Even if a helicopter had flown overhead, the curve of the mountains hid the Icemen so completely that it would be difficult to discern life below. The mountains enfolded the valley so that everything— the stone huts, the cultivated plants, the population of archaic humans who came to greet me—remained invisible to the outside world.

I walked over an expanse of moss-covered rock toward Aki's tribe.

I have never taken it lightly, that moment of contact with the Icemen. I knew that they were vulnerable to the modern world. Vulnerable to me. They had persevered through the millennia without contact with the rest of humankind. Only pure, inviolate isolation had protected them.

Through the vicissitudes of time and geography, through the cruel workings of evolution, through all the hazards of climate, of migrations, food shortages, sickness, invasion: we stood face to face there, then, together. It was a miracle. By all measures, they should have been extinct. Like their direct ancestors, Neanderthals, or their more distant relations, Cro-Magnon, or any of the other dozens of archaic hominids that had evolved and perished—they should have been crushed by disease and competition. If the Icemen were a rare treasure of biology, I was the most privileged person on the planet: their witness. What I did not anticipate, and what has remained a source of wonder through all the years since that day, is how our meeting would transform me.

"My name is Alberta," I said to the gathering crowd. "Granddaughter of Vittoria Montebianco."

At the sound of my voice, more Icemen emerged from the stone huts, men and women and a few children. They looked at me, staring at me in wonder. I couldn't help but imagine Leopold Montebianco there, standing at my side, his jet-black hair and flamboyant cravat, surveying these pale men and women as they crowded around. I imagined the thrill of discovery he must have felt upon realizing what he had found. I felt it, too, a buzzing in the chest, the rare privilege of seeing something only a handful of people had ever seen before.

The Icemen gathered around. There were fifty of them, perhaps fewer. I scanned their faces, looking for aberrant traits, but they were all eerily similar to Aki in appearance. The defining features of their kind—the lack of pigmentation of skin and hair, the enormous blue eyes, the rough-hewn brow, the high cheekbones and long limbs—showed little variation. The full lips and the flatness of the nose, the pointed ears, the particular mold of the chin—these features were uniform. There was nothing of Leopold in any of these people. Nothing of me.

There was no variety in their clothing either. The women wore white woven tunics over loose pants, while the men wore cargo pants and leather vests that revealed their hair-covered arms. I remembered the picture of the Yeti in Justine's article, thick white hair covering its body, and while the Icemen might be mistaken for such a creature from a distance, up close they were far more human than anything that might resemble a beast. They were all as beautiful as Aki.

It surprised me to find them so different from Leopold's descriptions. While Vita had told me of the community's progress, I had imagined a struggling and ragged community on the brink of extinction. I had imagined the Icemen to be primitive, without resources, suffering the elements like animals in a cave. But that was not at all how I found them. Theirs was a human civilization, one with all the elements we would recognize as such: cultivated plants, shelters, clothes, and tools. Their technologies were simple, but simple in the way materials of the medieval period would seem simple to the modern eye. They raised goats and stored the milk. They wove very simple rough fabrics on a loom. Although they needed Vita's assistance, they had developed all the basic skills that could lead, one day, to survival.

Jabi, the man I had met with Aki on the east lawn with Vita, stepped from the crowd and turned to the others. From the way he pointed at me, and the sharpness of his voice, I knew he was angry that Aki had brought me there.

One of the children started to cry. She hid her face in her hands to block me from view.

"Jabi is telling them to be afraid of you," Aki whispered.

"They have no reason to be afraid," I said.

"He is telling them that you are dirty. He says you will bring disease. That you will kill with metal weapons."

"I'm healthy," I said. "And I have no weapons." I remembered the knife in the leather sack. No weapons that I intended to use.

Aki listened to Jabi, his expression dark.

"I thought Vita has helped the village," I said.

"She has not been here for two generations," he said. "The oldest remember her. But most do not."

As Jabi spoke, the others turned their eyes to me, watching, assessing. I could feel them turning against me. I glanced back, to the opening in the mountain, aware of my precarious position. I wouldn't be able to protect myself if they attacked me. The narrow passage was the only way in or out of the village. If they blocked the passage, I would be trapped.

Just as I was assessing my chances of escaping, Aki came to my side, his arm brushing against mine.

He lifted an arm into the air, to announce that he would speak. The others quieted and listened. He opened the leather sack, showing them that I had brought gifts. The energy of the crowd shifted, and they came to me, touching me, greeting me in their strange, guttural language. They said the word "Simi," the word Joseph had written on his drawings of the blue men, a word I would come to learn meant "fellowship." It would be months before I would understand even the rudiments of their speech, but I saw from Aki's gestures—and the way his voice softened when he looked at me—that he had convinced them of my intentions.

"Now," Aki said, "give them the gifts."

I distributed jars of preserved fruit, a few rings of dried sausages, a container of goat cheese from the mews. I pulled out medicine and bandages, a sharp kitchen knife. Jars of aspirin and tubes of antibacterial disinfectant. Small things to us that could prove invaluable to them.

I removed a box of plastic freezer bags I'd found in the pantry, opened one up, and demonstrated how it worked. The bags interested them the most. They pulled the bags out of the box and passed them around, dropping in sausage and goat cheese, opening and closing them.

Aki gestured to a woman, who stepped close to meet me. It was Uma, the woman Vita had taught at the castle. She took the leather sack with its jars of painkillers and tubes of antibacterial ointment. The rolls of bandages and packs of antibiotics. A big bottle of rubbing alcohol and cotton. She threw the sack over her shoulder and smiled at me. "Welcome," she said.

I may have mollified the others with my gifts, but Jabi watched me, his expression filled with animosity and accusation. I didn't understand why he hated me so intensely, but it was clear that he wanted me to leave. He said something to me, and when I didn't respond, he moved closer, then closer still, until he stood inches from me, his blue eyes piercing, his smell overwhelming. I stepped back, alarmed by his proximity, ready to turn and walk away, when he struck me.

I understand now that this attack was much bigger than Jabi and me, or even the Montebianco family and the Icemen. This was a moment of reckoning, an evolutionary clash, a confrontation between past and the present. We were part of a war begun some forty thousand years before, when Homo sapiens surpassed other humans to become the dominant life-form on the planet. My people had survived through strength and intelligence, by taking over shared resources, by gradually pushing out the less adept hominids. We survived by creating communities to protect us. We ate well, formulated medicines, reproduced more often, lived longer. We developed speech and advanced tools, grew crops and built shelters. We created language, religion, writing. We became masters of our reproduction, our habitat, our environment. Our technologies allowed us to exist apart from nature and to regard it as something other than ourselves. From this position of dominance, I watched Jabi, knowing that he could easily kill me, but it wouldn't change a thing. His kind would die. Mine would survive.

Jabi pushed me to the ground. I fell, pain slicing through me. I pulled myself up and tried to stand, but a second blow knocked me flat onto my stomach, socking the wind from my lungs. I gasped, trying to breathe, as Jabi stood above me, growling, his long yellow teeth bared. There was a rock in his hand. A sickening, triumphant smile grew on his face as he brought it down on my head.

THIRTY

✦

U MA WALKED ME to her hut, where she pointed to a cot near the window. I sat as she unpacked the medical supplies I had given her. The hut was spotlessly clean, the thick medicinal odor of disinfectant creating a strange contrast to the rough, moss-covered stone ceiling, plants growing from its jointed slabs of granite. The hut had been equipped with three cots, white cotton blankets, kerosene lanterns—all of which must have come from the castle. A man lay sleeping in the last cot, half his face scraped away, his jaw bone exposed, his cheek swollen, a long suture tracking over his collarbone. This was the man who had been hurt hunting, I realized, the reason Aki had needed extra supplies to begin with.

"Are you in pain?" Uma asked. I nodded, too shaken to speak.

Uma put pills in my hand, gave me a glass of water, and gestured for me to swallow them. I recognized the capsules— they were the same pills Vita had given me after my surgery. I swallowed them and watched as Uma went to a stack of clear plastic storage boxes in a corner of the hut and put the supplies away. Bandages and ointments and pills and gauze— Uma looked at each gift carefully before putting it in the box.

There was a row of old medical texts on a shelf. When Uma saw me looking at them, she said, "From Vita. She gave them to me so I could understand your ways of healing." She said the word "your" with a particular resistance, and I understood how very foreign she found me and my people. She had learned from us, and she had accepted what Vita had given her, but there was a clear line between our civilizations. "Thank you," she added, as she closed the lids and stacked the boxes back in the corner. "Thank you for bringing these things to us. I am always afraid we will be without them one day. It would make our survival much more difficult. Your kind has created many things we need. Medicine is one of them."

She went to a basin of water in the corner, wet a cloth, and gestured for me to lie back on the cot, so she could examine the wound.

The rock had left a gash just below the hairline. A warm ooze of blood soaked my hair and dripped over my cheek. I touched the gash, feeling the sting. It was deep. Blood stained my sweater and my jeans. A headache bloomed through my skull, prickling and painful. If Jabi had been given the chance, he would not have stopped. He would have smashed in my head and broken my bones. He would have killed me without a second thought.

"Some time ago, we lost a child to a very bad sickness," Uma said, as she cleaned the wound with the wet cloth. "The child was covered in small red sores. They became infected, causing him tremendous pain. His skin was hot. His tongue was dry. I tried everything, read everything in those books, but I could not save him. Do you know what illness he could have had, and do you have a medicine for it?" She looked at me with hope. "You have a medicine for everything."

I tried to place what the disease could have been—measles, mumps, chicken pox, rubella, a list of possible diseases came to mind. But I only knew these names from the list of immunizations I had as a child. No one I knew had ever suffered from these diseases. I had no idea what they looked like, what symptoms they produced. "I don't know," I said at last. "I've never seen a disease like that."

"We have lost three children in the last five years. Two in the first month after birth. And the other to sickness, as I just mentioned. He was five years old. Do you know what it feels like to watch a child suffer? It is terrible. I knew if it was one of *yours,* living below, you could have saved him. You would have medicine to treat the sores. You will look for this medicine when you go back, and when you return, you will bring it to us."

"I can try," I said. "But I'm not a doctor. I don't know what medicine you want."

"You will find it," she said confidently. "Since the first *kryschia* came to us, we have come to understand that your ways can save us. What you do to survive does not always make sense to us. There have been, over the generations, many among us who reject your ways. But I am convinced your people are wise. I have urged all of our tribe to follow your customs of survival, even when we find them strange."

Uma threaded a needle and closed the wound, pulling three stitches tight before tying off the knot. Then she took a white cotton tunic from one of the plastic boxes and handed it to me. I slipped out of my stained clothes and put on the tunic.

Uma gave me a small mirror, and I saw the black thread holding my skin together, three tight tracks, a crust of blood at the edges. It had been some time since I had looked at myself, and what I saw startled me. My skin was dry, my expression worn, my hair dirty and matted with blood. I was no longer the naïve woman who had received a mysterious letter inviting her to Italy. I was no longer the person struggling to understand her failing marriage and her inability to have children. Pain had hardened me and made me strong. This battered woman was as powerful as any of the noble men staring down from the portrait gallery. As powerful as Vita.

"I am angry with Jabi for doing this to you," Uma said. "He does not like your kind, but he must not hurt you."

"Why did he attack me like that?" I asked.

"In the beginning, Jabi went with us to your home. He studied with us, but he became unhappy and left. He admired your kind, once, and wanted to learn everything you knew. But then he changed. He saw the castle and the way your family lived. He became"—she paused, thinking of the word—"*jealous.*"

I sat at the edge of the cot, trying to understand. "But Vita was trying to help him."

"He saw that you live while we die," she said quietly. "He saw that your kind has created unthinkable abundance, while we struggle. He knows that we suffer more than you suffer. And this made him hate you."

After the pain medication kicked in, and the throbbing in my head receded, Uma took me behind her hut, where a narrow path angled up the side of the mountain. It was late afternoon by then, the light soft in the sky, but so much had happened since that morning that it seemed a week had passed since I had found Aki on the east lawn. The air was colder up in the mountains, swelling with the sound of birds. The peaks surrounding the village were so high that I felt that they were pressing in on me, squeezing the air from my lungs. Chateaubriand's words—the words Leopold had written in his field notes—rushed back to me: *High mountains suffocate me.* The altitude was too high. I could not breathe.

Voices grew from somewhere in the distance. We walked

for a few minutes, closing in on the sound, until we emerged onto a plateau of rock overlooking the village. At the center of the plateau, surrounded by rocks, stood a hot spring. Water bubbled up from the core of the mountain and reacted with the cool evening air, sending gossamer sheets of steam across the water's surface.

"This is where we bathe," Uma said, as she slipped out of her tunic, threw it on a rock, and waded into the water.

Uma joined a group of women at the center of the pool, and I watched her transform from the woman I had spoken with in her hut to one of them: her gestures became forceful, her voice loud and guttural, even the way she stood seemed altered. It was as though by speaking my language, and understanding my culture, she had put on a mask. With the mask gone, I felt our similarities recede.

I studied Uma, and this group of women, looking for one who might be different from the others, a body giving some clue of an inheritance that diverged from the pure Icemen. I found nothing. They all looked strikingly similar, a homogenous group of women, all the same height and coloring, with the same white hair and the same white skin as the rest.

The women paid no attention to me at all. They talked and washed each other, glancing occasionally at a group of children nearby. There were four, all between the ages of five and ten, old enough to be alone in the water, but still young enough to need oversight. They laughed and splashed, behaving like any group of children in any pool of water. When it began to rain, they caught raindrops in their mouths, a game that reminded me how Luca and I had sat on the top of a slide in the playground of our elementary school and caught snowflakes on our tongues.

I squatted at the edge of the pool, cupped my hands, and

filled them. The water was bathwater warm, thick with minerals, sulfurous, giving the odor of rotten eggs. I brought the water over my face and washed the blood from my forehead. The wound stung. The water ran pink through my fingers. Through the haze of pain medication, a headache thrummed.

"Come, join us," Aki said, his voice startling me.

I looked up, finding him naked before me. Night was coming, and his skin took on the gray-blue hue of twilight. He was a wonder of nature—the tapering muscles, the impossible height, the span of his arms and chest, the perfect symmetry of his torso. His feet were wide, shaped like mine, the second toe hooked, proof that we were cut of the same ancestral cloth.

"Come in," he said, smiling. If he had noticed me staring, he didn't show it. "It is warm. The water will feel good."

"Okay," I said, standing and pulling off a shoe, still a bit shaky from Jabi's attack.

Just then, from the far edge of the pool, I saw Jabi. His gaze was unrelenting, one part fascination and another part disgust. I slipped off my other shoe, then my socks. I knew he was trying to intimidate me, and while I was afraid of him, I held his gaze without blinking. When at last he turned his eyes away, I felt a rush of triumph.

I pulled the white tunic over my head, feeling the cold mountain air pulse against my skin. I was bruised and covered with goose bumps, my thigh scarred pink from the gunshot wound. I was ugly compared with them. Damaged. Broken. But they didn't seem to notice. Nudity, I would come to understand, was no different from being clothed for the Icemen. There was no sense of shame or embarrassment. They wore clothes for warmth, but in the summer heat, they were often naked. Not one of them watched me as I stepped into the warm, swirling water of the pool.

I started toward Aki when I saw that a woman had joined him. She was pregnant, her hands resting on her stomach. Aki said something in her ear and she laughed. She was beautiful, even taller and more muscular than Aki, with long white hair falling over her shoulders. When she sunk into the water, her hair spread over the surface like tentacles of an octopus.

As I watched them together, a hard pit formed in my stomach. In the shadow of their love, I felt how terribly I missed Luca. All the moments of tenderness we had shared, the intimacy and understanding between us—I wished with all my heart that I could go back and change things. I regretted so much: asking him to move out, the fight in Turin, but most of all asking him to come to Nevenero. He had sacrificed himself for me and there was no way I could ever repay him. A wave of longing came over me. I wanted Luca back.

When I stood before them, Aki slid his arm around the woman. "This is Ciba," he said.

Ciba looked up, meeting my eye, and everything around me faded: her eyes were dark brown.

THIRTY-ONE

✧

WHEN THE SUN had set, the Icemen walked up the mountain to a grotto overlooking the hot spring. It was a natural formation, a deep cave that shielded them from the wind and—even more important—from detection from above. A fire blazed at the center of the cave and, as we walked inside, I saw how its flickering orange light glimmered over the walls, lighting up chunks of rock crystal and amethyst, geodes of pink and purple stone that clung to the walls like luminous arachnids. Animal skins had been spread over the stone floor and, one by one, everyone sat on the skins around the fire. A woman ladled brown liquid from a barrel into wooden cups. She passed a cup to me. I took a drink of bitter wine, feeling it warm in my stomach.

When the fire was going strong, some men pulled a skinned ibex onto a spit. The head and horns were intact, the light of the fire playing over its features in a macabre dance, as though they had caught the Krampus himself and were roasting the devil for our dinner. As the beast turned over the fire, its skin crackling from the heat, serpentine shadows cascaded over the crystals of the grotto. The entrance to the cave cut away to reveal the sky, a clear, moonless sheet of darkness. The Icemen talked and laughed. I watched them, fascinated by all that I didn't understand.

I had been watching Ciba carefully since the hot spring,

trying to see if there were other clues to her heritage. There was no evidence that she was any different from the others. Yet, her brown eyes were the only evidence I needed: Ciba, this young woman carrying Aki's child, was a Montebianco descendant.

Maybe Ciba had noticed how I stared at her, because she gestured for me to join her by the fire. Her manner was friendly, welcoming. She didn't seem to have any hesitation about me, no fear or prejudice. She moved over, making room on her deerskin for me. It was such a small gesture, this invitation, but it was one I hadn't been given in a very long time, and I felt grateful to her, the way I had felt grateful when Luca had sat with me at lunch at school when the others rejected me. Ciba's gesture opened a possibility to me, something that I had not considered: that I might find genuine friendship among the Icemen. That I might feel the same kind of connection that Leopold had felt with these people. That it was not my duty to be there, but my choice.

The smell of roasting meat filled me with hunger. I moved close to the fire, warming my legs and drying my hair. My feet tingled as the chill of the night melted away. How strange it felt, to sit there so openly, my feet exposed. A lifetime of hiding them had made me self-conscious to the point of neurosis. But there was no reason to hide my feet from these people. They were all like me.

Soon, everyone gathered around the ibex. Its charred head strained into the air, its horns curling, its eyes burned away. There were no plates, no eating utensils, nothing but a communal bowl filled with slices of the roasted ibex. The bowl was passed from person to person. By the time the bowl came to me, there was one piece of meat left, grizzled flesh on a knob of joint. I looked at the fat-marbled flesh, a dull brown bone lurking below sinew, feeling nauseated. I noticed that Aki was watching me, so I took the meat and passed the bowl. I couldn't imagine eating it with my fingers, but when I looked around, I saw that everyone else was doing just that: biting the meat off the bone and washing it down with wine. I reminded myself that Leopold had participated in their rituals, learned their language, ate with them, slept with them, learned their customs. I picked up the meat and took a bite.

"Are you in pain?" Aki asked, gesturing to my stitches. He sat on the other side of Ciba, putting his hand on her leg possessively.

"No," I said, sitting up straighter, trying to mask how uncomfortable I felt. Everything was so strange and disorienting. It took all of my strength to remain calm. "It's just . . ." I waved my hand to the others, to the fire, to all of it. "All of this is so strange for me."

"When I was below," Aki said, "I felt that way. I did not understand your ways. I felt afraid."

"How long were you at the castle?"

He gave me a blank stare, as if he didn't understand the question, and I remembered what Vita had said: the Icemen did not record time the way we did. Years and months and days, all the ways we tracked our experience of living in the world, meant nothing to him.

"You were a child then?" I asked. "When you lived with Vita?"

"I was a child," he said. "*Kryschia* brought me down the mountain, to her home. It was warm and dark, without the sounds we have here. There were so many windows in every room. She taught me to speak your language and to eat your food. It was very different from our life here, but I soon liked it."

I did a quick calculation. Aki looked to be between twenty-five and thirty years old. Basil had come over twenty years before, and Sal and Greta had not been at the castle until more recently. They hadn't been there when Aki and Uma were living at the castle, but Dolores had been.

"And Ciba?" I asked, fishing for information. "Has she ever seen the castle? Or met Vita?"

He shook his head. "Ciba was not alive when the *kryschia* last came."

I glanced at Ciba. She couldn't be older than twenty, I realized, which explained why Vita had not discovered her brown eyes.

Ciba was watching us, her eyes narrowed, as if trying to understand our foreign words. "Does she understand anything we're saying?" I asked Aki.

Aki shook his head. "She never learned your language. Very few of us want to learn it. Uma must fight, sometimes, to make the group understand that your ways can help us."

The bowl returned to me, this time filled with thick cuts of meat. I took a piece and ate. It was good, gamey and rich, and I was hungry. I took another bite and washed it down with sour wine. The meat was warm, tender, the skin crunchy, an aftertaste of salt lingering on my tongue. A rush of chemicals hit my blood as I ate. My strength was beginning to return.

We sat together, me and Aki and Ciba, in the warmth of the fire. It was our first meal together, and while I did not understand it fully then, I felt the significance of our meeting deep in my heart: with the three of us together, a perfect configuration had been put in place, a triangle that would form the foundation of my life thereafter.

Ciba leaned into me, and I could smell her wet hair, feel the heat from her body, see the veins snaking through the transparent skin of her hands. Aki poured me more wine and made sure the bowl of meat came to me again. Their proximity made me feel every inch of myself—my arms, my neck, my heart—everything tingled with the pleasure of discovery. Nothing had prepared me for it, that sense of belonging I felt when I was with them, but I knew that this was what Vita had tried to describe. I felt how rare and precious this sense of belonging was, and how much I needed it. For the first time, I understood what drove Vita to protect the Icemen at all costs.

After a while, Ciba stood and walked from group to group around the fire, her hand resting on her belly, laughing and talking as she swam between pools of firelight and shadow. Everyone loved her, and I understood why: she was warm and friendly and beautiful. Every angle of her pale, alien features was exaggerated in the firelight. Ciba must have thought me equally strange. Every so often I caught her staring at me, as if I were the most exotic thing she had ever encountered. The others' reactions to me fell somewhere between Jabi's violent dislike and Ciba's fascination: I was dangerous and invasive and marvelous, something to be watched with fear or wonder.

Aki opened the package of goat cheese I had brought from the mews and refilled our cups with wine. Another bowl went around, this one with roasted nuts, the shell charred black, the taste—when I put one in my mouth—buttery sweet. Eventually, Ciba returned to us, bringing a bowl of roasted beets from the fire. The food was simple, but it was a feast to me, a kind of homecoming celebration.

When the fire had burned down, a woman sang, her voice lifting into the still night air. Aki fell back onto the animal skin. Ciba lay by his side and gestured for me to join them, and so I lay next to her, listening to the music.

"That," Aki said, gesturing so I looked to the ceiling of the grotto, "is our past."

Above, the rock surface was covered with drawings. I saw the valley that led down to Nevenero. An avalanche falling over a group of people. A man with a spear, and a pack of ibex, their horns curling. Enormous figures standing on the top of mountain peaks. Then, at the far side of the ceiling, there was a representation of the arcade of caves, the stone huts, the pool of mineral water.

"There," Aki said, pointing to the figures standing on the peaks of the mountains. "We came from this place at the top of the world. Before us, there were no people, only giants made of ice. They were very powerful because they never felt cold. They had ice palaces and ice tools. But they were not happy. They were masters of all they saw, but they were alone. And so they created us from ice. We were tall and pale, like them. But we were not strong or immortal. We felt the winds and the snow. We needed fire and the fur of animals. The giants hated our fires. The heat melted their ice palace, and so they banished us from the top of the world. Since then, we have been here, far from the Ice Giants." Aki pointed to the very far end of the cave, to a castle in black coal, clouds hanging over it. "Now we are closer to you."

My gaze fell upon a figure with long white hair and a black dress. Vita. Their protector. The wise woman who brought medicine from another world. Their *kryschia*.

We sat there together, the three of us side by side, as the woman sang. The fire had died to embers by then, and a freezing wind blew down from the mountaintop. When the fire was gone, and the song faded to silence, the three of us stood and left the grotto together.

Aki and Ciba's hut was dark when we arrived. We slipped

inside and soon Aki had a fire going in the fireplace. It burned weakly, throwing dull light over the bearskins strewn over the stone floor. As the flames grew, I saw that the hut was furnished with a wood-framed bed, a wooden table and chairs, a shelf made of knotted birch logs, some wooden boxes, and a stack of blankets. The walls were bare, and there were no embellishments, but it seemed sturdy and, as the fire warmed the air, and the smell of burning cedar filled the hut, more comfortable than the large, drafty rooms of the castle.

I warmed myself by the fire. Seeing that I was cold, Ciba brought me a wool blanket, and wrapped it over my shoulders. I had eaten well and drank too much wine. Soon, I lay down on the bearskin and fell asleep.

I jolted awake at the sound of voices. Ciba and Aki sat together at the table talking. I tried to sit, and a rush of pain flooded through me. Everything hurt. The pills had worn off, leaving me sore and aching. The sensation began at the base of my skull and spread, warm and fluid as blood, leaving me dizzy. My vision blurred, and so I focused on the table, on Aki and Ciba.

How distant Bert Monte seemed to me then. How far from her I had traveled. It had happened in small steps, each one tiny in itself but—when I looked back at myself from the vantage of how far I had come—staggering in its distance. My old life was gone, burned to ashes, and there was nothing left ahead but these strange people and endless vistas of ice. All the pressure of the past months collected in my chest, heavy as a rock, pressing down, pressing hard, until I could not breathe. Panic, swift and electric, moved through me. My skin moistened with sweat. My breath quickened. The room spun around and around and around. I gasped for air, buried my face in my hands, and sobbed with fear.

I was dimly aware of movement from the table, and then Ciba pressed a jug of water into my hands. I recognized the jug—its pattern was the same as Dolores's china in the salon, the Bavarian farm scene with roosters painted in French blue, a gift from Vita, like so much else. It was a small thing, but seeing this familiar object, this human object, calmed me. I drank the water, my hands trembling. Ciba was clearly worried and gestured for me to drink more. In the face of her kindness I began to cry.

Ciba squatted down onto the fur, the weight of her stomach ready to topple her. She took my head between her hands and looked at me, her large brown eyes warm and reassuring. She wiped the tears from my cheeks and spoke to me. I didn't know what she said, but her voice was soft, maternal, and while she was younger than me, I was comforted in a way I had not felt since my mother died.

THIRTY-TWO

✦

For the rest of the spring and into the summer, I remained in Aki and Ciba's stone hut. Vita, and the castle, felt far away. I slept on the bear fur, warmed by the fire and a thin wool blanket. I ate with them at their makeshift table, walked with them on the trails above the village to gather mushrooms and nuts, worked in their garden, and slowly—over the course of many weeks—became part of their lives.

At the same time each day, Ciba, Aki, and I walked with the others to the hot spring, where we bathed together. They were a ritualistic group, so set in their ways that their patterns never changed. There was not a day without foraging or tending the garden. Never a day without going to the hot spring. Never a day without meeting in the grotto to feast and sing. They lived simply, without the comforts of modern life, but also without its anxieties. If it rained, they faced the tempest without question, their wet bodies tattooed by flashes of lightning. When it was hot, they stripped down, and their pale skin burned to blisters. They faced the sun and the snow and the rain with relentless heartiness, their bodies adapted to survive the brutality of nature.

At the grotto, we roasted whatever had been caught that day—rabbit or deer or ibex or marmot—and ate together before the fire. Over time, the others lost their wariness of me. Jabi stopped glaring at me. The children—three girls and a boy—were no longer afraid to approach me. I cooked with the Icemen and ate with them. I hunted with them and tended the garden with them. Ciba spoke to me in her language as though I understood it and gradually, after weeks of confusion, I began to recognize a word here, a word there, then more and more.

Some nights, I replayed the lineage that connected me to them, moving back in time, from me, to my father, to Giovanni to Vita, Vita to Ambrose, Ambrose to Vittorio, Vittorio to Leopold, and then, like a stream guttering into a river, this tribe. I imagined Leopold sitting with us, Zyana at his side, eating from the communal bowl. I was falling in love with these people as Leopold had fallen in love with them so many generations before.

In those moments of happiness, with my skin hot from the fire and the sky a sheet of stars, I thought of Luca, freezing under this same sky. We were so small, so insignificant, compared to the galaxies shimmering beyond, so powerless to change the realities of nature. And yet, such beauty, such marvelous beauty, was a tonic to our suffering. I hoped that Luca had died with the stars blazing above him, and that their cold beauty had given him comfort at the end.

MOST MORNINGS, I worked in the garden. I weeded the plants and carried water in a bucket from a stream and poured it over the rows of carrots and turnips and melons. The soil was rocky, and—at that altitude—the climate less than ideal, with the sun emerging only in spurts of warmth from behind the mountain peaks. And yet, by some feat of adaptation to the elements, these vegetables were coming in by the basketful. When we cooked them in the fire at night, they tasted unlike any vegetables I had ever tasted before. They were varieties that had grown from ancient seeds—roots and tubers and gourds that had adapted to the thin air and cold nights, hard apple-like fruits that tasted tart on my tongue. During the late summer, with so many vegetables, we had no need for meat. We didn't stop hunting, but with such an abundance of food, we cured and hung the carcasses in a cave near the grotto, in the deepest, coolest recess, where it was to be stored for the winter. I did not plan to be there when the meat was eaten. I told myself I would be gone before winter came, when the ice and wind would be bone-chilling and brutal.

I would miss the children most of all. There was Oryni, a boy of around seven years old, and three girls: Xyra, of a similar age to Oryni, and Laya and Saba, girls of about five or six. They sought me out, and I played games with them—hot potato with rocks, hide-and-seek, rock-paper-scissors. I spoke to them in English, and their minds were quick, so that by the end of the summer they spoke well enough to communicate with me. They gathered around me when I was in the garden, and sat near me in the hot spring, and squatted nearby as the fire blazed in the grotto. I told them stories about the world beyond the mountains, about cars and planes and ships. They wanted to know how my kind lived, and I would describe what I had done each day, when I lived in New York. My house was a wonder to them. My jobs. My school. We would sit talking for hours and hours. I would feed them and wash them and comb their hair. I would pick wild berries from the bushes above the village and carry them to the children in my hands. I would mend their clothes, cut their fingernails, remove ticks from folds of skin. When I didn't know a word in their language, they taught me.

I never knew which of the Icemen were their parents. The community raised them together, as Leopold's notes had described. The children belonged to everyone. I felt they belonged to me.

One afternoon, as I left the hut, I saw Oryni playing near the stream. He wore a bright-green T-shirt with a cartoon on the front, something manufactured that had come from my world. I walked to the stream to get a closer look. It was not only a cartoon, but a T-shirt advertising a children's festival. I read the German printed across the top of the shirt: KINDER-THEATERFESTIVAL 2012.

I caught my breath. There were many manufactured objects in the village. The medicines and plastic boxes in Uma's hut, for example, had all been made below, in a factory, by human hands. The sturdy boots that Aki wore hunting, his bow and arrow, the sharp butcher knife he used to slaughter his kill—these objects had been gifts from the castle, too. But this T-shirt could not have been brought in with our supplies. It was from a local festival in Germany in 2012. The year Greta had come to Montebianco Castle with her son, Joseph.

I complimented Oryni on the shirt. He ran his hand over it, smiling with pride. His teeth were decayed, crooked, in need of major dental care, but all I could see was the T-shirt. The character was a green dragon with batlike wings and a huge grin. The word "Tabaluga" was written across the dragon's body. "Where did you get this?" I asked in his language. He gestured for me to follow him, and we walked along the stream, past the garden, past Uma's hut, to the stone structure where the children slept.

Inside, there were four beds, one for each child. Oryni took a wooden box from under his bed. There was a pair of blue tennis shoes, a winter jacket, a yellow knitted hat, some gloves. I turned the clothes in my hands. They were all about the same size. The labels were written in German. I knew without a doubt that they had belonged to Joseph. My heart sunk as I realized that all the hope Greta had held for her son had been for nothing. Joseph had been here. And he had never returned.

BY THE END of the summer, Ciba was my constant companion. It was the last month of her pregnancy, or so I guessed. She didn't know when she had become pregnant, and Uma did not keep a record of the weeks that had passed. But it was clear that a shift had taken place—Ciba's legs had swollen and she had trouble walking up the path to the hot spring. She struggled to do simple things, like wash her clothes in the stream or make tea on the fire, and she was tired most of the time. She would curl up on the bed in the hut, her hair twisted over her body, and fall asleep for hours at a time.

Ciba's skin had become even more pale, if that was possible, dark circles forming under her eyes. I suspected she had become anemic. With all the medicine in Uma's hut, there were no vitamins, no iron pills, nothing to ensure she had proper nutrition. To make matters worse, she was too tired to walk far from the hut and was beginning to lose her appetite. Aki and I brought her a bowl of food from the grotto each night. She would eat a few bites and smile with gratitude, before turning over and falling asleep.

I was skeptical of Uma's ability to care for Ciba. The entire scope of the Icemen's prenatal care involved herbal teas, bathing in the hot spring, and extra food. I explained the kind of care a woman would receive below, the vitamins, the sonograms, the blood work to check for iron deficiency, the tests for high blood pressure, but Aki and Ciba had no idea what I was talking about.

Once, when Ciba was particularly weak, I told Aki we should bring Ciba down the mountain, to the castle. Greta would take care of her, and I could get her proper medical care, bring a doctor to look at her. I could get her vitamins and iron supplements at the very least. Aki only looked at me with his large, cool gaze, a gaze that contained the history of suffering and isolation his people had endured, and I knew that it was impossible. Ciba could not be seen by anyone below. Bringing her to my world would compromise her life. It would compromise all of them. This was the true dilemma of the Icemen. Not the harsh conditions of the mountain, not the lack of technology or medicine, not even their dwindling population. There was no place for them below. My kind had made sure of that. To survive, they must hide.

On evenings when Ciba felt strong, we ate together in the hut. Aki did not alter his routine and ate with the others in the grotto, often returning after we slept. And so we laid out bowls of food by the fire, sat on the bearskin, and did our best to communicate, speaking in fragments of her language I had picked up from the children. We spoke with gestures and laughter, and while there was much that was lost, I felt close to her even in the absence of understanding. We would drink herbal tea Uma had brought to soothe Ciba's discomfort, and I would tell her about my life before I had come to their village. My parents. My town. My school. She wanted to know more about Luca—had I loved him? Did we have a child? Did I want a child? For the first time, I expressed how bereft my inability to have a child had left me, how I wanted to hold a baby in my arms and see life flash in its eyes. Ciba put her arms around me, comforting me, heartbroken by my loss, as if it were her own.

Uma came every day to check on Ciba. She would sit with us and translate when we couldn't understand each other. It was on one of Uma's visits, a night when the air buzzed with the sound of birds and mosquitoes outside the window, that I tried to tell Ciba that we were related by blood. We sat at the table, the three of us, drinking tea and eating purple radishes Uma had brought from the garden. I told Ciba that Leopold and Zyana had had two children together, one of whom went down the mountain and another who stayed in the village.

"I am the descendant of the first child," I said, biting into a radish. "And you are a descendant of the second child."

After a full minute of silence, Uma said, "Why does this matter?"

I was totally unprepared for the question. My relationship to the people who came before me—to my parents, to my grandparents—had always seemed so important. "Because it connects us," I said weakly. "By blood."

"Leopold spoke to our ancestors about this connection," Uma said. "He taught us the importance of blood. But we do not care about the blood between us. We are one tribe."

I pointed to Ciba's eyes. "You see her brown eyes? They are the same as Leopold's. She is his descendant. She is connected to him, whether she wants to be or not. And so am I. This inheritance connects us. It makes us family."

Ciba and Uma discussed this. Finally, Uma said, "This is not our way. Who is born here is family. Who we feed and care for is family. There was an elder who taught me when I was very young. His name was Gregor and he was not born to our tribe, but he lived with us and became my teacher. My mother and father created me, but I am not my mother and father. I am not my grandparents. I am Uma, part of our tribe. And you, who are different from us, are part of this tribe, too."

I sat with them, trying to imagine Gregor, Nonna Sophia's brother, living among them. It didn't matter that he had been different; he was part of their tribe. Everything that had brought me to Nevenero, everything that had taken me to the Icemen, seemed suddenly secondary to this simple truth. Those who came before us, with their family names and genetic legacies, with their physical peculiarities, whether it be albino skin or brown eyes—none of this mattered. Family was who we loved and who we protected. Family was the tribe we created here and now.

THIRTY-THREE

✦

I WAS WORKING IN the garden when Aki and Jabi brought the new child to the village. They slid through the narrow crack in the mountain and carried her to the huts. The child was crying, and the others must have heard her voice, too. They gathered around her, just as they had months before when I had arrived. I followed them, joining the others to see who Aki and Jabi had found.

It was a girl, perhaps seven or eight years old. Aki held her in his arms, carrying her close. It was clear that she was terrified. She trembled, her face pressed to Aki's chest. He hoisted her up, showing her to all who had gathered at the entrance, as if she were some kind of trophy, and I saw she had been injured. Her arm hung limp. Her jeans were soaked with blood.

"Her parents called her Anna." Aki said the word with difficulty, as if it stung his tongue. "She was on the other side of the mountain. On a hiking path with her parents."

"She's hurt," I said, my gaze falling to her bloody clothes.

"She struggled," Aki said, glancing down at the girl. "She fell."

"Give her to me," I said, gesturing for her. "I'll bring her to Uma."

Anna had red hair and pale, freckled skin. She glanced at me furtively, her green eyes red from crying. She trembled as

I carried her to the medical hut. I whispered to her that everything would be okay, that she shouldn't worry, that I would
help her. She spoke Italian, I assumed, maybe German or
French, but I hoped the tone of my voice would soothe her.
She listened to me, her eyes wide, but said nothing.

Uma met us at the door, and seeing Anna in my arms,
gestured to a cot, where I lay the girl down, placing her arm
on a folded blanket. Uma cut away Anna's shirt with a pair of
scissors, revealing the damage. Her arm was fractured. The
bone had broken through the skin, leaving a bloody wound
the size of an apple on her forearm. Uma examined it from a
number of angles, and Anna whimpered with pain. Uma instructed me to crush some pills and dissolve them in water.
But when I brought the cup to Anna, she wouldn't drink.

"She is lucky it is just her arm," Uma said. "Aki is not very
careful."

I understood, then, that finding Anna had been no accident. Aki and Jabi had taken her, just as I suspected they had
taken Joseph and Nonna Sophia's brother, Gregor. Maybe
she had been hiking in the mountains with her parents, playing near the trees, when Aki and Jabi found her. I imagined
Aki and Jabi had watched her, waiting for her parents to turn
away for a minute. I never learned the details of how they stole
the children. I never asked Aki about their methods. And I
didn't know if they targeted certain villages—as they had
Nevenero—or if they took the children randomly, from the
ski resorts and hiking trails, one child here, another there, so
that the disappearances would not cause too much attention.
I only knew that Vita had been wrong. Children went missing.
The Icemen took them and brought them to the village. But
if this was the case, where were they? What had happened to
them?

Uma gestured for me to hold Anna down as she set the arm, cracking the bone quickly into place. Anna screamed and kicked, then collapsed in tears, sobbing in my arms as Uma lay a piece of wood on the wound, making a splint, and wrapped a bandage around it. When she had finished, Uma brought a clean tunic and a blanket, gesturing for me to dress the girl.

I sang softly, trying to soothe Anna. The songs were children's songs I knew from my own childhood, lullabies, as if she were a baby. My voice calmed her a little. She lay in bed, tears rolling down her cheeks, but she didn't fight when I gave her the pain medication.

After she drank it down, I stood to go. "No," she said, her voice filled with fear. "Don't leave me."

I started at the sound of my language.

"You speak English?"

She nodded, pale and terrified, her skin slicked cold with sweat. "I want to go back to my parents," she said, gazing up at me with tear-filled eyes.

"I know you do," I said. "Don't be scared. I'll help you."

I took her hand and squeezed it. This time, she didn't flinch. She held my hand. She met my eyes. "Stay with me," she said, and I understood that she trusted no one but me. She was so afraid, so vulnerable, that I couldn't bear it. A surge of anger overtook me. Aki had done this. And Vita—how could she have been unaware of this? When we sat together in her rooms, she had said that she didn't believe that the Icemen were capable of harming children. She believed that Joseph had been taken by his father. But I was certain, standing in Uma's hut, an injured child before me, that she was wrong.

Shooting a wary look toward Uma, who stood at the far end of the hut, Anna whispered, "Are they monsters?"

Our eyes met. "They are people," I said. "Like us."

She narrowed her green eyes, as if weighing what I said with what she had witnessed. "No," she whispered. "They are not like us."

"They won't hurt you."

She looked down at her arm, proving me wrong.

"That was an accident."

"Don't leave me with them," she said. "Please."

I sat by Anna's side until she fell asleep. I found a blanket and covered her, so that she would be warm. "I will help you," I whispered in her ear, wiping the sweat from her brow. "I promise."

It was not long after Anna's arrival that Ciba went to stay in Uma's hut. She had been having mild contractions, slow and irregular, for days. Uma was sure the baby would come any moment and wanted to keep her close by. "It is rare, to have a baby that survives," Uma told me, after Ciba was settled on a cot. Ciba was asleep, and she wouldn't have understood us, even if she had been awake, but I found myself whispering.

"This baby is healthy, though," I said. "It kicks all the time."

It was true—the baby could kick so hard Ciba's stomach would jolt. It thumped rhythmically, which led to Aki calling the baby their little rabbit. One night, Aki and I sat with Ciba, and Aki had put his hand on her stomach and the baby had pushed against his palm. "Is it a girl or a boy?" I had asked. "It is a boy," Ciba said, smiling with confidence. She was absolutely sure. "We will name him Sibi."

That night, after Ciba fell asleep, Aki and I walked to the grotto, where the tribe sat around the fire. Aki brought us cups of sour wine and a bowl of roasted carrots. I took a sip of the wine, remembering the rush of pleasure I had once taken in drinking—my gin hangovers, my addiction to genepy after my surgery, all the bottles of wine I had taken from the Montebianco cellar. I hadn't made a decision to stop drinking and yet, since I had arrived in the village, I had no interest in losing myself in that way anymore.

Aki gazed up at cave paintings. I loved the drawings. The Icemen may not have articulated time as we did, but they had recorded the history of their tribe, all the stories of men and women who had struggled to survive in that remote, un-known crevice in the mountains. Aki pointed to a cluster of pictures that showed a man with black hair: Leopold.

"When he arrived," Aki said, "the Icemen tried to kill him. We had never allowed such a man to enter our village before. We did not want him here. He was beaten and held in one of the caves of the arcade, left without food or water, to die. We were afraid of him, and all his kind. You did not know we existed, but our kind had watched you for hundreds of years. We knew you were more powerful than us. You had developed machines and weapons. We knew you grew food and manufactured clothes. And Leopold looked different from us. He carried objects that we had never seen before. A gun. Books. He spoke a language we could not understand."

Aki drank his wine down. He looked at my cup, full in my hand. I gave it to him.

"But Zyana, a direct descendant of the Ice Giants, a fearless woman, went to see Leopold. She found that he was not dan-gerous, as the others had believed. She taught him our language and she learned his. She insisted that this man was not so different from us. With time, she fell in love with this dark man. He began to teach her the ways of your kind. She called him *kryschia*.

"At first, we did not accept him. But soon, he spoke our language very well and explained himself to us. He was very"—Aki stopped to find the correct word—"*critical* about your kind. He told us about war. He explained what happened when one group of people dominated another group. With time, we came to understand he was our friend. We freed him. After this, Leopold and Zyana were happy. They had children. Healthy and strong children. This was a great joy for my kind. We were weak in those years. When a child was born, it was often small and sick. Sometimes a baby would live for a few days. Sometimes, it died later, after a year or two. Few grew to be men and women. Our population became smaller every year. *Kryschia* saw this. He examined all of us and said that we were in danger. He was a wise man. He told us what we needed to do to survive. We had lived too long in isolation, he said. The mountains protected us from outsiders, but such protection would also kill us. We must find others, he said. Find people different from us and mix their blood with our blood. It seemed very strange to us, who had always known only our tribe, but we trusted him. We did as he said. We wanted our children to be strong and healthy, like your children. Leopold taught us to go down the mountain, to the villages. Not only near the castle, but farther away, many days' walk. We found children and we brought them here."

"Like Anna?" I asked.

He nodded. "Yes, like her."

It made sense to me that Leopold would suggest such a thing. He had been a student of the earliest writings on heredity and genetics. The books of natural history in the library—Mendel, Huxley, Darwin—attested to his seriousness, and his field notes were filled with observations about mating and sexual habits and the diminishing population. He must have discerned that the tribe was too small and isolated, and that interbreeding over generations had caused infertility and sickness. He understood that bringing Homo sapiens into the tribe would strengthen it. But to suggest that the Icemen steal children was cruel. How many parents had been thrown into Greta's hell of uncertainty and longing? How many children had longed, like Anna, to go home? The pain such a practice had caused was immeasurable.

"How many children were brought here?" I asked at last.

"Many," he said, looking at me with a curious expression. He saw how his story upset me. I remembered everything Nonna Sophia had told me—people waking with their children gone, the village filled with terror. But even as I understood what the Icemen had done, I felt a small, niggling doubt: If these children had been integrated into the population, and grew up to mate with the Icemen, why didn't the Icemen look more like me? Why was Ciba the single person with brown eyes?

"Your population hasn't grown," I said. "It has only declined since Leopold was here."

He flinched, as if I had struck him. "Do not doubt us," he said. "One day there will be many children. And they will be strong, like Leopold and Zyana's children. Like the children of your people."

Because I had grown to care about Aki and Ciba, and because I had come to see the Icemen not as a foreign tribe but as my own people, I wanted this to be true.

I WENT TO Uma's hut the next afternoon, took Ciba by the arm and led her along a flat path near the village, where blackberry bushes grew wild. Uma thought walking would help relieve Ciba's discomfort. She had been in pain all morning, the pressure of the baby pressing into her organs so that she couldn't sleep.

It was a beautiful summer day. The sky was blue and the bushes bursting with berries. The plan was to find a shady spot and sit together. Ciba hadn't had fresh air for days.

The path was not far from the village. We could have filled our sack with berries and been back to the hut in a few minutes. But the blackberries were fat with juice, so ripe that they dropped with a brush of a finger, and we lingered. We ate as many as we collected. I held a leather sack open and Ciba shook a branch, sending a rain of berries down, until the sack was full. My fingernails were stained black. Sweet purple juice had tinted Ciba's lips, creating a stark contrast to her pale skin. In the past week, she had swelled. Capillaries had burst under her eyes, giving her a mask of bruises. She smiled and looked ghoulish. I reached out and took her hand in mine, to help her along the path.

It felt good to be there with Ciba, to feel her weight against me as we walked. She had been inside the stone hut for days and days, lying on the bed, doing nothing but sleeping and eating. It struck me that this stolen moment of sun and friendship was the first moment of pleasure Ciba had experienced in weeks, and I hoped it would give her a respite before the baby arrived, for it was sure to come soon. Two days before, Uma had examined Ciba and said the birth could happen anytime. At night I woke every few hours to check on her. If waiting was excruciating for me, I could only imagine how Ciba felt.

Ciba stopped near a birch tree, took a labored breath, and walked on. Sweat soaked through her white tunic. Her hair clung to her forehead and neck. The baby both anchored and unmoored her. It was misery, I thought, carrying a child. The heaviness and discomfort of it should have driven any woman away. And yet, the inconveniences of pregnancy—the bloated breasts, the swollen ankles, the body distorting under the weight of a new life—didn't detract from the magic of what was happening. Ciba would experience something I could not, and although I understood she would suffer, I felt a pang of jealously at this gift.

I was thinking this when the first wave of pain stopped Ciba cold. She bent over and groaned. As another contraction came, she clutched my arm so that her nails dug deep into my skin. I helped her stand, urging her to walk with me back to the village, but she couldn't move. I could feel her shaking against me. Another contraction came, and she doubled over again, clutching at me as she groaned with pain. I steered her back to the path, and we were making our way down to the village, when fluid slid over her bare legs. The baby was coming, and I needed to get her back to Uma, but another contraction came, then another, each one stronger than the one before, and soon Ciba was unable to walk at all. She fell against a birch tree, clinging to it. She panted and sobbed, trying to breathe. The baby was coming.

"Uma," she gasped.

I looked past her, toward the village. It was so close I could see the slate roofs. If I ran, I could be back in a few minutes. But a lot could happen in those minutes.

"There isn't time," I said. "I'll stay and help you."

She whimpered as another contraction shook through her. "Go," she said, her eyes filling with tears. "Please."

I ran to the village as fast as I could. Aki wasn't in the hut, but I found Uma right away, and soon we were running back up the path, rotting blackberries staining the ground. I heard Ciba cry out ahead. Every second seemed long and distended, thick as a minute. When we finally made it back, Ciba wasn't where I left her. She had crawled into the blackberry bushes, where she lay on a bed of crushed berries. She was giving birth. I heard her sharp breathing and her cries of pain.

Uma turned to me. "Water," she said. "Go back to my hut. Bring water and towels, a needle and thread. There is a scalpel. Get that, too."

I ran to the village again, collected the towels, found the scalpel in Uma's supplies, filled a jar with water, grabbed the sewing kit, and ran back up the path. I hadn't wasted a second, but as I reached the blackberry bushes, I knew something was terribly wrong. Ciba was still. There was blood everywhere. Pooled over the berries, around Ciba's legs. Soaked into her tunic. Blood on Uma's hands. Blood. Blood. So much blood that my stomach turned. There had not been nearly so much blood during the birth of my son.

I squatted at Ciba's side. I took her hand. "Ciba," I said. *Ciba. Ciba.* I said her name over and over. She didn't move. She didn't respond. I shook her shoulders, touched her forehead, tried everything I could to reach her. Her eyes were fixed open, and she stared up into the blue sky, lifeless.

Tears filled my eyes, so that the blood seemed to swirl at my feet, a hot magma burning around us. I had to leave. I couldn't see her that way another moment. My heart would break. I couldn't bear to see another dead baby.

That is when I saw it: a tiny foot. Bloody, thick with tissue, the foot was flat and wide, with a hooked second toe. The baby had arrived feetfirst, which had caused the problem. I put my hand on Ciba's arm, to steady myself, when, to my astonishment, the tiny foot twitched. A delicate toe flexed. I caught my breath. Ciba had died, but the baby was still alive.

Uma jumped up and grabbed the scalpel. I watched, frozen with disbelief, as the blade sliced into Ciba's abdomen, cutting through skin and muscle. The incision was wide, gaping. Blood spilled through the cut, over Uma's fingers. I looked to Ciba's face, half expecting an expression of pain, but it was waxen and still. Uma peeled Ciba's body open like the skin of a fruit and, pulling gently, removed the baby from her body.

Uma poured water over the baby, washing the blood away. It was not a boy, as Ciba had predicted, but a girl. A beautiful girl, white-skinned and shriveled, stunned to silence by light and atmosphere. Uma gave her to me and I held her close. She was warm and still, watchful. She didn't cry, only blinked in the sunlight. Then she turned her gaze to me, and I saw that this little being was a miracle, a creation so perfect that I couldn't help but believe her to be the highest expression of all who had come before her.

Something in my mind shifted, and I recalled Eleanor's account of Vita's birth—the monstrous teeth, the exposed spine. I couldn't help but remember my own child, dead in my arms, its body covered with hair, the sweet expression on its monstrous face. I looked for signs of these deformities in the baby. She had none of them—the spine was straight. The skin hairless. The only evidence of her lineage was the albino coloring and her large, flat feet with the hooked second toes. Soon, she would be hungry. Soon, she would need more than my arms. But at that moment, as we stood there together, the baby taking her first breaths, she only needed me.

I wrapped the baby in a towel, grabbed the leather sack stained with Ciba's blood, and walked back to the village to show Aki his daughter.

THIRTY-FOUR

❧

WHEN I BROUGHT the baby to Aki, he looked at her with a coldness that chilled me. We stood at the center of the village, the baby not an hour old, so new to the world that she struggled to open her eyes. I offered him the baby, but he would not touch her. He would not look at her. Ciba's death had made the child invisible to him.

"What will you name her?" I asked.

"Ciba must name her," he said, without meeting my eye. "It is our tradition that the mother chooses the name."

"But Ciba can't name her," I said. "Ciba is gone. You have to do it."

Aki looked so forlorn, so lost with grief, that I said nothing more. I understood that his silence was not indifference, but his way of expressing the pain he felt over losing Ciba. His rejection of his daughter was an act of mourning, one that took the opposite form of my own grief: I wanted to spend every minute with the baby. Ciba had given her life for this child, and I would care for her as if she were my own.

I named her Isabelle. If the tribe called her something different, I never knew it. Aki could not bear to have her near, and so Isabelle slept in Uma's hut, in a wooden box lined with fur. In her first days of life, I spent every minute with her, anxious that she would fall sick. I wrapped her tight in a blanket, so that she felt warm and secure, and held her close to me when she cried. I watched for signs of illness. She was strong at birth, and remained healthy for the first days, but soon began to grow weak. She needed nutrition, and there was no milk. Uma soaked a towel with warm goat's milk and put it to Isabelle's lips, but she wouldn't take it. She began to grow thin.

"There is no other way," Uma said, gesturing to my breast. "You are her mother now. You must feed her or she will die."

Uma lifted my tunic and positioned Isabelle at my breast, guiding the tiny mouth to my nipple. "You love this child," she said. "You will keep her alive." Of course, it wasn't possible to feed Isabelle. When I said as much, Uma replied, "It *is* possible. I have seen it before. Hold her. Sing to her. Keep her at your breast. Milk will come."

At Uma's urging, I slept on a cot near Isabelle, waking every few hours to bring her to my breast. It was Isabelle's instinct to nurse, and so she latched on and began to suck at my flesh, desperate for milk that did not arrive. She cried with frustration and hunger. It struck me as a futile endeavor. The very idea seemed absurd. Surely, there were hormones and chemicals swirling through a mother's body that I simply did not have. Uma made teas from mountain herbs, and I drank them religiously, but they did nothing. Isabelle would cry, and—more out of desperation than belief—I would try again, praying that Uma was right, and that my body would comply with Isabelle's needs. Some nights, I would hold her for hours at a time, rocking her, as she cried herself to sleep; I would whisper her name when she woke, calming her in my arms, bringing her to my breast. Days passed like this, and Isabelle grew weaker and weaker, her voice becoming no more than a whimper.

I saw her small body diminish, the tiny ribs becoming

visible through her pale skin, her arms and legs like twigs, her tongue dry and white. The horror of watching Isabelle wither cast an ominous shadow over my thoughts. I slept very little, and when I did, I was haunted by dreams of Ciba. Always, in every dream, I lifted Isabelle from Ciba's arms, carrying her away from her mother as if just for a moment, no more than a quick walk around the village. There was no blood. No scalpel. Just a simple exchange—I took Isabelle; Ciba kissed us both and then ran into the blackberry bushes alone. I interpreted this dream as Ciba's blessing to love and protect Isabelle.

One night, I was asleep on the cot, when I heard Isabelle crying. I woke, pulled myself out of bed, and went to her. I was used to waking up every few hours. The thin towels we used for diapers soaked through easily, leaving Isabelle wet and uncomfortable, needing to be changed many times a night. But when I went to the box, Isabelle was not there. I walked through the hut, looking for her, but there was only Anna, asleep at the far side of the room. A slap of fear stopped me cold. I imagined an animal sneaking into the hut, perhaps a wolf, sliding past my cot, taking my child in her teeth, and dragging her away. I understood with a terrible clarity the anguish Greta must have felt upon discovering Joseph missing. I felt a deep, instinctual longing for Isabelle, a physical need to have her against me, to feel the compact warmth of her, to see her hard, glimmering eyes, to hear her pink lips sucking at my body. This longing—this unbreakable connection between me and my child—was stronger than anything I had known before—stronger than hunger, stronger than pain. Even stronger than the loss of my own child. I was not Isabelle's biological mother, but nature had made me her mother anyway.

Isabelle cried again, and I followed the sound outside, just beyond the hut, where she lay cradled in Uma's arms.

"She woke up," Uma said. "You are tired, *Kryschia*. You didn't hear her."

I was so relieved that Isabelle was safe, so exhausted and emotionally unsettled from the weeks of watching her die, that tears came to my eyes. "Give her to me," I said, taking Isabelle in my arms.

But something had caught Uma's eye. She stared at me, her brow furrowed, as if she were not quite sure she could believe what she saw. I looked down and found my tunic wet. My breasts had swollen with milk and leaked. I gasped, overwhelmed by joy and confusion as Uma lifted my tunic and placed Isabelle at my breast. The milk came slowly, but Isabelle was soon full.

For many years after I left the village, I believed that the milk that saved Isabelle was a miracle. How else to explain such an impossible gift? But recently, after doing research online, I found that lactation without pregnancy is not impossible, and that in certain parts of the world where maternal mortality is high, it is still common for an adoptive mother to breastfeed. Certain natural protocols—all of which Uma had known—could produce milk and save a motherless baby.

With regular feeding, Isabelle grew stronger and stronger. But even as Isabelle thrived, Anna drifted further away from the world of the living. I sat by Anna's bedside, Isabelle at my breast, and tried to coax the girl back to health. I told her stories of dragons and princes and castles tucked into the mountains. I sang songs and asked her questions about her parents. But she rarely gave a sign that she heard me. She never smiled and she never spoke. If I brought her food—roasted vegetables and milk from the goats—she refused it. She took a bite or two of meat, if I brought it from the grotto, but it didn't help. She grew thin and pale as she wasted away. If I said her name, she turned away. Her only expression was a solemn, shocked stare, numb and terrified. She grew listless and dull-eyed. I wasn't sure if it was the broken arm or her terror of Uma, but her suffering had slowly begun to undo her.

Uma made medicines from herbs, distillations of mountain flowers and grasses that she gave Anna to drink. They had no effect. By the end of the first month of Isabelle's life, Anna eyes were glassy and unfocused, her skin pale and clammy. When I brought the other children to see her, a flicker of interest played over her face, but when Uma stepped near the bed with water, terror flitted through her eyes and she faded away again. Uma tried her best to heal Anna, but her best wasn't good enough. I knew Anna would not live long unless I got her real medical attention.

THIRTY-FIVE

✦

I WOKE IN A panic, Isabelle's cries ringing in my ears. I looked around the hut, ready to comfort her, but I had only imagined the crying. She slept soundly in her wooden box, a finger in her mouth. I pulled a blanket over her to shield her from the cool night air, when I saw that Uma's and Anna's beds were empty.

Possible explanations flooded my mind—Anna had been nauseated and Uma had brought her outside for fresh air; Anna had to go to the bathroom and left the hut. But I knew that these scenarios were unlikely. Anna had been too sick to leave her bed. She couldn't lift an arm, let alone walk. And besides, it was the middle of the night, the sky black and moonless—not the moment for Uma to take Anna outside. A sensation of dread filled my mind. Something terrible had happened.

Carefully, so as not to wake her, I wrapped Isabelle in a blanket and walked outside, wandering through the darkness in search of Uma. But a strange silence met me as I walked through the village. The stone huts were dark and quiet and, as I peered into them, one by one, I saw that they were all empty. In fact, the entire village was empty. Not a voice to be heard. Not a fire burning in the fire pits. Not a person asleep in her bed. I held Isabelle close, feeling her warmth, smelling the sweet odor of her skin, wondering what to do next.

I was on my way back to the hut when I smelled something odd in the air. An acrid scent, like burning pine. Then a noise from above, a low rhythmic humming, half song, half moan. I strained to hear it, half believing it to be the distant bellow of an injured animal. But the more I listened, the more I knew that this strange sound was not an animal. It was not the wind. It was the low, rumbling vibration of human voices. The Icemen had gathered together and they were singing.

Holding the baby close to my body, I climbed the long, steep path to the hot spring, then beyond, to the grotto, its wall of crystals shimmering black in the darkness. The tribe was not there but somewhere above, where the evergreen trees thinned to rock and sky. I had never climbed beyond the grotto, and it took some time to find my way through the tangled branches of trees, but I followed the sound of voices, and soon the air thickened with skeins of gray smoke. Finally, holding Isabelle tight, I hoisted myself over the ledge of a rocky promontory and emerged onto the flat of a stone plateau.

I found the tribe gathered around a bonfire. I had been right. Anna was dead, her body laid out on a pallet near the fire. Dressed in animal skins, with wildflowers woven into her hair, she looked more peaceful in death than she had in the weeks I had known her. I felt overwhelmed by regret and sadness. I had promised to take her away from there, and to reunite her with her family, and now it was too late.

I moved closer to the bonfire, transfixed by the spectacle. Half naked and chanting, dancing and drunk and frantic, the Icemen had worked themselves into a kind of fervor. Even the children—Oryni, Laya, Saba, and Xyra, whose hair I brushed and whose clothes I mended, who had taught me their language and treated me like a sister—were wild with a frightful energy. Perhaps demons inhabited me as well, because I couldn't turn away.

"Drink this," Uma said, coming to my side. She gave me a bowl. I took a long sip of a bitter and herbal liquid. A chemical rush moved through me as I finished and gave the bowl back to Uma.

"What are they doing?" I asked, gesturing to the dancing.

"We are calling our ancestors," she said. "We will ask them to take the child."

"You'll bury her up here?"

"After our ancestors accept her," she said, glancing at the bonfire, "she will burn."

My gaze returned to Anna, her long, fine hair gleaming in the light. Tears filled my eyes, tears of sadness, but also of anger. Her death was a terrible crime. I thought of what her parents must feel, never knowing what happened to her. I thought of what Greta felt after losing Joseph. Aki and Jabi had killed this child, and I had allowed it to happen.

"You must never take another child from below," I told Uma. "Speak to the others. Tell them I won't allow it. Tell them it is wrong. If you promise to stop, I will help you survive. I'll bring you medicine and supplies. Everything you need. I promise. But you can never bring another child here."

Uma looked at me, her eyes wide with surprise and, I thought, relief. "I will tell them," she said.

Just then, Aki saw us from across the fire and approached. He had been dancing, and sweat glistened on his skin in the flickering light. "Give her to me," he said, gesturing to the baby. A shot of fear spiked through me, an instinctual need to keep her away from the fire.

Isabelle gazed at Aki with her enormous blue eyes, assessing her father.

"He won't harm her," Uma said, touching my arm. "It is our custom to welcome a child this way."

"Be careful," I said, as Aki scooped her from me. He turned to the others and lifted her into the air, as if making an offering. As they cheered and called out Isabelle's name, Uma took Isabelle from Aki, twirled her around, then handed her to Oryni, who kissed her and gave her to another pair of hands that passed her to another, then another. In this fashion, Isabelle made her way around the fire, moving from person to person, shared between the tribe like one of the bowls of meat in the grotto.

I watched her rise and fall with their movements, alarmed by her proximity to the fire, ready to pull her away if she was in danger, but also moved by the tenderness with which each member of the tribe held her. They cherished her, this new member of their community, treated her as something precious and rare. I tried to imagine what her life would be like there, among the Icemen, playing in the hot spring with the other children, or feasting in the grotto, but I couldn't. Isabelle was not my flesh and blood, and Aki and his tribe had more right to raise her than I, and yet I felt a deep, maternal need to save her from them. With Anna lying dead at my feet, and the number of their children who survived into adulthood being so few, the very idea of giving Isabelle over to them seemed, suddenly, a terrible risk.

What happened next seems incredible, and even now, after so much time has passed, I struggle to find the words to explain it. There are evenings, when Isabelle is asleep in her room and I am alone by the fire, that I try to reconstruct the madness of the tribal dance and the chanting, the clapping and stomping, the serenity of Anna's frozen features bearing down on me, but the memories turn through me like a cyclone, whirling and whirling, so that, try as I might, I cannot see it clearly. I could blame it on the drink Uma had given me, and it is possible that some hallucinogenic herb altered my senses, twisting my vision so that I saw and felt what I did. But if I am honest with myself, I know that what I saw that night was real.

It began as a wisp of smoke from the fire, the slightest tendril of movement. I thought it was the heat distorting the air, or perhaps the wind in my eyes. But then, the smoke coalesced, and a figure stepped from the flames, a man dressed in clothes of another era—a brown suit and a white silk cravat. It was Leopold, his face as saturnine as the picture in the portrait gallery. I stared, awed by this vision, when his parents, Alberta and Amadeo, appeared by his side, and then their parents. The twins, Guillaume and Giovanni, and my great-great-grandparents Eleanor and Ambrose, and then the first Montebiancos, Frederick and Isabelle. My parents appeared from the smoke, and then my grandmother Marta, but when I stepped to them, they slipped through my hands. There were others I didn't recognize, the ancestors of Aki and Uma and Jabi and Isabelle, the ancient human beings who had lived and died in those mountains, the Ice Giants who banished the Icemen from their palaces. They stood together, joining the circle around Anna. They had come, I understood, to bless us.

And while our reunion was brief, and they faded into the fire as quickly as they had emerged, I knew, as they vanished in the half-light, that they were not gone. I carried them in my body. My ancestors lived in my bones and in my blood, in the connections of my nervous system, and in the unreachable recesses of my consciousness. They would always be with me, even when I was far away from that mountain. From the moment I was born, they had accompanied me through life. And when I died, I would join them again.

With the voices of my ancestors in my ears, and their blessing in my heart, I took Isabelle in my arms and—leaving the others to their delirious dance—held my daughter close and slipped away, gone before anyone knew we had left the village of the Icemen.

THIRTY-SIX

✤

V ITA HAD BEEN so ill when I left that I half expected to find the northeast tower empty upon my return. But when I arrived, a fire smoldered in the fireplace, and Greta stood by Vita's bedside, pouring one of Bernadette's herbal remedies into a spoon.

"Madame!" Greta said, looking from me to Isabelle wrapped in a blanket in my arms.

"Is that Alberta?" Vita said. Her voice was weak, and she didn't have the strength to lift herself up in bed, but it wasn't too late: she was alive. "Alberta? Is that you?"

"There's someone I would like you to meet," I said. Walking close to the bed, I held Isabelle before Vita. "This is Isabelle. Aki's daughter. She is a descendant of Leopold."

"What a beauty," Vita said, her eyes alight with pride.

Greta looked at the baby, startled, and turned to go, but I stopped her. "Wait a minute, Greta," I said, feeling all the sadness of what I was about to tell her. "There is something you need to know."

"What is it, madame?"

I pulled out the green Kindertheaterfestival T-shirt I had found in the village and gave it to her. She gasped with recognition. "He wore this the day he went missing," she said. "Where did you find it, madame?"

"In the mountains," I said softly.

"The mountains," Greta echoed, scrunching the T-shirt into a ball in her hands. "Where in the mountains?"

"Far from here," I said, tears coming to my eyes as I watched her take in the meaning of this, her expression changing from hope to despair.

"Joseph is not coming back," she said, "is he?"

Isabelle shifted in my arms, opened her eyes long enough to see that I was there, and fell back to sleep. "No, he's not," I said. "I'm so sorry."

Greta sat on the bench near the fire and sobbed, and I found myself crying, too, crying for Joseph and Anna, crying for my own sweet Isabelle, who would never know her mother and father, crying for Luca, who would never meet my child. Greta was overcome by sorrow, but she wasn't alone in her sadness. It was all of ours to bear.

"I'm going to be leaving the castle with Isabelle," I said at last. "I'll need help. Can you come with me?"

Greta looked to Vita. "But what about my work here?"

"Your work here is done," Vita said. "Bernadette will tend to me."

"Then I will go," Greta said, her voice unsteady and her eyes red from crying. "Gladly."

"I plan to leave as soon as possible," I said, giving Vita a challenging look, daring her to stop me. "If you could pack our things, I will ask Sal to drive us down the mountain today."

"Yes, madame," Greta said, turning to the door.

As she passed the fireplace, Vita said, "Bring me that box on the mantel before you leave." Greta lifted a wooden box with copper trim and carried it to Vita. "Thank you, Greta," she said, raising her eyes. "For everything."

"Pleasure, madame," Greta whispered, and hurried from the room.

I had intended to confront Vita after Greta left. My anger about Joseph's death and the lies she told about the children the Icemen had taken had enraged me. But when we were alone, I found that all my anger and indignation had drained away, leaving nothing but sadness.

"You are upset with me," Vita said, watching me with narrowed eyes.

"I'm devastated," I said. "All those children, Vita. They were not strong enough to survive the cold. It was all for nothing."

"I didn't know they took Joseph," she said, lowering her eyes. "They had access to the castle, and they must have taken him. But I didn't know. I wouldn't have allowed it."

"I won't let anything happen to Isabelle," I said. "That is for sure."

"Ah, then you have become a *kryschia* after all," she said, smiling weakly. "There is something you must see before you leave."

Vita opened the wooden box. Inside, there were notes of currency, bundles and bundles of francs and liras held together with string, outdated currency that she would never be able to spend. Digging below a stack of franc notes, she removed an envelope and gave it to me. The letter was addressed to Vittoria Montebianco and had been postmarked from Milton, New York. The name and return address was that of my grandfather, Giovanni Montebianco.

May 14, 1957

Chere Maman,

Marta has urged me to write a letter of reconciliation. She believes that, if nothing else, such a gesture will relieve the pain of our final unhappy encounter. She sees that I suffer from our altercation and, quite honestly, she is correct. I am alone, so very alone, in this foreign place. Losing my fortune, my birthright, my home, my mother and my brother, has left me bereft. And while I hold no illusion that a single missive can heal what has transpired, I do believe that there is the chance you will listen to me and alter the terrible commitment you have made to our ancestors.

When I think of what the creatures have done to the people of Nevenero, what they did to my Marta, I am utterly at sea. Anger seizes me, gripping my heart, and I am unable to forgive. How do you live, Maman, with the knowledge of what you are doing? Assisting these creatures to survive is one thing, but condoning their crimes is unforgivable. You accused me of abandoning my family, but you were wrong. I have not abandoned you, but them, and all they represent. If I am an orphan, it is they who have made me such.

The immigrants from Nevenero are strangers to me, and seem to hate me for my name and history, but it is they who have become my only connection to home. I will never see our mountains again, my children and their children will never know them, and I thank heaven for that. There is nothing but evil in our black mountains. Nothing but ice and snow and secrets.

Dearest Maman, we are not prisoners to our ancestors. We must resist our biology and be happy. There is still hope for you and for Guillaume. Abandon the castle, sell everything, and come to New York. I am here, waiting. There are ships every week. I beg you to break this monstrous chain holding us to the past. We are tainted, but our dark lineage can be left behind.

Yours,
Giovanni

I put the letter down and looked at Vita. She stared at me with an intensity that I had seen just once, just minutes before she had poisoned Dolores.

"When I felt they were old enough to know the truth," Vita said, "I took the boys to the village of the Icemen. I had hoped that, when they were older, they would work together to help our ancestors. But Giovanni found Marta in the village, and that was the end of everything."

I stared at her, astonished. "My grandmother was one of them?"

"Not by birth, but by integration. She had been taken as a girl from Nevenero and raised among them. She spoke their language and understood their customs. I believe she would have been a great asset to them, a strong peasant girl like Marta. But Giovanni took her from the Icemen. She, in turn, stole him from the Montebianco family. Together, they took my dreams with them."

I held Isabelle close, her smell filling me with tenderness, so that I almost felt, as I listened to Vita, capable of forgiving everything. But whatever sadness Vita carried, whatever disappointments and mistakes marred her life, I could not remedy them. I had made a commitment to Isabelle. I was not her mother, I was not even part of her tribe, but I would be her family. Gathering the baby up in my arms, I stood to leave, knowing that I would not see Vita again.

"One more thing before you go," Vita said. "You see from my son's letter that he wanted me to come to America. I don't know if you can imagine what a terrifying proposition it was, to leave these mountains. I considered it, seriously considered it, for years, all the while hoping to find the courage to do what my son did so naturally: defy my lineage and be free. Finally, I wrote to Giovanni at the address on that letter in

Milton, New York. He never responded, and thus I was not sure that my letter had ever made it to him. Not, that is, until you arrived."

"I don't understand," I said. "I never mentioned a letter."

"You didn't have to," Vita said. "You told me that Giovanni killed himself in July nineteen ninety-three. I sent my letter some weeks before, in June, telling him I would leave the castle to come to America. His response was suicide."

PLACE DES VOSGES,
PARIS, FRANCE

✣

I N THE BEGINNING, it was easy to hide Isabelle. I wrapped her in blankets and pushed her through the streets of Paris, her alien features hidden from view. If someone stopped to stare, I turned and walked away quickly, before I could be questioned. But now that she is older, my work is more difficult. Just the other day, I found Isabelle at the window, waving to an elderly couple below. They must have thought her bizarre features and luminous skin a trick of the light, or perhaps they doubted their eyes, because they stared and stared, gawking at my child as if at a horrible apparition. I came to the window, swept Isabelle aside, and closed the drapes.

My child may be monstrous, but she is mine, and I will protect her as best I can. The Montebianco family has given me the means to do so. The apartment is spacious and elegant, a *maison particulière* of four narrow floors filled with the treasures of Eleanor's ancient French family. The forestry business is thriving, and Enzo sees to all of our needs. We have discreet servants, and food delivered when we're hungry, and every kind of luxury imaginable. But still, we are prisoners of our heritage. Isabelle will never go to school. She will never have friends. Our outings in the city are becoming more and more difficult. I live in constant fear that someone will uncover the truth and take her from me, a Dr. Feist or a journalist, hungry to make a discovery that would change the world.

Sometimes, when I am most afraid, Eleanor's words come rushing back to me—*I have protected Vita and yet, in my weakest moments, I question the goodness of such protection.* There are moments when I agree with Eleanor and wonder how I can protect a creature that, if discovered, all the world would destroy. But then she laughs, and her whole being lights up with happiness, and I know that I will do anything to keep her safe.

Before I left Montebianco Castle, I found Aki on the east lawn. He had followed me down the mountain the night of the bonfire, determined to take Isabelle back to the village. We sat together near the pond, like generals negotiating a settlement. In exchange for Isabelle, I would continue to send supplies to the village. If I ever learned they had harmed another child, however, I would stop all aid to the tribe. There would be no medicine, no clothes, no blankets, no food. It would be a death sentence, he knew, and he promised never to bring another child to the village, even though this, as we both understood, made survival equally impossible. He gave me his blessing to raise Isabelle and, to my relief, we parted in peace, not exactly friends, but not enemies either.

That was nearly three years ago. In that time, Isabelle has become the image of her father—a beautiful, smart girl with a strong body and a sharp mind. I have done my best to protect her, and yet, it is becoming impossible to hide her. Soon, we will be forced to leave Paris and take refuge in the immense, geologic silence of the mountains. Sal and Basil are there now, waiting for our return. They tend to the greenhouse and the goats in the mews. I've installed a new telephone, and Basil calls every week with updates about the various projects I have started—the helipad on the north lawn, the renovation of the second-floor ballroom, with its hundred mirrors and crystal chandeliers. A flower garden has been planted around the mausoleum in tribute to Vita. She lies next to Eleanor now. Etched into the cartouche above her tomb are the words:

> *A LONG, long sleep, a famous sleep*
> *That makes no show for dawn*
> *By stretch of limb or stir of lid,—*
> *An independent one.*

I imagine her there, among the remains of our ancestors, laid out in that marble vault, waiting for me to come home.

Until then, I walk with Isabelle through Paris at night, when the streets are empty and she is hidden in shadows. I find comfort in memories of my time with the Icemen in the grotto, bathing with the tribe in the hot spring, playing with the children in the garden. I cannot help but believe that it is my destiny to be Isabelle's mother, a destiny as ancient and powerful as the codes in my blood. When I am in doubt, and feel I might fail, I recall my ancestors dancing at the fire, that rich and noble tribe, and know that I am not alone.

A NOTE ABOUT THE RESEARCH

✦

RESEARCH INTO THE evolution of Homo sapiens forms a significant part of this novel. I consulted many works, notably *Sapiens: A Brief History of Humankind,* by Yuval Noah Harari; *The Gene: An Intimate History,* by Siddhartha Mukherjee; *Neanderthal Man: In Search of Lost Genomes,* by Svante Pääbo; many articles by *New York Times* science writer Carl Zimmer; and the incredible exhibit at the Musée de l'Homme about Neanderthal man. Dr. Hannah Brooks of Hudson Valley Cancer Genetics gave me invaluable guidance in all things relating to family genetic inheritance.

ACKNOWLEDGMENTS

Much gratitude to my editor, Katherine Nintzel, for believing in this book.

Thanks Liate Stehlik, Jen Hart, Julie Paulaski, Amelia Wood.

And everyone at HarperCollins/William Morrow.

Thank you Eric Simonoff and Susan Golomb.

Thank you to Stephanie Koven.

Thank you Sally Willcox.

Thank you Dr. Hannah Brooks.

Thank you Angela and Jeffrey Bluske.

Merci beaucoup Yveline and Nicolas Postel-Vinay.

Love to Hadrien, Alexander, Nico and Sidonie, the home team.

Most of all, thank you to my readers, whose loyal support has sustained me.

About the author

About the book

Insights,
Interviews
& More . . .

Read on

Meet Danielle Trussoni

DANIELLE TRUSSONI is the *New York Times*, *USA Today*, and *Sunday Times* (UK) top ten bestselling author of the supernatural thrillers *Angelology* and *Angelopolis*. She is the co-creator with Hadrien Royo of the Crypto-Z audio series podcast, a companion to *The Ancestor*. She writes the horror column for the *New York Times Book Review* and has recently served as a jurist for the Pulitzer Prize in Fiction.

Trussoni holds an MFA in Fiction from the prestigious Iowa Writers'

Workshop, where she won the Michener-Copernicus Society of America Award. Her books have been translated into thirty-three languages. She lives in the Hudson Valley with her family and her pug, Fly. Learn more at danielletrussoni.com. ∾

Behind the Book Essay

The Ancestor is the story of a woman whose life is upended by a DNA test. After taking a genetic test, Alberta "Bert" Monte is shocked to discover that she is the last living member of an aristocratic dynasty whose estate— a castle dating from the twelfth century in the Aosta Valley of the Italian Alps— now belongs to her. But it is only when she travels to Italy, and uncovers the terrible truth about her ancestry, that she understands that her personal secrets are as much a part of her inheritance as the castle.

The inception of this story began when I took a DNA test and had the surprise of my life. I was raised in a tight Italian-American family, one where Catholic school and long Sunday lunches with stories of my great-grandfather's life in the Italian Alps were the hallmarks of our identity. I even have an Italian passport, and am a dual U.S.-Italian citizen, because my grandparents never denounced their Italian citizenship. Therefore, I was astonished to discover, after taking a 23andMe test, that I am exactly 1.7 percent Italian. My sister took the test and her results were the same. We are more Irish and Norwegian than Italian, more British and German than Italian, a fact that shatters the cultural identity that was so very powerful in our childhood.

This surprise made me wonder: What could be the most shocking discovery to be found in one's ancestry? We've all heard stories of a rich uncle dying and leaving an unsuspecting heir a fortune, but what about the windfalls (and pitfalls) of genetic inheritance? What does it mean for us that the genetic makeup of all human beings is 99.95 percent identical, and that only .05 percent accounts for all the differences of sex, race, health, disease, and so on? As a fiction writer, I was interested in what could happen when a character's genetic inheritance proved that her origins were outside of these percentages. What would it mean for Alberta? What would it mean for humanity? As Alberta discovers, everything that she believed about herself—and her species—can be turned on its head with one test.

My great grandparents had been born in the Italian Alps, and I decided that this romantic and foreboding setting would be perfect for *The Ancestor.* I went to the Aosta Valley, rented a car, and drove through the Alps near Mont Blanc. The novel is set in the fictional village of Nevenero, which means "Black Snow" for its ▶

position in the shadows below Mont Blanc. When Alberta goes to the castle, she has the same view of Mont Blanc that I had from the window of my hotel room, where I took this picture.

During my time in the Alps, I learned about the ibex, a variety of goat that had been hunted by the noble families of the region and mounted in their enormous trophy rooms. I took this picture in a castle once belonging to the House of Savoy. Killing an ibex used to be considered a sign of masculinity. There were two thousand ibex mounted in this particular trophy room.

I slept at a medieval castle with a
tower that inspired the northeast tower
where Vita, the eponymous ancestor of
my novel, resides.

And, of course, I tried all the local
food and wine (hardships undertaken
in the name of research!) from the
aged goat milk cheeses to the strangely
delicious red wines that embody the
drama of the landscape.

The Ancestor is about family secrets,
and the ways in which families transmit
and hide their particular histories. ▶

And while I may not be as Italian as I was raised to believe, I feel liberated rather than disappointed by the revelation. My conception of our ancestry as human beings has changed, and I now see that labels such as Italian or even Caucasian are insignificant compared to my history as a Homo sapiens. I hope that the advent of genetic testing, and the bigger view of our history as a species, helps us see that we are not limited to a tribe, but rather gives us membership to the human family.

Photographs courtesy of the author.

Reading Group Guide

1. Have you, or anyone in your family, ever taken a DNA test?

2. What does your DNA and family heritage mean to you? Do you identify with the culture of your ancestors? What does that mean to you?

3. Alberta learns that she has inherited a title and an estate in the Italian Alps, and that her family is utterly different from what she believed it to be. How much does honesty around inheritance (both genetic and financial) matter to you? Have you had conflicts or surprises around this issue?

4. What's the strangest thing you've learned about an ancestor? What would surprise you about your ancestry?

5. Do you have any famous/well-known ancestors?

6. What would you do if you learned you had different DNA than your parents? Would it matter to you? Do you believe that how we are "nurtured" matters more than "nature" (i.e., genetic relationships)? ▶

Reading Group Guide *(continued)*

7. Did the book or any of its themes remind you of any other literary works or films?

8. Were there any parts of the story you would like to know more about? What would your ideal sequel or spinoff story look like?

9. Were you surprised by Bert's ancestors? What would you have done in her position?

10. How does the cover art reflect the themes in the book? If you were to design an alternate cover, what would it look like? ∾

An excerpt from
The Fortress

Enchantment

Before the club in Paris, and before the Frenchman, I was a woman in a fortress.

Or, more precisely, I lived with my husband and two children in La Commanderie, a medieval fortification at the center of the French village of Aubais, pronounced "obey," as in "love, honor and . . . Aubais." Built by the Knights Templar in the thirteenth century, the fortress stood high on a hilltop and could withstand attack from every angle. There were arrow slits in the walls and a perch from which to spy the enemy coming. The foundation was sunk deep into the rock of the village, rock that millions of years before had formed the Mediterranean seabed. Occasionally, when I examined the rock, I would find imprints of fossilized shells, ancient swirls of disintegrated calcium that created the bedrock of the entire region. The fortress rose from this long-gone sea like a stone Leviathan, strong and unsinkable. It was a defensive place, a place of barriers, one meant to resist catapults and battering rams. ▶

A place in which we could shut everything out, even the truth.

An ancient granite wall surrounded the fortress. Outside the wall the sun scorched the streets to a sizzle. Inside, a deep shadow fell over a courtyard, where my family ate lunch at a weathered wooden table. I picture us now, as we were then: My two children, Alex and Nico, our pug Fly Me to the Moon (Fly for short), and our three cats: Napoleon, Josephine, and ChouChou. I see me, a thirty-six-year-old woman in an oversize sundress and sunglasses, walking barefoot over hot flagstones, slipping between slats of sun and shade as I make my way past the cats, to my husband, Nikolai. Tall and dark and handsome, he wears a black top hat perched on his head. He bought the top hat in a junk store and wore it as a joke, but the joke became a habit and the habit an eccentricity, and so the hat stayed, giving him the air of a dark magician, one who could—with a flick of his wrist—coax a dove from the depths of nothingness.

Under our feet, deep below the hot flagstones, was a treasure-filled tunnel, or so we liked to imagine. According to legend, the Knights Templar had constructed a system of tunnels between La Commanderie and the fortified city of Aigues-Mortes, where St. Louis launched the Crusades. These passages allowed the Knights to move in stealth to defend the king, to hide valuables, and to transport goods for their voyages to the Holy Land, but anyone looking at a map would have serious doubts that such a tunnel actually existed. The swampy port of Aigues-Mortes is more than ten miles from Aubais, the terrain rocky. Even so, I liked to believe that there was some truth to the story and that deep below the fortress, carved into the compacted limestone, was a hidden space, a tunnel guarding Templar treasure.

La Commanderie was eight hundred years old and had many owners after the Knights Templar. One built an olive press on the property. Another created an Italianate courtyard with flagstones and a window-lined salon to border it. One used the garden as an arena for bullfights—or *les courses camarguaises,* as they say in the Languedoc—and I liked to imagine the matador and the bull moving around each other in the courtyard, attacking and hiding, one beast pursuing the other. When the Nazis requisitioned the property in the forties, they used it as the center of their operations in the region, a legacy that older villagers remembered. The fortress had seen olive oil and bullshit and swastikas. And then we arrived.

We hadn't been in the market for a dark, drafty, thirteenth-century ▶

fortress, but we walked through the door, took one look, and knew that La Commanderie had been waiting for us. The realities of buying and living in a historic compound in a tiny village in a foreign country didn't strike us as daunting. The fact that we were thousands of miles away from family and friends didn't dissuade us. The problems with the house itself—the oil-sucking monstrosity of a heater, the leaky roof, the mold-infested bathroom, the broken sewage pipe—seemed manageable. It was precisely the scale of the fortress—so outsize, so unrealistic—that made it ours.

The day we moved in, we pushed open the gate together. Over ten feet tall, the blue ironwork speckled with rust, it was so heavy that it took the two of us with our combined weight to move it. It swung open, creaking on old hinges, and suddenly we were not a couple on the verge of divorce. We were the owners of La Commanderie, a structure more powerful than us, a place so solid that it would—*it must*—be strong enough to save us. I remember looking at the thick walls of the fortress, at Alex and Nico in the courtyard, and thinking, *This is it. This is where we will finally be happy.* ◖